PRIMARY PERIL

PRIMARY PERIL

The Gatekeepers of Democracy:
Book Three

BILL LEWERS

TABLE OF CONTENTS

DEDICATION

"To Mary, the love of my life, who has put up with the writing of this book (and so much more)."

That was the dedication that I wrote for *Six Decades of Baseball: A Personal Narrative.* Now, ten years and four books later, those words ring truer than ever. This book is dedicated to Mary Delphine Marlow Lewers whose love, understanding, patience, and support have exceeded, beyond all measure, anything that this poor soul could have ever hoped for or deserved.

AUTHORS NOTES AND ACKNOWLEDGEMENTS

I T's BEEN SAID that there are two types of authors: Plotters and Pantsers. Plotters are folks who develop a plot outline before they begin to actually write their novel. The author then writes "to the outline," flushing out the details that transforms the outline into a story. While modifications and digressions are to be expected, the final product remains pretty much how the author envisioned it.

On the other end of the spectrum are the Pantsers. Pantsers begin with a concept and not much else. They just start writing "by the seat of their pants," and go wherever the writing experience takes them. Hopefully a story emerges that readers (and the author) can relate to.

There are advantages and limitations to each approach. Plotters are able to write with the confidence that comes from knowing where they are headed. Pantsers get the freedom that comes from knowing that anything is possible. Plotters risk the loss of spontaneity. Pantsers risk losing focus.

When I wrote *The Gatekeepers of Democracy*, I was definitely a plotter. For over twenty years, I had been privileged to serve the election process in Fairfax County, Virginia, first as an election officer, then as a chief election officer, and finally as a "rover." Gradually over time, the idea of "a day at the polls as seen through the eyes of the election officers" began to take hold. I had seen so much that could be used to inspire such a story; things that had happened to me; things that I had seen happen to others. By the time I started to write, the essentials were all in place: The personalities of the characters; the key turning points of the plot; the additional details that would fill the pages and add texture to the story.

The first draft was written in six weeks. After that, one additional scene was added and a certain amount of tweaking took place, but the end product was essentially as I had envisioned it.

Now fast forward eighteen months.

A sequel titled, *November Third* had just been published. Except it wasn't called it a sequel. "You never call it a sequel," was the advice. Rather you call it "Book Two of a series." Sequels are usually considered disappointments (*Back to the Future, Part II*) while series are money makers (*Harry Potter, Star Wars*). So with that in mind, *November Third* was christened *"The Gatekeepers of Democracy: Book Two."*

The obvious challenge was that folks wanted to know if there would ever be a "Book Three." All sorts of ideas were offered, from having the Russians infiltrate the county Office of Elections to the chief election officer finding a severed head inside the ballot bin ("That's why our counts are off by one!"). While these ideas were intriguing, I didn't see any way that I could mold them into a novel. In truth, I wasn't sure if there would ever be a Book Three. Book One saw things through the eyes of the election officers; Book Two through the eyes of the rovers. That's where my experience was. That's what I knew. What more did I have to offer?

Then ever-so-gradually, a new idea began to take hold.

How about writing a murder mystery?

I had always enjoyed the Agatha Christie style murder mysteries. I had at my disposal a universe of characters that I had created along with an election type setting. Why not give it a go?

Almost immediately, I decided that it would take place during a primary election and the title would be "Primary Peril." But when do I want the murder to actually take place? How about Election Day itself? I quickly dismissed that as being unworkable. Precincts on Election Day are busy places with many people coming and going. Too difficult to isolate the killer and his/her victim. Too many suspects.

So it has to take place prior to the election. But who will be the victim? Who will be the killer? What's the motive? What's the murder weapon? Who's the sleuth who figures it all out? What is the motive for the sleuth to even get involved (assuming the sleuth is not the police)? Who are the other suspects? So many questions.

I consulted "how to write a murder mystery" books. Surfed the net. Researched different ways of rubbing people out. Gradually it came into focus. Sort of. But with a murder mystery, you need to get the details straight before you start writing. All the sources agreed on that. To write an air-tight murder mystery you need to be a plotter, not a pantser.

The challenge was that an air-tight plot continued to elude me. Whenever I felt I had the outline pinned down, flaws and inconsistencies reared their ugly heads. This continued for a number of weeks. Finally in a fit of frustration, I decided to go against the advice of the experts.

I just started writing.

There's a cliché in writing circles that says "you go where your characters take you." I'm not sure I totally believe that, but with a plot that was flawed, at best, I had no other choice. So I wrote. And wrote some more. Gradually the outline became firmer. And with that came the realization that much of the stuff I had written needed to be either revised or scrapped all together. Never mind that now. Just keep writing. The more I wrote, the more I understood where I was headed. Characters' motivations became more crystalized. Sometimes, it almost seemed like they were correcting me,

"No, I would never do that now," or,

"Please don't have me say that. It's so trite."

As the sequence of events fell into place, I became increasingly aware of a problem. A very significant problem.

The wrong person was being murdered.

I was several weeks and 20,000 words into the novel but it wasn't working. Too many things had to be twisted around in order to service my originally intended victim. Fortunately another candidate was readily available. The switch was made and now the flow of events was a whole lot easier. At this point it became a back-and-forth dance between the narrative and the emerging outline:

Write.

Modify outline.

Confirm that the narrative and outline are now in sync.

Write some more.

This continued for about three months until I had a first draft.

From there the usual editing and revision process took over. The final result is *Primary Peril,* a.k.a. *The Gatekeepers of Democracy: Book Three.*

It is a murder mystery with an election setting.

And it's quite a bit different from the story I originally envisioned.

It is written so that a person who enjoys murder mysteries, but has no great interest in the Election Day process, can read and hopefully enjoy it without having read the first two books in the series. On the other hand, events from *The Gatekeepers of Democracy* and *November Third* are referred to when appropriate. So I think it's fair to say that the reader will have a richer experience by having read the earlier books (hint, hint).

And, as with the two earlier books, *Primary Peril* is a work of fiction. Its people, places, and events exist only in my imagination. It is true that my experiences while working for the Fairfax County Office of Elections provided much of the inspiration for this book. It is equally true that, for the purposes of telling a story, I deviated, in ways large and small, from the election code and practices of both Fairfax Country and the state of Virginia. Ultimately *Primary Peril* is a story written to entertain, not an election documentary.

I cannot thank enough my three beta readers, Catherine Mathews of the Great Falls Writer's Group, Mary Marlow Lewers, and Barbara Lewers. Besides correcting countless typos, they made many constructive suggestions involving both the style and substance of the narrative. I am very much in their debt.

Likewise I am fortunate to receive the continuing support and encouragement from the Great Falls Writers Group and especially its founder and facilitator Kristin Clark Taylor.

As always, I conclude with my sons Mark and John and my wife Mary. Their love and support through the years has sustained me in every way possible. They are the joy and foundation of my life.

Chapter 1

TUESDAY, APRIL 20, 1:30 P.M.

WHAT LUCK! IT'S all falling into place.
Everything had gone so well. And that look of amazement that Carl had flashed in her direction had been priceless.

It was one of those beautiful sunny days that occur in late April, when the last reminders of winter are gone for good. Even the dirty warehouse parking lot, where county trucks were parked every which way, reflected the pleasure she felt as she entered her two seater sports car. The appropriate buttons were pressed and the roof of her car folded back. Putting on her sun glasses, she backed the car out of its parking place. She then shifted into forward, maneuvered around and through the trucks, and was on her way.

"How could I have ever doubted it?" she wondered as she drove down the road that led to the interstate. Of course, there were risks. She had known that all along. But thanks to Steve, the one obstacle in her way was being removed. Getting involved with Steve had been her best move yet.

It was hard to contain her excitement. As she pulled to a stop at the red light, she noticed how her hands were shaking. Perhaps a cigarette would settle her down. She rarely smoked now, certainly never in public, but perhaps this once…

She reached into her handbag and found the pack near the bottom. Fortunately it was a long light. She lit up and took a deep drag. Good. That seemed to help.

The light turned green and she was off. There's the ramp to the interstate. Foot on the gas. Onto the ramp.

Her hands started shaking again.

Steady, girl. It's not like you to get the shakes.

It was worse this time. She reached for the ash tray. Another drag might help. She tried to grasp the lit cigarette but her shaking fingers dislodged it from the ash tray and it fell to the floor.

Reaching back, she tried to get both hands on the steering wheel. But the hand that had reached for the cigarette didn't seem to respond. Her arm had suddenly become stiff.

Up ahead the merge lane was ending. She had to get over, into the flow of traffic. There was that truck in her blind sport. She needed to speed up. Or slow down. Or slam on the brakes.

For God's sake, do something!

Thirty minutes later paramedics extracted her lifeless body from the wreckage.

Chapter 2

SATURDAY, FEBRUARY 13, 1:00 P.M.,
EARLIER IN THE YEAR

A s USUAL, CARL Marsden answered the phone on the second ring, ignoring the number that flashed on the Caller ID screen.

"Hey bro," came the cheery voice on the other end of the line, a voice that Carl knew all too well. "How are things down by the Potomac?"

"Hello Brad," exclaimed Carl. "What a surprise to hear your voice. Mom told me that you were involved in some high power murder investigation. There was a bit of it on our news. That poor family."

"Yeah, we cracked it all right," said Brad. "Turned out to be the second cousin. Completely deranged. He's confessed so there won't be a trial, thank God."

"So now you move on to another grisly case?" asked Carl. He had always been fascinated by his brother's work as a homicide detective. He could not imagine having the stomach for such work himself but from a safe distance it was exciting to hear about.

"Funny you should ask," said Brad. "It just so happens that I've received an offer that I can't refuse; an offer which will put me down in your neck of the woods."

"Really! You're coming down here. To stay?"

"So it seems. I've got some paperwork to complete but as of March first, I will be a resident of the Commonwealth of Virginia. I'll be coming down next weekend to do some apartment hunting. Any suggestions where to look?"

"I think, I can suggest a couple of places. And of course, you can hang out at my place while you're looking."

"And does this mean I finally get to meet Cindy?"

"Yes, you get to meet Cindy," said Carl, feeling a bit vulnerable as he said it. Although he generally kept his personal life low-keyed, it had been impossible not to mention his girlfriend during the family Christmas gathering at his parents' house on Long Island. This had caused considerable interest from his parents as they had almost given up hope of ever becoming grandparents. Brad, as dashing as ever, was now in his early forties. He flitted from girlfriend to girlfriend without giving any indication of ever settling down. Carl, on the other hand, never a social butterfly to begin with, had become something of a recluse in recent years, married to his work and increasingly to his devotion to the election process. The existence of Cindy, whose name he had supplied only with reluctance, had been the primary item of interest around the Marsden Christmas dinner table.

Carl still remembered that night that he and Cindy had cemented their "boyfriend-girlfriend" status. It had come on the evening of Election Day, November third, a day that they would both long remember. It was now some three months later and things were going well. At least on the surface.

The thing was that with Cindy's easy charm and quick temper, you were never quite sure. At times, Carl found himself wondering if she was really content or was just using him as some sort of temporary "safe harbor," only to be lured away when someone more exciting (like Brad?) came along.

Chapter 3

Monday, March 1, 7:30 P.M.

CINDY WAS LATE. That meeting had run over. Way over. This messed up her plans. She had promised Carl that she would bring dessert.

Of course, "bringing dessert" was not the same thing as "making dessert." Cindy never made dessert. In fact, when it came to the kitchen she rarely made anything at all. Cooking had not been part of her domestic education and since graduating from college she had done little to expand her proficiency. But at least she had planned on stopping off at the supermarket to buy a cake, or a pie, or something. But now there was no time for that. She had promised Carl she would be at his townhouse by 7:00 p.m. and it was already seven-thirty. Fortunately there was some ice cream in the freezer. She grabbed it and hurried to the car.

Tonight she would be meeting the famous Brad, the homicide detective who had come to their county. Carl never talked much about his family, but from what he had said it was clear that he was proud of his older brother, who would be staying in his townhouse until he could secure his own accommodations. He had arrived a few days ago and today was his first day on the job. Carl wanted to make him feel welcome and as the dutiful girlfriend, Cindy was to be part of that process.

At 7:45 she pulled into the parking lot of Carl's development. She parked her car and hurried up the walkway to the townhouse. On the way she noticed a two seater Mercedes Benz, sporting New York license plates. While not exactly a car buff, Cindy enjoyed her Mazda convertible. A Mercedes, however, was something else. Out of her league, to be sure.

Not too shabby. I guess being a homicide detective pays.

Up the walkway and a knock on the door.

"That must be her now," came the voice on the other side of the door.

It opened and there was Carl, looking just a bit piqued.

"I'm sorry Carl. There was this meeting and—"

"That's OK", said Carl, in a tone that indicated that it was not quite OK. "Come on in, I'd like to introduce you to—"

"So this is Cindy," came a voice from behind Carl. "I have heard so much about you."

Brad stepped forward and before Cindy realized it, she was engulfed in a hug.

Extracting herself, she replied, somewhat breathlessly, "Well I've heard a lot about you too."

"This was Brad's first day on the job at the police dep—" began Carl.

"Oh, come on," said Brad. "Cindy doesn't want to hear a lot of boring cop talk. I understand you work for *MarketPro*. Tell me all about the world of marketing. Is it like that TV show?"

"Hardly," said Cindy. "But we do have our moments."

"I'm going to get dinner on," said Carl. "Have a seat, you two, and I'll announce when it's ready."

"OK," said Cindy. "And uh, here's dessert."

She handed the ice cream to Carl who gave her an "Is that the best you could do?" look.

While Carl put the finishing touches on dinner, Brad peppered Cindy with questions about the world of marketing. Cindy found him both attractive and personable. Much more outgoing than Carl. Confident. Assertive. And yes, handsome.

"I do have one question for you," said Cindy, not wanting the conversation to be a monologue about marketing.

"Yes?"

"Is that your Mercedes out there?"

"Well, yes," said Brad, sheepishly. "Mind you, I bought it used. Homicide detectives don't make that kind of money."

"It's a beautiful car," said Cindy.

"Would you like a ride in it?"

"Oh yes, I—"

"Dinner's on," called Carl.

It was not one of Carl's better efforts. The pork chops were tough and overdone as Cindy's tardiness had upset Carl's timing. Everyone, however, pretended to enjoy them. Dessert wasn't much better as Cindy's ice cream had partially melted.

As Carl was clearing the table, Brad turned to Cindy and said, "Why don't we take that ride in the Mercedes?"

It was so tempting.

"Yes I'd love to," said Cindy, brightly. "That would be so much fun."

"Then let's—"

Cindy held up her hand.

"But, not right now," she said, softy so Carl couldn't hear. "I think I need to mend some fences."

Brad nodded, indicating that he understood.

Cindy got to her feet and went into the kitchen where Carl was organizing the cleanup.

"I'm sorry I screwed up dinner. I should have called. Please let me do the dishes."

"No, it's OK. Go for that ride."

"Not tonight. Anyway, I have to leave in a bit. A new client tomorrow and I need to prep. Now give me the dishrag and get the hell out of the kitchen."

Forty-five minutes later, Cindy had said her goodbyes and left.

"She is something," said Brad. "How did you ever land her?"

"I'm not sure," admitted Carl. "But she seems content. At least for now."

"At least for now", thought Brad.

Chapter 4

"THANK YOU SO much for seeing me," said the gray haired woman.

"Of course, Emily," said Cindy, as she ushered the woman into her apartment. Her polite words failed to completely mask her bewilderment.

What could Emily Weston possibly want to talk to Cindy about? The last time they had met was that evening when she had practically begged Cindy to run for an open seat on the county Soil and Water Commission. The ensuing campaign had been a disaster, as even Cindy's considerable charm and attractiveness had been unable to mask her lack of qualifications. She had suspended her campaign after an embarrassing debate performance, and finished not only behind the two other announced candidates, but behind a write-in candidate as well. As she put it to Carl,

"I managed to finish fourth in a three person race."

They exchanged a few pleasantries. Cindy liked Emily and had always found her easy to talk to. The environmental activist had been a candidate for the State Senate in a special election to fill a vacant seat the previous year and had lost by the narrowest of margins. Cindy wondered if Emily was going to try again. State Senate was just one of the variety of state and local offices that were to be on the ballot this year.

It felt like she had read her mind when Emily declared,

"I've decided to run again for the State Senate. I believe I would have won last time if not for that ice storm."

"You certainly have my vote," said Cindy.

There was a pause.

"I expect this to be a difficult campaign," said Emily.

"I assume Jennifer Haley is running for reelection."

"Yes, she is." Emily's face hardened. "I didn't have a strong opinion about her in the last campaign. A bit too showy for my taste but at least she was from the moderate wing of the Republican Party. But since she's been in office, she's pretty much followed the downstate Republicans."

Cindy nodded but remained silent.

"And then there's that company she manages. There are a number of significant environmental concerns. I'm not sure if anything illegal is going on but…let's just say she's no friend of the environment."

There was another pause. Emily seemed to be struggling to get to the point of her visit.

"What do you want?" asked Cindy, softly.

"I need help," said Emily. "I need a campaign manager."

"Let me recommend Steve Winters," said Cindy. "He was campaign manager for my ill-fated effort last year. He's very competent and committed to winning."

Also quite charming, she thought. *Oh yes, I remember that all too well.*

"I must tell you however, that we did not part well so if you approach him, do not mention my name if you have any hope—"

"I've already approached Steve," interrupted Emily, "and he declined. He didn't say why but I think he is working for another candidate."

"So you're going to be opposed in the primary?"

"I don't think so. No one else has filed and the party likes to avoid primary contests, if they can. He's probably just working for a candidate in another race."

"Did he say who?"

"I didn't ask and he didn't offer. He seemed uncomfortable in my presence. It's so different from the last time when Biff Logan encouraged me to run."

Cindy understood. Biff Logan, the county Democratic chairman, could be very convincing. She remembered how he had recruited her to run for the Soil and Water Commission. Brushing aside her lack of qualifications, he proclaimed that her youth, personality, and attractiveness were what the party needed. And Cindy had allowed her ambition, and yes, her vanity, to cloud her better judgement. The memory of it made her feel both ashamed and angry. But with Emily it was different. She was qualified to serve in the legislature and had run a good campaign the year before. She deserved another chance.

"I want to help," said Cindy. "I could probably squeeze in some time to help pass out fliers or perhaps—"

"Would you be my campaign manager?" asked Emily. The expression on her face told Cindy that she was deadly serious. "I'd pay you the going rate for your time. I have some resources left over from my last campaign and—"

"Hold on," interrupted Cindy. "I said I would help and I will. It's true that I did pick up a certain amount of knowledge about campaign organization last year. But if I've learned anything, it's not to overreach. I'm sure there are others in the party who are far more qualified—"

"Perhaps, there are. But they're all spoken for. Or so they say."

"Can't Biff Logan suggest some alternatives?"

"Oh, Biff suggested an alternative all right," said Emily. "He suggested I move to the sidelines and become a party 'elder statesperson.' Share my wisdom with the next generation of candidates. Cindy, I'm not ready to do that, not yet anyway. I believe I can make a real contribution in the Senate on a variety of environmental concerns. One more chance is all I'm asking for."

"I'm not sure I'm the right person for this."

"Are any of us absolutely sure? But I've seen you in action. You're smart and you learn fast. And your heart's in the right place. The way you campaigned for Howard last year even after your own effort failed. That's the sort of person I want running my campaign. Plus," Emily added with a playful grin,

"I suspect you might enjoy showing Biff and Steve how it's done, after last year's uh…experience."

Cindy smiled.

"You're damn right on that," she admitted.

The room became silent.

"How about it?"

"There are all kinds of reasons why I shouldn't. Do you know I used up all my vacation time last year on election stuff? No travel, no nothing. I even had to work the day after Christmas. Carl and I were talking about going to Europe in late June, after the primaries are over."

"Sounds like you guys are serious. Do you think he'd be upset by you getting involved in another political campaign?"

"Shit no! He'd be pissed if I turned it down," said Cindy, laughing.

Once again, silence. For almost a minute Cindy sat, deep in thought, staring at her folded hands.

"I tell you what," said Cindy, at last. "Let's both of us think on it for a few days. I want you to go through your options once again. I've got to believe there is someone in the party more qualified than me to do this. In the meantime I will reflect on my own situation and priorities. What happened last year was both painful and humiliating and mostly self-inflicted. If I do this thing, I want to be confident I can do it right."

"All right. And then?"

"And then we'll talk."

They exchanged a few more pleasantries and Emily took her leave.

So once again I find myself at the brink, thought Cindy. She truly meant it went she told Emily of the pain of last year's election. What she hadn't said was that it had also been exciting. Very exciting.

Chapter 5

THURSDAY, MARCH 4, 7:30 P.M.

"**I** DON'T BELIEVE THIS. Cindy, are you insane?"

"Oh, come on Carl. It might be fun."

"Fun?!? Don't you remember what that campaign did to you last year? How exhausted you were. How short tempered you were. How humiliated you felt."

This wasn't what Cindy had expected. Carl, the ultimate election nerd, was trying to talk her out of this.

"Come on, Carl. That was different. You know it was. I had no business running for Soil and Water. But Emily is fully qualified. She should have won last time. And Biff Logan is trying to shut her out. He's hoping she'll drop out so he can recruit a younger candidate. Emily doesn't think she'll be opposed in the primary but I'm not so sure. None of the experienced campaign managers are willing to help her. She asked Steve Winters but he's busy helping someone else."

There was an uneasy pause. It happened every time Steve Winters' name was mentioned.

"Do you even know how to be a campaign manager?"

"Not entirely," Cindy admitted. "But I'm a quick learner, or so I've been told." A quick smile. "And I did learn a lot from Steve last year—"

Oops, why do I keep saying his name?

"This will probably take a lot of your time," said Carl, remembering how time constrained Cindy had been the year before.

"I know."

"It will probably eat into your vacation time as well."

Cindy knew what Carl was referring to. That trip to Europe they had been talking about. And although nothing had been said, they both sensed that it would go a long way toward revealing how well suited they were for each other.

"So you want me to turn Emily down?"

"You're a free agent Cindy. The choice is yours, not mine."

Cindy got to her feet and walked over to Carl, put her arms around his neck, and kissed him gently on the lips.

"I know I'm a free agent. I'm not asking for your permission. But I am asking for your opinion which happens to mean a great deal to me. Do you think I should turn Emily down?"

Silence. The seconds ticked by. Then,

"Do you really want to do this?"

"Yes, I do."

"Then I guess, Emily has herself a campaign manager."

Cindy burst into that radiant smile that Carl had never been able to resist.

"Thank you," she said, giving Carl a big hug. "This will be so much fun. You wait and see."

Chapter 6

Sunday, March 7, 2:00 P.M.

IT WAS EASIER this time. Perhaps it was the confidence that comes from having done it once. Or it might have come from a certain sense of detachment. He hadn't voted for Emily Weston in the last election and he probably wasn't going to vote for her this time either. And yet, here he was, in front of the supermarket, gathering signatures on her petition to run for the State Senate.

Mostly he was doing this for Cindy, who was beginning to feel the impact of what she had signed up for as Emily's campaign manager. But it was also from his commitment to the election process. Emily Weston was a legitimate candidate with a deep commitment to the environment. She deserved to be on the ballot. And since she was the only announced candidate on the Democratic side, it appeared that she would get her rematch with Jennifer Haley in November. Cindy had feared that there would be primary opposition but, so far, nothing had materialized.

Be that as it may, Carl was having some success in getting signatures. In two hours he had amassed a total of seventeen.

Not a great number, but still much better than he had done last year. Every little bit helped. Cindy had dispatched a number of volunteers to various shopping centers and malls. At the end of the day, they would assemble at her place and see if they had reached the magic number of 250.

It was a was a bright, sunny day and, while still a bit chilly, there was a definite feeling that spring was on the way. This seemed to put people in an upbeat, receptive mood.

"Yes, ma'am, you're not committing to vote for her. You just want the voters to have choices. That's what democracy is all about, letting the voters choose." And with that acknowledgement, he had secured signature number eighteen.

The only blemish on the afternoon had occurred about forty-five minutes earlier when Steve Winters had arrived with a folding table and what appeared to be his own set of petitions. They had acknowledged each other with a curt nod. Steve had been Cindy's campaign manager (and what else?) the year before and had interacted with Carl a number of times. While these exchanges had been civil enough, their relationship could be best described as "frosty."

Still, Carl felt they needed to, at least, talk. Cindy would want to know what he had been up to as she was still convinced that some last minute rival would jump out of the woodwork.

Steve seemed to be doing very well at getting signatures. His easy going manner, coupled with his good looks, made him a natural. Carl waited for an opening and walked over.

"Good afternoon," he said, as casually as he could. "I see that we're both in the signature harvesting business."

"So it appears," said Steve, with a measured smile. "I'm collecting for Dan Brodkin who is running for House of Delegates. He's an exciting new candidate, the sort we need if we're going to hold on to the House. There are no other Democrats running for the nomination. Still we have to get those signatures. Who are you collecting for?"

As if you don't know.

"Emily Weston, for State Senate."

Steve frowned.

"She shouldn't be running. She's had her chance. She will only make it easier for Haley to be reelected. She should get out of the way for new blood."

"Why? No one else in the party seems to be interested in running."

"That's because no one wants an intra-party bloodbath. Why are you involved in this anyway? I understood that your political leanings pull you in another direction."

"I'm doing it as a favor to Cindy who is—"

"Is she really doing it?" snapped Steve. "I told her not to. Being a campaign manager is way over her head. She doesn't know what she's getting into."

Carl was taken aback by Steve's intensity. He was aware that Steve had been bitter over her withdrawal the year before but that was all in the past.

"She believes in Emily," said Carl. "And she learned a lot from you last year about the election process. Or at least that's what she's been saying."

Carl expected some quick retort but Steve did not respond right away. He seemed to be thinking carefully about what to say. When he finally spoke, his voice was calm and measured.

"Tell Cindy that she needs to consider her position carefully. This is a serious business and not for anyone with vulnerabilities."

"I think you're underestimating Cindy. She's learned from her mistakes and this time she's committed for the long haul.

And she appreciates all you taught her—"

　　"Just tell her what I said."

　　"But I don't understand—"

　　"That's all right. She will."

Chapter 7

Sunday, 5:00 P.M.

"Fourteen signatures was all I was able to get. I'm sorry it wasn't more. I'll get these notarized at the bank tomorrow."

"That would be great, Howard. I really appreciate it," said Cindy, with sincerity. It had been a productive day.

Just as Howard was preparing to leave, the front doorbell rang.

"I'll bet that's Carl," said Cindy. "He's the only one that I haven't heard from."

She opened the door and it was, indeed, Carl with his petitions in hand.

"So you've been recruited as well," Carl said to Howard Morgenstein. The George Mason grad student had been a major advisor to Cindy the year before.

"On a limited basis," said Howard. "I'm happy to help out when I can but the deadline for my dissertation is coming up."

"Well, thank you again," said Cindy, giving Howard a parting hug. He departed and Cindy closed the door behind him. She turned to face Carl.

"Well?" she said, hands on hips, with a bemused expression on her face.

"Well what?" responded Carl, looking Cindy straight in the eye.

Cindy let out a sigh. "OK Carl, I know this isn't your thing. But really, every little thing helps. I don't expect—"

"Twenty-eight," said Carl, throwing the petitions down on the table.

"I don't believe it!" shouted Cindy, clapping her hands. They both remembered the previous year when a similar effort had netted Carl a mere five signatures. Then she added, sheepishly, "You beat me by one. I had twenty-seven. Deb, twenty-two, and Howard, fourteen."

"For a total of ninety-one," said Carl, doing the math in his head. "Exactly how many do you need?"

"The magic number is 250 for State Senate. But Emily already had about 200 when I signed on."

"Which puts you over the top."

"Not quite. Steve told me last year that you need extras. In case some of the signatures turn out to be bogus. I figure one more day, just you and I, should do it."

"Speaking of Steve," said Carl, with what he hoped was a serious expression on his face. "We ran into each other today."

"Oh."

"He was collecting petition signatures as well."

"Oh, shit," snapped Cindy. "They're running someone against Emily. I was afraid they would."

"No, it wasn't for State Senate. It was for some House of Delegates candidate. When I said that Emily seemed to be unopposed for the nomination, he didn't contradict me."

"That's a relief."

"He did, however, give me a message to pass on to you."

Cindy frowned.

"I'm not sure I want to hear it."

There was an uneasy silence for several seconds.

"Well," asked Carl. "Do you want me to say it or not?"

Cindy gave a resigned sigh.

"Yeah, go ahead. Tell me what he said."

"He said, and I quote, 'Tell Cindy that she needs to consider her position carefully. This is a serious business and not for anyone with vulnerabilities.'"

"That's weird," said Cindy, with a puzzled expression on her face. "I mean, we all have vulnerabilities but—oh…"

She stopped in mid-sentence. The puzzlement was replaced by something else. Was it fear? Carl thought he could see Cindy silently mouth the words "It can't be."

Carl didn't know what to say. He had always suspected that there were things between Cindy and Steve that he did not know. That he did not want to know. But before he could say anything, Cindy broke out into a bright smile.

"It's nothing. He's still bitter over last year. It's all bullshit. He's just trying to get in my head."

"But why would he care?" asked Carl. "If Emily is going to be the party nominee, they're all going to support her eventually, even if they had hoped someone else might run. I don't understand—"

"Stop," said Cindy, who suddenly seemed a bit angry. "There's nothing to understand. It's political gamesmanship. Let's leave it there. And if it's OK, we'll call it a night. I know we talked about having dinner together but I'm kind of beat. Long day and all."

Carl had no choice but to accept Cindy's dismissal. But it was a curious way to end the day.

Chapter 8

TUESDAY, MARCH 9, 7:30 A.M.

"**I** HOPE YOU ALL enjoyed that long break from election work," said Terrence, cheerfully, to the dozen or so assembled rovers. "As you know, we need to do the cleanup from last November's election. Normally that would have been done in January or even December, but as we all know, last November was not a typical election."

Some laughs and chuckles came from a number of the rovers sitting around the table, inside the government warehouse in Springdale. A number of them flashed grins in Carl's direction.

"To begin with, the number of write-ins for Soil and Water Conservation Board was sufficiently large that we needed to assign them to the appropriate persons which took some time. Then the margin was so close that a recount had to be ordered and that took additional effort. By that time, we were on top of the holidays so we had to push things back to the New Year."

"Then," Terrence continued, "there was the matter of the scanners that we acquired from Braxton County. As we all now know, thanks to Mr. Marsden and associates," - a slight bow in Carl's direction - "there was a manufacturer's defect that slipped through the cracks. I'm happy to report that the *ElectionPro* staff came out in January and performed the necessary upgrade. They have thoroughly tested the machines, leaving them on for multiple hours, and they all work fine."

There was a round of applause from the assembled rovers.

Three more rovers had come in while Terrence was speaking. One of them, a short gray haired woman named Brenda, was shaking her head in apparent disgust.

"Our mission for the next two days is straightforward," said Terrence. "Unscramble the carts and scanners that the delivery men left every which way in the cage. Clean out the leftover debris from the carts; remove the flash drives from the scanners; check for stray ballots; and get the carts and scanners back to their rightful positions. Form yourself into teams. Let's get started."

Carl remembered the year before when he first started as a rover. How lost he had been. Now he went confidently to one of the workbenches, even as Jack Vincent started to organize the extraction of the carts and scanners from the tangled confusion inside the cage. Jack was the senior rover, well into his eighties, whose specialty came from knowing the proper place in the warehouse for each item.

Carl was joined at his workbench by Scott, a man in his sixties, who Carl frequently paired up with.

"What's Brenda so upset about?" asked Carl, as they waited for the first of the carts and scanners to be rolled into place at the beginning of the assembly line.

"Oh, the usual," said Scott. "It's the laundry carts, containing all those old library books. Brenda thinks they should be donated to something or other—"

"As well they should be," said Brenda who was walking by, en route to one of the other workbenches. "So many places could use those books. Daycare centers. Senior citizen centers. Libraries in some of the less affluent areas. Even Goodwill stores. Instead they just sit here. And they won't even let us touch them. The warehouse manager nearly bit my hand off when I started looking through them."

"What will happen to them eventually?" asked Carl.

"I don't know," said Brenda, "but I intend to find out."

At that point, the discussion of the books was interrupted as the first of the carts was rolled into position.

Cleanup from a prior election was a low stress, somewhat monotonous task. Left over materials and forms, that should have either been thrown out or returned to the Government Center on election night, were removed from the carts and appropriately sorted. Flash drives were removed from the scanners. The auxiliary bins were searched for stray ballots (there were none). There was no attempt to restock the items for the next election. That would occur at a future time when testing for the next election would take place. Exactly when that would be, no one yet knew. November, certainly. But sooner perhaps, if the parties were to have primaries.

In Virginia there was an election every year. This November, both houses of the state legislature would be on the ballot, as well as a long list of local offices. County Council, School Board, Soil and Water Conservation Board, to name a few. Cindy's older sister, Valerie, had been elected to the school board the previous November to fill a mid-term vacancy. Carl supposed that she would be running for a full term in November. Cindy, of course, had made that disastrous run for Soil and Water. Never again, she had solemnly promised.

The question was if there would be any primary elections prior to November. Primaries in Virginia were generally held on the second Tuesday of June, which this year fell on June eighth. There would be no statewide primaries this year. That occurred only in the years when people were voting for President, U.S. Senate, or Governor. In this "off-year election," things were much more granular. State Senate boundaries were different from House of Delegate boundaries which in turn were different from county district boundaries. A primary election might affect only a small subset of the 240 precincts located in the county. Depending on how many nominations were being contested, there might be many primaries scattered throughout the county, or just a few, or none at all. They wouldn't know for sure until after March 25, which was the deadline for filing.

Carl, as a good election nerd, was hoping for all kinds of primary action on June eighth. He had scanned the newspapers each day to see if there were any contested nominations looming but had found no mention of anything. This was hardly headline stuff, however, so there was no telling what might be happening behind the scenes.

The clean-up work took two days, as Terrence had predicted. Each day at noon, Carl and a few of the other rovers went to the deli next door for lunch. Carl asked if any of them had heard anything about possible primary action but no one had.

Well I guess we'll know on the 25th, he thought as he departed from the warehouse on the second day.

Chapter 9

WEDNESDAY, MARCH 10, 10:00 A.M.

"NORBERT GILBERTSON."

"Norbert, this is Cindy Phelps."

"Why, Cindy. You're the last person I ever expected to be hearing from."

"I know. I realize that—"

"That was a rather abrupt departure you made last year."

"I realize that. Under the circumstances…you know, my poor showing in the debate…"

"Politics is not for the faint of heart, Cindy."

(An awkward silence)

"Norbert, I'm not sure if you know this but Emily Weston is making another run for the State Senate."

"I've heard something about that."

"She has asked me to be her campaign manager."

"A curious choice."

Good God, Norbert. You're not making this easy.

"And, I was wondering—we were wondering if you would be

willing to be her campaign treasurer. You did such a marvelous job on my campaign last year. And we would pay you the going rate. Emily is a bit more financed than I was last year and—"

"No."

"Please Norbert, hear me out."

"No Cindy, I don't think I want to hear you out. I don't mind serving on losing campaigns. Someone has to lose. It's all part of the process. But I don't like wasting my time on people who aren't serious about it. Don't get me wrong; I'm not unsympathetic to Emily Weston. She has served the party well. But the feeling in the party is that it's time for her to step aside, a feeling that's only going to be reinforced by her turning to an amateur like you for her campaign manager."

Please Norbert, don't hold back. Tell me what you really think.

"Please Norbert, don't take out my imperfections on Emily. She is a committed environmentalist; she ran a good campaign against Jennifer Haley last January. She is dead serious about making this run and so am I."

"As you claimed to be last year, as I recall. Cindy, I'm sorry to be sounding so harsh. On a personal level, I like you. You're a charming young lady. But I will not associate myself with any campaign that you are involved with. I must go now. Have a good day."

A click and dial tone sounded before Cindy could say anything more.

Chapter 10

C INDY'S HANDS WERE shaking as she walked up the stone walkway to the house that displayed an aura of rustic grandeur. With no bell visible, she opened the screen door and gave a few taps with the large bronze knocker. Footsteps could be heard coming from the other side. The door opened and a middle-aged lady appeared in the doorway.

"Good afternoon," said Cindy. "I'm Cynthia Phelps. I have a four-thirty appointment to see Mrs. Purvis."

"Yes, she is expecting you," said the woman. She stepped to one side and motioned for Cindy to enter.

The interior of the house had a warm, informal look, comfortable but not ostentatious.

"This way," said the lady, as she proceeded down a hallway. Cindy obediently followed and was led into a room that appeared to be a library. Various paintings of birds decorated the walls and in the corner was a large desk where Mildred Purvis was seated. Spread out before the elderly lady was what appeared to be the day's newspaper.

"Cindy," said Mrs. Purvis, getting to her feet. "So good to see you again. Can we get you something to drink? Helen is making me some tea."

"Tea would be wonderful," said Cindy.

"Excellent, Please sit down and we can talk. I was thinking about you just the other day. And then you called. Isn't it strange how that sort of thing happens?"

Cindy sat down on the chair nearest the desk while Mildred took her seat behind the desk. Her sharp eyes focused in on Cindy. Helen returned to the library with two cups of tea and then left the room, closing the door behind her.

"I gather this is not a social call," said Mildred.

"No, it's not," said Cindy. "I need your advice on something. You see—"

"Emily Weston is running again for State Senate and somehow you're involved."

"Why yes," said Cindy, failing to hide her surprise at Mildred's foreknowledge of the reason behind her visit. "I'm her campaign manager, actually. And I was hoping to pick your brain. We've been having a difficult time recruiting a campaign treasurer. None of the usual suspects seem willing to do it."

"That's what I hear," said Mildred. "I do have my sources."

"Yes, and I was wondering if you could give me the name of the person or persons who were treasurers on Norman's campaigns?"

Mildred smiled.

"That would be me."

"Oh."

"Norman was never much with numbers or forms or regulations. That's where I came in. It isn't that hard, you know. Just read the forms and follow the directions."

There was an uneasy silence as the two woman looked at each other.

"Ask me what you came here for."

"You see…I'm desperate."

"Ask me what you came here for."

Cindy looked down at her hands which once again were shaking.

"You always see right through me."

"I wouldn't say that," said Mildred, smiling. "But I see you as you are. A bright young woman with a good heart who sometimes overreaches. Now ask me what you came here for."

Cindy looked up at Mildred.

"Would you be willing to serve as Emily's campaign treasurer?"

"Yes I would. Emily Weston has always been a friend to the environment. I'd be happy to help her. But only if…"

Mildred paused and looked intently at Cindy.

"…only if she and you are in it for the long haul. Politics can be rough. You're going to make mistakes. That's fine but I need to know that you won't cut and run at the first sign of trouble."

"No, not this time," said Cindy.

"Good," said Mildred. "Let's set up a meeting with the three of us. I'll download the necessary forms and we can get this thing started. The sooner she can file her paperwork, the less likely it will be that Biff Logan and his cronies will find someone to oppose her in the primary. Although personally, I wouldn't mind if he did. It's high time someone knocked him on his ass and it might as well be us."

Chapter 11

SUNDAY, MARCH 14, 6:00 P.M.

"So PUTTING IT all together we have over 600 signatures. 612 to be exact," said Cindy, with a bright smile. "And here are the forms that Mildred and I completed. I'll take the whole package over to the Government Center tomorrow and you will be officially on the ballot."

"That is so wonderful, Cindy," said Emily, a look of warm appreciation on her face. "I love the environment, I want to be a State Senator, and I don't even mind a bit of campaigning. But all that paperwork. That's what weighs me down. Thank you so much for handling this for me."

"Don't mention it," said Cindy. "Now here is the layout I've created for your brochure. Fortunately we have the money from your prior campaign treasury to do a mailing. What I need from you are a few bullet points on the issues you want to emphasize."

"Well one of the main issues will be that natural gas pipeline that they want to build through the western part of the state. It would be an ecological disaster. But the Republicans and, I'm ashamed to say, some Democrats support it. And the public is mostly uninformed. Opposing this is one of the major reasons I am running."

While not completely unexpected, this was not exactly what Cindy wanted to hear.

Well, this is why she's paying me. To say what needs to be said even if it's not what she wants to hear.

"I know. Carl has mentioned it a few times," said Cindy, slowly. "Something about meeting energy needs. He seemed to think it has broad-based support. Perhaps you might want to emphasize other less controversial issues."

Emily looked fondly at Cindy.

"You know I really like you. You almost remind me of…Well no matter. And I am so grateful you are in this with me…"

Emily paused. It was as if she was looking for just the right words to say. Cindy, for her part, squirmed uncomfortably in her seat, somewhat embarrassed by this show of affection that she did not feel she deserved.

"You see," said Emily. "My goal really isn't to be in the State Senate. Don't get me wrong, I want to win, but that isn't the real reason I'm running. I want to make sure that the issues I care about, like that pipeline, are brought to the public's attention. I'd rather lose campaigning for what matters than win, just for the sake of winning."

Cindy couldn't help but reflect on her own abortive run for Soil and Water the year before. And the wild-eyed political dreams and fantasies that she had briefly entertained.

"You make me ashamed to even be here with you."

"No, please, that's not my intent," said Emily. "I want and need your practical advice. Just don't be offended if I don't follow it all the time."

"Well on a practical level, please let me work some other points into your brochure. Like education. Transportation. Job creation. You do need to broaden things a bit."

She could tell that Emily wasn't convinced.

"Please. Let me help you."

"Well, all right," said Emily, after a lengthy pause. "If it will make you feel better."

"Great. Consider it done," said Cindy. Then changing the subject before Emily could entertain second thoughts, "There is one thing that you won't have to worry about. It appears that you were right. It doesn't seem that anyone will be challenging you for the nomination. I haven't heard anything and neither has Carl. And he's pretty good about sniffing out such things."

"That's a relief," admitted Emily. "I know I said I wasn't worried but, in the back of my mind, I was afraid that Biff would tap some younger, more personable worthy to oppose me. This allows us to focus all the more on November and Jennifer Haley. She's the enemy."

"And she will be tough to beat," said Cindy. "You know that better than most. She's smart and personable and—"

"She's evil," snapped Emily. For moment Emily's face was twisted in an expression of raw hatred that Cindy did not imagine her being capable of. Then, just as quickly, the moment passed.

"No, I didn't mean that," said Emily who seemed embarrassed by what she had just said. "No one is totally evil. It's just that…there are things about her that need to be known. I'll need your help on this…as we get toward November…uh yes…but no primary…. that will be good…and I guess we're done here…"

It was an odd way for the meeting to end, reflected Cindy, as she drove back to her apartment. On one level, it had been very productive. She liked Emily, who seemed more modest and unassuming than the political people she had met the previous year. Emily seemed to have taken to her as well. Cindy knew that she was childless and had never been married.

She must be lonely. At least some of the time.

But then there was that moment. So unexpected. How could such a gentle woman feel so much hatred for another? It was a bit scary.

I guess we all have our dark side. Lord knows, I have mine.

Cindy pulled into her apartment complex and parked her car. Skipping up the stairs, she reflected on the week ahead. No big meetings at work. A bit of flexibility there. It would be easy tomorrow to slip away and drive to the Government Center with Emily's paperwork.

When she entered her apartment, she noticed that the telephone answering machine light was on. She pressed the button.

"Hi, Cindy. This is Brad Marsden. Say, on Wednesday I need to drive out to Stony Creek to file some reports. I'll be leaving about four p.m. How about you join me and get that Mercedes ride I owe you. Let me know if you can break away from work. Just text me, no point calling the house. Hope to hear from you."

Brad's invitation was completely unexpected.

But sometimes unexpected can be fun. Should be no problem leaving work a little early. Why not? And Brad's right. With the two of them sharing Carl's townhouse, no point confusing things with phone messages for different people.

Cindy opened her cell phone and texted,

"Sounds great. See you on Wednesday."

Chapter 12

MONDAY, MARCH 15, 9:00 A.M.

NICOLAS DELGADO WAS a member of the county council, representing the Springdale district. The council had regularly scheduled monthly meetings where issues of county concern were debated and voted upon. In addition his office served as an information clearing house for the citizens of his district and he tried to be responsive to the concerns of his constituents. Most of the time it was just referring someone to the right department but every once in a while an inquiry came across his desk that prompted an in-person investigation. It was such an inquiry that had brought him this morning to the county warehouse facility in Springdale.

Nicolas gave an inward groan as he got out of his car at the warehouse parking lot. Walking toward him with a bright smile on her face was the local TV reporter, Tracy Miller, followed by her ever-obedient cameraman.

"Good morning, Mr. Delgado," she said, extending her hand. "What a beautiful day it is to be roaming the aisles of the county warehouse."

"Good morning, Tracy," said Nicolas, forcing a smile. "A pleasure it is."

"You wouldn't be here by any chance to investigate that book scandal?"

"Hardly a scandal," said Nicolas. "Merely looking into a matter from one of my constituents—"

"Then you wouldn't mind a little on-screen attention," said Tracy, giving a quick nod to her cameraman.

"Tracy, while I always love doing interviews with you, there isn't anything here worthy of the public's time. We've had an inquiry from a citizen as to how the county disposes of some of its surplus books. Now, if you'll excuse me—"

"This is Tracy Miller, WMML news, here at the county warehouse facility with councilman Nicolas Delgado who is here investigating a situation regarding county property which appears to be, at best, irregular. Mr. Delgado, is it true the county is shredding perfectly good library books that could be donated to worthwhile organizations that would love to have them?" asked Tracy, shoving her microphone in Nicolas' face.

"I can't comment on that," said Nicolas, as he walked past Tracy up the ramp into the warehouse.

"So there you have it, ladies and gentleman," said Tracy, brushing some strands of her long blond hair out of her face. *"A rather cryptic and frankly unsatisfactory response from the county councilman who either knows or should know the situation. Rest assured that WMML will be returning to this story as further information becomes available."*

"OK, that was good," she said to the cameraman. "We'll run with that at the 10:00 a.m. news cycle. I'm going in now to see what dirt I can find. You stay out here and be ready when I come back."

Tracy handed her microphone to the cameraman and walked up the ramp into the warehouse. When she entered she could see Nicolas conversing at the front desk with one of the workman.

"...and how long has this practice been going on?" Nicolas was asking.

"I'm not rightly sure," the man was saying. "It was already in place when I got here three years ago. Once a month they deliver old books from the libraries to be shredded. They're put in laundry carts in the back. Then every six months a county truck comes and hauls them away. The next pickup will be in mid-June."

"To be shredded?"

"That's my understanding but don't quote me on it."

"You mean you don't actually know?" chimed in Tracy, with a tone of shocked incredulity.

"Who are you?" asked the man. "What are you doing here?"

"I'm Tracy Miller, WMML—"

"Do you have a county ID badge? If not then you'll have to leave. And I mean now."

"I represent the people and they have a right to know—" stated Tracy, indignantly

"I don't care if you represent the Holy Father in Rome. If you don't have a county ID badge—"

"Hold on everyone," said Nicolas, holding up his hands. "No need to go nuclear here. Rudy, this is Tracy Miller, reporter for WMML. Tracy, this is Rudy Matheson. He's the foreman here at the warehouse. He's also responsible for security at the warehouse. So we are his guests. Now Rudy, Ms. Miller will be with me at all times during our visit. I will take full responsibility for her. Would that be satisfactory?"

Please Rudy, I don't want to be on the six o'clock news.

"I guess so," said Rudy, grudgingly. "I'll show you where the books are. But try and be brief. There's a lot of work going on here and we don't want to disrupt the process. Also there's some heavy machinery in use, like forklifts and shrink wrapping machines. You just can't wander off. It's for your own safety."

"May my cameraman come inside?" asked Tracy.

Before Rudy could answer, Nicolas jumped in, "No Tracy. We're disrupting things enough by being here. Rudy will show us what we've asked to see and that will be that."

Tracy's face registered her displeasure but she said nothing.

Rudy turned around and headed into the heart of the warehouse, motioning for Nicolas and Tracy to follow.

"Now remember. This is county policy about the books. It's not something we, at the warehouse, dreamed up. I can't tell you why we're shredding these books. You need to talk to the folks at the Government Center."

Just then a forklift passed, carrying a mountain of boxes.

"It's back here, near the election area," Rudy was saying.

And there they were. Three laundry carts, each piled high with what appeared to be old library books. "Fascinating. I don't believe this," said Tracy, as she went forward to the first laundry cart and picked up a copy of *Moby Dick*. "May I have this?"

"No," said Rudy, indignantly. "This is county property. Hey, you can't do this!" Tracy had started rummaging through the cart.

Rudy turned to Nicolas.

"I thought you were going to keep the broad under control. She just can't rummage through county property," he hissed.

"No she can't," agreed Nicolas, in a commanding voice. "Tracy, we've seen what we asked to see. We must leave now."

Tracy looked down at the books in her hand for a few seconds and then lowered them back into the laundry cart.

"Of course," she said. "Excuse me. I got carried away. Education is very important to me and books have always been special. You're right. We need to leave. Thank you, Mr. Matheson for showing us around."

The three of them returned to the front of the warehouse. Nicolas and Tracy said their goodbyes to Rudy and left.

Once they were out of the warehouse, Tracy turned on Nicolas.

"Don't tell me you're satisfied with what you saw?" she demanded.

"Actually, I am very satisfied with what I saw," said Nicolas. "It's clear to me that they're simply following county policy. Now why we have that policy is a legitimate question, one which I will get answered. That answer, however, will come from the Government Center, not here at the warehouse. Tracy, I know you love to find scandals wherever you go, but there's nothing here. So if you'll excuse me, I'll be off."

And with that, Nicolas got into his car.

"Get a shot of him driving off," said Tracy to the cameraman.

You're wrong Mr. Bigshot councilman. The pieces are falling into place, oh so nicely. There is a nice juicy scandal here, even if I have to make one up.

Chapter 13

Wednesday, March 17, 4:00 P.M.

FORTY-EIGHT DEGREES WAS a bit chilly to have the convertible top down. Throw in a stiff March breeze and it was really a dumb idea. Cindy suspected that she would pay for it with a head cold later on, but for now all the concerns from her job, from Emily's campaign, and indeed from everything seemed to melt away.

"How fast have you taken it?" she asked Brad, as they sat idling in front of one of those annoying red lights.

"Close to a hundred on the interstate," said Brad. "Of course you have to know where you can get away with it. The cops are getting better and better at flagging down speeders. I should know. I'm one of them."

"One of what? A cop or a speeder?"

"Both," said Brad, grinning as the light turned green.

"Maybe we can take the interstate on the way back," said Cindy. It was more of a request than a statement. They had avoided the interstate on the way out. Much too congested, going in that direction, at that hour.

"Sounds like a plan," said Brad, who seemed most pleased with how things were going.

A few minutes later they arrived at the police academy parking lot where he needed to drop off the reports.

"I'll be just a few minutes," he said to Cindy. Reaching into his jacket pocket, he pulled out a pack of cigarettes.

"Do you want one while you wait?"

Cindy hesitated. Having smoked all through college, she had vowed on her graduation day to quit, cold turkey. And she had. Sort of. Only in moments of stress did she backslide. The last few months had been relatively stress free. Work was going well. She had a boyfriend that she genuinely cared for. Her once rocky relationship with her sister had been smoothed over. It had been two, no three, months since she had last been tempted.

Oh, what the hell.

"Sure."

"Here you go," said Brad, handing her the pack.

He grabbed several folders and walked toward the academy door.

Cindy lit up and then leaned over to look at herself in the rear view mirror. Her hair was a complete mess from the open-air ride. Using her comb, she struggled to bring it under some semblance of control.

Taking a drag, Cindy reflected on the two brothers who were now part of her life. Carl was so steady, reliable, and consistent. He was intelligent in a bookish sort of way but was a bit dense about everyday things. And of course, he was obsessed with election service.

"We all have to contribute something to our society," he would say. "This is my contribution."

And he certainly treated her well. With kindness. With respect.

And then there was Brad. Even from their brief acquaintance, Cindy could tell he was cut from a different cloth. Handsome yes, and a glib talker, but he seemed more than that. He seemed so sure of himself. And exciting. Yes, that was the word, "exciting." Even his job, homicide cop, resonated with excitement.

"Hey pretty girl, want a ride?"

Cindy gave a start. She had been so engrossed in her thoughts that she hadn't seen Brad approach.

Brad climbed into the car.

"You know, we should get to know each other better."

Brad reached over and took the cigarette from Cindy and put it in the ash tray. Then taking her hands in his, he said, "I don't think my brother realizes what a gem you are."

"No, I mean yes, I mean what are you—"

Brad leaned over and kissed her softly on the lips.

Like you didn't know this would happen.

They started kissing, tentatively at first and then more intently.

Then suddenly with a jerk, Cindy pulled back.

Brad tried to close in again, but Cindy held up her hands.

"Please, I can't do this," she said, breathing heavily.

Brad wasn't fazed by Cindy's reluctance. He had experience in these types of situations.

"It's all right, Cindy. I sense we have something special—"

"No, we don't," said Cindy, with unexpected firmness. "We hardly know each other. God knows you're tempting and a couple of years ago I would have been ready to go but that was then and now is now. I'm with Carl, and you need to respect that."

"And you really think my brother can satisfy you? For the long haul, I mean?" asked Brad, with a sense of incredulity.

"I don't know," said Cindy, honestly. "All I know is that before Carl, I bounced from one romantic adventure to another and all I have to show for it is a string of ex-boyfriends, none of whom I'm on speaking terms with. I intend to give this thing with Carl every chance to succeed and I'm not going to blow it by falling for the first temptation that comes along."

"And if it fails?"

"If it fails, I'll look elsewhere. But not to you. I would never cause Carl that pain," said Cindy, adding with a grin, "Besides, you're not the only stud out there."

Brad was intelligent enough to reads the signs. Cindy's refusal had been definitive. Also, her honesty about her past hit home. What did he have to show from all his past conquests?

"You're making me feel a bit ashamed," said Brad. "And contrary to my recent actions, I do care for my brother. I would appreciate it if you don't mention this to him."

"I'm not exactly blameless either," said Cindy. "I won't mention it if you don't. But it can never happen again."

"You have my word. But don't you think he suspects?"

"No," said Cindy, smiling. "Carl's a bit dense about these things. It's part of his charm, actually."

There was silence for a few seconds as Brad processed what had happened.

"Just one more question," he asked. "If this is the way you feel, then why did you agree to come with me today?"

Now it was Cindy who took a moment before responding.

"Because I didn't figure it out until just now."

Brad nodded his understanding.

"Now," said Cindy, her bright smile returning, "Show me what a Mercedes can do on the interstate."

Chapter 14

SUNDAY, MARCH 21, 5:00 P.M.

"*T*HIS IS TRACY *Miller, WMML News, standing outside the county government warehouse in Springdale, reporting with a fast-breaking story that threatens to reveal a county practice which is, at the very least, problematic.*

"*It would seem that this warehouse is being used as a storage facility for books that have been labeled as surplus by the county libraries and are stored inside in huge laundry carts. These are books that would, no doubt, be welcome in many parts of the county. Day care centers. Senior citizen residences. Community centers in some of our less affluent areas. Instead, WMML has learned, once a sufficient quantity of these books are received, they will be shipped out to be destroyed.*

"*To make matters worse, county officials here at the warehouse have forbidden WMML access to the inside where these books can be seen. This raises the question. What are they hiding? Here with me now is Republican State Senator Jennifer Haley.*

"*Ms. Haley, does this county practice strike you as problematic?*"

"*Problematic is an understatement, Tracy. This shows an utter*

*disregard by the county Democratic administration for the citizens
from the less advantageous parts of the county where these books would
be most welcome. These are exactly the folks that the Democratic Party
claims to care about. And now they are preventing public access to
see what's going on. An outrage; a pure outrage. I am demanding an
investigation..."*

Click.

"I'm sorry but I can't bear watching any more of this," said
Stan Turner, putting down the remote. "Why do they always try to
politicize everything?"

"It was one of the rovers, Brenda, who brought up the whole
question of the books," said Carl. "You met her last year at the
warehouse," he added, looking at Cindy.

"I remember her. She was nice," said Cindy. "And I remember
those laundry carts full of books during my various warehouse
adventures last fall. It seemed a bit strange at the time but there
were other things on my mind." She smiled, remembering her
nighttime raid.

Carl and Cindy were Sunday dinner guests at the home of
Valerie and Stan Turner and their grade school sons. This was
happening with increasing regularity. Valerie liked Carl and
sensed that his presence in Cindy's life was a good thing. Since
Carl's culinary skills were modest and Cindy's non-existent, the
Turners' hospitality was much appreciated.

"So why are they destroying those books?" asked Valerie.

"That's the question, isn't it?" said Carl. "I'd be interested
in learning what it's all about, but I suspect there's a simple
explanation. Nothing that could be called an 'outrage.'"

"It's all politics," said Cindy. "Jennifer Haley's election to the
State Senate last January was a very close thing. And since Emily
Weston is running against her again, she knows it will be another

— 47 —

tough campaign. She will do anything that will embarrass the Democrats."

"I can see why Haley wants to exploit this," said Stan. "What I don't understand is why Tracy Miller felt this was even worthy of a TV spot. She's no dope. She must know the whole thing is bogus."

"Actually it makes perfect sense," said Valerie. "Everything I've seen tells me that Tracy Miller is both an aggressive journalist and a self-promoter. She loves the journalistic spotlight. I wouldn't be surprised to see her run for political office someday."

"Oh," said Cindy, softly. Her expression suggested both surprise and instant comprehension. She looked over at Carl. "I wonder if that's why Steve Winters wouldn't be Emily's campaign manager."

"What do you mean?" asked Carl.

"Tracy is going to challenge Emily in the primary and Steve will be her campaign manager."

"No way," said Carl. "Steve is working for some House of Delegates candidate. Anyway, Tracy would have filed long before this if she was interested."

"But you told me that the actual deadline is the 25th. That's this Thursday."

"Perhaps. But no one waits to the last day to file. That only happens in cheap election thrillers."

"That's a lot of inside baseball you two seem to have picked up," said Valerie.

"Well, you see, I kind of—" began Cindy, looking away from Valerie's gaze.

"Kind of what?" said Valerie, giving her sister a measured look.

Cindy and Carl exchanged glances. Carl gave a shrug as if to say,

It's up to you. She's your sister.

"OK, OK," said Cindy. "I've agreed to be Emily's campaign manager."

Valerie gave Carl a look, as if to say,

"You're the one who's supposed to keep her out of trouble."

"Cyn, are you sure that's wise?"

"No, it's not wise," snapped Cindy, getting to her feet.

"The wise thing," she continued, pacing the room, "would be to tell Emily that she's on her own. Let Biff Logan push her off to the sidelines. But one thing I did learn from last year's fiasco is that the environment really does matter. And Emily Weston knows more about the environment than Tracy Miller, Jennifer Haley, and Anthony Palucci all put together."

"Who's Anthony Palucci?" asked Valerie.

"He's some Tea Party goon who's challenging Haley from the right. Anyway, I did learn quite a bit about campaign organization last year and if Emily thinks I'm her best shot, I'm going to give it all I got."

"Carl, what do you think of all this?" asked Stan.

"As the only Republican in the room," said Carl slowly, aware that his every word was being scrutinized, "I do think Jennifer Haley will be tough to beat. She's smart, hardworking, and has distanced herself from the down-state Republicans on some issues. I voted for her the last time out."

Cindy gave a derisive snort.

Any further political discussion was curtailed as Mathew and David Turner, ages ten and eight, burst into the room. Cindy had firmly entrenched herself as the "cool aunt" and they had learned to accept Carl as her regular companion.

Two hours later, well fed, Carl and Cindy said their goodbyes.

"So do you still prefer Haley to Weston?" asked Cindy pointedly, as they got into the car.

"I don't know," began Carl. "No wait, I do know. Yes, on balance I prefer Haley. I know the environment is important but it's not the only issue."

The car was silent as Carl pulled out into the road.

"OK," said Cindy, softly, breaking the silence.

"OK, what?"

"OK, I accept that. We just see things differently. Is this going to be weird, me being Emily's campaign manager?"

Carl considered. He liked Cindy a lot, no it was more than just "like," and it would be silly to let something like this stand between them. But to pretend to be something he was not, just to please Cindy, would, in the end, do neither of them any good.

"No, it will not be weird," he said decisively. "I think it's great what you're doing and I will help in any way you want me to. And I promise to keep my political opinions to myself."

Carl waited for Cindy's response but she remained silent for the next several minutes.

Then, out of the blue,

"Carl, do you ever think about having kids?"

It was not the question Carl had expected.

"Well...I'm not sure...I would think that is something...to be talked about..."

Cindy laughed.

"Didn't see that coming, did you?"

Chapter 15

MONDAY, MARCH 22

FROM: COUNTY REPUBLICAN Party
   To: Mr. Carl Marsden:

Dear Mr. Marsden,

This is to inform you that you are no longer eligible to represent the Republican Party as a county election officer. This decision was reached, after careful deliberation, by the county Republican Committee.

You may appeal this decision by contacting the committee at 446-REPB (7372).

Sincerely,

Seymour McNulty, secretary

cc: county Office of Elections

Chapter 16

Tuesday, March 23, 8:00 a.m.

ONCE AGAIN IT was time to "rescue the bins." In a few minutes, Rolando would open the door to the vault where the blue bins, filled with ballots from last November's election, were stored. It was necessary to bring these bins back to the warehouse where they could be inserted into the outer black casings, in preparation for primary day. The challenge was that although the bins needed to be returned to the warehouse, the voted ballots they contained had to be retained, by law, for two years. So today the rovers would build cardboard boxes and then transfer the ballots from the bins to the boxes. They would then label and seal the boxes and return them to the vault. The empty bins would be placed on pallets. Then in a few days' time, county workmen would take the pallets to the warehouse. This had been the drill for the past few years and everyone was familiar with it.

"I have a few announcements to make," said Terrence, to the team of rovers. They were seated in the courthouse cafeteria, waiting for the vault to open and the work to begin.

"The first involves primary day, June eighth. As you know, this is the year in the cycle that is mostly given to local elections. County Council. School Board. Soil and Water Conservation Board."

"Ah yes, Soil and Water," said Jack Vincent, winking in Carl's direction. "Is Cindy going to make another run?"

"No, she's taking a pass this time," said Carl.

"Well, tell her 'hey' from me," said Jack. "You should have been there last November. She took over the whole damn board meeting. Had those stuffy bureaucrats tied up in knots. Most fun I've had in ages."

"I'll pass it along. Cindy enjoyed all those stories you told—"

"If we can continue," said Terrence, looking sternly at both Jack and Carl.

"As I was saying, June eighth is primary day. The focus this year is local elections along with the two houses of the state legislature. There are no statewide elections. What this means is that, depending on who files, some precincts will have primary elections while others will not. If only one candidate files for a party's nomination, or if no candidates file, then there will be no primary for that particular office. The deadline for filing is March 25, two days from now. The parties have known for a while who was going to file, so the electoral board has ordered the ballots from the printer. They really don't expect any last minute changes. Now these are the primaries that we know are taking place. House of Delegates, 34th District Democrat. Scott that's mostly your route; State Senate, 30th District, both Republican and Democrat. Brenda, that's yours..."

Terrence read down the list of primaries to be held on June eighth. Carl waited eagerly for something that would impact his route but he heard nothing. This was disappointing. Being on the sidelines on primary day was not his idea of being a rover.

"...and finally the State Senate, 48th district. The Republicans are having a primary. Carl, I believe this is on your route."

That's right. The Republicans are having a primary for State Senate. He had forgotten about that. He'd be in the field on primary day, after all. All was right with the world.

"Isn't that the Jennifer Haley district?" asked Brenda. "I know the Democrats will challenge in the fall but why would the Republicans challenge a sitting member in a primary?"

"She is being challenged by Anthony Palucci," said Carl.

"Palucci!" scoffed Brenda. "That weirdo runs for something every year. What's he pushing for this time? More Confederate statues?"

"If we can continue," said Terrence, in a tone that suggested that he was tired of repeating the phrase.

He looked around the room. There had been a certain amount of buzz among the rovers while the various primary matchups had been announced. Now Terrence waited for complete silence.

Once silence had been achieved, he continued.

"As some of you may be aware, our county warehouse was the subject of some unfortunate publicity these last few days," said Terrence. A number of the rovers looked over at Brenda.

"And I say to all of you what I said behind closed doors to Terrence," said Brenda, defiantly. "I did nothing wrong. As a concerned citizen, I felt it my duty to contact my elected county representative to investigate why the county is shredding those perfectly good books, when there are so many organizations that could use them. Organizations that serve the less affluent areas of our county. I had no idea that Tracy Miller would get involved and make a spectacle of it."

"An attention grabbing self-promoter if ever there was one," grumbled Jack. A number of the rovers nodded in agreement.

"Be that as it may," said Terrence. "A spectacle was created that put the county in a bad light. So Brenda, could you tell the group what was explained to you yesterday."

Brenda gave Terrence a sour look, as if to say "Is this necessary?" and then spoke in a monotone that suggested that this was a rehearsed speech that she had been directed to give.

"The books are coming from libraries. It's been years since any of them have been checked out. Yes, they will be shredded but it's part of a recycling program. The recycled pulp with be used to create new paper products that can be used and enjoyed by county residents. It's the paper industry's 'Circle of Life.' All is as it should be. Nothing is wrong. Over and out."

"Thank you, Brenda," said Terrence. "Unfortunately it is not quite 'over and out.' The folks at the warehouse have reminded us that we are their guests. We are not to interfere with the regular working of the warehouse. The concern is that things have gotten too lax. There is also a genuine concern for safety. Some of the equipment and piles of supplies at the warehouse are potentially hazardous to the unaware. Therefore, we will be much more limited as to where we can go within the facility. Also our comings and goings will be more closely monitored. All the details haven't been worked out yet, but things will be quite a bit different when we assemble for testing which, I will remind you, begins next Tuesday."

A few grumbles, greeted Terrence's announcement.

"Ah yes, I think Rolando is ready for us," said Terrence. With that the rovers proceeded through the cafeteria doors on their way to "rescue the bins."

Six hours later, their mission complete, the rovers headed for the parking lot. Carl, however, lingered.

"Terrence, Can we talk?"

"Of course."

Carl took out the letter he had received from the county Republican Party.

"Do you know what this means?" said Carl, showing the letter to Terrence.

Terrence studied the letter.

"It means, pretty much what it says," said Terrence. "In the eyes of the Office of Elections, you no longer represent the Republican Party."

"Does that impact the work I'm doing?" asked Carl, anxiously.

"Potentially, it does," said Terrence, "You see, the chief election officer must represent the party of the sitting governor while the assistant chief represents the other party. So if you are not representing either party, you are considered an independent. You can serve as an election officer but not as chief or assistant chief."

"But does it impact my position as a rover? I like to think I've been doing a good job."

"And you certainly have," said Terrence. "You saved our bacon last fall by identifying those bad scanners. With an assist from your lady friend, of course," he added with a smile.

"But unfortunately there is more to it than that. The electoral board has decided that all rovers in the field need to represent one of the parties. So yes, you can continue to be a rover but you will lose your route. You will have to work in the Command Center on Election Day."

"This is crazy," said Carl. "It should be based on how I do my job. Not whether some party endorses me. Once we take the oath, we cease to be Republican or Democrat. Just public servants. This isn't right."

Carl was working up to a fit of righteous indignation, something that was very unusual for him.

"I agree with you," said Terrence, with a helpless shrug of his shoulders. "But that's the way it is. We live in contentious times. So unless you can get some party to endorse you, I'm afraid you will lose your route."

Chapter 17

Tuesday afternoon, 3:00 P.M.

"**S**URE, COME ON over," said Cindy. "Val's over here now. They bought a new china pattern and they're giving me some of their old stuff."

Thirty minutes later found Carl in the living room of Cindy's apartment. His meeting with Terrence had given him the need to vent.

"So let me get this straight," said Valerie. "Everyone at the Office of Elections thinks you're doing a good job, but you can't continue to serve because the Republican Committee thinks you are not 'Republican enough.'"

"That's pretty much it," said Carl, sadly.

"Wow. And I thought the school board was screwed up."

"Why do you suppose the Republican Committee did that?" asked Cindy.

"I don't know," said Carl. "I always vote Republican. Well, almost always. And I agree with most of their positions. Smaller government, less taxes, pro-life, energy independence. There is a phone number I can call to appeal. Maybe I can use it and try to get back in their good graces."

"Of course, there is another solution," said Cindy, with a mischievous smile on her face. "There's another party you could join."

"No."

"The party of Thomas Jefferson," said Cindy.

"And Franklyn Delano Roosevelt," added Valerie.

"And Roger B. Taney," countered Carl.

"Who's Roger B. Taney?" asked Cindy.

"Don't worry about it," said Valerie. Then turning her attention back to Carl, "And Harry Truman and John F. Kennedy and—"

"Stop, no," said Carl, trying to smile. "I should have known better than trying to get support in this devil's den."

"Seriously Carl," said Cindy. "Give the party a call and plead your case. You are the most Republican person I know. It must be some mistake."

"I'm not sure it's a mistake," said Valerie, thoughtfully.

"How so?" said Carl and Cindy in unison

"Carl, you supported Cindy in her race last year and she ran with the Democratic Party's endorsement."

"Yes, that's true but it was a special case and—"

"And as I recall, you contributed to her campaign—"

"Five hundred dollars," chimed in Cindy.

"—and you held a fundraiser for her at your townhouse and you secured signatures on her petition and—"

"OK, I supported Cindy and she's a Democrat, but that's only one race."

"And you supported me in my school board race, thank you very much. And both Cindy and I had opponents endorsed by the Republicans."

The room grew silent.

"You're a RINO," declared Valerie.

"I am not a RINO," said Carl indignantly.

"What's a RINO?" asked Cindy.

"Republican in Name Only," answered Valerie. "The GOP Border Patrol is constantly trying to ferret them out and you, Mr. Marsden, got your hand caught in the cookie jar."

"My word," said Cindy, in mock surprise. "You mean I've been dating a RINO and never even knew it."

"I am not a RINO!" repeated Carl, practically shouting.

"RINO! RINO!" the sisters chanted in unison.

Even as she was saying it, however, Cindy sensed that the teasing had gone as far as it should. Carl looked so miserable. She flashed a warning look at her sister.

"Carl, just call them and explain it. Tell them your girlfriend drugged your coffee. Tell them you're sorry and it will never happen again. It's sort of like going to Confession. You Catholics are good at that. I'm sure they'll listen."

She's right. I need to call the committee and do whatever penance they require.

Carl nodded. He knew what he had to do. He then offered to help unpack the dishes that Valerie had brought over but Cindy declined.

"Go home and make the call," she said, seeing him to the door. "And good luck. I know this will work out."

And with a kiss and a hug she sent him on his way.

"He gets so emotional over that election stuff," said Cindy, returning to the living room. "Last Sunday, after Mass, he outlined the entire rover schedule from now to primary day."

"After Mass?"

"Yeah, he goes every Sunday and sometimes I go with him"

There was a pause of several seconds.

"You really like him, don't you?"

Cindy, slowly nodded. "Yes, I do."

"Cyn."

"Yeah?"

"Don't screw it up."

Chapter 18

TUESDAY, 4:30 P.M.

"**G**OOD AFTERNOON, REPUBLICAN Party headquarters."

"Yes, good afternoon. I'd like to talk to someone about this letter I received."

"Oh, you're one of the election officers who've left the party."

"That's it. I have never left the party."

"Name, please."

"It's Marsden. Carl Marsden. I've been serving as an election officer for the past six years. Always representing the Republican Party."

"It says here that you publically supported two Democratic endorsed candidates in last November's election."

"Yes, but—"

"And there were viable Republican alternatives. Candidates who could have used your support. One of then, Janet Hayes, lost her school board race by the narrowest of margins."

"Yes, but there were special circumstances—"

"Mr. Marsden, every election is special."

There was an uneasy silence.

"What do I need to do to be able to represent the party again?"

"Let's see. You're in the 48th district. Jennifer Haley is running for reelection to the State Senate. If you were to become an active supporter of her campaign, it would go a long way toward reestablishing your status."

"Consider it done. I voted for her in the last election."

And my girlfriend is managing her rival's campaign. No need to mention that.

"And a campaign contribution would always be appreciated."

Ten minutes later and a hundred dollars poorer, Carl completed the call. He and the Office of Elections would be receiving a letter shortly, indicating that once again he would be representing the Republican Party as an election officer/rover. His exile was over. He was no longer a RINO.

Chapter 19

THURSDAY, MARCH 25, 6:30 P.M.

I T HAD BEEN a long day. The meeting on the Donaldson account had started at 7:00 a.m. and had lasted well into the afternoon. Normally these all-day affairs energized Cindy. But not this time. They had gone over the same points over and over again. When things were finally brought to a halt, she was completely exhausted.

Fortunately, she had not scheduled anything for the evening. No campaign strategizing with Emily. No date with Carl. No babysitting her nephews. Some takeout food. A hot bath. Maybe a little TV. All followed by a good night's sleep.

Forty-five minutes later, she was unlocking the door to her apartment. After turning on some lights, she proceeded to the kitchen area, holding a bag containing her recently purchased Peruvian style chicken dinner.

She was transferring the dinner to a plate when she noticed that the call button on her phone was flashing. She walked over to the phone and saw that there had been two calls. She pressed the button.

"Cindy, this is Emily Weston. Could you call me when you get a chance? We need to discuss how this changes things. Talk to you soon."

That was a weird message, thought Cindy. *How "this" changes things. What "this" is she referring to?*

Cindy gave a sigh. She really didn't want to get involved in election stuff this evening but it sounded like Emily was concerned about something. She'd give her a call after dinner.

She pressed the button again.

"Hi Cindy. It's Carl. Just wondering how you are holding up. I can tell you I was shocked. Turns out you were right. I guess this changes things. Call me when you can."

Carl's message, on top of Emily's, was a wake-up call. Something was up. Cindy was beginning to feel like Rip Van Winkle. What was it that Emily said?

" We need to discuss how this changes things."

And from Carl,

"...how are you holding up...I was shocked...I guess this changes things."

Dinner can wait. I need to find out what's happened.

She placed the call.

"Carl, this is Cindy."

"Cindy, I've been thinking about you all day. How are you doing?"

"Uh...OK, I guess."

"You saw it coming. I sure didn't."

"Carl, you need to help me out here. I'm not exactly sure what you're referring to?"

"You mean you haven't heard? It was announced early this morning. But I guess you've probably been involved in one of those nonstop all-day meetings you have over at *MarketPro.*"

"Yes, work's been intense. Now please tell me, what was

announced?"

"It's Tracy Miller. She's taking a leave of absence from the TV station."

"Whatever for?"

"She's running for office. Today was the deadline and she filed for the 48th State Senate district as a Democrat. She will be running against Emily Weston in the primary and Steve Winters will be her campaign manager."

Chapter 20

SATURDAY, MARCH 27, 10:00 A.M.

"*T*RACY, *AFTER SEVERAL years of being the face of political news in our county, why have you decided to leave your position in news journalism and throw your hat into the ring?*"

"*Jimmy, it was not an easy decision, I tell you. But with so many of our constituents' needs not being met by the Republican controlled legislature, I felt compelled to act.*"

"*But hasn't the Democratic Party already put up a full slate of candidates for both the House of Delegates and State Senate for November's election? And let's be specific. Emily Weston received the party's support in that special election last year and made a close run of it. Why not give her another chance?*"

Tracy flipped her long blond hair and gave a bright smile.

"*Now Jimmy, don't try and get me to say anything negative about Emily Weston. She is a dear, dear lady, one of the true matriarchs of the county Democratic Party. And she certainly has shown leadership in the area of the environment. But if we are going to capture control of the State Senate, we need to make sure we have the candidates who can best resonate with the widest spectrum of voters and whose interests and passions encompass many issues, not just the environment. As a news reporter, I have investigated and uncovered a wide range of abuses. I have exposed incompetent election officers. I uncovered the scandalous destruction of precious books. But Jimmy, I am tired of simply reporting government's failures. I want to be in a position to actually do something about them."*

Toward the end of the discourse, Tracy's demeanor had turned deadly serious and she looked straight into the camera.

"Finally, on a personal note," continued the interviewer, *"after having interviewed so many of our county's political personalities, how does it feel to have the tables turned and to be the subject of an interview?"*

Tracy laughed.

"It does feel different. But having you here with me, Jimmy, makes all the difference. I take my leave of absence here at WMML knowing that everything is in your capable hands," she reached out and took her interviewer by the hand and gave it a squeeze.

"And there you have it, ladies and gentlemen," said Jimmy. *"I'm sure we all wish Tracy Miller the very best in her upcoming campaign for State Senate. We now close out this segment with videotaped highlights from Tracy's Miller's five year career here at WMML. I am Jimmy Forbes and this is..."*

"I think we can put it on mute," said Emily Weston. Cindy complied and the room was silent, even as video images of Tracy Miller continued to fill the TV screen.

"This is the first time I've ever been described as a matriarch," said Emily.

"At least, you're not one of those 'incompetent election officers,'" said Cindy, even as the image of that interview of her with Tracy from the previous January flashed on the screen.

"So where does this leave us?" asked Emily.

Cindy considered. "I think our brochure's layout is still good. But we'll need to spend some of our capital that we were saving for the general election. Plus we need to come up with some way to show Tracy as a lightweight. Superficial. Looks good on the surface, but no depth."

"I'm not going negative," said Emily.

"You may have to," said Cindy. "She going negative on you. All that milk and honey about being a matriarch."

"She is good at what she does," admitted Emily.

"She's a self-serving opportunist," said Cindy. "She's in no way qualified—"

Emily gave Cindy a concerned look.

"I think you're being a bit harsh. Tracy has been covering the political scene for five years. She's obviously been exposed to a wide variety of issues."

"Exposed, perhaps. But without any real understanding. If we don't challenge her, she'll skate by on her looks and personality."

Like I tried to do last year.

"We will challenge her when we differ on the issues, especially when it concerns the environment," said Emily. "But I've already told you, I'm not going negative. And I have also decided that I want to revisit those bullet points in the brochure. I want to go back to primarily stressing my environmental concerns. The pipeline. Off shore drilling. A revenue-neutral carbon tax. Crack down on animal abusers. Clean Energy. These are the things I care about."

"Are you sure? It's just that—"

"I am very sure."

For the next two hours they discussed the direction of the campaign. Cindy felt it was a mistake to focus solely on the environment but in the end she yielded to Emily's insistence. They worked out the changes to the brochure's layout. They discussed the radio/TV ads that their budget allowed them to have. Finally they scheduled some time for debate prep for the first candidate forum to be held in a couple of weeks. In all these matters, Emily's wishes were respected. They would emphasize the environment. They would not go negative.

At least, not yet, thought Cindy.

As they were ending the session, Emily smiled at Cindy.

"I hope this doesn't make you uncomfortable but you remind me so much of my niece. My brother's girl. Like you, Grace was so full of energy. So full of life. She loved the outdoors. Went camping every chance she got."

Cindy didn't know what to say. She was conscious of Emily's use of the past tense.

"Thank you," said Cindy, slowly. She felt some sort of response was called for. "Are you—were you close?"

"Close, oh yes," said Emily with a faraway look in her eyes. "So full of life. Just like you."

Chapter 21

TUESDAY, MARCH 30, 8:00 A.M.

"GOOD MORNING EVERYONE," said Terrence, cheerfully. "Welcome to the start of our testing in preparation for the June eighth primary. Before we get organized and swear you all in, we need to go over some of our revised procedures for working at the warehouse. The first of these changes you are holding in your hands. These mesh lime green vests are to be worn whenever you are working here. It identifies you as guests of the warehouse and will be used to help ensure that you are only in authorized areas. So let's all put on these vests."

A few grumbles greeted the announcement.

"How come you and Michael have orange vests?" asked Jack.

"As Machine Coordinator and Assistant Machine Coordinator, we have a bit more flexibility in our movements," said Terrence. "Now to outline the new procedures, I've asked the site foreman, Rudy Matheson, to say a few words."

Rudy, a muscular man who appeared to be in his mid-forties, stepped forward. Most of the rovers knew him by sight and a few had chatted with him informally over the years.

"First of all, let me assure you that the changes are nothing major," said Rudy. "None of your work here in the election area will be affected. Your pathway from the front door to the election area will not change. No one will have to be escorted to the bathroom."

There were a few sighs of relief.

"But," continued Rudy, "just as we respect your space here in the election area, you need to respect what we are doing in the rest of the warehouse. This is for your own safety as well as the smooth working of the facility. Equipment like forklifts and shrink-wrap machines are hazardous to people who are not familiar with them. Our workers need to be able to concentrate on their jobs without having to look out for the unwary. In addition, we're having a bit of a problem with rodent infestation. We have set some traps, baited with rat poison, at a number of locations in the warehouse. With that in mind, you will see over on this bottom shelf, an area reserved for hazardous materials." He pointed to the shelf.

"Do not touch any of those items. They are all toxic. There's a similar shelf near the front entrance, by the bathrooms."

Carl looked over at the bottom shelf. He could see the box, clearly labeled "Rat Poison." Also on the shelf were containers of what appeared to be industrial strength cleaning solvents along with an open container of antifreeze. They all appeared to have warning labels on them.

"Do we really have rats?" asked Scott.

"There was some evidence of that last month," said Rudy. "The traps caught a couple and the exterminator inspected the outside for possible entry points so we think it's been resolved. But we're still keeping a watchful eye."

There was a pause as the rovers assimilated the information.

"What about the books?" asked Milton.

Rudy and Terrence exchanged looks.

"Do you want to address it?" asked Rudy.

"I think it's better if you do," was Terrence's response.

Rudy nodded.

"As many of you know," began Rudy, "the county has a policy concerning these old library books. They are stored in those laundry carts you see over there." Rudy pointed to the laundry carts in question. "Twice a year they are picked up to be recycled. The next pickup will be in mid-June. I know some of you would like to see them donated. Perhaps you would like to take a book for your own use. Unfortunately the county has a strict policy about this and they have directed me to enforce it. I know it sounds silly but hands off the books. They are county property and we are no more entitled to them than we would be entitled to take office supplies home for our own use."

Silence greeted Rudy's announcement. A few of the rovers looked in Brenda's direction but most of them were sick of the subject and just wanted to move on with the testing.

"One last thing," said Rudy. "All guests have to log out of the warehouse when you leave the building. That's a change from before when you only had to check in. And that's pretty much it. Are there any questions?"

There were none.

"All right, I will get out of your way. Do realize that these changes are for your protection and that you are all welcome guests here in the warehouse."

Carl thought he saw Brenda mouth the words "Liar, liar, pants on fire" as Rudy nodded to Terrence and departed.

Chapter 22

TUESDAY, 8:30 A.M.

"**N**OW THAT WE have those administrative details out of the way," said Terrence, "we can get to the business at hand: Our testing for the June eighth primary. As you know, it's all local offices on the ballot plus both houses of the state legislature. No federal offices. That means we don't have to worry about testing for 'federal only ballots.'"

Scott flashed a grin in Carl's direction. One of his early "rookie mistakes" was to forget to account for these special ballots, that were used only by citizens who had moved from Virginia to a permanent overseas residence.

"Because there are so many different races," continued Terrence, "we have many different ballot styles to work with. Some precincts have only Republican primaries or only Democratic primaries. Some precincts have primaries for both parties and some have no primaries at all. We have a total of thirty-one different ballot styles. We could not create multiple test decks for each ballot style so there will be some waiting."

Carl listened attentively to everything that was being said. Last September had been his first experience in testing so it was still relatively new to him.

"Then we have the situation with the 48th Senate district..." Carl's ears perked up. That was his route. "As some of you know, there was a last minute filing so the printer has not yet delivered ballots for that State Senate district. I'm told it will be a couple of weeks. Let's see...Carl, the 48th is on your route. So when those ballots come in, Carl and one or two others will have to come in to test those precincts. But for now, we'll skip them. Jack, here's a list of the precincts in the 48th as well as the other precincts that won't have primaries at all. Just skip those when we start rolling the carts and scanners in for testing."

Jack nodded and took the list. He was the expert as to where each of the carts resided in the warehouse and generally supervised the process of forming the assembly line.

"I think that covers the particulars," said Terrence. "Since this is our first day of testing, we cannot start until 9:00 a.m. So until then you can review the testing procedures in your handbook. But remember, after today we start at 7:00 a.m. In the meantime please stand and I will swear you all in."

Once the rovers took the oath, they resumed their seats. Some like Carl started to review the appropriate sections in the manual. Others attended to crossword puzzles or chatted amicably

"Why do we have to wait till 9:00 a.m. to start testing?" asked George, one of the less experienced rovers.

"It's the official day and time that's communicated to the parties and candidates. That way if anyone wants to observe the testing process, they will know exactly when it starts. It's pushed back from 7:00 a.m. to 9:00 a.m. on the first day, as a courtesy," said Milton.

"Do many of them come?" asked George.

"They almost never come," said Milton. "Perhaps at one time they did but not anymore. Occasionally some party rep will drop by, but that's more of a social call than anything else."

"Cindy came last year," said Carl. "When she was running for Soil and Water."

"And how long did she stay?" asked Milton.

"Not long" said Carl. "Maybe twenty minutes. But she really wanted to see how the process worked. It was not just a social call."

"Of course not," said Milton, smiling.

Chapter 23

Wednesday, March 31, 7:30 P.M.

I T HAD BEEN a long day. Tiring but good. Work had gone well; she was on a winning streak there.

If only things were going equally well with Emily's campaign.

Tracy Miller's entrance into the race had put a cloud on everything. Cindy wished that Emily had not been so insistent on emphasizing only environmental issues. She had tried one last time to convince her to put other things into the brochure, such as education, job creation, and transportation, but Emily had held firm. Opposition to the pipeline would be the marquee item in the brochure with other environmental issues like opposition to offshore drilling close behind. In the end, Cindy had acquiesced. It was Emily's campaign, after all. Tomorrow Cindy would work with the printer to get the brochure into production.

Driving home, Cindy's mind drifted back to her earlier encounter with Brad. Yes, she had been tempted; she had wavered. But in the end she had done what was right. Earlier that day she had talked briefly with Carl to plan the weekend. Dinner and a movie on Saturday night. Typical evening with Carl. Totally predictable and for the moment at least, totally satisfying. Then on Sunday, Valerie and Stan had invited them over for dinner. They were getting increasingly used to seeing Cindy and Carl as a pair. Cindy was thankful she had not put it all at risk for a few hours of excitement.

She pulled into her assigned parking spot at her apartment complex. Locking the car, she proceeded up the walkway to the front door, pausing to open her mailbox.

Two bills, the latest issue of that woman's magazine she never had time to read, a flier from a carpet cleaning company, and…

…a large plain brown envelope.

Cindy frowned. There was no address on it. It must have been hand delivered. Several strips of adhesive tape secured the flap.

She unlocked and opened the door to her apartment and immediately went to her desk and slid open the top drawer. Taking out a pair of scissors, she cut through the tape and reached inside.

And then she saw what the envelope contained.

There was an involuntary gasp as the envelope fell from her hands onto the desk.

This was not possible! They had all been deleted. Destroyed. But here they were. She suddenly felt the need to cry but no tears came.

Then she remembered the message from Steve.

"This is a serious business and not for anyone with vulnerabilities."

She looked one more time at the envelope and then turned around and walked slowly over to the kitchen, almost in a trance. Her hands started to shake as she took the bottle of wine out of the refrigerator. She then opened one of the cabinets and reached up for a glass. The glass fell through her trembling fingers and landed on the kitchen floor, shattering into multiple pieces.

Cindy looked briefly at the mess on the floor and then returned her attention to the wine. She twisted off the top and started to drink directly from the bottle.

An hour later she went to bed. The bottle was empty and the broken glass was still on the floor.

Chapter 24

Thursday, April 1, 8:30 A.M.

"**N**o Gary. I don't think it's anything serious... Probably the twenty-four hour bug...hit me last night....Didn't sleep a wink...I'm sure I'll be fine tomorrow...No, I think the Thornton account can wait another day...I'll put some time in this weekend, if necessary...Thank you for understanding...Not at all...Really appreciate it...Goodbye."

Cindy put down the phone and turned her attention back to the bucket that had been her constant companion throughout the last several hours.

There can't be anything left in me to lose...Oh my God, here it comes again.

Cindy couldn't recall ever being so hungover. In college she had been something of a party girl without ever suffering anything more than a mild headache. Well, there was nothing mild about either the headache or the nausea that had greeted her a few hours before sunrise. Only the greatest amount of will power had enabled her to make the "sick call" to her boss. Having completed the call, she walked slowly and painfully into the bathroom where she emptied the contents of the bucket into the toilet. She then returned to the bedroom, climbed into bed, and curled up into a ball, desperately wanting to go back to sleep.

It was several hours later when she began to emerge from her stupor. Still bleary eyed, she leaned over to get a better look at the clock on her nightstand.

Four in the afternoon. Do I bother to get dressed? Do I even bother to get up?

After about twenty minutes of silent deliberation, Cindy thought that, yes, it would be wise to get dressed and try to reconnect with the world. Tentatively she got out of bed and put on a pair of jeans and an old sweatshirt. Deciding that she should eat something, at least some cereal, she left the confines of her bedroom and shuffled ever so slowly into the kitchen area where she was greeted by the sight of the shattered pieces of glass on the floor.

"Oh, shit," she moaned, as she turned around and went over to a closet which contained a broom and dust bin.

Securing the two items, she returned to the kitchen and commenced with the cleanup. Within a few minutes, the shards had been swept from the floor. She then poured some milk and cereal into a bowl, hoping that she would be able to keep it down. She ate her cereal slowly, deliberately, not wanting to do anything to upset the delicate sense of equilibrium she was trying to establish.

Cindy looked over to the living room area and noticed that the call button on her phone was flashing. She walked over to the phone and saw that there had been two calls. She pressed the button.

"Ms. Phelps, this is Mainstreet Printing. Do you still intend to

send over the layout for those brochures? You said we'd have it by 1:00 p.m. Please advise. Thanks.

Cindy slowly shook her head.

It seems the world doesn't stop when you get a hangover. Hold your water Mainstreet. I'll get it to you.

Then Cindy's eyes were drawn over to the brown envelope on the desk. The envelope whose contents had thrown her off the rails the night before. The envelope that reminded her that in spite of her quality education and professional success, she still could be, at times, a silly and stupid creature.

Her thoughts went back to those heady days last year when all those dreams of political stardom had seemed so real. Soil and Water serving as a springboard to the state legislature. And then what? Congress? Governor? Steve had made it seem so doable. So real. It had all been so wonderful. Steve had been wonderful. And then that night she had been drinking. Not that much really. Just enough to cloud her judgment.

But he told me he would delete them. He promised.

Of course, she had promised things too. Or had she? She couldn't quite remember. But even before her disastrous debate performance, she had realized how shallow the whole thing was. Running for an office she had no business running for and not even any interest in holding.

And Steve had been so bitter. Not so much about the personal connection. But her withdrawal from the race had been a professional betrayal. That night in the parking lot when she had tried to explain. So bitter.

But still he promised me they would be deleted!

But what was that message that Steve had sent via Carl?

"This is a serious business and not for anyone with vulnerabilities."

She would have to call Steve. Find out what that envelope

meant. Put a stopper on this. Those photos could be disastrous. To her professional reputation. To her relationship with her sister and her family. Her nephews. Her parents out in California. To Carl.

To Carl who has been so unfailingly loyal. Of course, they hadn't been officially together then. But still...

She pressed the button again.

"Hi Cindy. It's Emily. I know we are scheduled to meet tonight at my house for debate prep at 7:30 pm. But why don't you come early, say 6:00 p.m. for dinner. I've ordered a spread of Indian food. It will be a real treat for both of us..."

There was more to the message but Cindy didn't hear it. Somehow the mere mention of a platter of Indian food had sent her back to the bucket.

Twenty minutes later, she reemerged from the bathroom.

She picked up the phone and called Emily. Fortunately the answering machine picked up and Cindy was able to leave a message, saying that she was sick and had to cancel.

Once again her thoughts went back to the brown envelope. And the conversation she needed to have with Steve. She was sitting on the floor of her living room, staring at the envelope, with the bucket next to her. At that moment she never felt so vulnerable. So alone.

Her eyes drifted over to the refrigerator. She shook her head and began to laugh.

I'm not that stupid. I tried Plan A last night and it didn't work out so good.

She then got to her feet and slowly walked back to the bedroom where she climbed back into bed and turned out the light.

Chapter 25

Saturday, April 3, 7:00 P.M.

CINDY COULD TELL Carl was excited when he picked her up for their Saturday night date. He had made it clear that they could eat anywhere she wanted. Expense was no object. Carl was celebrating. Not only had he been reinstated into the Republican Party's good graces but there was something else as well. But first things first.

"So, where do we eat?"

"Oh, Luigi's is fine."

Carl was puzzled. Luigi's was the Italian greasy spoon they ate at when no one could think of anything more exciting. Still, if that's what Cindy wanted…

"OK, Luigi's it is. I just received the letter from the Republicans saying that I can represent the party again. Part of the deal is that I do volunteer stuff for Jennifer Haley one night a week, but I was going to vote for her anyway. So Terrence has confirmed that I get to keep my rover route."

"That's nice," said Cindy.

"But then Terrence asked me to come in yesterday afternoon. It seems that Michael is leaving. He's a boating enthusiast and he indicated that he and his wife want to sail around the world in their yacht. Wants to do it while they still have the energy. They're both retired and all."

"OK."

"Now as you know, Michael is second in command to Terrence. Deputy Machine Coordinator. So his departure leaves an opening."

Cindy was silent.

"So, Terrence asked me if I wanted it. To be Deputy Machine Coordinator. Can you imagine that? So, I asked what about Milton or Scott or Brenda. They are so much more experienced than I am."

"Yeah, I guess it would be—"

"None of them were interested. They're all retired and not looking for a career. So they figured this would be an ideal stepping stone for me to get into the office. The next step might be a full time position. This will reduce my consulting time with *Software Solutions* but still…"

They pulled into the parking lot at Luigi's.

Carl turned off the engine and looked over at Cindy.

"Cindy, are you all right?"

"What. Yeah, of course I am."

"You seem a bit distracted. Did you have a good week?"

A good week. Let's see, I drunk myself into oblivion and I think I'm being blackmailed. Other than that, the week was great.

"I'm sorry," said Cindy, regaining some of her focus. "All this business about Tracy Miller being a candidate. It kind of makes this campaign manager thing more complicated."

"I should have known," said Carl. "Of course, it was a surprise.

Does it change your strategy at all?"

"Yeah, it changes it a lot," said Cindy. There was a bitter edge to her voice. "How could it not? We were supposed to have an easy ride to the nomination and now we get this shit thrown in our face."

"I would think Emily's commitment to conservation would give her a real boost—"

"Emily's obsession with conservation is sinking us," said Cindy, her voice rising. "She won't listen to anything I say. I should probably get out now and preserve my sanity."

"I'm sorry you're under such pressure. If there's anything I can do to help—"

"To help?" said Cindy, almost shouting. "You're in bed with the goddamn Republicans. Anything I say, you'll just blab to the other side. Why don't you go work for Tracy too, while you're at it?"

This was too much.

"Do you really think I'd betray you? I did everything I could to support your effort last year. I would never—"

"This evening's a waste," snapped Cindy. "Just take me home."

Cindy's words were like a slap across the face. Carl resisted the temptation to lash back. When he spoke his words were soft and measured.

"I'll take you home if that's what you want. But please don't create an artificial quarrel. I would never betray you and you know it."

The ride back to Cindy's apartment was a silent one. The car pulled into the parking space nearest to her apartment.

"I'll manage. You don't need to see me to the door."

Carl said nothing. Cindy was ending the evening on her terms. He was a bit resentful that his promotion had scarcely been acknowledged but he also realized that something larger was in motion. Time would let it play out.

When he got back to his townhouse, the message light on his phone was on. He pressed the button.

"I'm sorry I trashed our date tonight. Please forgive me. I wouldn't have been good company anyway. I'm cancelling our dinner with Stan and Valerie tomorrow. I just need some space. Please don't call. We'll talk soon...sometime. Again, I'm sorry."

Chapter 26

Thursday, April 8, 3:30 P.M.

THE DOOR HAD been closed for an hour.

"I need to get those reports done," Cindy had said.

Well here she was, sitting at her desk, staring off into space as the unfinished reports lay in front of her.

Tonight would be the first debate. Technically it was a "Candidate Forum." The 48th Senate Race would lead off the evening. Emily and Tracy would be squaring off at 7:00 p.m. Then at 8:00 p.m. the Republicans, Jennifer Haley and Anthony Palucci, would be on stage. A couple of other contests would follow.

For the last two evenings, Cindy and Emily had done debate prep. Emily's strategy would be simple. Emphasize her expertise on the environment. This was what she was best at. This was what energized her. Unfortunately she was determined to focus on her opposition to the pipeline which Cindy felt was a mistake. It was so controversial. Better to say that this was an issue that needed careful study and let it rest at that.

"Cindy, I have to stand for something," she had said, making

Cindy feel a bit ashamed, not for the first time.

In addition, Cindy had reviewed various talking points in other areas. Job creation. Transportation. Education. Emily had listened attentively and was able to address the relative talking points more-or-less adequately but it was obvious that this was not where her heart was.

Cindy sensed that it would be a tough night. In so many ways the deck was stacked against them. Tracy Miller was a marquee figure. She was more than just attractive. She was stunning. A polished speaker. Experienced in working the media to her advantage. Cindy feared that measured against Tracy's youthful relevance, Emily would seem dull and old-fashioned.

Even the choice of moderator would play to Tracy's advantage. Her protégé, Jimmy Forbes from WMML, would be serving as MC.

And then Tracy would have Steve Winters in her corner as campaign manager. Steve was one of the best, as Cindy well remembered.

Steve. How many times in the past week had Cindy almost called him? To confront him. Those photos he swore he had deleted. Had he been the one to send them? Or had he handed them off to someone else? It didn't really matter. All that mattered was someone had the power to expose and humiliate her. And the anxiety that this caused was taking its toll.

While she had (just barely) been able to keep her focus at work, the rest of her life seemed to be unraveling. She had rejected a number of overtures from her girl friends to get together. She had bordered on being rude to Valerie when she cancelled their Sunday dinner plans. Then Carl had called the other night in direct defiance of her "Don't call me; I'll call you" instructions. Claimed he was worried about her.

I'm worried about me, too, she thought, bitterly.

Anyway, she had told Carl that she needed her space. Just leave me alone.

Well tonight she would end it. She would confront Steve and find out what was going on. It would happen right after the debate was concluded. She did not want her personal troubles to make her lose her focus as campaign manager. But then she would get it resolved. Somehow.

Chapter 27

THURSDAY EVENING, 8:00 P.M.

"*T*HIS CONCLUDES THE *first part of our evening with the candidates. We would like to thank both Tracy Miller and Emily Weston for being here this evening. There will be a ten minute break and then the second portion of the evening will commence with the two Republican candidates, Jennifer Haley and Anthony Palucci."*

That could have been worse, thought Cindy, with relief. Although lacking Tracy's sparkle, Emily's expertise and passion for the environment had come through. She had even done a creditable job on some of the other issues as well. Cindy allowed herself to feel a bit of self-satisfaction. She had prepared Emily well.

"Emily, you were great," she said. "If it's all right with you, I need to talk to my counterpart for a bit." She motioned over to Steve, who was huddled with Tracy.

Emily gave Cindy a quizzical look for just a moment and then broke into a smile.

"All right, Cindy. Do what you have to do. I'm just so relieved we got through this evening relatively unscathed. I knew I made the right choice for campaign manager. I'll be heading on home."

She gave Cindy a parting hug and departed.

Cindy took a deep breath and looked over at Steve. He was looking at her, as was Tracy.

Here goes nothing.

Cindy walked over to where they were standing.

"Good evening, Cindy," said Tracy, offering her hand which Cindy shook briefly. "So good to see you."

Good to see you too, bitch.

"Hello Tracy," replied Cindy, trying to smile. "Always good to see you."

Then turning to Steve, she said as casually as possible, "Can we talk?"

She expected either Steve or Tracy or both to protest. To say that "anything you say to one of us, you can say to both." Tracy, however, putting on her most winning smile, said,

"Of course. You two need to talk shop. Best not to let the candidates see how the sausage is made. Steve, I'll be standing over here." Tracy immediately went over to where a few of her well-wishers had been hovering.

Steve had stood, pleasantly serene, during the exchange. Once Tracy was out of earshot he assumed a sterner countenance.

"What do you want, Cindy?"

For the past week Cindy had been rehearsing what she would say. What approach she would take. But now that the moment was upon her, all she could think of was to ask the question,

"Did you send me the envelope?"

"What envelope?"

"Don't give me that 'what envelope' shit. The envelope with the pictures. Those pictures that you promised to delete last year."

Steve seemed surprised by what Cindy was saying. Slowly he responded,

"I wasn't aware that you received an envelope. It wasn't from me."

"And those pictures? The ones that you deleted from your smartphone? They just happened to magically jump out of your phone and image themselves somewhere else after you hit the delete button."

Steve was silent.

"You didn't delete them, did you?"

Steve gave Cindy a hard look.

"Cindy, this isn't for amateurs. You really need to rethink what you're doing."

"If you didn't send the pictures then who did?"

"Cindy, I'm afraid I have to reclaim my campaign manager," sounded a voice from over her shoulder. Tracy had rejoined them. "We need to do some strategizing for the next debate. It's been so good talking to you." She leaned over to give Cindy a hug.

"I wonder who else will be receiving an envelope in the next few days," she whispered in Cindy's ear.

"Ladies and gentlemen, if you could clear the aisle, we will be starting the next part of our evening," Jimmy Forbes was saying from the podium.

Released from Tracy's embrace, Cindy nodded to the pair with a shocked expression on her face. She hadn't expected such a blatant admission of guilt. Slowly she walked from the auditorium. On the steps she saw Carl, who was handing out Jennifer Haley fliers.

"Cindy," he said, trying to sound upbeat. "People coming out seemed to say that Emily held her own tonight. You must be so relieved."

"Relieved, yes. Relieved," said Cindy, with a blank expression on her face. She was anything but relieved.

Cindy started down the steps. Carl went along beside her.

"Don't ask if we can go out this weekend. I said I'll call you when I'm ready."

He tried to look her in the eye but she averted his gaze.

"Cindy please, don't shut me out."

But Cindy had already hurried past him down the walkway to the parking lot.

Chapter 28

SUNDAY, APRIL 11, 12:30 P.M.

"**H**ELLO"

"Hi Carl. It's Valerie. Just wondering if you would be free to join us for dinner this evening."

"Well...uh...I'd love to...but you should know, I haven't been with Cindy in over a week and—"

"That's her loss. Dinner's at five. Come any time after three."

"Sure, great. Is there anything I can bring?"

"Oh, I don't know. Maybe a mallet to knock some sense into that girlfriend of yours."

Carl laughed.

"It will take more than a mallet. Thanks Valerie. I'll see you in a little bit."

Shortly after three, with a bottle of wine for his hosts, Carl arrived at the Turner house.

"They're all in the back," said Valerie. "Stan's trying to jumpstart the baseball season with the boys. Tell him you're his relief pitcher. He needs to help me in the kitchen."

Carl went around to the backyard. Stan was indeed pitching to Mathew Turner who seemed to have developed a pretty good batting stroke. His younger brother David along with Cindy were in the "outfield," retrieving the batted balls although David's interest appeared to be waning. Cindy had an old baseball glove on her left hand and was wearing a Washington Nationals cap.

"Hi Carl," called Stan. "Little League starts this week. Getting the boys ready for the tryouts. I think Mathew has a shot at AAA."

"I'm afraid I'm your relief pitcher," said Carl. "You're wanted in the kitchen. Unless Cindy wants to pitch."

"No, not Cindy," cried Mathew. "She throws like a girl."

Carl looked out at Cindy. She gave him a bit of a wave and a sheepish smile.

Carl had never been much of an athlete but he was able to do a passible job pitching to Mathew. With David it was a bit more of a challenge but eventually he was able to lob it over so the boy could hit it.

"David was just in tee-ball last year," explained Mathew.

Shortly before five, they were called in for dinner. Carl went to join Cindy, who was collecting the baseballs that were scattered over the yard.

"Can you forgive me?" she asked, quietly.

"There's nothing to forgive. And it's nice seeing you smile again."

"We both know that's not true. But thank you for understanding," she said, leaning over and giving Carl a quick kiss on the cheek.

The thing is, I don't understand. What's made Cindy so fragile?

Dinner was an upbeat affair. The conversation went in many directions ranging from Mathew's science project (design and build an insect) to the latest superhero movie. The one thing that was not discussed was politics and elections. Stan, and especially Valerie, seemed determined to keep that out of the mix. The two boys obviously adored Cindy and it was equally obvious that the feeling was mutual.

Then, out of nowhere, as they were finishing dessert, Mathew said,

"Mom's quit the school board."

"Val, no!" said Cindy.

"It's true," continued Mathew who added, turning to his mother, "I heard you talking to Dad."

"Matt, that will be enough," said Stan, sternly.

"But—"

"No," said Stan, with an air of authority.

An awkward silence engulfed the table. At last Valerie spoke.

"It's no big deal. I have not quit the school board. I've simply decided not to run for reelection in November. That's all. No big deal."

Carl and Cindy exchanged glances. Ever since he had met Valerie, her signature passion had been the county school system. At first an indifferent campaigner, she had risen to the challenge last fall and had run a successful campaign. Something did not seem right.

"Mom, can Cindy and I go downstairs and watch TV?" said David who was getting fidgety.

"Yeah, me too," said Mathew, getting up from the table.

Valerie nodded her approval. Cindy gave Carl a grin and a shrug as she got to her feet. As they headed downstairs, he thought he heard David say,

"We want to watch one of your channels, not Mom's."

Valerie looked at Stan.

"Don't worry, I'm on it," said Stan, getting to his feet.

"Which leaves me and you to do the dishes," said Valerie to Carl.

They commenced the cleanup with Carl clearing the table while Valerie worked in the kitchen. Once the dishes had been cleared, Carl felt emboldened to say,

"So you got tired of working on the school board?"

"Yeah, kind of. No biggie. I just don't feel like doing it anymore."

She seemed determined to avoid Carl's glance.

"I don't believe you," said Carl.

He could hardly believe what he had said. Here he was, a guest who had just been fed a delicious dinner, accusing his host of lying.

I've endured Cindy's wrath. I might as well get her sister's as well.

"Excuse me."

"There's got to be more to it than that. You're not the sort of person who just gets tired of doing something."

Valerie put her dishrag on the counter and looked Carl straight in the eye. Her demeanor was deadly serious.

"Carl, I like you. And I happen to think you're the best thing that's happened to Cindy since...perhaps ever. But you have crossed way over the line. The reasons for my decision are personal. I share them with my husband and no one else. Do I make myself clear?"

"Yes, I'm sorry," said Carl, retreating in the face of Valerie's rebuke. "It's just that..." He paused, looking for the right words. "It's just that I so clearly remember how passionate you were during last year's campaign. I had never seen anyone so committed to bettering the county schools. But you're right. It's none of my business. Please accept my apology."

Valerie nodded and they continued working in silence. Once

the last of the dishes was cleaned and dried, Carl said, "I probably should be on my way. Thank you so much for having me. I'll say goodbye to Stan and Cindy and be off."

He turned to leave.

"Wait."

Carl stopped and turned back to face Valerie. Her earlier severity seemed to be softening.

"Three weeks ago, after the school board meeting, I was approached by Biff Logan. He is the county Democratic Chair—"

"I know who Biff Logan is."

"Well, he told me that Emily Weston's decision to run for the State Senate was hurting the party. She was keeping the nomination from some younger, more electable candidate. He also claimed that this was being facilitated by my sister's involvement in the campaign. He said that the party would be indebted to me if I could talk Cindy into quitting as campaign manager. That somehow would convince Emily to withdraw."

Carl was silent.

"I happen to believe that Cindy made a mistake in signing up to be her campaign manager. But it's her decision to make. Not mine and certainly not Biff Logan's. So I told Mr. Logan 'to go to hell.'"

"In so many words."

"No, those were my exact words," said Valerie with a faint smile. "Then three days ago I received a letter from the county Democratic Committee, informing me that the party would not be endorsing me for another term on the school board. So to save a bit of personal dignity, I've decided that I simply will not run at all."

"You could run as an independent."

Valerie shook her head. "Independents never win a school

board race. It would be a total waste of time and effort. But Carl, now that I have shared this with you, I need you to promise never to tell Cindy. Something is weighing on her right now. I'm not sure what it is but she's in a delicate state. I had to practically kidnap her to come here today. The last thing she needs is a guilt trip about her causing me to drop out. Will you promise?"

Carl readily agreed. So Valerie had sensed it as well. Something was eating at Cindy. But what?

Chapter 29

MONDAY, APRIL 12

Election Office Integrity Called into Question

By J.C. Styles, Washington Herald

The drama that is unfolding in this spring's primary season notched up today when representatives for one of the candidates in the upcoming Democratic primary for Virginia's 48th State Senate district called into question the integrity of the county's election procedures.

"It has come to our attention," declared Steve Winters, campaign manager for Senate candidate and former television reporter Tracy Miller, "that a key member of the county's Office of Elections is in a personal relationship with the campaign manager of a rival candidate."

Upon further questioning, Winters revealed that the players in question are Carl Marsden, who has recently been promoted to the positon of Deputy Machine Coordinator, and Cynthia Phelps who is currently serving as campaign manager for Senate candidate Emily Weston.

"It is an unfortunate situation," said candidate Miller. "As I

discovered earlier when I unearthed that scandal with the books, there does seem to be some serious lapses in the judgment shown by county officials. I personally don't doubt the integrity of Mr. Marsden but the optics of the situation do raise questions. Perhaps the best thing for everyone would be to have Ms. Phelps remove herself from the Weston campaign."

The "scandal" candidate Miller was referring to was the county practice of shredding old library books, in lieu of donating them to worthy organizations.

County officials were quick to respond, emphasizing the many procedures the Office of Elections employs to ensure fairness and transparency.

"Mr. Marsden has our complete confidence," said Machine Coordinator Terrence Bucholtz. "Like all election officers, he has taken an oath to perform the duties for this election according to law and the best of his ability. In addition I would emphasize that candidates and their representatives are always welcome to observe the process by which the voting equipment is tested and prepared for Election Day. We will begin testing the voting machines for both Democratic and Republican primaries for the 48th Senate district next Tuesday, April 20 and will continue for as many days as is necessary."

Response has also come from the Republican candidates in the race.

"Tracy Miller has a knack for raising issues where none exist and creating controversies that mask her own lack of substance," said Republican State Senator Jennifer Haley, who is seeking the nomination from her party for another term. "We are sure this will be amply displayed in the upcoming fall campaign."

In the meantime, Republican candidate Anthony Palucci has chimed in, noting that "Mr. Marsden was observed passing out Jennifer Haley brochures during last week's debate. His embrace of the Haley candidacy by day coupled with pillow talk no doubt received from his Democrat sweetheart at night, suggest that Mr. Marsden is a rather confused young man. Hopefully, none of this will interfere with the performance of his duties for the county."

Chapter 30

"**H**ELLO."

"Hi. It's me."

"I told you not to call."

"I don't care. We're going out Saturday night."

"No, we're not. Please leave me alone."

"I'll pick you up at seven."

"Damn it, I said no."

"And damn it, I said yes."

"I can't. I'll be over at Val's."

"No, you won't."

"How do you know?"

"Because I just talked to her."

"So now you clear everything with her?"

"I'll see you at seven."

A pause.

"We won't talk politics. Or elections."

"You have my word."

"But those are the only things you know."

"You have my word."

"So we'll eat dinner in total silence."

"Apparently."

Another pause.

"Don't be late."

"I wouldn't dream of it."

"Carl…"

"Yes?"

"Thank you."

Chapter 31

"**A**ND I WOULD like to thank you for all the effort you have put in these last three weeks. It appears that by noon today the last of the precincts will have been tested. We will do a bit of cleanup this afternoon but if any of you have other things to do, feel free not to come back from lunch."

Terrence was in an upbeat mood as he was giving the rovers his 7:00 a.m. morning briefing.

"I think we should all come back after lunch for cleanup," said Brenda. "I've said it before and I will say it again. This place is a pigsty. Our conference table is littered with food items, newspapers from the past two weeks, half-done crossword puzzles. And look at the floor. Discarded boxes, bubble packing, empty bottles and containers, tools that need to be put back in the cabinet, those 'Attention All Voters' signs that got ruined in the rain but never got thrown out. This is our work area and we need to treat it with more respect..."

Brenda went on about the lack of cleanliness of the election area. Most of the rovers shifted uncomfortably during her monologue, aware that they all had contributed to the mess.

"Your point is well taken," said Terrence. "How many of you can come back this afternoon and help with the cleanup?"

Carl and one or two others raised their hands. Carl thought he heard phrases like "doctor's appointment," "need to drive to Baltimore," "company's coming," and "just let Brenda do it."

Terrence considered. "There are a number of things that I should do back at the Government Center. So why don't we postpone the cleanup until sometime next week..."

Sighs of relief could be heard as well as a snort from Brenda.

"Now one thing that is definitely on the horizon is the testing for the 48th State Senate races, both Democrat and Republican. There are only a dozen precincts impacted and they're all on Carl's route. We should have the test decks and flash drives ready for testing next Tuesday morning. Carl and maybe one or two others can handle the actual testing. So most of you will get a bye on this. It should take one or, at most, two days."

"Since we're all getting a bye," said Brenda. "Why don't I come in Tuesday and clean up this mess while Carl is doing the testing. Does anyone wish to join me?" She looked around the room as various rovers shifted their eyes so as to avoid her menacing glare. Eventually George, one of the newer rovers, raised his hand.

"There's one interesting development concerning next week's testing," said Terrence, eager to change the subject to anything but the cleanup. "As you know, the candidates and their reps are permitted to observe the testing process. In practice, they rarely bother to come. That seems to have changed for the 48th Senate contest resulting, I suspect, from a certain amount of media attention."

A number of eyes focused on Carl. He thought he heard

someone whisper "pillow talk."

"We will have a number of observers next Tuesday. Representatives from all four candidates, Democrat and Republican, have indicated that they will be in attendance."

"Representatives or the candidates themselves?" asked Scott.

"I believe it may be both. At least for the Democrats. But for now, let's get started and knock out those last few precincts."

The morning's testing went smoothly. By noon, it was complete.

"How's Cindy holding up?" asked Milton, as they were preparing to leave.

I wish I knew.

"She's hanging in there."

"That article was complete garbage," said Jack. "Tell Cindy that we're thinking of her."

Milton and Jack were the two rovers who had gotten to know Cindy. Milton had been the rover when she had been chief while Jack had seen her in action during that impromptu board meeting the previous fall. It was obvious that they both had a soft spot for her.

"Thanks," he said to both. "I'm sure she will appreciate it."

The following evening Carl and Cindy had their date. While they did not exactly eat in silence, it was a quiet dinner as each of them, sitting at the table in Luigi's, ruminated about his/her situation. Carl's thoughts normally would have been focused on the upcoming Tuesday when they would be testing the voting machines, under the watchful eyes of the candidates. Superseding that, however, was his realization that Cindy was in pain. He desperately wanted to help her but for now at least, was powerless to do so.

Cindy, for her part, knew only that her whole world was about to come crashing down on her and she had no idea how to prevent it from happening. She had to think of something. She just had to.

Chapter 32

"WELCOME BACK, CINDY," she said, under her breath, as she got out of her car. The ramp to the warehouse loomed ahead. How well she remembered the last time she was here. When she had boldly walked-in on that emergency meeting of the electoral board. And the night before that when she had hid in the shadows in order to turn on all those scanners.

She walked up the ramp, opened the door, and entered. She then paused to look around and take the measure of her surroundings. Much of it looked familiar. Piles of boxes. Dumpsters filled to overflowing with supplies. A forklift to one side, currently not being used. But something was different. That counter where the check-in log book had been. The counter was still there but in place of the log book was a laptop computer.

"All guests must log in and log out," read the sign.

Cindy stepped forward and looked at the screen. There were huge buttons that said Check in and Check out.

"Move the pointer with the mouse," said the man at the desk, behind the counter. The sign on the desk identified him as Rudy Matheson, site supervisor.

Cindy did as directed and logged herself in.

"You need to log out when you leave," said Rudy. "We've beefed up security here. Ever since that after-hour's break-in last fall."

It wasn't a break-in. I just didn't leave when you all went home.

"Yes, sir," said Cindy. She turned around and looked at the door through which she had entered. There was a surveillance camera that she had not noticed last November. Also a panel had been installed next to the door.

"We finally installed that security system," said Rudy. "No more break-ins. At the end of the day I turn on the camera and set the code."

"It's reassuring that everything is so secure," said Cindy, with a bright smile. "I'm the manager for Emily Weston's campaign and it's a relief that so many precautions are being made. Should I head on back?"

"You have to wear one of those mesh lime green vests," said Rudy, motioning to a bin on the floor. "All guests need to be properly identified."

"Of course."

She put on a vest and then looked at the shelves across from the bathrooms.

"Excuse me," she asked, "but do you have a pest problem?" She motioned to the box labeled "Rat Poison."

"We did," said Rudy. "So we baited some traps a while back and that seems to have solved it. In a way, it was a good thing because it forced us to rethink where we store all our toxic substances. Cleaning fluids, antifreeze, and the like. Now they are all on the same shelf. One here and one in the back in the election area."

Cindy nodded. "Well I better get back there."

"I'd appreciate anything you can do to get them to speed things up. I'm the only worker in the warehouse today. Everyone else is offsite on some sort of team building exercise. The sooner you all can complete what you're doing, the sooner I can lock up here and go home."

"I'll do what I can," said Cindy.

But not until I have a very important conversation.

Chapter 33

TUESDAY, APRIL 20, 9:00 A.M.
(TIMELINES FOR CHAPTERS 32 AND 33 OVERLAP)

IT WAS EXACTLY 9:00 a.m. when Carl logged in at the warehouse. He had been assured by Terrence that the flash drives for the scanners and the ballots for the test decks would be available. Carl would have an hour to mark the ballots for the test decks. The candidates' reps had been told that testing would begin at 10:00 a.m.

Carl put on his vest and went back to the election area. George was seated at the table while Terrence was on the phone.

"What do you mean you are still programing the flash drives? The candidates were told the testing would begin at 10:00 a.m. They all said they would be here...Well get them done as soon as you can and send them over here...Very well, I'll expect Jack by 10:30 a.m.....Please no later..."

"Are you here for the testing?" Carl asked George.

"Not really," George replied. "I think Terrence intends for the two of you to handle that. I'm supposed to meet Brenda for the cleanup. She just called. Running a bit late. Something about the dogs. I don't want to start until she gets here."

"Smart move," agreed Carl. "You want to make sure it's up to her specifications. You don't want to risk being on the receiving end of the 'wrath of Brenda.'"

Terrence walked over to Carl.

"The flash drives are going to be late," he said, with a grimace. "We do have the ballots so you can start creating the test decks. I suppose we can entertain our 'guests' for a bit by showing them the decks but they're not going to be happy that things are delayed."

Terrence gave the ballots to Carl who sat down and got to work. His initial task was to stamp "Test Ballot" on each of the blank ballots. Once done, he studied the grid which showed how each ballot should be marked. There were two sets of ballots. The Democratic ballots had Tracy Miller followed by Emily Weston; the Republican, Jennifer Haley followed by Anthony Palucci. Their positions on the ballots had been determined by lot.

While Carl worked diligently at his tasks, the candidates began to arrive. Emily Weston was first. She accepted Terrence's apology about the delay and sat down at the far edge of the table.

After a few minutes, Jennifer Haley arrived. She walked over and shook hands with Emily.

"I was hoping we would get to face off against each other this fall," she said to Emily.

Emily nodded but said nothing. Jennifer then walked over to Terrence.

"I trust this will be starting on time," she said, curtly. "I have a busy schedule today."

"All right, George. Let's get started."

Brenda had arrived and started barking instructions. "I'll start with the table. You work the floor. Get all that c-r-a-p into the dumpsters. The ruined signs, empty containers, those bubble wrappings, boxes. Look under the shelves for lose items. Just don't get your fingers caught in any of the rat traps."

Brenda's appearance and the resulting activity provided enough of a cover so Terrence could move to another area and pretend to be busy, and thus avoid responding to Jennifer.

Even as Brenda and George were commencing their cleanup, Cindy arrived. She and Carl exchanged quick nods. They had agreed that in view of the current scrutiny, they would limit their interactions at the warehouse to whatever formalities were required but nothing more. Cindy went over and sat next to Emily.

Next to come was Steve.

"Is Tracy here yet?" he asked to the room in general. A few "no's" were heard and he went over and sat on the other end of the table, as far away from Cindy and Emily as possible.

For the next fifteen minutes, most of the warehouse sound came from Brenda and George as they worked on their tasks. None of the guests seemed in much of a mood to talk. Jennifer stood to one side, sending messages on her smartphone. After a few pleasantries, Emily and Cindy let their conversation lapse. From time to time, Emily would glance covertly at Jennifer. Cindy remained silent, lost in her own thoughts. On the other side of the table, Steve seemed to be scrutinizing Cindy. Eventually Brenda and George had filled one of the dumpsters with trash.

"We're done," Brenda announced. "We're taking this to the front and transferring everything to trash bags. Rudy told us that the county generally picks up the garbage between eleven and noon. Terrence, Carl, have a good test." With that, Brenda and George departed with the dumpster.

"Good morning everyone. I'm so sorry I'm late,"

Tracy Miller burst onto the scene with a dazzling smile.

"So good to see you all," she said, nodding to the assemblage. "Emily. Ms. Phelps. You're looking well. Jennifer, good to see you."

Steve had risen.

"Steve, I'm so glad you could make it," said Tracy, shaking his hand. For a moment they gazed at each other. Then Tracy broke off and began to walk around the room.

"Ah, those famous books," she said, approaching the laundry carts containing the books. "I wonder if that copy of *Moby Dick* is still on top of the pile. No, it seems to have moved. What have we here? *In Cold Blood*. Well that's a classic in its way." She picked up the book and started thumbing through it.

Terrence looked up from his papers.

"Excuse me, Ms. Miller. We're not allowed to be handling those—" he began.

"What a fine assemblage we have here," came the voice of Anthony Palucci, "Now don't all get up from your chairs. I seem to be the last one to arrive. Perhaps we may begin."

Palucci then proceeded to walk around the area, greeting each of his rivals individually.

"Shouldn't you be seated next to your gentleman friend?" he whispered when he got to Cindy.

Cindy said nothing, but returned what she hoped was her dirtiest look.

Palucci walked over to where Tracy was standing.

"Catching up on your reading Ms. Miller?" he began.

"You! You, there!" came the voice from the entry point of the election area. Rudy Matheson, obviously very agitated, came into the election area, pointing at Palucci.

"You need to log in, sir. You did not log in."

"Don't be silly," said Palucci. "This isn't Fort Knox. None of us are going to steal any of your precious supplies. Or are you afraid

I will walk off with a bushel of 'I Voted' stickers?"

For a moment Rudy looked like he would explode with rage. Then his demeanor changed. His gaze at Palucci was intense, almost like he was looking through him. He said in a measured voice.

"These are the rules, sir. I am required to enforce them. You must return to the front, log in, and put on a vest, like everyone else here has done."

"All right. All right," said Palucci, holding up his hands in mock surrender. "Let us return to the front, if return we must." With that, he walked past Rudy and headed back to the front. Rudy briefly looked around the room to confirm that everyone had on their vest. Apparently satisfied, he turned around and went back to the front.

There were a few snickers. "He's only doing his job," said Carl.

A few minutes later Palucci returned, wearing his vest.

"Now that we're all here, can we get started?" said Jennifer.

Terrence and Carl exchanged glances.

"Have you finished creating the test decks?" asked Terrence.

"Just about," said Carl.

Terrence nodded, took a deep breath, and began.

"I would like to thank you all for coming out today. This is the first day of testing the equipment that will be used for the upcoming June eighth primary for the 48th State Senate district. You will be seeing us test two different machines, the *ElectionPro* scanner and the *CreateBallot* device. Both of these machines are manufactured by the *ElectionPro* Company which is based in Madison, Wisconsin. Now each precinct will be assigned two scanners, although for the primary a chief may decide to only use one…"

Even as Terrence was giving his introductory remarks, Carl was busy completing the creation of the test decks. When he finally had them done, he gave Terrence a quick nod.

"Now, let me explain to you how the test decks have been prepared," continued Terrence.

"Excuse me, but I think we all know this," said Jennifer, impatiently. "We're here to observe, not to be lectured at. Just start the testing and we'll figure it out."

Steve, Tracy, and Palucci nodded in agreement.

"I for one, appreciate Terrence giving us an overview of the process," said Emily, glaring at Jennifer.

"Ah, well...you see," said Terrence. "The fact is that the flash drives needed for the test have not yet arrived. I am assured that they are on the way here, even as we speak. So Carl why don't you go over the test decks that we will be using."

There were a number of audible groans. Carl then started describing the test deck process. Only Emily appeared to be paying attention. Cindy seemed lost in her own world. The others displayed outright annoyance.

For the next twenty minutes, Carl soldiered on. It was only then that Jack Vincent came into the election area, wearing his vest, and carrying a large brown envelope.

"Excellent," cried Terrence, taking the envelope from Jack. "We can start the test. Jack why don't you and Carl wheel the carts and scanners into the assembly line. The rest of us will go back to the workbench and wait for you."

Jack and Cindy exchanged smiles of recognition. They had bonded the previous fall during that impromptu four and a half hour board meeting. Jack, who was in his mid-eighties and something of a raconteur, had regaled Cindy with all sorts of tales, some true and some tall.

"Don't let those newspaper stories get you down," he whispered to her. "You and Carl have more integrity than the rest of those goons put together."

For a moment, Cindy regained a bit of her old spark. "Are you trying to sweet-talk me, Mr. Vincent?" she whispered back, grinning.

"Ah, if only I could. OK, Carl, let's go find those carts for the 48th."

Jack and Carl proceeded to enter the cage area where all the precinct carts and scanners were.

"Most of the 48th vote in schools," said Jack, "and they are all stored together. Ah, here we are. Let's start with precinct 301, Cooper."

Jack pulled the cart out of its assigned place while Carl took charge of the two scanners. The cart had been fully loaded with supplies the previous week, so all there was to do was roll it and the scanners to the workbench area where Terrence and the others were waiting. Carl noticed that Jennifer and Tracy were off to one side, engaged in a hushed, yet animated, discussion.

"OK, Carl and I will get this started," said Terrence. "Jack, you can get the items for the next precinct."

Carl went over to the workbench to retrieve his cheat sheet of instructions. This was mostly for show. Having spent the past three weeks testing the other precincts, it was ingrained as muscle memory by now.

Once the first scanner had gone through the preliminary setup, Carl inserted the flash drive.

"It takes a few minutes for the scanner to recognize the flash drive and go through the opening sequence," he explained.

Carl pressed the appropriate button. Almost immediately the screen displayed the message,

"Election file invalid."

"Oh, shit," said Terrence, softly.

"What's going on?" said Tracy, who had extricated herself from Jennifer.

"I'm afraid, we have a bad flash drive," said Terrence.

General groans greeted that announcement.

For the next forty minutes various scanners for various precincts were wheeled into place. In every case, the same error message was displayed.

Terrence got on the phone with the Government Center.

"None of them are working. Who programed these? They will have to be redone."

While this was going on, Jennifer and Tracy resumed their previous discussion with Jennifer becoming increasingly agitated. Steve tried to join them but Tracy waved him away. Cindy stood by, at a respectful distance. Emily returned to the table and sat patiently. Only Palucci seemed to be enjoying himself.

"Ah, another fine day for the Office of Elections," he said cheerfully.

Finally Terrence put down the phone and called for order.

"Folks, let me apologize for the delay we have encountered. I've talked to the Government Center. The person who normally programs the flash drives had a personal emergency so they handed off the assignment to a less experienced person. The good news is that the original person has resolved the situation and is now at work. So Jack is going to return to the Government Center with these flash drives where they will be reprogramed. As it is now 11:30 a.m., why don't we break for lunch and we can resume at 1:00 p.m.? There is a deli next door. A number of the rovers eat there regularly. I'm sure you will find it satisfactory. Thank you for your patience."

This announcement brought the expected groans and

complaints. Jack put all the flash drives back in the envelope and departed.

"Are you going over there?" Cindy asked Carl, quietly.

"I brown bagged it," said Carl.

Similar conversations occurred among various combinations. It gradually became apparent that the men had all brought their lunches.

"Come on, Cindy," said Emily. "It will do us good to get out of here." They proceeded to the front where Tracy and Jennifer were already shedding their vests. The four then departed together.

Palucci chuckled. "If ever there was a catfight waiting to happen…"

Chapter 34

TUESDAY, APRIL 20, 12:15 P.M.
(TIMELINES FOR CHAPTERS 34 AND 35 OVERLAP)

"TRACY, I'D REALLY like to talk with you. Privately, I mean," said Cindy, as the two of them waited at the counter for their deli order to be filled.

Tracy stared straight ahead, a faint smile on her lips.

"I bet you do. Ah, here's my order now."

Tracy received her plate and quickly walked over to the self-serve beverage machine, leaving Cindy to mull over her next move. She suddenly wished she had ordered something that could be prepared quicker than the Rueben that was still in a half-cooked state on the grill. She looked over at Tracy and sighed, feeling helpless and vulnerable.

At last her sandwich was ready. She put the plate on her tray, filled her cup with Coke at the self-serve machine, and went over to the table where her three companions were already seated. Tracy and Jennifer Haley appeared to be having an intense conversation.

"You have absolutely no proof of that," snapped Jennifer. "No proof at all. That's pure bullshit and if you try to publish that, our lawyers will sue you into the dark ages."

"Of course we would never publish anything without proof," said Tracy, smiling. "So if everything is on the up and up as you say, then you have nothing to worry about. I do so hope we get to face off in the general election. It would be such a shame if Mr. Palucci upsets your reelection plans."

"What have I missed?" asked Cindy, taking her seat and trying to be as upbeat as possible.

"Nothing that shouldn't be hammered out elsewhere," said Emily. She looked at Cindy's Rueben and fries. "Oh how I wish I was thirty years younger and could eat as you do. Tuna on rye can get a bit monotonous."

An uneasy silence pervaded the table as they continued to eat their lunch. Tracy clearly enjoyed being the center of attention. From time to time Jennifer glared at Tracy, a look of utter loathing on her face. For her own part, Cindy stayed focused on her meal. She was vulnerable and did not want Tracy to have any more of an advantage than she already had.

At last it was time to get back to the warehouse. They took turns refilling their drink cups and left the deli.

"You would think they'd have lids for these cups," said Emily to Cindy.

"My understanding is that they usually do. They must have run out today," replied Cindy.

"Hopefully, they can begin testing this afternoon. I don't want to waste any more time on this," said Jennifer. She broke ranks from the others, walking briskly. Her body language clearly said that she wanted to be by herself.

The others stood by, watching her go. Then Cindy looked

over at Tracy.

"I believe I left something inside," said Emily. "If you'll excuse me…"

Emily turned and went back into the deli.

"So," said Tracy. "Now we're alone. What do you have on your pretty little mind?"

"I think you know."

"Perhaps, I do," said Tracy as they started to walk toward the warehouse. "You know, Steve is a great campaign manager. He knows how to win. He would have secured you a victory last year if only you had possessed the character to stick it out. And he will help me win as well. Because he and I will do whatever it takes. Whatever it takes."

"What do you want?"

Tracy stopped and turned to face Cindy.

"What I want is for you to resign as Emily Weston's campaign manager."

Cindy was shocked. She wasn't sure what she had expected but it wasn't this.

"I can't do that. Losing her campaign manager this late would ruin her campaign. Emily would never understand."

"Of course, she would. Make up some story. You're good at making up stories, aren't you? As I recall from your campaign last year."

Cindy winced. Yes, she had made up some stuff during her Soil and Water effort last year. Not her proudest moment.

Tracy turned and continued walking to the warehouse. Up ahead, Cindy could see Jennifer opening the door to the warehouse and entering. To the rear Emily could be seen, having apparently retrieved whatever she left in the deli. For a moment Cindy stood frozen to her spot, not sure what to do, who to approach.

There has to be a way out of this. Maybe if I plead with Tracy one last time.

She turned and broke into a half trot, catching up to Tracy at the base of the ramp leading up to the warehouse door. Cindy tried to think of something to say but no words came out. Tracy opened the door to the warehouse and they entered, allowing the door to close behind them. Tracy proceeded to put on her vest.

"Tracy, please—"

Tracy turned on Cindy.

"You think you're so clever," hissed Tracy, barely above a whisper. "Go ahead. Stay on as Emily's campaign manager. When Steve and I finish exposing your dirty little secret, her campaign will be as good as dead."

The desperate look on Cindy's face encouraged her to go on.

"And what will your precious Carl think when he learns of this? Not to mention those darling little nephews of yours. Won't they be surprised when they learn what their favorite auntie does when the sun goes down?"

It happened so fast. Something in Cindy snapped. Even as Emily was opening the door, Cindy hurled the contents of her drink cup into Tracy's face.

Tracy stood, frozen in shock, her face and blouse completely soaked.

"Cindy? What in the world?" exclaimed Emily.

"My God," gasped Cindy, reeling in horror over what she had done. "Tracy, I am so sorry."

Tracy looked down at her own drink cup. For a moment Cindy thought she would retaliate.

Go ahead. I deserve it.

For a few moments Tracy, Cindy, and Emily stood in their positions, each waiting for someone else to make the next move.

Over by the check-in desk, Rudy Matheson suddenly became engrossed in his paperwork.

At last, Tracy made the first move. She carefully put her cup on the table, turned around, and went into the ladies room. After a moment's hesitation, Cindy made to follow suit.

"Don't," said Emily, putting a restraining hand on Cindy's wrist. "This needs time. Just go back to the election area."

"I have to try," said Cindy, releasing her arm from Emily's grasp. She then followed Tracy's footsteps into the ladies room.

Tracy was by the sink. She had rinsed her face off and was patting it down with a paper towel.

"You'd think they'd give us softer towels," said Tracy, looking at her reflection in the mirror. "Look at me. And it just came back from the cleaners."

"Tracy, I'm sorry."

"And in front of witnesses, too. You do need to control your temper, Phelps."

Cindy looked down at the floor. The desperation she had felt a few minutes earlier had changed to defeat. Utter defeat. When she spoke, her tone was listless, void of any emotion.

"I'll do what you want. Just give me some time."

Tracy's lips gradually curled into a triumphant smile. Still staring at the mirror she said, "Today. Do it today and I might even forget about this assault just now. Take one minute longer and you're dead meat."

"You must really hate me."

"Quite the contrary. We are actually quite a bit alike. I just happen to be better at it. Once you are out of my way, we'll get along fine. Now if you would be so kind as to provide me some privacy so I can tidy up and reclaim some of my dignity..."

Cindy recognized the dismissal and left the ladies room.

Anthony Palucci was sitting in the chair by the table on which Tracy's cup rested. He looked up at Cindy with a mischievous grin.

"The ladies have returned to the election area. You must have had a most enjoyable lunch hour. I would have so loved to be a fly on the wall."

Cindy looked over to the table on which rested Tracy's drink.

"Will you be throwing that in her face as well?"

Cindy went over to the table and picked up the cup.

"Maybe I'll throw it in your face instead."

Palucci got to his feet, laughing. "Oh, please. Don't throw a hissy fit on my account. I think I will beat a hasty retreat."

With that, he turned and went back toward the rear of the warehouse, leaving Cindy alone, holding Tracy's cup.

I need some air.

Putting the cup down, Cindy opened the door and went outside.

Rudy was sitting on one of the picnic benches, smoking a cigarette.

Good idea.

Cindy opened her handbag and quickly found the pack. Matches were another story. They were in there. Somewhere.

"Cindy, what is the matter with you?"

Cindy looked up. It was Steve, looking at her with an incredulous look on his face.

"Attacking my candidate? She's still in the ladies room composing herself after your assault. What were you thinking?"

"Don't judge me," hissed Cindy. "You're the reason I'm in this mess, you little—"

"Of course, as I recall, fits of temper are your specialty," said Steve. "That night in the parking lot. Just because I said your sister is a bore. She is, by the way."

Cindy tried to think of a response but nothing came. She turned her back to Steve and resumed her search for the matches. Why couldn't she find them?

"Is this what you're looking for?"

Steve had knelt down and retrieved the book of matches that had apparently fallen from Cindy's handbag. He handed them to her.

"Thanks," she mumbled, putting them in her handbag. She had suddenly lost any urge to smoke.

They stood in silence, each taking the measure of the other, for about a half a minute. When at last Steve spoke, it was with an air of calm severity.

"You need to get out Cindy, or people will get hurt, especially you. Politics is not for you. You should have learned that last year."

He turned around and went back into the building.

Cindy looked out into the parking lot. The warming rays of the sun had a soothing effect. She did not want to go back inside.

"You know this is my favorite part of the day," said Rudy. "To take a few extra minutes and relax out here. Really nice."

Cindy gave what she thought was a minimal nod. She did not want to get into a conversation with the warehouse foreman.

"Now you election folks are a different breed altogether. Always intense. Serious. Work. Work. Work. And inquisitive, too. Take that blond. You know, the reporter. Easy on the eye but always snooping. I sure wouldn't want to have any secrets. Not with her nosing around."

"No," said Cindy, sadly. "No secrets."

Chapter 35

*T*HERE IT'S IN *place. Finally.*

Carl looked, with satisfaction, at the precinct cart and two scanners which he had wheeled into place in front of the workbenches. The stenciled name on the cart identified it as being for the Tower precinct. Tower was one of what the rovers called "specials." Precincts that were located in venues other than schools. It had recently been added to the 48th Senate district, the result of a court ordered redistricting that had taken place the previous year.

Twenty minutes earlier Jack had arrived at the warehouse to give them the reprogramed flash drives for this precinct. He was now heading back to the Government Center to obtain the other flash drives that were being reprogramed. Once they were done, he would bring them back to the warehouse but at least Tower would allow them to make some progress. Carl felt for Jack, who it seemed would be spending his whole day driving between the two locations.

Satisfied that the equipment was ready, Carl returned to the gathering table, just outside the election cage. Steve and Palucci were seated, having finished their lunch. Terrence was off to one side, reviewing some papers.

Jennifer Haley, having apparently just entered, was on her cell phone.

"I know. The whole thing has been a complete fiasco. A complete waste of time."

Jennifer was angry and she didn't care who knew it. She slammed her drinking cup onto the small table by the entrance to the cage, spilling some of its contents in the process.

"Understood. Just try and keep things on an even keel until I get back."

Emily then came into the area, holding her cup. Seeing Carl, she hurried over to his side.

"I'm worried about Cindy," she said, in a hushed voice. "She completely lost it back there. Threw the entire contents of her drinking cup into Tracy's face."

Before Carl could respond, Palucci weighed in with,

"Oh my, that does sound delicious, doesn't it?"

"Will you excuse us?" said Emily, sternly. "We are having a private conversation."

"Oh, of course," said Palucci, with a malicious grin. "I think I'll take a stroll to the front. See which way the wind is blowing and all that." With that he got to his feet and strolled toward the front.

Carl and Emily exchanged helpless looks.

"I'm sorry," said Emily. "I thought I was being discreet. But with that creep hovering about, you can't be too careful."

"Where's Cindy now?" asked Carl.

"She followed Tracy into the ladies room, in hopes of making amends."

Carl considered. "I'll talk to her when she gets back. I'm not sure what I can do before then."

"There is nothing you can do. I just thought you should be aware."

Carl took a seat at the main table while Emily started wandering around the election area. Steve got to his feet.

"I think I'll go up front. Use the restroom," he said to no one in particular. He then proceeded in the same direction that Palucci had gone a few moments earlier.

Terrence looked up from his papers.

"Where's everyone going? We'll be starting as soon as people get back from lunch."

"Well I certainly don't intend to hold things up." Palucci had returned. He walked over to Carl.

"There is a fair amount of drama going on up front," he whispered. "Your lady friend threatened to assault me with a drinking cup."

Feeling helpless, Carl said nothing.

For a few minutes, everything seemed to be in a holding pattern. Jennifer completed her call. Emily continued wandering around, examining the items on the shelves.

"I hope I'm not holding up the proceeding."

It was Tracy. Both her blouse and vest had brown strains.

"What an invigorating lunch we had over at the deli. Old friends catching up," she said cheerfully. She looked over at Jennifer's cup on the table.

"Oh Jennifer, you seem to have lost part of your drink. There must be some sort of epidemic. Cindy lost hers, just a little while ago. I guess I better be extra careful." Tracy placed her cup on the table next to Jennifer's. "Now let's do some testing."

Jennifer glowered at Tracy.

"It looks like all the candidates are here," said Terrence. "We just need the two campaign managers and we'll be ready to start."

"This campaign manager is ready." It was Steve, who had come hurrying back from the front. "And I see that it's 1:00 p.m. so let's get started. That was the agreed upon time."

"We will wait until everyone is here," said Carl.

Carl realized he was overstepping his authority. It was Terrence's call when to start, not his.

Before Terrence could speak, Tracy walked over to Steve.

"Oh Steve," she said, putting a hand on his shoulder. "I think we can be flexible on this. It would seem that Ms. Phelps needs some time to compose herself. Surely we can be accommodating."

It was a few minutes later when Cindy walked into the area. She looked neither to the left or right, her face expressionless. She seemed to be aware that all eyes were on her.

Emily quickly took her by the hand and escorted her to the main table.

"We are now all here. Excellent," said Terrence. "While you were all at lunch, we had delivered to us the flash drives for the Tower precinct. Carl has moved the cart and scanners into position by the workbench. The flash drives from the other precincts are being reprogrammed as we speak and they will be arriving in a little while. So Carl, why don't you lead us all to the workbench and we can get the testing started."

Carl got to his feet and proceeded to lead the way through the opening of the cage back to the workbench where the cart and scanners were. Jennifer, Tracy, Steve, and Palucci followed.

Emily and Cindy remained seated.

"We need to talk," whispered Cindy.

"Yes. But not now."

"Are you coming?" called Terrence, who had already started walking to the testing area.

"We'll be along soon," said Emily. "Go ahead and start without us."

Emily got to her feet and, taking her cup, started to go back to the testing area. Then as she reached the small table, she stopped and turned around.

"This is ridiculous," she said. "I have to trust the system."

Looking over to Cindy, she asked, "Are you going back there?"

Cindy shook her head. "I've seen it all before." For the moment she seemed content to remain seated and stare at the surface of the table. She was leaning forward, elbows on the table, fingers pressed to her forehead.

Emily looked over at the precinct map on the wall and then proceeded to wander around the area, picking up random items from the shelves.

Suddenly there was a burst of noise coming from the testing area. The sound of angry voices could be heard.

"That's it. I'm out of here," said Jennifer, as she emerged from the cage. She grabbed her cup, made as if to take a final sip, but instead threw it into the same dumpster that Brenda and George had emptied hours earlier. "Call me if you ever get your act together," she said to the room at large and exited the election area, passing Emily who was standing by one of the laundry carts which held the books.

The others began to emerge from the testing area.

"Please folks, just wait till I get an explanation," Terrence was saying apologetically to anyone who would listen.

"For once I have to agree with my opponent," said Palucci who was shaking his head. "As entertaining as this has been, I need to take my leave." With those words, he too was gone.

Even as Terrence was dialing the Government Center, Carl emerged.

Cindy looked up at him.

"Same error message," said Carl.

"Oh Carl, I'm sorry," said Cindy, temporarily distracted from her own problems.

Terrence was speaking on the phone.

"Yes, it's the same error...I thought Naomi was back at work... No, don't have Henry try it again. He doesn't know how to do it..."

Tracy and Steve came out of the area, deep in conversation.

"So I'll see you later," Tracy was saying to Steve. Steve nodded and turned to leave. Before leaving however, he took a long look at Cindy.

"What?" said Cindy.

Steve said nothing but slowly shook his head and left.

"Attention, everyone," Terrence was calling out to the dwindling crowd. "There will be no more testing today. I will personally reprogram the flash drives this afternoon. We will resume tomorrow at 9:00 a.m. On behalf of the county I would like to apologize..."

Meanwhile, Tracy took a sip from her drink and walked over to where Carl and Cindy were seated.

"Carl, your girlfriend is so photogenic. You simply must take some pictures of her." With one last triumphant smile, Tracy exited from the testing area.

"OK, everyone," Terrence was saying. "We all need to vacate the warehouse." With that, he locked the entrance to the cage and they all made their way back to the front.

Rudy was there, turning on the security system for the night.

Lights were being turned off.

"You all logged out?" said Rudy. "Good. I checked everyone as they left. All hands accounted for. Another day at the office."

One by one they exited the warehouse. Rudy was the last to leave. He closed the outer door and pulled the handle a few times to ensure it was locked. It was done. They would try again tomorrow.

Chapter 36

"**C**INDY!"

"May I come in?"

"Of course."

Emily opened the front door and allowed Cindy to enter. "Do have a seat. Can I get you something?"

"No, thank you," said Cindy, taking a seat on the couch. "This won't take long."

"Are you sure," said Emily, sitting next to Cindy. "These things always take longer than we imagine. The world of politics is so complicated isn't it? That unpleasantness at the warehouse today—"

"I'm resigning as your campaign manager."

Emily did not respond right away. For the better part of a minute she remained silent as she digested Cindy's announcement. Finally she spoke.

"May I ask why?"

I'm being blackmailed and I'm trying to avoid total humiliation.

"I'm not doing you any good," Cindy began. She had been rehearsing this in her mind. The things she would say. "You saw what happened today. I let the pressure of the campaign get the better of me. I'm an amateur who's been pretending to be a professional..."

Cindy want on, describing and embellishing her imperfections and why they were hurting Emily's effort. How Emily would be so much better without her. For her part, Emily was content to be silent. To let Cindy talk until she ran out of steam which eventually she did.

"May I speak?" said Emily, with a gentle smile.

"Cindy, I know you're upset," she began. "That incident today was unfortunate—"

"It's not just that—"

"Cindy," said Emily, with a touch of firmness in her voice. "I've allowed you to speak uninterrupted. I ask that you extend me the same courtesy."

Cindy felt trapped but couldn't think of any way to overrule Emily's legitimate request.

Please, I said my piece. Just let me go!

"You are obviously under a lot of pressure and you feel things deeply. So much like my niece..."

Not that again. I am nothing like your niece.

"...but I always believe that when things seem darkest, something happens to brighten the skies. When things calm down in a few days we can craft a note of apology to Tracy. But to be honest, I don't even think that will be necessary—"

"No, it's not going to work. I have to quit—"

Emily reached over and took Cindy's hands into her own.

"Cindy, if in a few days you still feel this way, then we can talk. But I don't think it will be necessary. I'm sure that in a few days, perhaps even in a few hours, things will seem so much better. Life has a way of doing that."

"Please, no—"

"And you know, if I lose to Tracy, it won't be so bad. What matters is that we eliminate Jennifer Haley. That must happen. And if the voters think Tracy is the better option to accomplish that, then so be it. And now I must ask you to take your leave. There are some things I need to attend to. But don't worry. All will be well."

With that, Emily stood up and motioned for Cindy to do the same. She walked Cindy to the door and ushered her out of the house.

"Not to worry," were her parting words. "All will be well."

Chapter 37

Tuesday, April 20, 5:30 P.M.

C INDY'S CAR WAS parked at the outermost extremity of the parking lot in Carl's townhouse complex. It had been there for the past half hour. She did not want Carl to be aware of her presence. Not until she was sure.

Why should this be so difficult? He knows I led an active social life, long before I met him.

But, she realized all too well, this was different. Yes, it was true that they had not been officially "boyfriend-girlfriend" when this had happened. No promises had been made. And she and Steve had been working so closely on the election. Carl must have known. Carl must have suspected.

Perhaps, but never openly acknowledged. He never asked. And why should he? It was really none of his business.

Still, he should hear it from me. Before it goes viral on the internet.

She went over it, again and again. What she needed to say. Then at last with a sigh, she opened the car door. Getting out of the car, she started walking the length of the parking lot. She could see Carl's car in its customary place. Brad's car was not there. Good. This had to be only the two of them.

She walked past the car and went up the short walkway to the townhouse front door. She rang the doorbell.

Carl, there is something I need to tell you...

The door opened.

"Cindy, I'm so glad you're here. It's been all over the news."

Cindy was confused. Carl seemed agitated and obviously concerned about something. But not really angry.

"It's on the news?"

"Yes, they had a big feature on the five o'clock news and they've been replaying it—"

So the photos are out. He knows.

"Carl, I am so sorry—"

"Of course you are. But please don't let it eat at you. You had no way of knowing this would happen. It's just one of life's nasty twists. None of it was your fault."

What are you talking about? It's all my fault.

"Carl, it's sweet of you to say this but I need to take ownership for what I've done."

"What you did was lose your temper. Not your finest moment perhaps but I'm sure it had no impact on her. After all as we both know, Tracy was tough as nails."

"Don't I know it? And I tried so hard to keep Tracy from— what do you mean 'was'?"

Carl gave Cindy a bewildered look.

"You don't know?"

"Know what?"

"It's Tracy. She's dead."

Cindy was stunned.

"Dead but how—"

"It happened on the Interstate. She apparently lost control of her car. Smashed through a guard rail. Car was demolished."

"Did it say where on the interstate?"

Carl paused. When he spoke again, it was in a more somber tone.

"She was coming off the entrance ramp from Buford Drive."

"Which means—"

"It was just minutes after she left the warehouse."

Cindy suddenly felt she was about to collapse. Sensing her distress, Carl led her over to the couch.

"Can I get you something? There's beer in the fridge. Or do you need to smoke?"

Cindy never smoked on her dates with Carl but he knew she sometimes indulged when under stress.

Cindy shook her head. "I hated her," she said, flatly.

"I know but—"

"And I threw my drink in her face. And now she's dead."

Carl took Cindy's hands and gave a gentle squeeze. For several minutes they sat in silence.

At last Cindy got to her feat.

"I guess I better go. I'm sorry she's gone. As much as I hated her, I'm sorry she's dead. You do believe that don't you?"

"Of course. And don't worry. Everyone else will believe it as well."

Cindy nodded. "Will you be at the warehouse tomorrow?"

"I guess so. Unless they cancel it out of respect. I'm not sure what the rules are when a candidate dies."

Cindy nodded. Carl walked her to the door. There was a hug and she departed in silence. She was halfway to her car when she realized,

I still haven't told him.

Chapter 38

TUESDAY, APRIL 20, 7:30 P.M.

CARL WASN'T HUNGRY but he knew he should eat something. Some ground beef in the fridge. Some frozen French fries. An unimaginative dinner but it would suffice. He was in the process of cleaning up when Brad came through the door.

"Good. You're home," said Brad. "That was a shock today, wasn't it?"

Carl nodded. "I still can't believe it. Cindy is devastated. I had to break the news to her. I'm just about to call Terrence to see what the schedule is. My guess is that they will postpone the testing out of—"

"Don't."

"Excuse me."

"Don't call Terrence. There won't be any testing tomorrow."

Carl looked skeptically at his brother.

"How do you know what my testing schedule will be?"

"Trust me, I know," said Brad. "You will receive a phone call—"

Almost as if by magic, the phone started to ring.

The two brothers exchanged glances.

"Just pick it up."

Carl did as directed.

"Carl, it's Cindy." She sounded breathless. "Have the police called you yet?"

"No. Brad's here, though. He said I would be receiving a call but he didn't say from who."

"It will be from the police. They're asking us to come to the warehouse tomorrow at 9:00 a.m. They want to get as full a picture as they can concerning the lead-up to Tracy's accident. At least that's what the cop who called said to me."

"Who are they calling in?"

"He didn't say exactly but I get the impression that it was everyone who was at the warehouse yesterday."

I don't understand. A tragedy to be sure but shouldn't they be focusing on where the accident occurred. What do the people at the warehouse have to do with it?

"Carl...?"

Cindy had been saying something but he must have missed it.

"I'm sorry, I didn't catch what you were saying."

"Should I be worried?"

"No, of course not," said Carl soothingly. "We'll answer their questions and be done with it."

They talked for a few more minutes and Carl reassured Cindy as best he could. They said their goodbyes and hung up.

"She's very upset," said Carl. "I tried to reassure her that this was normal under the circumstances and not to worry."

Brad remained silent.

Chapter 39

WEDNESDAY, APRIL 21

Democratic Candidate Perishes in Tragic Accident
By J.C. Styles, Washington Herald

Followers of the county political scene were shocked yesterday to learn of the tragic death of popular TV and radio reporter Tracy Miller. Miller, 28, had covered the county's political scene for WMML radio and its sister TV station WMML-TV for the past five years, having first received her bachelor's degree in broadcast journalism from the University of Florida. During that time she earned a reputation as a charming on-screen personality as well as a tenacious news reporter who did not hesitate to embarrass interviewees. She recently took a leave of absence from her position to seek the Democratic nomination to the State Senate for Virginia's 48th district.

Miller's death came as the result of a single car accident which occurred on the county interstate, just north of the Buford Drive entrance. "It appears that she lost control of her vehicle as she was trying to merge into the flow of traffic," said Officer Phillip Jenkins of the county police department. "Witnesses say that her car swerved into a guard rail, penetrating the rail, and then smashed head-on into a tree. Death must have been instantaneous."

"This is a shocking and sad day for all of us," said Steve Winters, who had been serving as Miller's campaign manager. "She was such a lovely person and had such a bright future." When asked what impact this would have on the upcoming June eighth primary, Winters bristled saying, "This is neither the time nor place for such speculation. We are all in deep mourning."

"We are all greatly saddened by this," said Emily Weston, Miller's rival for the Democratic nomination. Weston indicated that she would suspend campaigning for the foreseeable future, "out of respect." Similar expressions of sorrow have been issued by the two Republican candidates for the Senate seat, current State Senator Jennifer Haley and Anthony Palucci.

Political commentators are unsure what this means for the upcoming Democratic primary. Miller's death leaves Emily Weston as the sole Democratic candidate for the nomination. The county Democratic establishment had lined up behind Miller, believing that Weston, 66, had passed her peak as a campaigner.

"This tragic event leaves us in a rather fluid situation," said county registrar Gordon Carruthers. "Normally the date for filing has long passed. However, there is a provision in the election code that if a candidate dies forty-five days or more before the day of a primary, an alternative candidate may file if he/she turns in the necessary paperwork within thirty-five days of the primary. As we are now forty-seven days away from primary day, we could theoretically see an alternate candidate enter the race."

Chapter 40

WEDNESDAY, APRIL 21, 9:00 A.M.

ONE BY ONE they went into the room. Each of them had come voluntarily and without a lawyer present. It had been explained that each would be free to go after his/her "conversation." Very informal. Just so they could get an understanding of the events immediately preceding the tragedy. If they chose to stay, they were requested to refrain from talking with the others. A police officer was on hand to ensure that this request was honored.

In spite of all the assurances from the police, the fact that the warehouse had been sealed off with crime scene yellow tape told them that this was anything but routine.

Terrence had been called in first. Then Rudy, the warehouse foreman. Both were interviewed for about twenty minutes and both chose to remain on site after questioning. Next was Jennifer Haley. She was in for a bit longer, perhaps thirty minutes. She exited her session with a solemn expression on her face, gathered up her things, and left.

Anthony Palucci was called in next. Giving a smirk to the others, he strode in to the room.

"I'm glad somebody is enjoying this," muttered Carl, under his breath.

Palucci's time in the room was about twenty-five minutes. When he exited, the smirk was gone. He left quickly.

Next it was time for Steve Winters to be called in. Earlier in the day when Cindy had offered him her condolences, he had eyed her coldly and said,

"It makes things so much easier for you, now that she's gone, doesn't it?"

Cindy hadn't known how to respond so she just murmured "I'm sorry," and retreated.

Steve was in for about twenty minutes. He too came out with a solemn expression on his face. He seemed determined not to make eye contact with anyone in the room and quickly left the scene.

"Ms. Weston," said the police officer and Emily Weston got to her feet. She exchanged glances with Cindy and entered the room.

The minutes ticked by. Fifteen. Twenty. Twenty-five.

"This is killing me," said Cindy. For the past hour, she and Carl had been holding hands, trying to comfort each other. Was there some reason for the order of questioning? Tracy's accident had been a tragedy, but even if she had been upset when she left the warehouse, she was still responsible for her own actions. It was an accident involving a single car. One occupant. Each of the individuals in the warehouse had been miles away.

The door opened and Emily Weston emerged. She and Cindy exchanged looks. Carl tried to decipher Emily's expression. Was it fear? Disappointment? Pity? Emily turned around and departed.

"Mr. Marsden. Could you step inside please?"

Carl and Cindy exchanged looks. Cindy grimaced and nodded. Carl gave her hand an extra squeeze and got to his feet.

He followed the inspector into the room and gave a start. Brad was sitting in the corner of the room, with an open laptop in front of him.

"Mr. Marsden, if you would have a seat. I am Inspector Dan Fellows and I will be conducting this conversation. Deputy Inspector Brad Marsden is observing only. He will not be participating in this conversation. Is that clear?"

Carl exchanged a quick look with Brad and nodded.

This is more than just a car accident. They suspect something. But what?

"Mr. Marsden, we have here a difficult situation. A popular news reporter and political candidate, apparently in the best of health, with a spotless record as a driver, suddenly drives her car into a tree. A personal tragedy to be sure. All we are trying to do is understand, as well as we can, how this sad state of affairs came to be."

Carl remained silent.

"Mr. Marsden, could you describe your relationship with the decedent, Tracy Miller."

"My relationship with Ms. Miller was virtually non-existent," said Carl. "I have, of course, been aware of her as a television reporter for the past few years. She did a short news segment last January during a special election when I was serving as assistant chief—"

"Did she interview you at that time?"

"No, she interviewed the chief election officer."

"That would be Cynthia Phelps."

"Yes."

"What was your recollection of that interview?"

"It was short. I was processing voters at the time so I didn't really focus on it."

Inspector Fellows considered this for a few moments.

"Did you have any dealings with Ms. Miller since she became a candidate?"

"Not really. We were trying to get the testing for the primary started yesterday morning. We might have exchanged a word or two but I'm not sure—"

"You and Cynthia Phelps are seeing each other socially, I believe."

It was more of a statement than a question but it seemed to require a response. Carl tensed but there was no point avoiding the obvious.

"Yes."

"Was Ms. Miller happy about this?"

"I'm not sure I'm qualified to judge Ms. Miller's state of happiness."

Carl realized almost immediately that his snarky response was a mistake. Out of the corner of his eye, he could see Brad frowning.

"What I mean," said Inspector Fellows, giving Carl a warning look, "is did Ms. Miller complain to anyone that the boyfriend of her rival's campaign manager was involved in the testing of the voting machines being used in the primary?"

"It was mentioned as a concern in a newspaper article. She might also have complained to Terrence. But you'd have to ask him to be sure."

Once again, Inspector Fellows paused. He seemed to be considering how best to resume the questioning. At last,

"Could you describe the events at the warehouse leading up to

Ms. Miller's departure?"

Carl recounted the events, as best he could recall. The inspector allowed him to give his narrative uninterrupted.

Once again there were several moments of silence. Then,

"Are you aware that Cynthia Phelps, apparently in a fit of rage, threw the contents of her drinking cup into Ms. Miller's face?"

"Yes. I am aware of that."

"But you did not actually see it happen?"

"No, I did not."

"Do you know why she did that?"

Carl paused. There was something unfolding here and they seemed to be zeroing in on Cindy. He suddenly felt in over his head. He harbored suspicions but nothing was certain. He did not want to lie but he did not want to say anything that might harm Cindy.

"Do I have the right to remain silent?"

Fellows and Brad exchanged looks.

"Yes, you do."

Carl suddenly felt thirsty and was aware that he had been perspiring.

"Then I wish to exercise that right."

There was silence for several moments as Inspector Fellows started writing something in his notepad. Then he looked up at Carl and smiled.

"Thank you Mr. Marsden for participating in our little chat here today. You are free to go."

The inspector got to his feet and, with what seemed to be undo haste, ushered Carl from the room.

"Ms. Phelps," said Inspector Fellows, displaying a dazzling smile. "Could you step in here please?"

Looking absolutely terrified, Cindy got to her feet. She gave

Carl a pleading look. Carl returned her gaze, giving a slight shake of the head. He hoped she understood.

Please Cindy, be on your guard. They mean business.

Chapter 41

THE HOURS OF waiting had taken its toll. A sense of acute anxiety gripped Cindy as she took her seat. She wished she could smoke but knew it was not allowed in the warehouse. Her throat suddenly seemed dry. Incredibly dry.

"May I have a glass of water?"

"Certainly. Brad will you do the honors?"

Brad got to his feet and left the room. While he was gone, Inspector Fellows went through the preliminaries. Cindy nodded her understanding but remained silent.

"Ms. Phelps, here is the water you requested."

Cindy took the glass, with a nod of appreciation. She took a small sip and placed it on the table.

"Ms. Phelps, you and the deceased had a number of interactions over the past couple of years. Is that correct?"

"Yes, a few, I guess."

"Can you describe the first time she interviewed you? That would have been last January, the day of the special election to fill the State Senate seat."

"It was a very brief interview, early in the day. I was chief election officer, you see. She asked about how things were going, how many people had voted. That sort of thing."

"Didn't she also confront you with the fact that one of your officers had been expelled from the polling place?"

"That's right, you see there was—"

"And didn't your response turn up on a YouTube video later in the day? A video which almost got you removed from your position as chief election officer?"

Cindy was confused. What did any of this have to do with Tracy's tragic accident?

"I guess you could say that," said Cindy, slowly.

For a few moments there was silence. Then Inspector Fellows added in a tone that suggested sympathetic understanding,

"I bet that made you mad."

It was a statement, not a question. Cindy took another sip of water, neither confirming nor denying what Fellows had said.

"You ran for political office last year, I believe."

"Yes. I was a candidate for Soil and Water Conservation Board."

"And I believe the deceased moderated a debate in which you participated."

Cindy nodded.

"How did that debate go?"

As if you don't know, you bastard.

"I did not do well."

"And you dropped out of the race soon after?"

"Yes."

"Because of your poor debate performance?"

"Partly."

"You were observed to be very angry after that debate. Is that a fair assessment?"

"Yes, I was angry."

"You were angry at Ms. Miller because her questions exposed your lack of qualifications?"

"No," said Cindy. "I was not angry with Ms. Miller. Her questions were honest and fair. I was angry with myself for not being better prepared. Now may I ask, what does all this have to do with Tracy's—I mean, Ms. Miller's tragic accident?"

Inspector Fellows leaned back in his chair and gradually gave a relaxed smile.

"Almost certainly, nothing at all. We're just trying to get the complete picture. Now would you describe, in your own words, what happened yesterday at the warehouse?"

Cindy took another sip of water and then recited, as best she could, the sequence of events that took place, starting from when she arrived that morning. Inspector Fellows was content to let her talk uninterrupted. In fact, he didn't seem interested at all, until she reached the point where the four women went to the deli for lunch. He then listened attentively, taking notes, as Cindy described the lunch and events occurring afterwards, culminating when they all left the warehouse.

"Thank you, Ms. Phelps. Now returning to the lunch. Would you describe it as a harmonious event?"

"For the most part, I guess."

"No disputes. No one got angry?"

Cindy looked down at her water glass. It was empty.

"Well Jennifer Haley seemed to be angry at Ms. Miller. I wasn't sure why."

"And that was it. A dispute between Ms. Haley and Ms. Miller. Nothing else?"

Cindy was silent. Her head started to throb. She looked again at the empty water glass. The seconds ticked by.

"Ms. Phelps," said the inspector, He spoke softly, gently. "Did you throw the contents of your drinking cup into Ms. Miller's face?"

Unable to speak, Cindy nodded. Tears were beginning to trickle down her cheeks.

"May I ask why?"

Cindy shook her head.

"No. It was nothing to do with what happened…it's personal… nothing to do…"

"Ms. Phelps," the inspector continued to speak gently. "I know. Sometimes these things happen. But we do need to know. To have some idea."

Cindy suddenly felt out of breath. The dryness in her throat was suffocating.

I have to say something. This won't end until I say something.

"It was the pictures…I was drunk…please…no one knows…"

With that Cindy broke down into a fit of sobs.

For several minutes the room was quiet except for Cindy's muffled sobs. At last she seemed to regain a modicum of composure.

"I'm sorry about that. You see it was—"

"Not at all," said the inspector with a relaxed smile. "Not at all. We were all young once. I believe that completes our questions. So sorry we had to put you through this. We needed to get the full picture. Brad, if you could show Ms. Phelps to the door?"

Brad rose and went over to Cindy. Taking her by the hand, he led her to the door.

As Brad opened the door, Cindy whispered in his ear, "If you tell Carl, so help me I'll throw something in your face and it won't be a cold drink."

Cindy walked over to Carl who had risen and engulfed him in a hug.

"Please, just hold me."

Chapter 42

THURSDAY, APRIL 22

*A*LL *I* CAN *say is thank heavens for MarketPro.*

On Thursday, the day immediately after the questioning, Cindy was back at her job. It was such a relief to get back to her regular routine. To return to the environment that had defined her professional existence and had consumed so much of her energy and talent in recent years. She was even able to resurrect some of the easy charm that she had learned to turn on at will.

The police questioning had been draining but in a way she was glad she had been forced to endure it. The police seemed satisfied and it looked like the tawdry little secret that the pictures embodied would be allowed to fade away.

She was aware that Tracy's funeral and burial would take place on Saturday. Cindy would not attend. They had never been friends and to pretend otherwise would be hypocritical. Emily would attend. The word was that Jennifer Haley would be there as well.

Cindy talked with Emily by phone for some length Thursday

evening. She agreed to remain as campaign manager, at least through the primary, although with only a single candidate it doubtless would be cancelled. This would give them the time and resources to plan for the fall showdown with Jennifer Haley. Things were so much simpler with Tracy out of the way. Cindy found herself alternating between relief on one hand and profound guilt on the other. At times she felt like she was dancing on Tracy's grave.

She had agreed with Carl to "play it by ear" with respect to the weekend. The events of the past couple of weeks had caused her to fall behind at *MarketPro* and Cindy knew she would definitely be working Saturday and possibly Sunday. Carl indicated he might be working this weekend as well. He did consulting work with *Software Solutions* and would continue to do so until such time as he might gain full-time employment with the Office of Elections.

It was late Friday afternoon when Cindy's phone rang. She could see on the screen that the call was from Carl. Cindy frowned. Carl almost never called her at work. He respected Cindy's need to keep her personal and professional lives separate. So there was a bit of apprehension when she picked up her phone. Her usual bright "This is Cindy Phelps. How may I help you?" was replaced with "What is it Carl?"

"Two things," said Carl. "I've been working today at the Government Center and Steve Winters came in."

"What did he want?"

"Are you ready for this? He's running for State Senate, in place of Tracy. He submitted the filing papers, the signed petitions, the whole thing."

Cindy was stunned. "But Tracy died just three days ago. How did he—"

"Get it all done? Beats me. But he did. The appropriate people are reviewing the materials now."

"So much for his grief," said Cindy. She found it hard not to feel cynical. "I guess there will be a primary after all. Any idea when testing for that will begin?"

"No idea," said Carl. "They'll have to print the ballots and all. I don't think anyone has even given that a thought."

"What's the second thing?"

There was a pause. A long pause.

"Carl?"

"Are you sitting down?"

A sinking feeling.

"Please Carl. Just tell me."

"I just received a call from Inspector Fellows. You'll be getting one too. They want to interview everyone again."

"Good God," gasped Cindy. "Please no."

"I know. It's awful," said Carl.

Silence. Then finally,

"When do they want us to come in?"

"Originally they were going to do it tomorrow but since the funeral is tomorrow…"

"So is it pushed back to Monday?" said Cindy, dreading more lost time at work.

Another pause.

"Sunday 11:00 a.m. at the warehouse."

"Oh, shit," said Cindy, softly. "They really mean business, don't they?"

"I'm afraid so," said Carl. "I'm afraid so."

Chapter 43

SUNDAY, APRIL 25, 10:30 A.M.

H E RANG THE doorbell and waited. Ten seconds. Fifteen. His mind wandered to all those times he had rung that very bell. How the door would open and she would flash that radiant smile, showing how happy she was to see him.

He could hear the footsteps now. A turn of the latch. The door opened. There was no smile. She was tight lipped, her face drawn. Carl thought he could see lines around her mouth and eyes. Lines he had never noticed before. She had not bothered with any makeup. Her hair hung loose, barely combed.

Carl was about to ask, "Are you ready?" but he saw she had a book, water bottle, and jacket so he just stood to one side. She came out, closing the door behind her. After locking the door, they proceeded down the walkway to Carl's car. He opened the door for her and she got in. Carl then walked around to the driver's side of the car. He got in and started the engine. He backed the car out of the parking place, changed gears, and exited the parking lot onto Carter Road.

Neither one had spoken a word.

"Did you go to Mass this morning?" asked Cindy.

"Yes, seven-thirty."

"I'm sorry I didn't join you. I just didn't have it in me—"

"It's OK."

The silence resumed.

The Sunday morning traffic was light and in a few minutes they were on the interstate. The exits flew by.

"You can smoke if you want to," said Carl, trying to be helpful.

"If I start, I won't stop."

At last they reached the exit. For a few moments, Cindy allowed her eyes to drift to the other side of the interstate where the accident had taken place.

The car exited the interstate. In a few minutes they would be there.

"Cindy, if there is anything you want to talk about, anything at all…" Carl tried to sound as soothing and understanding as he could.

Cindy remained silent.

They pulled into the warehouse parking lot. A number of cars were already there. The crime scene tape was still up.

They got out of the car and went up the ramp to the warehouse entrance. A policemen nodded and opened the door.

"They're in the workers' lounge to the right," he said.

Carl followed Cindy into the room.

"Ah, we have two more," said Inspector Fellows.

Carl looked around. They were seated in various chairs sprinkled throughout the room. Terrence. Rudy. Jennifer Haley. Emily Weston. Steve Winters. There were also several persons who were obviously policemen. Brad was among them.

"Who are we waiting for?" asked the inspector.

"Anthony Palucci," said Brad, looking at his clipboard.

An uneasy silence engulfed the room. No one seemed to have any desire to speak. Then they heard voices and footsteps. The door opened and Anthony Palucci entered.

"Very good," said Inspector Fellows. "We are all here. And I see you have all brought books with you. That's good because we are going to be here for a while."

The inspector paused, looking around the room. All eyes were on him. Waiting.

"I realize that calling you in, on short notice, on a Sunday morning is an inconvenience and I thank you for your cooperation. I had hoped that our interviews the other day would have concluded the matter before us but unfortunately they have not. As before, all of you are here, without legal representation, by your own free will and for this we are grateful. We will be calling you in, one at a time, for further questioning. Before we begin, however, I need to advise you of one additional development."

Once again, the inspector paused. All eyes were completely focused on him.

"I must tell you that the police department, at twelve noon today, will be issuing a statement to the media that the death of Tracy Miller is being treated as a homicide."

There were gasps from all parts of the room. The inspector waited for silence.

"One of the deceased's effects inside the car was a beverage cup that came from the deli where a number of the people in this room had lunch with said deceased, shortly before the accident. The cup was not completely empty and the residue from the cup consisted of a soft drink poured from the fountain of the deli. Mixed in with the soft drink was a rather deadly poison."

There were no gasps this time but many of the faces registered shock at what was being said.

"I will be asking each of you to recount the events between the time that Tracy Miller returned to the warehouse after lunch and the time she left to go home. For it was within that period of time that the poison had to have been administered to the drink. I will request, no I will demand, that you describe the details, as best you can. Who went where? Who said what? Even the most insignificant detail matters. Because—"

"Because," interrupted Mr. Palucci, "one of us murdered Tracy Miller."

Chapter 44

ONCE AGAIN THE wait seemed interminable. Terrence, twenty minutes. Rudy, a half hour. Palucci, twenty minutes. Steve, a half hour. At that point Rudy was called back in for fifteen minutes. Jennifer, twenty minutes. Emily, a half hour.

Cindy tried to read her book but it was no use.

"Why are they saving me for last?" she would occasionally ask Carl.

Carl tried reassuring her. "Just tell what happened as best you can remember. That's all they can expect."

The door opened and Emily walked out, stone faced.

"Mr. Marsden, will you please come in."

Carl gave Cindy's hand a quick squeeze, stood up, and walked into the room. Once again Brad was on one side, taking notes. In addition to Inspector Fellows, there was a uniformed woman, about forty years of age.

"Mr. Marsden, this is Deputy Inspector Hamlin. She will be assisting today."

Carl nodded to Hamlin and sat down.

Fellows took a seat at the other end of the table, next to Hamlin. Several pages of paper were spread out before them.

"Mr. Marsden, perhaps we can begin with your recitation of the events of last Tuesday from the moment the four ladies left for lunch to the time when everyone left the warehouse at the end of the day."

Carl repeated the story he had told previously. He was conscious that Inspector Fellows was constantly referring to the pages laid out in front of him. Now and then he would ask Carl to repeat something but, in general, he seemed satisfied. Once Carl was finished there was silence for about a minute as the inspector shuffled his papers. Then,

"Mr. Marsden, are you aware that certain toxic substances are stored at the warehouse?"

"Yes."

"Do you know where these substances are kept?"

"To the best of my knowledge, two places. The bottom shelf in the front of the warehouse, across from the restrooms. And on a bottom shelf in the election area next to a cabinet that stores some tools."

"What sort of substances are there?"

"The most obvious is a box labeled 'Rat Poison.' It's my understanding that they use it to bait some traps that are placed in different spots in the warehouse. Otherwise there are cleaning compounds, antifreeze, and I'm not sure what else."

"And these materials are stored on both shelves."

"Yes, I've seen them on both shelves."

"Including last Tuesday."

Carl paused.

"I'm not sure I can swear to that. They aren't things we use in our election work. So while I am conscious of their being part of our environment, I can't say I specifically noticed them on any one particular day."

"Try. Think back to that day."

Carl frowned.

"Perhaps I noticed them up front...Yes I did."

"And in the rear."

Carl thought for a minute.

"I'm sorry, I just don't recall."

"But if they had been missing, you would have noticed it."

"I can't really say that. We don't access those lower shelves that much. I don't focus on them. I'm sorry."

It was clear that Inspector Fellows was sorry as well.

"All right. That's all for now. You may step outside."

Brad opened the door for his brother.

"Ms. Phelps, if you would step inside."

Chapter 45

SUNDAY, APRIL 25, 2:45 P.M.

*J*UST TELL THE *truth. That's all you can do.*

Cindy kept repeating it over and over again as she took her seat. She opened her water bottle and took a sip. She was barely conscious of the inspector's introductory remarks.

His opening question brought her into focus.

"Ms. Phelps, why did you throw the contents of your cup in the victim's face?"

"I already told you. She claimed to have pictures of me that showed me in a compromising light."

"Could they possibly be these pictures?" asked Deputy Inspector Hamlin, as she pushed a large brown envelope across the table.

Cindy stared at the envelope.

Stay tough, girl. Just answer the questions.

She took the envelope and opened it.

"Yes. These are the same photos that were anonymously delivered to me."

"Do you know who took these photos?"

"Yes. Steve Winters."

"Did you pose for them voluntarily?"

Cindy's fear and shame were gradually being replaced by anger.

"Yes," she snapped.

"We have talked with Mr. Winters. He has assured us that the photos have been deleted. The only ones in existence are the ones that you received and these, which were retrieved from the passenger seat of Ms. Miller's car."

Cindy remained silent.

"So the photos will never be released."

Continued silence.

"That must be a big relief to you."

"I won't dignify that with a comment," she said, looking daggers at the inspector.

If the inspector was upset at Cindy's belligerence, he did not show it.

"Ms. Phelps, are you aware that certain toxic substances are stored at the warehouse?"

"Yes."

"Did you see them when you were at the warehouse last Tuesday?"

"Yes. I noticed them in the front of the warehouse when I checked in. The warehouse foreman pointed them out to me."

"What were they?"

"Rat poison. Antifreeze. Some sort of cleaning compound. I think I might have seen them back in the election area as well."

"So you recall seeing the antifreeze in both locations. Front and back." Inspector Fellows suddenly seemed much more focused.

Cindy thought.

"Definitely the front. And yes, I saw a container in the rear as well."

"Are you aware that antifreeze is toxic?"

"I think I read that somewhere."

"Are you also aware that it's sweet tasting...?"

"No, I didn't know that."

"...so that its taste would not be noticed that much if added to an already sweet soft drink?"

Cindy did not answer.

"Ms. Phelps, some antifreeze was found in the residue of Ms. Miller's cup that was retrieved from her car."

Cindy remained silent.

"Preliminary reports from the lab indicate ethylene glycol in the victim's body. Which is contained in antifreeze. We are not sure if it killed her or simply rendered her incapable of driving her car safely. Either way, it was the cause of her death."

"So," said the inspector, leaning back in his chair, "It would appear that one of the eight people in the warehouse at the time spiked Tracy's Miller's cup. It all comes down to the classic three things. Motive. Means. Opportunity."

Cindy felt the need to say something.

"Let the record show that I deny being that person."

"Ms. Phelps. Would you agree to being fingerprinted?"

"Yes, I would," said Cindy, who was suddenly hopeful. "I never touched either container of antifreeze, front or back—"

"The problem is that the container in the front has been completely wiped of fingerprints. Nothing. Not even the warehouse staff."

"And the one in the rear?"

"Ah yes. That's where it gets interesting. You see, it is gone.

Missing. The warehouse foreman swears that there was a container there. Others, including yourself, report seeing it. But somehow it has disappeared. And the disappearance could not have occurred after you all left the building as no one reentered before the police secured the premises the following morning. Data from the security system verifies that."

The inspector continued. "But when it comes to Tracy Miller's drinking cup, there were fingerprints. The victim's, of course. But another as well. I wonder whose that would be."

As if you don't know.

"Those would be mine."

"When you picked up the cup and threatened Mr. Palucci."

"...and which I immediately put down after he left."

"...and which you were still holding when Mr. Winters arrived from the rear of the warehouse."

"Yes, I mean no. I put the cup down and went outside immediately after Palucci left. Winters did not approach me until I was outside."

"Yes, Mr. Winters did confront you outside. That's been confirmed by the warehouse foreman. But he also approached you earlier. When you were across from the ladies room. Holding Ms. Miller's cup."

"No!"

Inspector Fellows zeroed in on Cindy with penetrating eyes. "You were holding the cup when Mr. Winters arrived. You were holding the cup the whole time. All alone. You. The cup. The antifreeze. Like I said before. Motive. Means. Opportunity."

Cindy let out an audible gasp.

Oh my God. He's accusing me. He really thinks I did it.

"Are you arresting me?"

The inspector continued to fix his gaze on Cindy.

"All in good time, Ms. Phelps. All in good time."

Then almost immediately his demeanor changed.

"I think we're done for now. You may go."

He then called over to Brad.

"They can all go."

Cindy got up and hurried from the room.

She was only vaguely aware of Inspectors Fellows saying, "You may all leave. Thank you for coming in."

Thud.

Without looking she had collided with Steve.

They stood, frozen in place, staring at each other.

"Why did you lie about me?"

Steve said nothing, but gave Cindy a look of pure loathing.

Carl rushed to her side.

"Come on Cindy. Let's get out of here."

They quickly left the warehouse. Once they were settled in Carl's car, Cindy buried her face in her hands. Then ever so slowly she raised her head and looked up at Carl.

"I'm screwed."

There was complete silence all the way back to Cindy's apartment. She chain smoked the entire journey.

Chapter 46

WEDNESDAY, APRIL 28

*T*HEY CAN'T DO *anything to you. You're innocent.*

That was what Carl said repeatedly during their numerous phone conversations over the next few days. As the work week began and the memory of Sunday's interrogation began to fade, Cindy gradually felt better. Work at *MarketPro* was a welcome distraction. There was also a fundraising event scheduled for Wednesday evening at Emily's house.

In a matter of eight days, the primary opponent had gone from Tracy Miller to unopposed to Steve Winters. Steve's late entry would intensify the importance of the fundraiser as these monies would be used in the primary campaign rather than in the November election. Cindy would play the gracious hostess, steering Emily from one potential contributor to another. She would also ensure that their campaign treasurer, Mildred Purvis, would be centrally located and prepared to accept contributions. At the appropriate time, Cindy would call things to order, make a few introductory remarks, and turn everything over to Emily.

Cindy wanted to be at her best for this event. The stress of the last week had taken its toll. She had not eaten well and had neglected her appearance. But now with her hair perfectly in place and makeup applied, she felt she was ready to get back in the game.

"The only candidate truly committed to the environment."

Those were the words that Cindy used over and over again during the event. She had learned enough during her abortive run for Soil and Water Conservation Board to discuss the environment, albeit at a fairly superficial level. This combined with her signature charm, which she could turn on in an instant, was promising to make this a very special evening.

From time to time she checked in with Mildred. Contributions were coming in at a brisk rate, at least during the early portion of the evening. At 8:00 p.m., Cindy called for order and gave her introduction of Emily. She had rehearsed her remarks during the day and she delivered them well. Or so she felt. There was polite applause but not the ovation that she had been hoping for. Something wasn't right.

"How are we doing?" she asked Mildred, shortly after Emily had concluded her remarks.

"We're doing all right," said Mildred. "It's been a pretty good evening."

"But how much in the last half hour?"

"Some," she said, returning a nervous smile. "It's a work night. People don't stay late on a work night."

Cindy frowned. She went over to the side of the room and looked at the thinning crowd. And that's when she heard it.

"...suspect in the Tracy Miller death...they're calling it murder...what was Emily thinking when she hired that woman... unstable...ran for office last year...complete meltdown...what nerve even being here..."

Cindy forced herself to rejoin the crowd and work it as best she could. Smile in place. Eye contact. Offer your hand. No one was outright rude but people seemed to be guarded. By 8:45 the room was virtually empty.

"Thank you so much for doing this," said Emily warmly. If she was disappointed, she seemed determined not to let it show. "Mildred tells me we have enough for some more brochures and perhaps some radio time."

"We should meet later this week to strategize what we do now that Steve Winters is in the race."

"I'm not sure that's necessary," said Emily. "Tracy's death casts a shadow on all of us, I know, but as an opponent Steve will be pretty much the same. They were very close, I believe."

Cindy nodded.

"And the most important thing is to take out Jennifer Haley. Whether I do it or Steve, what really matters is to take her out."

They said their goodbyes and Cindy left to drive home. While hardly a disaster, the evening had not gone as well as she had hoped. And those remarks she had overheard were truly unsettling.

When she got home, there were three messages on her answering machine. The first two were from reporters, requesting interviews. She wrote down their numbers. The third was from Carl.

"Hi Cindy. How are you doing? I hope the event was successful. If you want to talk, just call. No matter how late."

A strange message. Cindy dialed his number.

"Cindy, I'm so glad you called. I let Brad have it in no uncertain words. This is a disgrace."

"I'm not sure I —"

"He denies he had anything to do with it. Denies that anyone in the room had anything to do with it. 'Who then?' I asked. He couldn't answer. I am so sorry."

"I don't understand. What are you sorry about?"

A pause of several seconds.

"It's the whole Tracy Miller thing. The Herald is running a story in tomorrow's print edition but it's on the net right now. You've been identified as a 'person of interest.'"

Cindy sat down, trying to absorb this new development.

How stupid I was to think this was just going to fade away.

"...Cindy...Are you all right...Please say something..."

The urgency of Carl's voice brought her out of her reverie.

"I'm sorry, Carl. I'm OK. I guess."

"Is there anything I can do? Do you want me to come over?"

"No need for that...but could you answer one question for me?"

"Of course. Anything."

"Do you...do you think I'm innocent? I know you keep saying it...but do you really believe it?"

"Cindy, how can you ask such a thing?" He sounded hurt.

"I sorry but it just suddenly became very important to hear you say it."

"Cindy, you are completely innocent. And once the police finish their stupid investigation, they will know it too."

Somehow she found that simple declaration to be soothing. Hopefully, it would help sustain her in the days and weeks that lay ahead.

Chapter 47

Thursday, April 29

Dramatic Turnaround in TV Reporter's Death
Political Operative Identified as "Person of Interest"
By J.C. Styles, Washington Herald

The investigation into the death of TV reporter and political candidate Tracy Miller has taken its most bizarre turn yet when it was learned from a reliable source that local political operative Cynthia Phelps has been identified as a "person of interest." What was initially reported as a single car accident occurring on Tuesday April 20 has subsequently been categorized as a homicide. Police spokesperson Hannah Wilkens declined to answer questions as to the reclassification, nor was she willing to confirm or deny that Phelps was a target of suspicion.

"We do not comment on cases under investigation," was Officer Wilkens' response when questioned by reporters.

Phelps is currently serving as campaign manager for Emily Weston, candidate for the Democratic nomination for State Senator from Virginia's 48th district. Weston and Miller were due to square off against each other in the June eighth primary.

This is not the first instance of controversy surrounding the mercurial Phelps. Her brief run as the Democratic Party's candidate for Soil and Water Conservation Board last year ended abruptly after the party withdrew its endorsement. This followed an embarrassingly weak debate performance, a debate that was moderated by Tracy Miller.

Miller's place on the primary ballot has been taken by her campaign manager, Steve Winters.

"I am running for elective office with a heavy heart as a tribute to a magnificent person who would have been a great public servant," said Winters, when he announced his candidacy. When asked about the apparent interest the police have shown in Phelps, Winters refused to speculate.

"We must all hope for a speedy determination of all the factors that led to Tracy Miller's tragic death and that anyone so involved be brought to justice."

Attempts to reach out to Phelps for a reaction have been unsuccessful.

Chapter 48

SATURDAY, MAY 1, 11:00 P.M.

"I WONDER," SAID CINDY, "if they will ever make bobbleheads for famous criminals. You know like Jack the Ripper or Al Capone?"

They were sitting in the Metro car as the subway was making its way from downtown DC to the Virginia suburbs. Although Cindy was not much of a baseball fan, she readily agreed with Carl that a night at Nats Park might be just the escape she needed. And it turned out to be a fun evening, accented by the free bobblehead of the head groundskeeper that was given to each attendee.

"I suppose," said Carl, with a yawn. Unlike Cindy, he was a baseball fan and he had rooted hard for the Nats as they squeaked out an 8-7 win over the Phillies.

"So, if they find me guilty, then someday there might be a bobblehead of me."

"Yeah, I guess...no wait," Carl looked incredulously at Cindy.

"You keep telling me to look at the bright side," said Cindy, with a mischievous smile. She looked down at the bobblehead in her hands. "I think I'd make a pretty good bobblehead. Better than, what's this guy's name anyway?"

"I think that's enough gallows humor," said Carl, with a serious look on his face. "I'm not sure it's doing you any good."

"I've got to do something to keep from going mad," said Cindy, as she continued to study the bobblehead. "I wonder how long this spring mechanism lasts. Mathew and David have a number of them but they seem to break easily. I wonder—"

"Cindy," interrupted Carl. "We're getting off at this station."

Cindy looked out the window as the train was slowing down.

"Virginia Square. This isn't our stop. We go all the way to—"

"'Get up,' said Carl, in his most commanding voice. "We'll get on the next train. But we need to move now."

"But I don't understand—"

And then she saw it. The man directly across from them was staring at Cindy. In his hands was a copy of one of the grocery store tabloids. The headline read,

Battle of the Vixens
Brunette topples Blond. But will she pay?

Underneath were photos of Tracy and Cindy. The photo of Cindy had clearly been taken during the previous year's debate when she had begun to lose her poise. The unflattering, slightly out of focus, photo made her look not only confused but slightly unhinged as well.

The train came to a stop.

"She's the one," said the man to his companion, pointing at Cindy.

Others in the train started to look at Cindy who sat frozen in her seat, unable to think, unable to move.

Then before she realized what was happening, Carl had pulled her to her feet and, putting his hands on her shoulders, pushed her through the door and out onto the platform.

Even as the train door closed, Cindy could see the faces in the window looking at her. The train then mercifully began to pull away. In a few seconds it was gone.

Cindy looked at Carl. He could see the tears running down her face.

"When is this going to end?" she asked.

It was a question Carl could not answer.

"When is this going to end?" This time she was shouting.

"Excuse me, miss."

It was a transit policeman.

"Is this man bothering you?" he said, pointing to Carl.

"No, not at all," she said, regaining her composure and taking Carl by the hand. "I was just upset. You see I left my bobblehead on the train."

"Oh, I wouldn't fret about that," said the policeman. "They always break in a day or two anyway. Very fragile. You folks have a pleasant evening." He nodded to them both and departed.

Cindy turned to Carl, a look of panic in her eyes.

"You see, Carl, it's OK," she said, trying to laugh, her voice unnaturally shrill. "They're fragile you see...They'll break in a couple of days...Not like...not like me... you see, I'm not fragile...I won't break...I'm not..."

Chapter 49

MONDAY, MAY 3, 9:00 A.M.

IT WAS SO upsetting. No, "upsetting" wasn't the word. "Maddening" was more like it. Not to be informed of a key meeting. Normally Cindy dealt with these misunderstandings in a peer-to-peer way but this was too much. She got up from her desk and walked down the hall to her supervisor's office. This had to be set right and someone had to be held accountable.

Fortunately the door was open. Cindy took a deep breath to calm herself and tapped gently on the door.

"Gary, do you have a minute?"

"Yes, Cindy. Have a seat. I was about to call you."

Even as Cindy was sitting down, her boss crossed to the entrance of the office and closed the door. He then went back to his desk and sat down.

The hell with being calm.

"Gary, I just found out that there was an unscheduled meeting of the Jacobson account on Friday. Apparently it lasted four hours. Four friggin hours! How the hell am I supposed to make sure everything is working right when Dan and Liz pull shit like that? I know they're new but that's no excuse—"

"Cindy, stop right here," interjected Gary.

"Damn it, Gary. I will not stop. This is so—"

"I said, stop," said Gary, almost shouting.

Cindy looked at Gary, in amazement. Gary never raised his voice. In the high stress world of marketing, he was always the rock of tranquility. But the look on his face told Cindy that she had crossed a line. For several moments there was silence. At last, with deliberate calmness, Cindy spoke.

"I'm sorry. But this is so upsetting."

"I understand," said Gary, in his most soothing voice. "But Dan and Liz didn't screw up. They only did what they were instructed to do."

"I don't understand," said Cindy, her anger replaced by bewilderment.

"The client has asked that you be removed from the project," said Gary.

Cindy couldn't believe what she had just heard.

"No. There must be some mistake. They've always liked my work. Did I do something wrong?"

"No, it's not...well...sort of...It's this unpleasantness in the newspapers. Being a 'person of interest' in a murder case. They just weren't comfortable with—"

"But the article specifically said that I was *not* a person of interest—"

"The article said that the police could not comment which is not the same thing as denying."

This can't be happening.

"This is so unfair," she said, more to herself than Gary. Then in an attempt to rally, she gave what she hoped was a semblance of her best smile.

"I guess I better get back to the Benson proposal and—"

"Cindy," interrupted Gary.

"What?"

"You have to understand. Tracy Miller was a very popular figure. Her apparent murder has attracted a lot of attention. The tabloids have picked it up as well as some of the media outlets in different parts of the country."

There was silence as Gary's words took the desired effect.

"What are you saying?"

"What I am saying," said Gary solemnly, "is that none of the clients want to work with you—"

"Then I'll get new clients," said Cindy, a note of desperation in her voice.

Gary shook his head.

"Cindy, the partners have directed me to put you on administrative leave. For the moment it will be 'with pay.' But I cannot promise how long that will last. If this thing doesn't resolve itself soon, they may decide to invoke a more permanent solution. But for now you need to gather up your things and leave. I need to have your badge by noon."

"But…" It was all Cindy could say. For five years she had been the young superstar. It had been the foundation that had defined her life in so many ways. And now it was about to end.

Gary got to his feet.

"I'm going out for a bit. Take some time in here to compose yourself. But you do need to be off the premises by noon."

"Gary, you do believe I'm innocent, don't you?" She was almost pleading.

Gary was suddenly unable to look Cindy in the eye. Staring at the door he said, "Of course, I do."

"Then fight for me."

Gary shook his head.

"There's nothing more I can do."

He then left the room, shutting the door behind him.

Chapter 50

"**H**ELLO"

"Hello, Carl this is Valerie. Do you have a minute to talk?"

"Sure, what's up?"

"It's Cindy, She's been put on leave at her job."

"What?"

"They had her pack up her things this morning. Cindy thinks this is phase one for her eventual termination."

"This is awful. How is she handling it?"

"Not well. She wanted to contact you. To go over to your place actually but with Brad being a cop assigned to her case, she felt she couldn't."

"That's ridiculous. I'll go over to her apartment right now and—"

"Don't. That's the reason I'm calling. With all that's happening and those phone calls coming into her apartment and all, we decided that it's best to get her out of there. So she'll be staying

— 183 —

at our house, at least for a little while. But please come over here and visit whenever you can. She needs all the support she can get right now."

They talked for a few minutes more. When the call finally ended, Carl put down the receiver and turned to his brother.

"Cindy's been suspended from her job. I'm going over right now and—"

"Before you go," said Brad. "I need to ask you something."

"Sure, what is it?"

Brad paused. He wanted to choose his words carefully. Very carefully. At last,

"How well do you know Cindy?"

"That's a dumb question," said Carl. "She's my girlfriend and—"

"I mean, how well do you really know her? I know she's hot. I know she can be a lot of fun. I also know that she is loyal to you. But do you really know her? What she's capable of?"

Carl looked at his brother in amazement. What was he suggesting?

"I know she is not capable of killing someone if that's what you mean," he said angrily.

"She has a quick temper, doesn't she?" said Brad.

"Well yes," conceded Carl.

"And we know the poison was administered in the warehouse over about a one hour period between when Tracy returned from lunch and when she drove away."

"So, there were eight of us there. Anyone could have—"

"And she was seen having a heated argument with Tracy."

"Yes but—"

"Culminating in throwing her drink in Tracy's face."

"So she lost her temper."

"And then she was seen holding Tracy's cup. The very cup that she drank the poison from."

Carl tried to think of a comeback. All he could think of was to say weakly,

"She didn't do it."

Brad looked intently at his brother.

"Nothing I have told you compromises the secrecy of the police investigation. It's all common knowledge that you and I know. Now I ask you the question, 'What was it that made Cindy so mad at Tracy that she threw the drink in her face?'"

Carl shook his head. "I don't know. What I do know is the homicide division of the county police force leaks like a sieve. One of your esteemed colleagues has made her out to be public enemy number one."

"I know and there is no excuse for that," conceded Brad. "But you still need to face reality—"

"The reality is that there are eight different persons who could have poisoned that cup. I know I didn't do it. I know Cindy didn't do it. That leaves six. You need to thoroughly check them out. What each of them was doing, every minute during that hour. Plus you have to examine them for motives. You need to look into all that."

The look on Brad's face told Carl that he knew more than he was revealing. Things he wanted to say but couldn't. After a silence that endured for a number of seconds, he repeated his original question.

"How well do you know Cindy?"

Carl looked solemnly into his brother's eyes.

"I know her well enough. She did not do it. You need to check out those other suspects."

Brad returned his brother's look and declared with equal solemnity,

"Right now, there are no other suspects."

Chapter 51

TUESDAY, MAY 4

FOR THE NEXT week, the Turner household was a welcome sanctuary for Cindy. She reciprocated by doing the dishes, helping the boys with their homework, and otherwise keeping to herself as much as possible. She spent a fair amount of time working on Emily's campaign, organizing a phone bank as well as generating labels for a mass mailing. In addition she spent time at Emily's house, helping her prep for Thursday's second and final debate. She had finally given up trying to influence the direction of Emily's message. The environment was what she cared about; the environment was what she knew. Cindy's job was to help her refine her talking points and hope that Emily's passion and expertise in this area would carry the day.

On Wednesday, Carl joined them for dinner. While he had never been one for idle chatter, he seemed even more silent than usual, as if he was trying to come to grips with what they were all going through. He reported that the police had finally removed the crime scene tape from the warehouse. He and Terrence had visited it earlier in the day to see if anything had been disrupted, but it looked pretty much as they had left it.

Testing of the 48th Senate district scanners would not take place for a couple of weeks. This was because the ballots were not officially frozen until thirty-five days prior to the primary which happened to be today. Now nothing, not even withdrawal or death, could alter the candidates on the ballot. The electoral board had decided to wait until this day before ordering ballots from the printer. They had already spent a fair amount of money on ballots with Tracy Miller's name on it, ballots that could never be used. They did not want to get stung again.

Cindy, for her part, was rather downcast about Emily's campaign. Once dessert had been cleared and the boys excused, she told them that a number of volunteers for the phone bank had backed out as well as everyone who had agreed to hand out fliers at the debate.

"They don't come out and say it but it's obvious they're uncomfortable working on a campaign led by a suspect in a murder investigation."

Carl, Valerie, and Stan all tried to reassure Cindy that the truth would win out. Valerie had arranged for her to meet a lawyer at the end of the week to help assess the situation. In the meantime Emily's campaign would have to limp along without volunteers. Carl offered to fill in by handing out fliers but Cindy refused to let it happen.

"You're going to all this trouble to convince your Republican brethren that you're the real deal. Then suddenly you switch from Jennifer to Emily. I don't think you could explain that one away. Just stay out of it, Carl. It's my mess. I'll deal with it."

Carl yielded in the face of Cindy's insistence. He would continue to hand out Jennifer's fliers.

But if you think I'm going to stay out of this, you're crazy.

Chapter 52

THURSDAY, MAY 6, 5:30 P.M.

C INDY EXITED THE large stone building feeling moderately better. *When all else fails,* she thought grimly to herself. Getting into her car, she contemplated the evening ahead. Once again, the Democratic candidates would speak first at 7:00 p.m. The Republicans would follow. Cindy had reserved for 6:30 a room located in the hallway that ran parallel to the auditorium. There, she and Emily would go over any last minute strategizing. More important, it would keep Cindy out of the public's view. She did not want her presence to be a distraction.

She drove into the parking lot of the East County Civic Auditorium at 6:25. People were already trickling into the auditorium. From a distance she could see volunteers passing out fliers for the various candidates. Somewhere in the mix must be Carl, working for the Haley campaign. Cindy felt a twinge of guilt. There would be no one passing out the brochures that they had for Emily. It seemed that no one wanted to work for her toxic campaign manager.

Determined to keep as low a profile as possible, Cindy put on a pair of dark glasses and walked from her car to the entrance, face down, as quickly as possible. Across the parking lot. Onto the sidewalk. Up the steps. Suddenly, there was a figure in front, blocking her way.

"Would you like a flier for one of the candidates? I understand she's very good."

I know that voice, thought Cindy, looking up.

It was Jack Vincent, the crusty octogenarian rover who Cindy had bonded with during that elongated electoral board meeting last November. In his hands were a stack of the Weston brochures.

"You see, Emily Weston. She knows about the environment and stuff."

Throwing caution to the wind, she engulfed Jack with a big hug.

"Jack, what are you doing here? How did you know—?"

"—and she's got this great campaign manager so we figured—"

"We?"

"Don't I get a hug too," called Milton, from the other side of the staircase. Cindy quickly obliged.

"Thank you, both," said Cindy, a touch of mist in her eyes. "I am deeply touched."

"Don't let the cops and the press get you down. Do what you need to do in there. We have you covered out here," said Jack.

Cindy nodded, her face showing the appreciation that she felt. With a parting wave, she continued up the steps. Carl was at the top, handing out his fliers for Haley.

"Did you see that?" said Cindy. "How did they know I needed help? How did they get the brochures? For that matter, are they even Democrats?"

"You seem to have a lot of questions," said Carl, with a blank expression.

"I don't suppose you have any answers," she said, giving him a kiss on the cheek and whispering in his ear, "RINO."

Chapter 53

THURSDAY, 7:00 P.M.

"**G**OOD EVENING LADIES and Gentlemen. Welcome to our second and final debate for the primary elections for both the Democratic and Republican parties for the State Senate from Virginia's 48th district. I am Jimmy Forbes of WMML news, your moderator. Before we begin, I would ask everyone to please rise for a moment of silence. On April 20 our county lost a champion and I lost a dear friend and colleague with the untimely passing of Tracy Miller. For five years she championed the cause of journalistic integrity and most recently had offered her services to the county and state as a candidate. We are all deeply saddened by her passing and shocked by the news that this may have been more than just a tragic accident. Even as we turn our eyes to the upcoming primary, we do so with the determination that those responsible for this heinous act will receive the justice and humiliation that they so richly deserve."

OK, I knew something like this was coming, thought Cindy as she got to her feet.

Is everyone in the auditorium looking at me? Sure feels like it.

"Thank you. It's now my pleasure to introduce the Democratic candidates…"

Jimmy Forbes gave the introductions and ground rules.

"…the first opening statement will be from Steve Winters."

Cindy watched as Steve went to the podium. All her interactions with Steve had been one-on-one where he was very effective. But how good a public speaker was he? A great campaign manager does not necessarily translate into a great candidate.

"I never wanted to be here," began Steve. "All I ever wanted was to help launch the public service career of an individual who was destined to be a great public servant. But fate and, it would appear, treachery has forced me into this race. And I do pledge to you this evening, with every ounce of fiber that I possess, that I will try to carry forth the torch of truth and integrity that Tracy Miller stood for…"

Intense applause engulfed the room.

It appeared that Steve was indeed a gifted public speaker. With almost biblical intensity, he recounted the highlights of Tracy's career. He expounded over and over again how unworthy he was to carry her torch even as the audience was led to believe that no other choice was thinkable.

There was prolonged applause when Steve completed his remarks.

Oratory had never been Emily Weston's strength. Expertise and quiet sincerity was what she attempted to convey in her opening remarks which she had practiced under Cindy's guidance. The over two hundred species that would be endangered by the pipeline. The risks involved with off-shore drilling. The need for a revenue-neutral carbon tax. Alternative forms of energy. All the points were made but they seemed dry and remote compared to

Steve's opening oration.

Her statement ended with polite but muted applause.

"Our first question is directed to Ms. Weston. In view of the cloud that hangs over us all, how can you justify having your campaign led by someone who has been identified by the police as a prime suspect...?"

Cindy could not believe what she was hearing. Murmurs of protest could be heard from various parts of the auditorium. But were they objecting to the question or were they objecting to her?

Emily tried.

"...police have not identified any suspects in this tragic case... presumption of innocence...avoid rushing to judgment..."

There were scattered boos from the crowd. Cindy thought she heard, "Fire her," but she wasn't sure.

"Mr. Winters, you have thirty seconds to respond."

"...need for transparency...a campaign must be above reproach...would never tolerate in my campaign anyone whose integrity is in question..."

Somewhere during that initial exchange, Cindy disengaged. There was only so much she could process. She sat in her seat, motionless except for checking the time on her cell phone every few minutes.

"...would like to thank the candidates...don't forget to vote..."

She was vaguely aware of Steve and Emily shaking hands. Of Emily coming down the stairs from the stage. They exchanged glances. Emily gave a resigned smile and wave and departed from the auditorium.

"Cindy."

She looked up. It was Carl.

"Come. I'm taking you back to Valerie's."

"But my car?"

"We'll get it tomorrow."

"But don't you have to hand out Haley's fliers for a while more?"

"They can do it without me. I'm a RINO, remember?"

Cindy stood up. For a moment she felt lightheaded and shaky on her feet but Carl steadied her. Then together they walked up the aisle and out of the auditorium.

Chapter 54

FRIDAY, MAY 7, 10:00 A.M.

THIS TIME SHE had prepared for the conversation. This time it was final. She would do it by phone and make it as formal as possible.

"Emily, I am resigning as your campaign manager, effective immediately."

"Cindy, no. Don't let what occurred at the debate—"

"It's not just the debate. It's everything. You can't have a campaign manager who is afraid to be seen in public. One whose very presence distracts from the message you're trying to deliver."

"Please, come over to my place and we can talk—"

"No. I've already contacted the media. It's a done deal. Now, listen. I'm not deserting you. I'll still do whatever I can to help you behind the scenes. In a way, nothing will change. I just won't be officially linked to the campaign. I've talked to Mildred and she's agreed to be identified nominally as your campaign manager."

A sigh could be heard from the other end of the line.

"All right Cindy, if you're sure."

"Very sure. It's the only way."

They said their goodbyes and hung up.

Well Tracy, wherever you are, you finally got your wish.

Chapter 55

SUNDAY, MAY 9, 3:00 P.M.

VALERIE OPENED THE door and stepped out onto the rear patio. Her sister was seated on one of the lawn chairs, staring out into the wooded area that ran adjacent to the property line. Valerie looked down at the saucer in front of Cindy, on which rested a lit cigarette as well as two crushed butts.

Cindy looked up at her.

"Don't give me that judgmental look of yours. You know I never do it around the boys."

Valerie smiled.

"I was going to ask if I could have one."

"No?!" said Cindy, in amazement. "After all those times you ratted on me to Dad."

"To Mom," corrected Valerie. "If you remember, Dad let you get away with anything. Anyway, as a mother with two active boys, I've earned a guilty pleasure or two. So hand them over."

Cindy handed her the pack along with the book of matches.

"Thanks," said Valerie. She studied the pack for a few seconds and then put it into her handbag.

"I thought you wanted one."

"Maybe later."

Cindy looked, in astonishment, at her sister as she gradually realized what had happened.

"I had forgotten why I hate you so much," she said at last, with a bit of a smile.

For several minutes they sat, looking out at nothing in particular, each one lost in her own thoughts.

"You know you can't stay here forever," said Valerie at last, breaking the silence. "It's not that I mind. The boys love you. Stan loves you…and yeah, I love you too, I suppose. But sooner or later you have to get back to reality."

"Right now my reality sucks," said Cindy, bitterly. "I'm on administrative leave at *MarketPro* indefinitely and probably permanently. The police think I did it. The press thinks I did it. My boss thinks I did it. Everyone in the friggin world thinks I did it. So tell me, oh wise sister, what am I returning to?"

"I can't tell you," said Valerie, honestly. "How did your conference with that lawyer go?"

"He said that while the evidence pointed toward me, there was not enough of it, yet, to indict. So assuming nothing more is found, the case should drift its way into the 'committed by person or persons unknown' file. The way he said it made it sound like he thought I did it."

"What about Emily's campaign? Does she believe you?"

"She says she does. I'll continue to help her as best I can, even though I'm no longer her official campaign manager. But it's going to be tough for me to do much with this cloud hanging over me."

"How about Carl? He believes in you, surely."

Cindy smiled.

"Yes, Carl's been great. First, last, and always, he believes in me. But that doesn't count. He thinks I'm perfect, regardless."

"No, he doesn't," said Valerie. Then she added, laughing, "Anyone who has spent twenty minutes with you knows you're not perfect."

"Well thanks sis. I like you, too."

For a few minutes silence returned. Then as Cindy gazed into the wooded area a realization gradually formed in her mind. For the past few weeks she had allowed outside forces to define her life. Some of those forces had been the consequences of her own follies while others had been things beyond her control. But either way, she had been in react mode. She could continue down that path, waiting in seclusion for the next bad thing to happen or she could attempt to reclaim at least a modicum of control in her life. Yes, it was true that, with a few treasured exceptions, the world seemed to have decided she was a murderer. She, however, possessed a truth that trumped all else. The knowledge of her innocence. It was time for that truth to assert itself. It was time to act.

"You're right Val," she said, getting to her feet. "I need to get back in the game. 'Not being indicted' is not good enough. I need to prove my innocence."

"And how do you intend to do that?"

The answer was obvious.

"By proving someone else is guilty, of course."

"Oh come on, Cyn. You can't be serious."

Cindy reached down and picked up her handbag as well as the cigarette from the saucer. She took an exaggerated drag and blew the smoke in her sister's face.

"I'm completely serious," said Cindy, even as Valerie was

wheezing and coughing from the cigarette smoke. "Thanks for everything, Val. Give my love to Stan and the boys. You know where you can reach me."

They stood, looking at each other for a moment, and then embraced in a final, parting hug.

"Oh Cyn, please be careful."

"Of course."

Chapter 56

SUNDAY EVENING, 8:00 P.M.

THE FIRST FRUITS of Cindy's pro-active posture were relatively modest. Fifty-eight messages on her phone's mail box deleted. Some rather disgusting food products in the fridge, which had overstayed their welcome, into the trash (along with several packs of cigarettes).

The next step would be harder but necessary.

"Cindy?"

"May I come in?" In her hands was a large brown envelope.

"Please do. What can I get you?"

A little bit of courage would be nice.

"Nothing. I'm good. Uh...Is Brad here?"

"No, he's out for the night."

Good, that makes it easier.

They went over and sat on the couch.

"I've left Val's. I'm back at my apartment."

Carl nodded. "Do you think you're up to it? Those phone calls and everything."

Cindy gave a faint smile.

"I guess I'd better be."

There was silence. Ten seconds. Twenty. Half a minute.

Carl started to say something but Cindy interrupted.

"No, let me...I have to say..."

It was so easy when I rehearsed it.

"Carl, I need you to promise me something. I need you to promise that you'll stand by me until this murder thing is resolved. After that you can dump me but until—"

"What are you saying? I would never dump you—"

"Yes, you will. When you see what's in here—" She gestured for Carl to take the envelope.

"I don't want to see it."

"You must."

"No, I don't. Plus I already have a pretty good idea what is in there."

Cindy's expression indicated extreme skepticism.

"No, you don't—"

"The envelope contains photos that were taken last year during the time when you and Steve were intimate," said Carl, dryly. "I suspect they reveal a bit more of you than would normally be seen if you were standing on a street corner."

Cindy looked at Carl in amazement. "How did you find out? Did Brad tell you—?"

"Brad didn't tell me anything," said Carl. "I'm not as clueless as you think I am."

A burden seemed to be lifting.

"And you'll stay with me until this thing is resolved? I'm going to do it, you know. Someone killed Tracy Miller and it wasn't me. The police are useless. They're convinced it was me. And so I'm going to crack it, one way or another."

"And I'm with you."

"For the duration?"

"Forever, if you'll have me."

It was a giddy feeling. Carl was with her. He knew the worst and he was still with her. They talked. About the case but also about their dreams. Carl's as well as Cindy's. The hours passed. Carl wasn't exactly sure when it happened. He just remembered waking and seeing Cindy asleep on the couch. He obtained an extra blanket and pillow from the closet, tucked her in, and planted a kiss on her forehead.

It was the first night they slept under the same roof.

Chapter 57

MONDAY, MAY 10, 10:00 A.M.

"A NEW DAY AND I feel like a million," said Cindy, as she entered Carl's townhouse. She had returned to her apartment earlier to shower, change, and delete ten more messages on her answering machine. Now she was back, ready to work. Ready to find the answer to "Who murdered Tracy Miller?"

"I've written the names of all the suspects," said Carl, pointing to a notepad. "These are the people who were at the warehouse between the time you returned from lunch at the deli and the time everyone left the warehouse."

Cindy looked at the list. There were no surprises.

Jennifer Haley, Republican candidate
Anthony Palucci, Republican candidate
Emily Weston, Democratic candidate
Steve Winters, campaign manager and later Democratic candidate
Cindy Phelps, campaign manager
Terrence Bucholtz, Machine Coordinator
Rudy Matheson, warehouse foreman
Carl Marsden, Assistant Machine Coordinator

"One of these eight killed Tracy Miller," said Carl. "But to complete the picture, they were not the only people in the warehouse that day. Jack Vincent dropped in twice, delivering flash drives, and Brenda Greenwold and George Metnick were there in the morning doing cleanup. But since none of them were present during the time in question, they could not have done it."

"Agreed," said Cindy. "It's one of the eight."

"But we have one advantage over the police," said Carl.

"And what would that be?" said a sleepy Brad, emerging from the spare bedroom. "Oh, hi Cindy. Sorry Carl, I didn't know you had company."

Cindy looked at Carl. "Should we be doing this here?" she asked, gesturing to Brad.

"We can move to your place if you want," said Carl. "Just remember, the police are not the enemy."

"I would hope not," said Brad, looking over at the pad. "Trying to sleuth it out, are you? Have a go at, it if you must. Just don't get in our way." He turned around and returned to his bedroom.

"As I was saying," said Carl. "We do have an advantage over the police. We know that two of us are innocent. So we only have to worry about six suspects."

"OK, six suspects," agreed Cindy. "So where do we start?"

"I would think we start with the three classic criteria. Motive. Means. Opportunity."

"Means is easy," said Cindy. "The antifreeze was clearly visible in two different locations. Locations that we all had access to. So we can't eliminate anyone here. Everyone had the means."

"Agreed. How about motive?"

There was silence as they both started thinking about the events of the day and the six individuals under suspicion.

"There was something going on between Tracy and Jennifer

Haley," said Cindy. "Jennifer was angry about something but I didn't catch what it was."

"I noticed too, that she was upset," agreed Carl. "And at one point Tracy seemed to be goading her…"

"I wonder what it was," said Cindy, slowly and thoughtfully. "Tracy had something on Jennifer, I just know it."

"All right, that gives Jennifer a potential motive. Anyone else?"

Again there was silence as they considered the suspects.

"I suppose you could say Emily Weston had a motive," said Carl, tentatively. "After all she and Tracy were competing against each other for the nomination."

Cindy looked skeptically at Carl. "Do you really think that's much of a motive? We have elections all the time without the candidates killing each other."

Carl agreed. "At least not in this country."

"I can't see Emily murdering anyone," said Cindy. "She's such a nice old lady."

"Ah, nice old ladies do it all the time," said Brad who had emerged from the bedroom and was on his way to the kitchen.

Cindy shot him a dirty look and continued. "And she had sort of accepted the notion that she might very well lose. She didn't seem to bare Tracy any ill will at all. All her venom was reserved for Jennifer."

Once again there was silence as Carl and Cindy retreated to their own thoughts.

"I think it's fair to say that Rudy, the warehouse foreman, was irritated by all that publicity concerning the books," said Carl. "That was one of the reasons they felt the need to put in all those new rules."

"Things are definitely tighter than they were last fall," agreed Cindy. "And no one likes to see their routine disrupted."

"Of course, to be fair, Tracy's 'book exposé,' if you can call it that, was aimed at the officials at the Government Center that created the policy, not the warehouse people. They were just following the directives that they were given."

Once again the conversation lapsed. It was apparent that neither of them felt that having your work routine altered was much of a motive for murder.

"What about Palucci?" said Cindy. "There's something going on there. He is one creepy guy."

"Being a creepy guy doesn't make you a murder suspect," called Brad, from the kitchen.

"No, but it might make you the next victim," retorted Cindy. "Carl, where do you keep the antifreeze?"

"Come on, Cindy," said Carl. "Palucci's not that bad."

"I wasn't talking about Palucci," said Cindy, looking at Brad.

"Cindy, this isn't helping," said Carl. "Back to Palucci, I agree he's a bit much. All those sarcastic remarks. He seems to enjoy seeing others in distress. But I'm not sure I see a motive for murder."

"Perhaps he thought Tracy would be the tougher candidate to beat in November."

Carl shook his head. "Anthony Palucci runs for something every few years. He never gets even 20% of the vote. He just likes to have a forum to vent his extremist views. But he's not delusional. There's no way he's going to defeat Haley in the primary so who gets the Democratic nomination is irrelevant to him. Maybe if we dig harder we can find something but right now I don't see any motive at all."

"So who does that leave? Terrence?"

Carl shrugged his shoulders. "Terrence is a hardworking, sincere public servant. Not the smartest guy perhaps and easily rattled. He was a bit of a basket case last fall when we had all those testing problems. He was down on me for a while but once we, I mean you, cracked the case concerning the Braxton scanners he was all smiles. Of course he got me promoted to Assistant Machine Coordinator—"

"Does he have any connection to Tracy?" said Cindy, bringing Carl back to the subject at hand.

"Not that I'm aware of."

"So," said Cindy. "The last man standing is…"

"Steve Winters."

They looked at each other. Intently. It was like they were testing the state of their relationship as much as trying to solve the murder.

"You know him best," said Carl.

"Yes," said Cindy with a grimace. "He's driven. He's focused. He carries a grudge. What's more he lied to the police."

This was the first Carl had heard of this. He could also sense Brad's ears perking up in the kitchen.

"Come on in, Brad," called Cindy. "You might as well hear this."

Brad entered the area where they were working but kept his distance.

"After I threatened Palucci and he left, I put down Tracy's cup and went out the front entrance of the warehouse. That's where Rudy was. A few minutes later Steve came out and we had words. What he told the cops, though, was that he met me inside and I still had the cup in my hand. That's what the inspector said when he questioned me the second time. It was a lie, plain and simple. There's no way he could have been confused."

Cindy and Brad exchanged looks, each taking the measure of the other. Eventually Brad shrugged and returned to the kitchen.

"All that being said," continued Cindy. "I can't imagine him as a murderer. But perhaps I know him too well, if you know what I mean."

"I'm not sure I see a motive either," said Carl, thoughtfully. "But there's stuff here that doesn't add up. For example, within three days of Tracy's death, he had all the paperwork and petitions filed at the Government Center. That's no small task. It's almost like he expected something to happen."

"I can't explain it," said Cindy. "If he wanted to be a candidate so bad, why didn't he just file? Tracy was a last minute filing as it was. I have a tough time thinking that he was all in favor of her candidacy, then suddenly got jealous, and then bumped her off so he could run in her place. It's theoretically possible I suppose but not really..." Her voice trailed off.

"Plus the two of them were lovers," said Carl.

"I thought the same thing," agreed Brad, coming out of the kitchen.

"How do you know?" asked Cindy sharply.

Carl hesitated. Did he really want to say it?

"How can you be so sure?" she demanded.

"That last day at the warehouse. I saw the way she looked at him."

"And...?"

Please don't make me say it.

"And...?" Cindy repeated.

"It was exactly the same way you looked at him last year."

Chapter 58

Monday, 11:00 A.M.

BRAD MUMBLED SOMETHING about needing to use the bathroom and quickly fled from the scene.

There was an awkward silence after he left.

"Sometimes I'm amazed that you have anything to do with me," said Cindy, looking down at the notepad.

"To summarize," said Carl, letting the moment pass. "Jennifer Haley had a potentially strong motive. Emily Weston and Rudy Matheson had motives that seem weak, to say the least. And none of the others had any motives at all. At least that we can presently identify."

"Agreed," said Cindy. "Now we move to opportunity. Just because we were all in the proximity of the antifreeze doesn't mean we had the same opportunity to use it."

"Right. The prime opportunities are for those who were alone with Tracy's drinking cup with the antifreeze nearby."

"That would include Palucci, who was all by himself when I exited the ladies room, and Steve, who later passed through on his way outside where he confronted me. Both had clear opportunity. How about back in the election area where you were?"

"I'm trying to recall," said Carl. "For the most part we were all grouped together. People arrived pretty much one at a time. Then we all went back to the testing area together. I don't remember any stragglers."

"There was one," said Cindy, grimly. "Me. I stayed behind after you all went to the test area. And earlier, up front, after I had confronted Palucci, I was all alone with Tracy's cup in my hand. So in both locales, I had opportunity. And I certainly had a motive with Tracy threatening to release those photos. Actually, it's not hard to understand why I'm police suspect number one. Sometimes I wonder if perhaps, I really am guilty."

Carl gave her a startled look.

"Just joking."

"I hate to say this," said Carl. "But the person with probably the least opportunity is Jennifer Haley. Coming back from the deli, she entered the warehouse and came back to the election area before you doused Tracy. Then she was among the first to go back to the testing area. And when the test failed to pan out, she was the first person to leave the warehouse. I remember her being in such a huff. I don't see any opportunity there, no matter how you stretch it."

"Damn," said Cindy, softly.

For a few minutes there was silence as each of them tried to mentally reconstruct the movements of Jennifer Haley.

"She could have doubled back to the front before reaching the election area," offered Cindy.

"No, she couldn't have."

It was Brad, who had rejoined them.

"Emily was asked about that. She said that she, that is Emily, went back to the election area, immediately after you entered the ladies room. That was confirmed by the warehouse foreman. When Emily arrived at the election area, Jennifer was already there. There was no doubling back."

"And don't forget," added Carl. "Emily is no friend of Jennifer. If they had crossed paths, she would have been most happy to say it."

"Maybe," said Cindy, not wanting to let it go, "Jennifer doubled back, taking an alternative route. So she and Emily would not have crossed paths."

Carl shook his head. "That's not likely. This was Jennifer's first time in the warehouse. It can be confusing back there. She wouldn't have known how to do it."

"It's not that confusing," said Cindy. "Remember last fall when I—"

"Cindy, you're missing the point," said Brad. "Even supposing she could have doubled back, spiked Tracy's drink, and then hurried back to the election area before Emily arrived…" He paused, allowing it to sink in as to how improbable that scenario was. "Even if she did all these things, why would she have wanted to? She would not have seen the incident between you and Tracy. And she would not have known the cup was Tracy's. No, I'm afraid I agree with Carl. In terms of opportunity, Jennifer Haley is on the bottom of the list. Anyway, I need to get out of here. Got a full day ahead. And please limit your activities to brainstorming. Let the police do the real work."

With that, Brad departed by the front door.

"Please limit your activities to brainstorming," said Cindy in a bitterly mocking tone. "Let the police do the real work."

"Actually, that's not what he meant."

"What do you mean 'that's not what he meant.' You heard

him. Let the police do the real work. So they can fry my ass."

"That may be what he said. But that's not what he meant."

"I don't understand."

"Cindy, just now Brad was telling us things from the investigation. Things that should not be shared with people like us on the outside. He could get in real trouble for doing that."

"Then why is he—"

"Because he believes you're innocent. Maybe he didn't at first but he does now. We have an ally. He's on our side."

"Yeah, right," said Cindy. "Brad's a great guy. Hooray for Brad." Her tone indicated less than full conviction. "I still think Jennifer Haley did it."

Carl looked at Cindy with surprise. It was the first time she had come out and made the accusation.

"You weren't there at the deli. Jennifer was furious with Tracy. I mean livid. Tracy had something on her and she was turning the screws. Just like she was doing with me. And even later, back in the testing area. You saw how short tempered and angry Jennifer was. Remember last year when she came to our precinct to vote in that special election. How polished and gracious and in control she was. I tell you, Tracy was doing something to knock her off the rails. And she snapped. She saw the opportunity and took it."

"Cindy—"

"I know what you're going to say. The opportunity wasn't there. But there's got to be something that we've missed. And for the time being at least, I'm not going to worry about that. We need to find what it was that Tracy had on Jennifer."

Carl facial expression indicated that he was far from convinced.

"I'm doing this, Carl. Alone if I must. But I'd rather have you—"

"You're not alone. What's your plan?"

Silence.

Then Cindy started to laugh. "You ask hard questions. OK, a plan. Let's see. I'll start by doing all the research I can on Jennifer. The net should have lots of stuff. Her Company. Her record as a State Senator. Political activity. Family. Education. The works."

"Got it. We can divide categories and start googling and—"

"Actually," said Cindy, thoughtfully. "There's something else you can do. Some work in the field, as it were."

Carl eyed Cindy, skeptically.

"I'm listening."

"You work for the Jennifer Haley campaign."

"Y-yes."

"Every Wednesday evening you are at county Republican headquarters, stuffing envelopes, making phone calls, etc. Am I correct?"

"Yes." Carl wasn't sure where Cindy was heading on this.

"I wonder what secrets the Republican headquarters might have."

"Cindy, there are no secrets there. It's just a big room with tables, chairs, and phones."

"And that's the entire facility? One big room?"

"No, there's a smaller conference room as well. Sometimes the Republican Committee meets in there. I've never actually been inside…" Even as he was saying the words, Carl realized he was making a mistake.

Cindy smiled at Carl but said nothing.

"No! I am not sneaking into the conference room. What do you expect me to find in there? A note on a whiteboard saying 'I did it. Please don't tell the media.'"

Cindy's smile was gone. "I don't know, Carl. All I know is that I am desperate. The cops think I did it, regardless of any conversion you think Brad may have had. Of all the suspects, Jennifer is by far the most promising. You wanted a plan. Now we have one. The internet coupled with a little old fashioned skullduggery. What can possibly go wrong?"

What indeed? thought Carl.

Chapter 59

WEDNESDAY, MAY 12, 4:45 P.M.

I NEVER THOUGHT OF *myself as a stalker. And yet, here I am. Desperate times call for whatever, I guess.*

Cindy felt rather silly as she sat in her car with sunglasses on, pretending to read a newspaper. She was parked in the far corner of the *Haley Enterprises* parking lot, waiting for something to happen. Something. Anything.

So this was the plan. Become a stalker. Not much of a plan. But she had to do something. She and Carl agreed that they would each do their own research on Jennifer Haley. Then they would compare notes. And tonight was the night that Carl would infiltrate Republican headquarters. A Hail Mary pass if ever there was one. And this was her version of the same thing. Their website had identified it as a nine-to-five company, so since 4:30 Cindy had been here on stakeout duty.

There was movement. People were leaving the building. Cindy raised her binoculars to her eyes. Yes, it was quitting time all right. First a trickle and then a steady stream of people exiting the building.

And there she was. Jennifer Haley, looking every bit the successful businesswoman that she was. The man she was talking to. Arm and arm. Real friendly. Had Cindy seen him before?

No, I don't think so.

He was opening the door of a car and she got in. He then went around to the other side and entered. They were still talking. Now he was backing out of the parking place.

Am I really going to do this? I guess so.

Cindy turned on the engine. She was pulling out of her parking space when she saw him. A young man. About thirty, she guessed. Rather unremarkable in appearance. He went to his car and entered. He pulled out of his parking spot and merged into the queue of cars waiting for the traffic light to turn green.

Cindy steered her car into the queue, several cars behind. The light turned green. Up ahead she could see Jennifer's car turning right. The line of cars moved slowly. The light turned red. Cindy waited patiently as the cars on the main road went back and forth.

At last the light turned back to green. The young man's car was making a left turn into the street. Cindy hoped she would make it this time. The cars were moving so slowly.

Shit. It's turning yellow. Why isn't that goon ahead of me moving?

The car ahead made the left turn into traffic just as the light turned red. Cindy followed suit.

There were honks from two of the cars on the main road. Out of the corner of her eye, she could see an obscene gesture. But that wasn't her focus.

There he was. About a half block in front. Cindy tried to get closer, to maneuver around some of the other cars. She was determined not to lose contact. Running a red light. Speeding. Sounding the horn.

Whatever it takes.

Fortunately it did not take too long and Cindy was able to avoid any traffic infractions. She followed him into a parking lot that seemed to serve a string of garden apartments. He got out of his car and walked over to the nearest the building. It looked like he lived on the first level. Good. That would make it easier. He opened the door and entered.

Cindy waited. Five minutes. Ten minutes. That should be enough.

She got out of her car and walked across the parking lot to the sidewalk leading up to the building. Up the short flight of stairs. There were a pair of doors, side-by-side. The door on the right. A name in the slot.

"Edmondson"

The name meant nothing to her. She knocked on the door and waited.

She could hear footsteps coming to the door. It opened.

He looked at her and gasped. Amazement on his face. And something else. Fear.

Cindy said nothing but just looked at him, straight in the eye, allowing her presence to have its maximum effect.

Then ever so calmly, she asked the question.

"Do you know who I am?"

Slowly, he nodded his head.

Chapter 60

WEDNESDAY, 5:30 P.M.

*I*F IT'S WEDNESDAY, *it must be the county Republican headquarters.*
Once again, as penance for having supported two Democrats the previous year, Carl found himself sitting at the large conference table, sorting Jennifer Haley brochures.

"There's a rumor that she may be dropping by this evening," said an elderly lady.

"I doubt if she has time for the likes of us," said the man next to her, sourly. "She has that company of hers to manage as well as preparing for the November election."

"What about the primary?" asked the lady. "What about Palucci?"

"No one takes him seriously, Dot," replied the man. "He runs every year for something. The man's a crackpot."

"Now Herb," said Dot. "We all have a right to run for office. He could possibly be our nominee."

"It would be the death of the party if he is," said Herb, who by now Carl deduced was Dot's husband. "The party wants nothing to do with him. That's why they're letting us use this space even though she won't officially be the nominee until the primary."

"What exactly does her company do?" asked Carl.

No one seemed to know.

"Something to do with energy, I think," said Dot. "Or else it's mortgages. Or something. I'm told it makes a lot of money."

The door opened and a man and a woman entered.

"It's her," said the Dot, excitedly.

"Folks, if we could have your attention please," said the man who had just entered. "I am Lester Miggins, Republican Party county chairman. It is my honor to introduce the gracious lady we have all been working so hard for. Jennifer Haley has agreed to take a few minutes out of her busy schedule to say a few words. Let's hear it for our own State Senator, Jennifer Haley."

Even as cheers sounded from around the room, Carl slouched down in his seat and partially hid his face behind some papers. He wasn't sure she would remember him from the warehouse but he wasn't taking any chances.

"Thank you so much for being here," said Jennifer, beaming at the group. As always she was immaculately groomed with her platinum blond hair perfectly in place. Her bio listed her as being in her mid-forties, but in the relatively dim light she looked ten years younger. "We live in difficult times but it warms my heart to see you out here, working hard for our Republican values of small government, free enterprise, energy independence, and American exceptionalism."

There was another round of enthusiastic applause. A number of the workers came forward to shake her hand and a few of them had her pose for selfies.

"Jennifer insisted on coming here tonight," said Lester. "Unfortunately her schedule is very tight and she has to leave now. There is so much that needs to be done to prepare for November."

"I'm afraid that's true," said Jennifer. "But once again, from the bottom of my heart, thank you all. Now on to November!"

They all applauded one final time as Jennifer gave a parting wave and left. Lester remained behind. He stood, looking at the group. Clearly he was about to say something and gradually the room became silent.

"We're all committed to Jennifer Haley and that's great," he began. "But there will be many other offices on the ballot this November. We want to make sure we have an exceptional slate of candidates from top to bottom. Now one of our challenges is to find three candidates for the at-large positions on the county school board. As you know, while the parties don't nominate school board candidates, they do endorse them. In last year's special election we had an excellent candidate in Janet Hayes."

There was lukewarm applause. "Too extreme for me," said Dot, quietly to her husband.

"Too divisive," agreed Herb.

"At the current time, we are struggling to come up with a slate of viable school board candidates," continued Lester. "So I'm asking you, some of our best activists, if you can think of some names we might consider to run under the Republican banner?"

There was silence as the volunteers pondered the request.

"What about Morgan Dietrich?" asked Dot.

"Isn't he dead?" said Herb.

"No, he's not," retorted Dot. "Perhaps not as spry as he once was but he'd be great. He was on the board once before if you remember—"

"That was twenty years ago," said Herb. "I think he's dead."

A discussion broke out as to whether Morgan Dietrich was

alive and who remembered seeing him last. Lester frowned. This was not the sort of input he was hoping for.

Without thinking, Carl blurted out, "How about Valerie Turner?"

There were a few gasps. Then silence. People looked at Carl with shocked expressions on their faces. Finally Lester spoke.

"She's a Democrat."

"Not anymore," said Carl. "She's left the party."

Actually the party left her but let's not quibble.

A flurry of remarks greeted that statement.

"Think of the headline. 'School board member repudiates Democrats; Joins GOP.'"

"But is she a Republican? What are her views?"

"Who cares, Think of the headline."

"I think I saw Morgan Dietrich at the Walmart last week."

"That was the son. He's dead, I tell you."

"Do you think Turner would accept our support?"

Lester held up his hand for silence.

"Perhaps if Mr. err…"

"Marsden"

"…if Mr. Marsden would join me in the conference room." He motioned to a door, off to one side.

Carl followed Lester into a small room. Lester closed the door.

OK, I'm here, Cindy. Now what am I supposed to look for?

Carl noticed a whiteboard on the wall listing corporate contributors to the Jennifer Haley campaign. Top of the list was *Haley Enterprises.*

No surprises there, thought Carl.

"Now Mr. Marsden," said Lester, taking a seat and motioning for Carl to do the same. "Perhaps we might start with you telling me how you have come to know Ms. Turner."

She's the sister of my girlfriend who's involved in the campaign of a Democratic rival and who also, by the way, is a suspect in a murder investigation.

"Ms. Turner is a personal friend."

About halfway down the list of donors was *"Virginians against Fraud."*

Now where have I seen that before?

"She ran as a Democrat last year. Have her views altered?"

"Not that I'm aware of."

"But she has left the Democratic Party?"

"Absolutely."

"Would she accept the Republican Party's support?"

"You would have to ask her."

Lester fell silent, pondering the situation. At last he spoke.

"Mr. Marsden, it's true that we're looking for credible candidates for this election. But while victory is important, it does not supersede principle. I'm not looking for a RINO..."

Carl squirmed uncomfortably in his seat at the mention of that word.

"... but if she really has left the Democratic Party and is interested, I would be willing to talk to her to see if some sort of...uh...accommodation can be reached that would be mutually beneficial."

"I would be happy to convey the message," said Carl.

What an interesting evening, thought Carl, on the way home, later that night. He had memorized the list of contributors to the Haley campaign that had been on the whiteboard. Hopefully, that would help Cindy. In the meantime he wasn't exactly sure how Valerie would react to his spontaneous use of her name. But Carl had never met anyone before so committed to education and the children of the county and if this would keep her on the school board then it was a good thing.

Chapter 61

Wednesday, 5:40 P.M.

"**I**'VE OFTEN THOUGHT about that day. I never wanted to hurt you."

"Within an hour it was on the internet."

"I know."

"It almost got me removed as election chief. I was publically humiliated."

"I said, I am sorry." He was almost in tears.

Careful Cindy. Don't push him over the edge.

"What are you going to do to me?"

"What do you mean?"

"Well the other one. The reporter. She said she was going to publically expose me. All over the newspapers and TV. How I subverted democracy. How I could be arrested. Unless I told her what she wanted to hear."

Cindy tried to control her excitement.

Gentle now. Ever so gentle.

"And just what did you tell her?"

Chapter 62

"**S**O YOU TELL me about your day and I'll tell you about mine," said Cindy.

"Why don't you go first? You seem eager," said Carl.

"Do I? I guess that's because there is quite a bit to Madame Jennifer Haley. Let's see, where should I begin?"

Cindy had several pages of notes and printouts spread out before her.

"To begin with, your tribe thinks quite highly of her. She's apparently gearing up for a run for Lieutenant Governor and has some well positioned early backers."

"But that's over two years away."

"It doesn't hurt to plan, now does it? Hence it's critical that she be reelected to the State Senate. She pretty much follows the mainstream Republican line. Pro-business. Low taxes. Minimize government regulation. Just let the corporations alone and everything will be great. Your basic Robber Barons 2.0."

"Thank you for that unbiased opinion," said Carl, dryly. "I've been concentrating mostly on the personal level. Her husband, one Sidney Johnstone Haley, is a big time mover and shaker. He's currently in Argentina finalizing some sort of deal. A real power marriage."

"Check that. Hubby is in Argentina, you say."

"That's what the article said."

"That's interesting because she was walking-arm-in-arm with someone yesterday. Quite chummy they seemed."

"Cindy, even if what you're hinting at is true, that could hardly be something that Tracy had on her. That stuff goes on all the time with the bright and beautiful. Plus it doesn't sound like they were being secretive about it, whatever it was."

"No, I suppose not," said Cindy. "Now back to my internet research. *Haley Enterprises* appears to be a conglomerate. One of its subsidiaries is an outfit called *Gibbs Manufacturing*."

"What do they manufacture?"

"I don't know…whatever. They were involved in a suit a couple of years back. Supposedly they were polluting the James River. They paid an out of court settlement and agreed to put in more safeguards but the environmental groups are less than satisfied."

"That might be the reason Emily is so negative on her. What's her background anyway? How did she acquire all this wealth?"

"As nearly as I can tell, it was inherited. Wikipedia doesn't go into her formative years other than to say she attended the Vanderbilt University. Anyway, enough from me. How did your evening go? Were you able to break into the Republican conference room?"

"No, but I got invited in."

"How did you manage that?" asked Cindy, in surprise. "Did you have to sell your soul to the Republicans?"

"No, but I might have sold your sister's."

Cindy gave Carl her *"You better be joking"* look.

"They need candidates to run for the school board," he explained. "So I mentioned Valerie. They want to meet her."

"To run? As a Republican?"

"Yes."

"Did you tell them she'd be interested? Because I can guarantee you that she won't be. She wants to retire from the school board. You heard her say that. If she wanted to run, she would do it as a Democrat. So what the hell are you doing, dangling her name in front of the Republicans?"

Carl was silent.

"I can't imagine what you were thinking," Cindy continued. "I mean..." She stopped in mid-sentence and gave Carl a questioning look.

"What do you know that I don't?"

Carl looked down at the table.

"I can't say. I made a promise."

"To Val?"

"I can't say."

Silence, and then,

"Actually," said Cindy, calming down, "I was shocked when she said she wasn't running. She's always been so dedicated to the whole education thing...OK, you made a promise. You need to keep it. Let me talk to her. Better that way. Val has a temper."

"As bad as yours?"

"Worse. I flame out. She smolders. Trust me, you don't want to get on her bad side."

Carl nodded. "Sounds like a plan."

"So we may have solved my sister's problem but how about mine? Did you uncover any dark secrets in the Republican lair?"

"Actually, I may have found something. It dates back to that special election last January—"

"You mean the one where we spent most of the day hating each other."

"I was going to say the one where we found each other, but anyway, if you remember late that morning when the person tried to vote, impersonating a dead man. And then they caught it on video—"

"The video that almost got me fired. How can I forget?"

"The organization that produced that video called themselves *Virginians against Fraud.* Guess what. According to the list on the whiteboard, *Virginians against Fraud* is one of the major contributors to the Haley campaign. That might suggest, and I'll admit it's a bit of a stretch, that the Haley campaign a year ago may have had something to do with that voter fraud scam that *Virginians against Fraud* pulled against us."

"It's not that much of a stretch," said Cindy, thoughtfully. "Do you remember the young man who actually tried to do it?"

"You mean Mathew David Kreigson?"

"Yes, well I met him tonight. Not Kreigson, he's dead. But the person who impersonated him, whose name is Edmondson. It seems he works for *Haley Enterprises.* I followed him home from work and presented myself at his front door. The poor guy was scared out of his mind. I almost felt sorry for him."

"What did he have to say for himself?"

"It seems he was a volunteer for the Haley campaign. Offered to do whatever he could to help her get elected, not fully realizing what he was signing up for. The ruse was set up where he would be secretly videotaped while checking in to vote, impersonating the dead voter. Once he received the ballot card they'd stop taping and he'd make up some excuse to leave. The tape would then be released if not enough Republicans voted in the first four hours that the polls were open. Supposedly an allegation of voter fraud would energize the faithful to get out and vote. According to Edmonson, Jennifer Haley signed off on the plan. And get this. At the last minute some low level operative tried to convince Edmondson to actually vote."

"That would have been a felony."

"Exactly. That's why he was so nervous, standing in front of us. Fortunately for him, he got cold feet and bolted. Anyway, somehow Tracy Miller got a hold of this. Now I can't believe Haley would have intended him to vote. She's far too smart for that. But I can believe Tracy Miller could have crafted the story to appear that way."

"And if Haley got wind of this," said Carl. "Do you think that could be a motive for murder? Actually taking someone's life?"

"It's impossible to say for sure," said Cindy, "but I do know two things. Number one, Jennifer was extremely angry. I mean, it was intense."

"Got it. She's mad. And the other."

"Everything I've read says that Jennifer is on the fast track. Politically, I mean. Lieutenant Governor in two years. The logical follow-on is Governor after that. Then who knows? It can be intoxicating. I remember last year during my brief political fling. I'm ashamed to think now of all the political fantasies that rattled around in my brain. And Jennifer's path to stardom is real, so much more than mine ever was. It could very well happen. Then Tracy comes along with a juicy little exposé that could derail the whole thing. So yes, I do believe this is a motive for murder. The motive we've been looking for. Jennifer Haley killed Tracy Miller."

Carl shook his head.

"No."

"It has to be Jennifer. She's the only one with any kind of

plausible motive."

"I'm not questioning that. But she didn't do it."

"How can you say—?"

"Because she did not have the opportunity," said Carl, raising his voice. "We've been through this. She never had access to either Tracy's cup or the antifreeze when others weren't present. I agree, it appears she has a motive. She may be a miserable, evil person but she did not kill Tracy Miller."

Cindy looked at Carl with tears in her eyes. "It has to be Jennifer. There must be something we've overlooked." She was almost pleading.

Carl reached out and took Cindy's hands in his own. "OK, we'll continue to try and think of an opportunity Jennifer may have had. One that we missed. But in the meantime, we need to turn our attention to some of the other suspects. Is that a deal?"

Cindy slowly nodded her head. "Agreed. I...I just want it to be over."

"I know," said Carl. "I know."

Chapter 63

Thursday, May 13

WITH JENNIFER HALEY temporarily on hold as a suspect, Carl and Cindy spent whatever free time they had researching the others. Emily Weston and Steve Winters both had professional websites. In fact, Cindy had put together most of Emily's. In contrast, Rudy Matheson and Terrence Bucholtz had virtually no internet presence. Neither, for that matter, did Carl Marsden. Cindy's campaign website from the previous fall had been taken down but there was a Wikipedia article which briefly described her run for Soil and Water. It also contained the same unflattering photo that had been in the tabloid.

But it was Anthony Palucci that they focused on. He was by far the most unpleasant of the remaining suspects and that made them believe (or hope) that he was the most likely killer. They poured over his campaign website as well as the numerous internet items that could be found on his career.

A lawyer by training, he was associated with a number of conservative organizations. Many of his views were things that Carl was uncomfortable with and Cindy found outright repulsive. While he gave nominal support to most conservative causes, the three issues that seemed to motivate him most were guns, immigration, and the heritage of the Confederate States of America. He had written a number of provocative articles on these subjects. His website prominently displayed photos of him and his son (there was no mention of a Mrs. Palucci) in full hunting regalia, sporting various forms of military hardware. His position on immigration was simple and unyielding. Illegal immigrants should be rounded up and sent away. No delay. No exceptions. Just do it.

He had run once for the U.S Senate, twice for Congress, once for attorney general, and twice for State Senate (this would be his third try). In every instance he had tried to secure the Republican nomination and each time he had fallen short. These efforts would be followed by initial silence and eventually a lukewarm endorsement of the Republican nominee.

By the end of the weekend, they felt that they had a good handle on "Palucci the candidate," although perhaps not "Palucci the man." What they were unable to come up with was any reason why he would want to harm Tracy Miller.

Chapter 64

Tuesday, May 18, 9:00 A.M.

And here they were again. Back at the warehouse. Not to be questioned by the police but rather to finally do what had brought them together in the first place: the testing of the voting machines for the Democratic and Republican nominations for the June eighth primary.

The atmosphere was different. Their earlier gatherings had been filled with suspicion and intrigue. Now the participants just wanted to get it over with as expeditiously as possible. There was no requirement that they be here. Yet each felt compelled to put in an appearance. To show that they were not concerned about the cloud of suspicion that hung over all of them.

Each had each checked in at the warehouse entrance and donned his/her lime green vest under Rudy's watchful eye. Now they all were seated around the table in the election area. Jennifer Haley. Emily Weston. Steve Winters. Anthony Palucci. Cindy was there as well. Although she was no longer Emily's official campaign manager, she felt, perhaps more than any of the others, that she needed to be there. To show she wasn't in hiding. To show she wasn't afraid.

"Once again we assemble the dream team," said Mr. Palucci, as he looked around at his fellow candidates. "It's a shame Inspector Fellows won't be able to join us." His declaration yielded a few sour looks but no one really wanted to initiate any dialogue. Just get this over with.

Standing off to one side were Terrence and Carl. "If I may have your attention," said Terrence, "I think we're ready to begin. The flash drives that gave us so much trouble before have been reprogrammed and we believe they are now fully operational."

That declaration was greeted with skeptical looks from the candidates. They had heard this before. They would believe it when it happened. Carl and Terrence, however, exchanged knowing smiles. They knew that the flash drives worked. They had run the whole battery of tests the day before, just to be sure. Today would simply be a repetition of what had already been proven to work. Also in attendance were additional rovers, six in all, who would actually be executing the test. In view of all that had happened, both Terrence and Carl agreed that it would be best if neither of them did the actual testing.

"Now, there is one change," said Terrence who shifted uneasily from one leg to another. "Because of, well because of… well everything, the Democratic ballot reflects the current state of affairs. The candidates listed are Emily Weston and Steve Winters. All other candidate names have been removed."

Stony silence greeted that announcement.

"So now if you follow me, we can commence the testing," announced Terrence.

With that, Terrence led the rovers and the candidates plus Cindy over to the workbench area where the carts and scanners for the first precincts to be tested were in place. Carl did not join them. His job was to make sure that the carts and scanners were lined up so that the other rovers could roll them into place when the time came.

In spite of the dress rehearsal that had been done the day before, Terrence was visibly nervous as Scott and Milton began the activities involved with testing the first precinct. As they performed each of the tasks according to the instruction sheet and the machines responded in the appropriate way, his mood improved. But it was not until the first set of printouts came out of the scanners, showing the correct number of votes for each candidate, that he relaxed.

Meanwhile, Carl was not witnessing any of this, as he worked with Jack Vincent moving the carts and scanners.

"I'm not hearing any groans of protest," said Carl. "I hope that means everything is going fine."

Indeed everything was going well. With three teams of rovers, the precincts were getting tested in assembly line fashion. By noon, it was done. The equipment for each of the twelve precincts had been successfully tested. While Carl and some of the other rovers would remain on site to do some cleanup, the candidates could leave. There would be no lunch at the deli.

Cindy had kept a decidedly low profile throughout the morning, keeping to herself as much as possible. Although she thanked Jack and Milton once again for helping with the fliers at the debate, there was no attempt to converse with any of the candidates. Now as she prepared to leave, she caught Carl's eye and gave a quick nod. She then walked over to the far end of the election area, removed from the others. Carl followed.

"I'm cooking you dinner. Be at my place at six. Oh, and please pray for me. I'm about to break the law."

It wasn't just the message. It was the almost robotic delivery. No expression, no eye contact.

"But Cindy, don't you think—"

But before Carl could get out his response, she had already left his side and was walking quickly toward the front of the warehouse and out of sight.

Chapter 65

TUESDAY EVENING, 6:00 P.M.

EVEN AS CARL engaged in the warehouse cleanup activities, his mind struggled with Cindy's parting words. What awful crime had she decided to commit? The fact that her intention was communicated so calmly made it even more unsettling. On the way home that afternoon, he listened to the local radio news station, half expecting to hear about some heinous crime committed by an unidentified woman in her late twenties.

It was exactly 6:00 p.m. when he knocked on the door of her apartment. The door opened almost immediately.

"Great, you're on time," she said. Her face was flushed and she had a cooking apron on. This was a first. She ushered him in.

"It's just about ready. I used a lasagna recipe that Val gave me. I hope it turned out OK."

It was better than OK. Carl was amazed. In all the time they had been dating she had never once cooked dinner. Pizza. Take out Chinese. Deli sandwiches. Something in the microwave.

All during dinner, Cindy seemed determined to keep the

conversation light. How was the Nationals' season shaping up? What would she get her friend Deb for her birthday? When were they going to finish the repaving work on Carter Road? Although not one for small talk, Carl did his best to stay with the mood. Afterwards he helped with the dishes and they were soon done.

"I never realized you were such a good cook."

"I'm not. Just 'follow the directions.' That's what Val told me and it seemed to work. I thought you deserved one home-cooked meal before, well before..."

Her voice trailed off. Carl remained silent. It was up to Cindy to say whatever it was she needed to say.

"Do you know what obstruction of justice is?"

It was not what he expected. He looked intently at Cindy. She was deadly serious.

"I think's it's when you do something that gets in the way of the police doing their job. Something like that."

"That's what I did today. I obstructed justice."

Carl nodded, not knowing what to say.

"This is when you say 'Cindy, I think we should take a break from each other. Have a good life.'"

"Aren't we being a bit dramatic?" said Carl, dryly.

"I just don't want to drag you down in the muck. I don't want—"

"I'm already in the muck. And I did not come over here to rehash old conversations. Now tell me what it was that you did."

"I'll be right back."

She got up and went back to her bedroom. A minute later she returned. She was holding a mesh lime green vest.

"That's it? That's your big crime? You stole a vest from the warehouse?"

"Take it."

Carl hesitated.

"You want to be in the muck. Take it."

Carl reached out and took the vest.

"Tell me what you see."

Carl examined it closely.

"It's the same vest that we've been required to wear in the warehouse the past few weeks. Part of the effort to beef up security. This one is rather grimy. Rudy should really get them cleaned from time to time. It's even a bit sticky. There is a large brown stain…" Then, gradually, he began to understand. He looked up at Cindy.

"Was this—?"

"Yes, this is the vest that Tracy wore the day she died. That brown stain was from the drink I threw in her face. Halfway through this morning I realized what I was wearing. It was so creepy. I felt like somehow I was violating her."

"I would have thought the police would have taken this to have it analyzed or something."

"One would think. They had that crime scene tape in front of the warehouse for four friggin days. You would think one of those geniuses…anyway, tell Brad they need to get their act together."

Carl nodded but remained silent. He sensed there was more.

"Did you know these vests have pockets?"

"Yes, but I never use them. I'm afraid I'll leave something in them at the end of the day."

"Check out the pockets on this one."

Carl reached in and felt something. He pulled it out. In his hand was a business sized white envelope. It looked like it had been opened with a letter opener.

"It was unopened when I found it. Look inside."

Carl gave Cindy a questioning look. "You opened it?"

"How does it feel to be in the muck?" said Cindy, who couldn't help flashing a mischievous grin.

Carl reached in and took out a single folded sheet of paper. He unfolded the paper. Cindy moved next to him so they could read it together.

Carl read the note out loud.

You need to try harder. We don't want your tawdry little secret to get out, now do we?

It was written in cursive. The flow of the well-formed letters gave an almost elegant appearance.

Then underneath there was more. The handwriting was different. Different shade of ink as well. It read,

I've already told you. I can't help you.

For a few minutes they both studied the note. At last Carl spoke.

"And this would have been in the pocket of Tracy's vest, unopened, the day she died."

"Can't prove it, but it's more than likely," agreed Cindy.

"So," said Carl, "she had either just received this note or was preparing to give it to someone else."

Cindy nodded.

"Do you recognize any of the handwriting?" asked Carl.

"Neither of these are Emily's," said Cindy. "I've seen enough of her's to be certain. Otherwise, I don't know. I don't suppose we can assemble the gang one more time and collect handwriting samples."

"Actually," said Carl, thoughtfully, "I may be able to do the next best thing."

Chapter 66

"SO WHY DID you need to go to the Government Center in the first place?"

"I thought I told you. I had to take this self-study course called 'Harassment in the Workplace.' It's required now. A test and everything."

"Did you pass?"

"Certainly. Why do you ask?"

"Well, that first election we worked together...you weren't always nice to me."

"It's not about being nice. It's about, you know, not bothering people or saying bad things about their ethnicity or religion or whatever. Anyway, I passed."

"Good boy. Now did you fulfill your real mission?"

Carl smiled and placed the folder on Cindy's dining room table.

"Mission accomplished. And it wasn't that easy. The forms were out in plain view. That's required. Anyone can look at them.

Making a photocopy, I'm not so sure. I had to do it discretely. I couldn't scoop them all up and take them to the copy machine. But eventually…well here they are."

Cindy opened the folder and examined the pages, reading off each of the names.

"Jennifer Haley, Anthony Palucci, Emily Weston, Steve Winters…and even Tracy Miller. I would think they would have removed her 'Declaration of Candidacy' form since…well, you know…"

Carl shrugged. "All the Declaration of Candidacy forms that the candidates submit are placed out in open view for anyone who wishes to inspect them. I suppose no one thought to remove Tracy's. For that matter, all the petitions that are submitted are in the Government Center as well. They are not out for public viewing although anyone can ask to look at them."

"OK, then let's have a look," said Cindy as she sat down and picked up the piece of paper that had been lying on the table most of the day. It was a photocopy of the note that they had extracted from the green vest. "Oh, and before we start, how did it go with Brad?"

"I explained to him that you took the vest home by accident and only after you opened the note did you realize that it might have something to do with the murder. He accepted the vest and note and will turn it over to Inspector Fellows. While he's still in the loop on this case, he's been temporarily transferred to the narcotics unit. There's been an uptick in cocaine distribution in the county. Anyway, he seemed to accept our explanation concerning the vest. Hopefully, you're off the hook."

"Good," said Cindy, with a grim smile. "I can handle being indicted for murder but obstruction of justice as well…that's a bridge too far."

While Cindy had been talking, Carl spread the five candidacy forms out on the table. "Maybe there won't be any matches at all. In that case, I suppose we'll have to get handwriting samples for Rudy and Terrence."

"I don't think that will be necessary," said Cindy, studying one of the forms. "Look Carl. Tracy Miller. See how she made her 'r,' and the loop on the 'y,' how it curls. She wrote the note."

Carl nodded. "It's her writing all right. You weren't the only one she was turning the screws on."

"That's right. She seems to have been a master at it. Why did she feel the need to do that? She was so successful..."

"I don't know. Why does anyone...what is it?"

Cindy seemed visibly upset.

"That last day. In the ladies room. She said that we were a lot alike. She was just better at it."

Carl shook his head. "On your worst day, you would never have blackmailed anyone."

Cindy gave a slight nod, apparently lost in her own thoughts.

"I stopped off at St. Mark's this afternoon. I do that sometimes when no one is there. I don't feel so much like an outsider then... anyway, let's get back to that note."

"The question is, 'who wrote that reply at the bottom?'"

"It's not Emily," said Cindy, looking over the forms. "Or Jennifer, not at all the same."

"What about this one?" asked Carl, pointing to Palucci's form.

"Maybe," said Cindy. "Let's see..."

They studied Anthony Palucci's signature on the form carefully, comparing it to the note. The match wasn't as obvious as it was with Tracy Miller. The bottom part of the note had been hastily written while the signature on the candidacy form had been made with greater care.

"I'm pretty sure it's Palucci," said Cindy, at last. "The flow looks the same. And the way the 'h' is made. And the 'n.' It's Palucci."

"You're probably right," said Carl, a little less convinced than Cindy. "But assuming that's true, what do we do with it?"

"Let me think on it. Next Monday is the Memorial Day festival and parade. I'll be meeting with Emily tomorrow to go over our preparations. All the candidates will be there, peddling their causes. This might provide me with an opportunity to—"

"Opportunity to do what?"

"Oh, never mind…you'll be there too, won't you?"

"Yes, I'll be passing out fliers for Jennifer."

"Right, part of your penance for being seen in public with Democrats…It could be an interesting day. The last time all the candidates will be assembled together before the primary. Yes, it could be a very interesting day."

Chapter 67

"THANK YOU SO much for coming in to see me, Ms. Turner," said Lester Miggins, motioning to a chair in front of his desk.

"It's Mrs. Turner. But please call me Valerie. And the pleasure is mine."

Once she was seated, Lester began.

"The Republican Party is looking for candidates to support for the three at-large positions on the county school board. One of our volunteers, Carl Marsden, thought you might be interested."

"That is correct."

Lester looked intently at Valerie.

"Before we begin, there is one item we need to discuss, however painful it may be. That is the matter of your sister. The media has referred to her as a 'person of interest' in the Tracy Miller murder investigation. If asked, how would you—?"

"My sister is absolutely incapable of doing what she apparently is being accused of. I support her totally, now and always, regardless of what may play out in the legal system. If asked, that's what I will say. If that's a problem, say so now, and I'm out of here."

Lester nodded his understanding. "All right, I appreciate where you're coming from on this. Now let's move ahead to the specifics of your candidacy. The fact that you are already a school board member is a huge plus. The issue, however, is that everything we know about you suggests that you're a Democrat. In your campaign last year, you were endorsed by the Democrats. You have consistently voted in Democratic primaries. So let me start by asking, do you support the principles of the Republican Party?"

"Mr. Miggins, I support the children of this county. I believe that every child should have the opportunity to develop his or her potential regardless of race, gender, creed, IQ, native language, sexual orientation, or any other category you want to come up with. They should be able to do this in an environment that is both encouraging and secure. We should strive to obtain and retain the best possible teachers. I also believe these things cost money and quality education must be a county priority. To the extent these things coincide with the principles of the Republican Party, then I am a Republican."

"Well said," said Lester. "But the question remains, why aren't you running for reelection as a Democrat?"

"The party has decided not to endorse me."

"Why?"

A pause.

"They didn't say why."

"Were they dissatisfied with your work on the board? Did you take any position they disagreed with."

"I generally sided with the majority. I did push for more consistent enforcement of the dress code and that may have upset some people."

"The dress code?"

"Yes, we have a good, common sense dress code but the school principals don't always enforce it. I thought more could be done to ensure uniform compliance."

"Really?" said Lester, his tone indicating both surprise and approval.

"Yeah, I thought you might like that," said Valerie, with a smile.

"But, in general you are satisfied with the direction our county schools are headed?"

"That is correct."

Lester considered.

"Let me ask you a few questions about society, in general. Are you pro-life?"

"I am pro-life in the most meaningful way possible."

"Which is?"

"I'm pregnant."

"Oh."

"Does the Republican Party have a problem with that?"

"No. But as a political issue, are you—?"

"Yes."

"Is that what you told the Democrats last year?"

"They never asked. Can we move on?"

"All right. Let's touch on immigration. Do you believe children of illegal aliens should be in our schools, which are being paid for with our tax dollars?"

"I think there should be a place in our schools for every child who resides in our county."

"Even though they are here illegally?"

"Would you rather have them on the streets?"

"I'd rather have them not here."

"And I'd rather have a million dollars."

Lester plodded on.

"What about guns. Do you support the second amendment?"

"The second amendment exists whether I support it or not. But it is the county's responsibility to keep guns out of our schools and to have an armed uniformed policeman assigned to every school."

"Couldn't we arm the teachers?"

"My husband teaches middle school English. He is a dedicated professional who loves his calling and loves the kids. The idea of him packing heat scares the crap out of me."

Lester took a deep breath and looked down at his notes. He scribbled a few things in the margins and looked up at Valerie.

"You know, the county Republican Committee has given me a blank check. If I say yes, the endorsement is yours. If you were to receive the party's nomination, would you be willing to attend joint appearances with other Republican candidates"

"Yes."

"Including fundraisers."

This time there was a pause.

"Y-yes."

"Would you openly support the entire ticket?"

"Not necessarily. I would focus entirely on my own campaign, offering a token endorsement to those who I feel I could support in good conscience, and silence on the rest."

Once again Lester paused, taking stock of the situation.

"I suspect," said Lester, "that if we were to drill further down, we would find many things that we disagree on."

Valerie said nothing.

"Things that would make your endorsement by the Republican Party difficult, if not impossible."

"And yet, here we are," said Valerie.

"Are you mocking me?" asked Lester, smiling. It was becoming increasing apparent that they both liked and respected each other, regardless of their differences.

"Perhaps just a little," replied Valerie, returning his smile.

Then turning serious she continued, "Lester, we are standing on opposite sides of a river. We have a choice. We can remain steadfast, each on our own side, reciting our talking points at ever increasing decibel levels, or we can build a bridge that will bring us together somewhere in the middle. I have, I believe, built half of that bridge. The Republican Party has a marvelous heritage dating back to Abraham Lincoln and Theodore Roosevelt. I would be honored to be part of that tradition. But it can only happen if you build the other half of the bridge."

"Am I going to regret this?" asked Lester.

"Probably," said Valerie laughing.

"Be that as it may," said Lester, getting to his feet. "I am officially offering to you, Mrs. Valerie Turner, the endorsement of the county Republican Party for the position of school board member at-large in the upcoming November election. Do you accept?"

"It would be my honor."

Chapter 68

Thursday, May 20, 4:00 P.M.

"So we have Mildred at the table from 10:00 a.m. to eleven. At that point Jack Vincent takes over."

"Jack Vincent. I don't believe I know him," said Emily.

"He's one of the rovers. Amazing fellow, in his mid-eighties, still going strong. He has sort of a soft spot for me. He'll be at the table till 12:30."

"At least I have the octogenarian vote covered."

"Then at 12:30 p.m. Milton Ayres takes over. He's another one of the rovers."

"And how old is he?"

"Not as old as Jack or Mildred but there's some mileage on the odometer," said Cindy. "Look I wish I could have gotten some younger faces for the festival but most of my friends are hitting the Delaware beaches that weekend. Start of the season and all."

"Of course, you're doing your best," said Emily soothingly. "I didn't mean to criticize."

"And then at 2:00 p.m. Howard Morgenstein takes over. He's

still in his twenties."

"Chronologically, I suppose. Howard is a dear. So knowledgeable on environmental affairs. Not exactly the most charismatic figure around. Why don't you take a turn at the table?"

"I'm sort of toxic right now," said Cindy. "I'll be working the crowd as best I can. And I can fill in when someone needs a break. But I should probably make myself as mobile as possible."

"I suppose you're right," said Emily. "I'm sorry this campaign has taken such a toll on you."

"Here are the brochures that just came in," said Cindy, changing the subject. She did not want this to turn into a pity party. "I think they did a good job highlighting the risks intrinsic to the pipeline project. I only wish you would have allowed me to put in more about your qualifications."

"The earlier set of fliers does a good enough job with that," said Emily. "I wanted these to let everyone know what a terrible thing this pipeline is. So it can be used by whoever wins the primary."

It's almost like she expects to lose.

"Emily, try to think positively. You've been in this race from the beginning. Steve is the latecomer. And your experience vastly exceeds his. I am confident—"

"Of course you are, dear. You are so much like my niece. Grace was full of optimism. And she loved the outdoors. Went camping every chance she got..."

Please, I'm not your niece. I hate camping. I did it once and I'll never do it again.

"...and I'm so sorry the shadow of Tracy's death has fallen on you—"

"It's fallen on all of us."

"But on you especially. I read the newspapers. It's so unfair," Emily's face hardened. "Especially since we both know who did it."

Chapter 69

"THANK YOU so much for helping out on this," said Cindy, helping Mildred Purvis to her feet. "You really went above and beyond. Emily and I are so grateful."

"You're most welcome," said Mildred. "I had a wonderful time. I only wish I could have done more. I'm afraid I was outflanked by the competition." She gestured toward the young lady at the other end of the table who was wearing a "Winters for State Senate" T-shirt that was obviously a couple of sizes too small.

Cindy offered to help Mildred to her car but was assured that it was not necessary. She then briefed Jack Vincent on the process. Give out as many fliers as possible. Both the one that stressed Emily's qualifications as well as the new one that focused on the pipeline. If someone seemed interested, offer them a lawn sign and campaign button and then add them to the list of volunteers. Also keep the dish of hard candy full. And try not to stare at the competition.

Jack laughed. "I only have eyes for you, my dear."

Cindy grabbed a handful of fliers, gave Jack a playful slap on the wrist, and headed back into the crowd.

It was a bright, warm, late spring day. Cindy wore sun glasses in the hopes that it would prevent people from recognizing her from the photos that had appeared in the media, but in truth it wasn't necessary. Everyone was in a festive mood, out for a pleasant day of meet and greet, eating junk food, and waiting for the parade to follow. There would be a solemn Memorial Day ceremony at 1:00 p.m., but otherwise it was to be a day of fun and sun.

Cindy strolled among the people, handing out fliers and repeating "Emily Weston for State Senate" in a pleasant tone to anyone who seemed remotely interested. She wasn't paying a whole lot of attention to where she was going. Otherwise she would have picked a different route. But suddenly there he was, standing right in front of her.

"Cindy!" proclaimed Steve Winters, flashing a bright, disarming smile. "So great to see you." And then he added with an awkward grin. "Shall we exchange fliers?"

Cindy returned what she hoped was her best smile, all too aware that her hands were visibly shaking.

"Of course, Steve. What a beautiful day."

People all around stopped to observe. Two young adults, each sporting shirts for rival candidates, each wishing each other well. Many of them smiled. This was what America is all about.

They exchanged fliers and then Steve leaned over to give Cindy a kiss. His lips grazed her cheek and continued up to her ear.

"Rot in hell, you murderous bitch," he whispered.

Pulling away, he smiled again and loudly proclaimed, "Well you have a wonderful day." With that, he walked past her to continue his rounds.

Meanwhile Cindy, shaken to the core, stood riveted to her spot, completely unaware that most of her fliers had fallen from her hands and lay scattered on the ground.

Chapter 70

Monday, 11:45 A.M.

CARL, WHO WAS handing out Jennifer Haley fliers, saw the exchange from a distance. Weaving through the crowd as best he could, he made his way to Cindy who was down on her knees picking up the brochures she had dropped.

"Are you all right?" he asked anxiously, as he helped Cindy complete her task.

"Yes, I'm fine," she said, getting to her feet. "Steve just said something very hurtful and it caught me off guard. I'm OK now. Really."

Carl wasn't so sure but before he could say anything they were interrupted.

"Cindy! Cindy!"

David Turner, wearing an oversized red "Jennifer Haley for Senate" shirt, came running up to her.

"Mom's been traded," he declared. "She's been traded to the Publicans."

"Re-publicans, stupid," shouted Mathew Turner, as he arrived on David's heels. He, in turn, was wearing a blue "Cindy Phelps for Soil and Water" shirt, left over from last year's campaign.

Their father was the last in the entourage to arrive. "A house divided," said Stan, gesturing to the two boys who were vying for Cindy's attention.

"Where's Valerie?" asked Cindy.

Carl and Stan exchanged looks, each trying to keep a straight face.

"What is it?" she demanded.

"You tell her," said Carl.

"All right," said Stan. "Even as we speak, she is serving her required shift at the Republican Party booth. I have never seen her look so miserable."

"Well she asked for it," said Cindy. "That's what she signed up for."

"She knows that," said Stan, "but still...could you go over there and cheer her up?"

"I'll go over there," said Cindy, brightly. "But it won't be to cheer her up. Carl, do you want to come with me?"

"No way," said Carl. "I'm not getting between the two of you. Besides I have these fliers to distribute. Go enjoy."

"Oh, I will," said Cindy. "I will."

Chapter 71

MONDAY, 12:10 P.M.

"DO YOU KNOW they have Spanish printed on the ballots? And some weird Asian language. That should not be. They should speak English like regular people. That's what America is all about."

"I think it's the law," said Valerie. "If a certain percentage of the population—"

"Then change the law," said the man, almost shouting.

"You're certainly entitled to your opinion—"

"Damn right I am."

"Sir, would you like some hard candy?" she said, offering him the dish.

"Well yes, thank you," said the man. He took a couple of pieces, nodded to Valerie and took his leave.

Valerie put the dish back on the table and checked her cell phone. She still had ninety minutes left on her shift.

"Excuse me. I have a couple of illegal immigrants tied up in the trunk of my car. I was wondering if you could help me dispose of them."

Valerie knew the sound of that voice. Turning around, she vented a couple of choice expletives at her sister.

"Why, Mrs. Turner," said Cindy, in mock surprise. "I didn't know you used such language."

"You'll hear a lot more of it if you don't get off my case."

"Is it that bad, Val?"

Valerie let out a sigh. "The Haley people aren't too bad, I suppose—"

"I hope so. Carl is one of them."

"But Palucci's a nutcase. It's all guns, send back the foreigners, and the south will rise again. And he's so obnoxious. I don't think I could vote for him even if I agreed with him, which of course I don't. Cyn, I never should have signed up for this. I don't belong here."

"Is Palucci here?" asked Cindy, looking around.

"No, he picked up a bunch of fliers about five minutes ago and headed off to the food truck area."

Cindy nodded. "I need to talk to him."

"Oh, about the…"

"Yes."

"Are you making any progress?"

"I'm not sure. Carl's been working with me and we're finding some stuff but we're not sure what it all means."

Valerie nodded.

"Well, I'm off to find Mr. Palucci. Hang in there, Val. You're doing this so you can stay on the school board. That's what really matters. That and…how are you feeling these days with…you know."

"Not too bad. A couple of rough mornings."

Cindy reached over and gave her sister a hug. "Your shift will be over before you know it. And if I never tell you this again, I'm so proud of you."

Chapter 72

H E WAS STANDING by the truck that was selling chicken teriyaki on a stick. Cindy circled around him so as to approach from the rear. She wanted to catch him off guard and have their meeting be as spontaneous as possible.

"Support the cause of American Exceptionalism," he was proclaiming as he distributed his fliers to anyone who would accept them. He seemed to be doing well. In an event like this, many would accept anything that was dangled before them.

"So did you try harder?" said Cindy, softly.

"What the—" Then turning around, "Why it's you Ms. Phelps. I'm not sure what you mean. We all try harder all the time—"

"Or was your tawdry little secret revealed?"

The momentary look of surprise on Palucci's face told Cindy that she had scored.

"I'm not sure what you mean."

"Tracy Miller was giving you a hard time." She had removed her sunglasses and was looking straight into Palucci's eyes.

"Are you actually trying to investigate this case? How pathetic. Of course, with you being the primary suspect, it's more like 'how desperate.'"

"I'm only a suspect because the police think I have a motive."

"You certainly appeared to have one. That nasty fit of temper you displayed with the cup throwing incident—"

"But someone else had a motive...you."

"How ridiculous."

"The police have the note."

"How did you know—I mean what note?"

"And you had the opportunity. When I came out of the ladies room, you were alone. All alone with Tracy's cup and the antifreeze so available. That must have been a really bad secret that you had."

"It was nothing. Just...it was nothing."

"What I don't understand is, what did Tracy want you to do? What was so important to her—?"

"She wanted dirt on Jennifer Haley." The words seem to explode from Palucci's mouth. Like something that had been bottled up and had to burst forth, sooner or later.

Palucci continued. "She wanted things she could use on Haley for the fall campaign. She assumed that since I was running against her, I must have done some opposition research. But I don't do opposition research. I could afford it but I don't do it. I want people to vote for me because they agree with my positions, not because they think my opponent is a skunk. I'm not like the rest of you, groveling in the gutter, throwing mud at each other. The people who vote for me truly believe."

"How's that strategy working for you?" Cindy taunted. "Win many elections lately?"

"My day will come," said Palucci solemnly. "It will come."

There was a pause as Cindy digested what he had said. Palucci's whole demeanor had changed. Gone was the detached smart aleck. It had been replaced by a zealot. Misguided yes, but, Cindy suspected, telling the truth.

"So you couldn't help her? And she was going to reveal your secret?"

"That's where it seemed to be heading. It would have hurt me some. And hurt others more. But I would never have killed her. I'm pro-life, you know, and that includes not killing anyone." He added that last part with a smile.

Cindy considered. She had the information she had come for. There was a motive. There was opportunity. There was a denial.

"OK," she said. "Thank you for your time." She turned to leave.

"Don't you want to know what my tawdry little secret was?"

Turning back she replied, "Mr. Palucci, we all have our own tawdry little secrets. Managing mine keeps me fully occupied. I don't have any time for yours."

"For what it's worth. I don't think you did it."

"Nor I, you. Have a good day."

Chapter 73

Monday, 3:00 P.M.

"So all total, I distributed about 150 of the fliers."

"Good work, Carl," said the Haley field captain. "I'm sure the candidate will be most grateful. Have you ever met her, by the way? I can set up an introduction."

Carl hastily assured the captain that he and Ms. Haley were old acquaintances and that no introduction was necessary.

"OK. Your call. We'll see you Wednesday night. We're on the home stretch."

Carl nodded and immediately went off to find Cindy. He was about halfway to the Democratic table when he saw her talking to Emily Weston. Cindy saw him and waved.

"I think we did well, Emily," she was saying. "And I think having two styles of brochures sent an especially strong message. We might not have the glitter of the Winters campaign but we have the substance."

"Well thank you again," said Emily, with what was obvious heartfelt sincerity. "I think we'll be in good position to finish off

Jennifer Haley in November. Oh, hi Carl. Cindy we'll talk later this week."

Fortunately Carl had changed from his "Haley for Senator" shirt, about the time the parade was ending. Emily said her goodbyes and left.

"So how did it go?" asked Carl.

"Mixed," said Cindy. "We've got a stronger message than Steve Winters, but Steve oozes with charm and his volunteers are bursting with energy. We did give out a lot of fliers though."

"What did Steve say that upset you so much?"

"It wasn't just what he said. It was how he said it. Such venom. Such hatred. He really thinks I killed Tracy."

"Or wants you to think that?"

"Let's let that slide for now. It's been a long day and I'm not sure I can handle it. But on another note, I had a most interesting conversation with Anthony Palucci."

"Was he as snarky as ever?"

"At first, but I then sort of disarmed him. Tracy wanted his opposition research on Jennifer and he refused. That was what the note was all about. Palucci said he hadn't done any opposition research."

"Do you believe him?"

"The strange thing is that I do. I also think he was prepared to tell me what secret Tracy held over him."

"'Prepared to,' you say. But in the end, he didn't?"

"No, I told him I didn't want to know. And I don't. Then we ended the conversation by saying we both believed in each other's innocence."

Carl wasn't convinced. "But he had a secret. And Tracy was applying pressure as that note shows. And he did have opportunity."

Cindy nodded. "I agree with all those points. I can't explain it but I just don't think he's the murderer."

"Because of your conversation?"

"Because of our conversation."

"Fortunately I was not part of the conversation so as far as I'm concerned, Mr. Palucci is still very much a suspect."

"Understood. So where are we now?"

"I'm working at the Government Center tomorrow. I'll come over to your place afterwards. We can have a working dinner. It's time we take a fresh look at Steve Winters."

Chapter 74

TUESDAY, MAY 25

ONE OF CARL's duties as Assistant Machine Coordinator was to pack the "kit" for each of the twenty rovers who would be driving a route on primary day. This kit was almost identical to the "chief's kit" that each of the chiefs would receive. These kits contained many of the forms and signs that were needed in the precincts on Election Day. Ideally the chief would have everything that was required, but if additional supplies were needed during the day, the rover would make the delivery.

Packing the kits was straightforward work and a bit dull. Nonetheless, Carl attended to it with his usual efficiency. There was a lunch break at noon. By 1:00 p.m. he was back on the job. By 2:30 he was done, ready to go home.

He wasn't sure why, but on his way out of the election office suite he was drawn to the Declaration of Candidacy forms on the table by the front door. These were the same forms that he had photocopied earlier when they were trying to decide who wrote the note in the vest. There was something about one of the forms that had earlier caught his eye but it had been lost in the flurry of amateur handwriting analysis that he and Cindy had undertaken.

He started thumbing through the forms. There it was.

Of course. How could I have missed it?

"Excuse me ma'am, I understand that anyone is allowed to examine the nominating petitions for the candidates."

"Yes, it's allowed. But no one ever asks."

"I would like to see the petitions for this candidate," said Carl, placing the candidacy form in front of her.

There was a pause. The receptionist seemed to be at a loss. Finally she said, "Wait right here. I'll get someone who can help you."

Carl waited. Five minutes. Ten minutes. Then the receptionist returned with Terrence.

"What is it, Carl?" said Terrence, with a note of disbelief. "Wanda here says you want to examine the nominating petitions for—"

"I believe I have that right."

"That's true but—"

"I wish to exercise that right."

Terrence looked intently at Carl.

"I know we've all been under a lot of pressure with the investigation and all. But why would you even want to examine—"

"Terrence, I wish to examine those petitions. That's all I want to say." Carl looked Terrence squarely in the eye. He hoped his expression mirrored his determination.

Terrence shrugged. "Very well. Wanda, I believe they are sealed in the third cabinet. Please retrieve them for Mr. Marsden."

Wanda got up and left, presumably on her way to the third cabinet. Terrence remained in place, staring at Carl.

Carl remained silent. He did not want a conversation.

Wanda returned with a large bundle of papers.

"Wanda, remain with Mr. Marsden while he examines the petitions," said Terrence. "When he is finished take them back to the cabinet." His message was clear. Carl would have no opportunity to take or even copy the documents.

Terrence turned and left. Wanda remained in place, not exactly looking over Carl's shoulder but close to it.

Carl sat down and started with the top page. Almost immediately he saw it. It was what he suspected. He went down the page, line by line. Every line was as he expected. He turned to the next page. Exactly the same. And the next. And the next. He started leafing through the pages, selecting some at random. Every one was as he suspected.

"Are you going to be much longer?" asked an obviously irritated Wanda.

Carl looked up at the clock. Had he been here that long?

"No, thank you," said Carl. "I'm done. I have what I need."

Chapter 75

TUESDAY EVENING, 6:00 P.M.

C ARL HAD BEEN emphatic.
We need to talk!

He had apparently discovered something at the Government Center. Or thought of something. Or…who knows what?

Looking out the window of her apartment, she saw Carl getting out of his car. She hurried over and opened the front door.

"What is it?" she asked as he hurried through the entrance.

"Do you still have those Declaration of Candidacy forms that we were looking at last week?"

"No, I burned them. You see I never use the fireplace and I thought why not now, so I gathered some logs, but I needed something to start it with and…"

Her voice trailed off under the scrutiny of Carl's withering gaze.

"OK, I just thought a little bit of levity might…never mind… my bad…I moved them over to the side table."

Carl went over to the table and picked up one of the forms.

"What do you see?" he said, showing the form to Cindy.

"I see exactly what I saw when we studied them last week. It's the filing form for Steve Winters. We verified that his handwriting did not match those on the note."

"I'm not interested in the handwriting. Look at the content."

Cindy studied the document.

"It's looks straight forward enough. Filing to run for the State Senate; 48th district; Democratic Primary; June eighth." She looked up at Carl.

"What am I supposed to be looking for?"

"Look at the date on the form."

"June eighth?"

"No, not the date of the primary. Look at the date that it was notarized."

"OK, here it is. It's…" and suddenly Cindy understood.

"…April fifth…"

She looked up from the form. "Carl, that was a full two weeks before Tracy died."

"That's right," agreed Carl. "Now remember how I said that anyone can examine the nominating petitions. That's what I did today. Terrence and company were not especially accommodating but eventually they let me see them. I didn't examine each of them but I saw enough. Page after page of signatures. Each one signed during the week of April fifth."

"I remember how impressed we were that he got all those forms signed and delivered so soon after Tracy's death," said Cindy. "It would seem that he had them already prepared. It's almost as if he…"

"…expected something to happen to Tracy," said Carl, completing the sentence.

"Carl, this doesn't make any sense," said Cindy, who began

pacing the room. "We've been through this before. If he wanted to run, he could have filed weeks earlier. But no, he signs on to manage Tracy's last minute entry, then changes his mind, decides he wants to run himself, and then bumps her off. I can't believe that. It's too bizarre. Plus you and Brad seem so sure that they were lovers. I agree that the dates on the forms are weird but it's got to be something else."

"Then what else explains it?"

"I don't know," said Cindy. "But I just can't see Steve as a murderer. I know he's ambitious and all but..." She looked intently at Carl. "There something you want to say, isn't there?"

Silence.

"Damn it. Just say it."

"I think," said Carl, tentatively, slowly, "that you have a bit of a blind spot when it comes to Steve."

He braced for the explosion but none came.

"You're probably right," agreed Cindy. "He certainly has proven himself a liar. He lied when he said he deleted those photos."

"And don't forget that he lied when he said he saw you holding Tracy's cup."

"I think I know why he did that," said Cindy. "He truly believes I did it. You should have been there yesterday. The intensity. He absolutely loathes me. He must have really had feelings for Tracy. No, blind spot or no, I can't see him as the murderer."

"He had the opportunity. After you went outside, he would have had a clear shot at both the antifreeze and Tracy's cup."

"Agreed."

"And the dates on those forms do raise the question."

Cindy gave a sigh.

"You're right," she said. "OK, I'll go see him and get his

explanation."

"You?"

"Yeah, I know where he lives and all."

"No way," said Carl, his voice registering firmness. "Either he is the killer or he believes you are the killer. Either way, having the two of you all alone is not a good thing."

"Are you going to stop me? Or are you afraid I still have feelings for him?" snapped Cindy. Then almost immediately her face registered the shock of her own words. "Oh God no, I'm sorry. That was a mean thing to say."

"I'll go see him," said Carl, allowing Cindy's words to pass. "My position with the Office of Elections might make him feel he needs to own up as to why he was gathering petitions which would have been useless had Tracy lived."

"There needs to be an explanation," agreed Cindy. "But in the end I think you'll find that Steve is not the killer."

"He had the opportunity," said Carl. "Just like Palucci. But you don't think either one of them is the killer. And Haley, who you want to believe did it, did not have the opportunity. We are running out of suspects. I just hope we're not running out of time."

Chapter 76

NOW IT WAS Carl's turn to be a stalker. Armed with Steve's address and car make and model, all supplied by Cindy, he waited patiently in the parking lot of the high-rise apartment complex. Steve's assigned parking place (also supplied by Cindy) was empty. Now it was a matter of waiting. With the primary less than two weeks away, the campaigns were in high gear. Even as he waited, Cindy was coordinating a phone bank effort out of Emily Weston's home.

It was shortly after 10:00 p.m. when Carl saw a car matching the description enter the lot. He got out of his car and walked quickly toward the parking space, managing at the same time to stay in the shadows. He had gone over in his mind how he would approach Steve. How he would get him into a dialogue.

The car pulled into the parking place. Headlights off. Engine off. Door opening.

"We need to talk," said Carl, as forcefully as he could manage, even as Steve was getting out of his car.

If Steve was surprised by Carl's appearance, he did not show it. "I think not," was his curt response.

"That was quite a feat, generating all that paperwork so soon after Miss Miller's passing."

Steve elbowed past Carl and walked as quickly as possible toward the front door.

"Of course, it helps that you had all those signatures collected two weeks before she died."

Steve turned around. "She didn't 'die' as you put it. She was murdered by that foul creature you choose to associate with. And those signatures are valid. There is nothing improper or invalid about any of them."

"You collected those signatures after the original filing date. That means, according to law, there was only one conceivable instance where they would be of any use. Check it out, 24.2-538. When a candidate dies forty-five days or more before the primary, the petitions for an additional candidate may be entered. Poor Miss Miller passed away just forty-nine days before primary day. Just made the cut, didn't she? And you were ready to step in."

"I had nothing to do with her death. I lov—I had nothing to do with her death."

"But the question remains. The question that the media will be asking. Why did you get all those signatures, signatures that would only be valid if she died? There would seem to be only one explanation, that you either knew she would die or else actually caused—"

"The answer is that I was sloppy!" said Steve. "I thought that the law applied when a candidate dropped out, not just when they died. I was hedging my bets. There. Are you satisfied?"

"Hedging your bets? Against what?"

"Against Tracy doing exactly what Cindy did last year. I

poured everything into Cindy's campaign. She was nothing when we started. And then the little tramp stumbled in the debate, decided that it wasn't so amusing after all, and quit, leaving me holding the bag. So I hedged my bets so that if Tracy turned out to be a fraud like Cindy, then at least I would be there to give the Democrats a chance at winning. But Tracy wasn't a fraud; she was the real deal. Until…until…"

"…until she died."

"…until Cindy murdered her."

"You can't believe that."

"Believe it. I know it. I saw her with my own eyes. Standing there, holding Tracy's cup in her hand. All by herself, by the table outside the ladies room."

That was the lie that you told the police.

"No, when you saw Cindy, it was outside, in front of the warehouse where she went—"

"Is that what she's been telling you?" said Steve, in a mocking tone. "And you actually believe her? She can be so charming, so believable when she wants to be. You poor slob. I almost feel sorry for you."

With that, Steve turned around and entered his apartment, leaving Carl to contemplate what he had just heard.

Chapter 77

Friday, May 28, 9:30 A.M.

"So this is the famous map that I've heard so much about," said Carl, in awe, as he looked at the projected map that was on the largest screen he had ever seen outside of a movie theater.

"See, we have little squares for each of the precinct locations," said Terrence. "Then by using the Election Tracker app, we will see little dots which will tell us the location of each rover."

"Will the dots identify the specific rover?"

"No, the county chose not to pay for the upgrade. They're just generic dots. It will simply say that one of the rovers is there. But we are able to superimpose the rover boundaries and since we are confident that each rover will be inside his boundary, we'll know pretty much who is who."

"Yes and you can tell how long we take for our lunch break," said Brenda, caustically as she headed to the election office's conference room where the rover pre-election meeting would start in a couple of minutes. Terrence would conduct the meeting but Carl, in his new capacity as Assistant Machine Coordinator, would be assigned to go over a few points, mainly so the rovers wouldn't have to listen to the same person talk for the full two hours.

At 10:00 a.m., Terrence called the meeting to order. Rovers had their handbooks in front of them and were studying the precincts on their routes, noting the chiefs that were assigned.

"Once again, that same bozo for the Golden precinct," complained Brenda. "When will they ever listen to me?"

"Now, Brenda," said Terrence. "He has a lot of experience."

"Experience in screwing up, you mean."

Other rovers began to chime in. It seemed that everyone had someone that they felt should be replaced.

Carl scanned his list of precincts and assigned chiefs. They were all familiar to him.

Nancy Jordan at Chesterbook, Dan Pitcairn at Tower, Sharon Goldman and Mandy Evans at the two Manchester precincts. All solid.

Then there are the two who had been rookies the last time out. Marianne Tomkins at Wallingford and Kathy Gibbons at Hagerman. Both had done well.

After that, things got a bit more interesting.

Patty McGrath at Happy Acres. She will demand more signs.

Rosemary Pennington at Carter Run. Nervous Nelly of the first degree.

Jessie McComber at Pikesville. I guess we could do worse.

Sylvia Moran at Danby. She'll ignore everything I say.

Millard Hazlet at Seneca Grave. Can't they find anyone else?

And then, Carl gasped in disbelief.

Julia Hopkins at Cooper. She must be ninety years old!

It was Julia Hopkins that he and Cindy has rescued on Duncan

Hill Road the night of the ice storm. A dear, dear woman and an outstanding chief for many years, she had reached the point where she could barely function as an election officer, let alone chief.

Carl was about to add his protest to the din, when Terrence reclaimed control of the meeting.

"I know some of you are a bit...disappointed in some of your chiefs, but the office had a challenging time getting people to step up. Many of the regulars had vacations and other commitments. And don't forget that these primaries don't have anywhere near the number of voters that we get in November. On the other hand, be aware that schools will be in session so parking will be an issue if your chiefs don't mark off their parking spaces early."

"There is an additional item that the Registrar has asked me to address. It is regarding the Prohibited Activities signs."

Scattered groans could be heard.

"As you all know, these signs, printed in four different languages, list all the things that voters are not allowed to do in the voting place."

"We, know, Terrence," said Scott. "Voters may not loiter..."

"...or hinder..." said Milton.

"...or chew gum..." chimed in Brenda.

"...or stare at the ceiling," said George

"Please, let's be serious," said Terrence. "It is a state law that these posters must be placed *outside the main entrance* of the building. Surveys taken last November indicated that many of the chiefs posted them *inside the building*, usually in the room where the voting took place, but also in other locations such as the hallway, door to the cafeteria, and believe it not, the door to one of the rest rooms. So please remind all of your chiefs where these very important signs should be placed."

The meeting continued as Terrence reviewed the various items that the rovers would have in their car. The kit and canvas bag containing signs, forms, and other supplies. Two extra Electronic Pollbooks (EPBs). An extra scanner. Two extra *CreateBallot* devices. A two way radio for most communications. Sensitive information, however, would be communicated by cell phone.

"This brings us to a sticky point," said Terrence. "Normally you use the county issued cell phones for Election Day work. However, they were sent to the vendor for a software upgrade and unfortunately they have not yet been returned. So you will be using your own personal cell phones for this election. Before you leave, check in with Abdul from our IT group. He will load the Election Tracker app onto your cell phone. Turn it on when you get home to make sure it works. Then turn if off until the morning of the election when you will turn it back on. We need to know where every rover is at all times on Election Day so we can allocate resources in the best possible way."

A few groans greeted that announcement.

Cell phones, thought Carl. *What a pain, but how did we ever get along without them?*

Carl's cell phone had in fact died earlier in the week. He had a replacement on order but wasn't sure when it would arrive. Cindy had loaned him hers and that's what the Election Tracker app would be loaded on. He would then give it back to her until the night before the election when he would use it for the day.

"...and now Carl has a few words to say about signage."

"As you know," began Carl, "all carts have six of the so called real estate signs, each of which consists of a plastic sleeve and wire frame. These are especially useful, and in many cases necessary, in directing voters to the polling place and voter parking area. With schools being in session, many of the precincts get locations within the schools that are different from what they usually get in November. Rooms that are different. School entrances that are different. Voter parking locations that are different. Some of your precincts will require extra signage to handle this. We have at the warehouse an ample supply of plastic sleeves and wire frames in some laundry carts that are located in the election area, outside of the locked cage. You'll find them by the large table, near those laundry carts with the old books."

"Ah, the books," said Brenda, with a touch of nostalgia.

"So," continued Carl, "you can swing by the warehouse any time it's open prior to Election Day for any extra signs that your precincts might need. However, there is one thing you need to be aware of. Because of some roof leakage at the warehouse, they are tarring the roof. This will probably cause a fair amount of dust and debris to come down from the ceiling so it could be messy. Just be advised."

Terrence then reminded the rovers that on the day before the primary, sheriff's deputies would be delivering to the home of each chief an envelope containing flash drives for the EPBs, containing the complete voter data file for the precinct. A hardcopy list of the absentee voters for that precinct plus any last minute memos from the electoral board would be included in the envelope.

Soon after that the meeting ended. Carl had the Tracker app loaded on Cindy's phone, picked up his kit and canvas bag, and took them to the car. The other items would be picked up the day before the primary. He had found the meeting both refreshing and energizing. The shadow of Tracy's death and Cindy's vulnerability had been so consuming; this meeting had provided Carl with a break. A welcome break, yes, but Carl knew that nothing would be returned to normal until the mystery surrounding the murder of Tracy Miller had been resolved.

Chapter 78

FRIDAY EVENING, 7:00 P.M.

"**S**O HERE'S YOUR cell phone back," said Carl. "It now has the Election Tracker app on it and it seems to work."

"So they can track me wherever I go," said Cindy, holding her cell phone. "How reassuring."

"They could if it was turned on, which it's not. The day before the election we check it by turning it on. At that point, you give it to me and I can use it on Election Day. Once it's over, I'll delete the app and return it to you. And thanks once again for letting me do this. I really appreciate it."

"No problem. So, have you entered the blackout period?"

"The blackout period?"

"You know, the zone where you don't think, talk, or do anything that's not directly related to the election. I forget whether that begins with the rover meeting or the following week when you start calling the chiefs."

"There is no 'blackout period,'" said Carl, a bit peevishly. "If you remember we have a murder to solve."

"Don't I know it," said Cindy. "But I have my own election stuff to prep for. There is enough money left for Emily to book a half hour radio infomercial. She wants to do it entirely on the pipeline and I'm helping with the research. I've been charged with looking up and documenting past pipeline accidents. There have been a fair number of them. In some cases lives were lost. That will pretty much be my weekend."

"Actually," said Carl. "I have quite a bit to do this weekend to prepare. I need to confirm the contents of the kit and canvas bag against the supply lists."

"Didn't you pack the kit at the Government Center earlier this week?"

"Well, yes."

"So you're confirming what you already did this week."

"Yes, but I can make mistakes. You can never be too careful. Then I want to drive over to Manchester High School to see if that construction mess from last fall has been resolved. And then I need to…"

Carl started rattling off the election related duties that would consume him over the next few days.

Although neither of them wanted to say it, an understanding had been reached. When it came to solving the murder, they were at an impasse. They had followed a number of leads which had provided interesting information but no solution. With the date of the primary fast approaching, it would be necessary for them to put on hold their search for Tracy's killer. That is, provided that circumstances and the police would allow them to do that.

Chapter 79

Monday, May 31, 11:45 A.M.

"No, Terrence," said Carl. "It's not that I don't like her. I've met the woman. She is a pure delight. But she's not capable of being a chief."

"I don't understand your concern. Her resume says she has over twenty years of service as a chief and she served as recently as last January's special election."

"That's right. She was chief then."

"So what's the problem?"

"Let's see, where do I start? She failed to post any signs. She was late in calling in the numbers during the day. She failed to call the Government Center with the results at the end of the day. She ignored the instructions not to drive to the Government Center because of the ice storm. And she drove her car into a tree. Besides all that, she did fine."

"I appreciate your concern, Carl. But we're short on volunteers to be chief."

"What about Tom Nelson? He was chief there last fall. He's

stubborn, judgmental, and altogether unpleasant but at least he functions."

"Yes, we read your glowing report last November. He's not available. We asked him but he'll be out of town. Carl, you're just going to have to work with Julia and her assistant chief to make it work. Look, I'd be happy to continue this talk with you later but I need to prepare for this afternoon's chiefs meeting. How did the morning meeting go for you? Were any of your chiefs there?"

The week before each election, a number of chiefs meetings were scheduled to help them prepare for the upcoming event. Each chief, as well as each rover, was required to attend one of these meetings and Carl had chosen the Monday morning meeting which had just been concluded.

"Yes, I got to talk to a number of them, although none of the one's I'm most concerned about."

"Good," said Terrence with a smile that suggested a certain detachment from reality. "I think everything is coming along nicely. Tomorrow we can take care of what remains to be distributed to the rovers. Also, I've received a call from the vendor. It's possible that the county cell phones may come in by the end of the week. So the rovers may not have to use their personal cell phones after all. That would be nice, wouldn't it? Anyway, thanks for coming in."

Having been obviously dismissed, Carl left the election suite and went down to the ground level. He was about to leave when he noticed the room off the lobby. Next to the door was a sign reading "In-person absentee voting."

I suppose I should vote.

Last January, in the special election he had voted for Jennifer Haley. Her pro-business, limited government message appealed to him as well as her position on social issues. In addition, she was obviously a very capable individual…capable of polluting the James River…capable of signing off on the effort to embarrass the election process with the impersonation of a deceased voter… and maybe, just maybe, capable of murder.

Carl walked into the room. There was no line.

"Your name and address please. Your ID."

It was provided.

"Do you wish to vote in the Republican primary or the Democratic Primary?"

"The Republican primary, please."

He was handed a ballot card (colored red).

Over to the ballot table. Turn in the card. Receive the ballot.

Next it was to the ballot marking privacy booth where he made his selection.

Then it was over to the scanner, with the ballot in its privacy folder.

"Just insert the ballot in the scanner. Any orientation."

The ballot was inserted.

"Excuse me sir. The scanner is questioning your ballot. Would you like to reexamine…"

"No thank you. Just accept the ballot as it is."

"You mean, you want to—all right sir, as you wish."

The appropriate button was pushed and the ballot was accepted by the machine. The sign on the panel read, "Thank you for voting."

Chapter 80

WEDNESDAY, JUNE 2, 9:00 P.M.

"YES, ROSEMARY. EVERY precinct will have a policeman stationed nearby on Election Day...that's right, they'll be in a squad car, a couple of blocks away so there isn't any reason,... no, if a 'person of interest' or any other bad person shows up, the squad car will be there at a moment's notice...I really don't think you have anything to worry about...Yes, we can't be too careful... well thank you, I look forward to seeing you too. Goodbye."

Carl put down the phone and took a deep breath. Rosemary Pennington was actually one of the better chiefs. Super conscientious. But she worried about everything. Getting through a pre-election phone conversation with her was always a struggle.

He looked at his list. He had reached half of his chiefs. For the most part it had gone well. Both Sharon Goldman and Mandy Evans had been delighted to learn that the worst of the construction at Manchester High School was behind them. And it was always a pleasure to chat with Nancy Jordan. The two of them went way back, some five or so years to the first time Carl had served as chief.

Just then Brad walked through the door. Carl had gotten used to his comings and goings at all sorts of hours. The life of a cop, he supposed.

"So how are things with the Narco unit?" he asked. "Have you broken up that cocaine ring yet?"

"I couldn't tell you even if we had," said Brad. It had been a couple of weeks since Brad had been pulled off the Tracy Miller case and temporarily assigned to the drug enforcement division.

Carl sensed a seriousness in Brad's demeanor that was not usually there. Although Brad took his profession seriously, he was usually able to totally disconnect when not on the job. To relax. To joke around. To have fun.

But not tonight.

"Carl, you know I'm no longer on the Tracy Miller case."

Carl nodded.

"...but I still have my sources...and I'm hearing things."

This doesn't sound good.

"What I'm about to tell you is classified. I could get fired or worse for sharing it."

"I understand," said Carl.

"You know this is a high profile case. A prominent, personable, and very attractive TV personality. Pressure is being applied. Why can't the police figure this out? Murder in the middle of the day... limited number of suspects...an obvious person of interest... there has been pressure..."

"What are you saying?"

"I think," said Brad, slowly, with the emphasis on 'think,' "that they are planning to arrest Cindy and ask the Grand Jury to indict her for murder."

Carl couldn't believe what he was hearing.

"No! She's innocent."

"I agree," said Brad. "I think she is too. But the circumstantial evidence is there. The motive. The opportunity. Her temper. And like I said, there has been a lot of pressure. Does she have a lawyer?"

"Her sister got her someone to talk to but I don't know if he's actually been retained."

"He probably should be."

"When is all this supposed to happen?"

"Not before the primary. With so many people in the investigation involved in the primary, the police don't want to be accused of meddling. But it will probably come soon after. Perhaps as early as the end of next week."

Carl shook his head in disbelief. "I have to tell her. She has to be prepared."

"You really like her, don't you?"

Carl looked up at his brother with tears in his eyes.

"I love her."

"Then make sure she sees that lawyer."

Chapter 81

Friday, June 4, 11:00 A.M.

"*So it looks like the rain will continue, heavy at times, through the afternoon and into the evening. Temperatures should hover in the uppers 70s. Then later tonight...*"

Carl snapped off the radio and turned the windshield wipers on high as he sat in the stalled interstate traffic. The weather matched his mood. Why had be waited until Friday to get those extra real estate signs?

Even as he waited for traffic to move, Carl contemplated the scene that had unfolded the previous evening in the Turner's living room. How the Turners, aided by Carl, had lured Cindy over to their house with a last minute dinner invitation. How it was arranged for Mathew and David to have dinner at a friend's. And then, as gently as possible, how Cart had shared the information he had received from Brad.

At that point, plans were put in motion. Stan volunteered to contact the lawyer and set up another meeting. Carl would ensure that sufficient funds were available for Cindy's bail. Valerie would choose the right moment to tell the boys. Her message would be that "the police have made a terrible mistake."

This was when Cindy had jumped in.

"You're all acting like I just died," she exclaimed.

Then she told them, in no uncertain terms, how it would be. Yes, she would meet with the lawyer, but not until the day after the primary. Until then, her schedule was quite full, bringing Emily's campaign across the finish line. And Carl, you know where you can stick your funds. Cindy would handle her own bail, thank you very much. Only when it came to Mathew and David did she relent, acknowledging that their mother knew best how to handle things.

Valerie then suggested that Cindy spend the night at the Turner's. At that point Cindy completely lost it.

"You're all afraid I'm going to stick my head in the oven! Damn it Val, you always think you're so goddamn wise but all you are, all you've ever been, is a bossy, sanctimonious—"

"Cindy, you're not being fair—," began Carl.

"Shut up Carl. When I want your opinion I'll ask for it."

"I will not shut up!" said Carl, his voice trembling with rage. "How dare you speak to me like that? You think you can do this all by yourself. Go right ahead and try. It's your decision. It's your life. But I will not listen to you trash the people who care about you and love you. You will not disrespect your sister. And you will not disrespect me. Is that understood?"

There was, for what seemed an eternity, complete silence. When Cindy finally spoke it was in a measured, calm voice.

"Valerie, Stan, thank you for inviting me to spend the night. I truly appreciate the offer but I will be fine back at my place. Carl, perhaps I could use some help in having the funds available for the bail. I will certainly reimburse you for anything spent on my behalf."

The evening had ended shortly after that. On his way out, Carl had received a discreet high five from Stan.

Carl was abruptly brought back to the present as the traffic began to move. Twenty minutes later he arrived at his warehouse destination. Unfortunately all the parking places close to the entrance were taken. Carl eventually found a spot at the far end of the lot. The rain was coming down hard with no sign of letting up. Large puddles seemed to be everywhere. He had neglected to bring a raincoat or boots.

For a few minutes he sat in his car, hoping for a break in the rain. Several minutes passed and, if anything, it was raining even harder. There was no getting around it. He was going to get wet. Very wet.

The worst part was running through the puddles which could not be avoided. When he finally reached the warehouse entrance, he was completely soaked. Once inside, he dried off his face as best he could. The rest of him would wait till later.

"It's a mess back there," advised Rudy. "All that ceiling debris. We haven't had a chance to sweep it out yet."

Carl saw what Rudy meant. All around, there were layers of dust of different colors. Only the main passages seem to have been swept.

Carl logged in, put on his vest, and went back to the election area where he was greeted with more dust and debris. Brown dust was everywhere. The dust appeared to be black over by the tool shed area and around the shelves where the supplies were stored. There was some white dust from the ceiling plaster near the books. Meanwhile by the conference table, the dust had a decidedly reddish hue. Probably from some rust, coming from the area near the ceiling lights. Looking inside the now empty cage, Carl could see the dust on the floor. Brown. Black. Red.

This is going to require a concerted cleanup, sometime after the primary, no doubt.

Turning his attention to the matter at hand, Carl found the laundry cart with the wire frames and plastic sleeves. He had already determined the number of signs he would need. Happy Acres, which was a sprawling retirement campus, always needed extras. In addition, a couple of the other precincts would be using entrances that differed from the previous November. They would require a few extra signs.

It was dirty work. Using a rag, Carl cleaned off each plastic sleeve and then placed it on the floor. Gradually, a small pile was created. The floor became slippery as the debris on the floor was changed to mud under Carl's wet shoes. At last he had what he needed.

It had eased to a drizzle by the time Carl loaded the sleeves and wire frames into his car. It was an uncomfortable ride home in clothes that were completely soaked. Entering his townhouse, he kicked off his shoes that were wet and caked with mud. It had been a most unpleasant trip but now it was done and they were one step closer to the primary. And one step closer to whatever lay beyond.

Chapter 82

FRIDAY EVENING, 10:00 P.M.

ONCE AGAIN, CINDY was searching the internet. Once again, scrutinizing the articles on pipeline accidents and explosions. Earlier in the day she had met with Emily and the local actor who was going to narrate the infomercial on the pipeline. They reviewed the proposed script and all agreed that it was too "academic." Too many dates and places. They needed more humanity and more accountability. People who had suffered. Companies that should have acted but did not.

It was dreary and depressing work. In many instances, the article was written on the day of the accident when the cause was not yet known. Gradually, however, some patterns began to emerge. Pipelines that carried liquid fuels like gasoline tended to have more spills than explosions, although there were tragic exceptions. Most of the explosions resulted from natural gas pipeline accidents and that's where the loss of life was more prevalent.

It was getting late but she keep on, in spite of her growing fatigue. They would be meeting again tomorrow to go over things. She wanted to have as much material as she could possibly provide.

One article caught her eye. A pipeline explosion in western Tennessee. Stone Hill Pipeline. There had been campers nearby. Sixteen lives lost...tents and sleeping bags completely melted. Her eyes slid from one name to the next. Most of the victims were young...Paul Higgins, 23 from Austin, Texas...Phyllis Landau, 18, from Raleigh, North Carolina...Grace Weston, 20, from Front Royal, Virginia...Jose Ruiz, 21, from Chattanooga, Tennessee...

Cindy came to with a start.

Grace Weston, 20, from Front Royal, Virginia.

Could this have been?

You remind me so much of my niece. Like you, Grace was so full of energy. So full of life. She loved the outdoors. Went camping every chance she got.

As the full impact of what she was reading took hold, Cindy began to feel for Emily as never before. How this childless woman must have suffered. She then wondered,

Should we use it in the infomercial? I would think that Emily would have specifically mentioned it if she had wanted it used. It would be a natural fit for the infomercial but Emily is not your conventional politician.

Even if it was not going to be used, Cindy felt the need to know. How had it occurred? Why had it happened? It was a bit of a search. Looking through various articles, trying to find the one that traced back to that tragic day in western Tennessee.

At last she found it.

...corrosion in the area of the weld joints...

...deliberate misclassification of the pipeline...

...reduced number of inspections...

…insufficient government oversight…

…"We did everything required by the government regulators," declared Stone Hill spokesperson, Jennifer Gibbs…

…must never happen again…

…new corrosion identification program put in place…

…a bright, new, future with safe, dependable natural gas…

Cindy looked up at the clock.

Shit, is it 3:00 a.m. already?

In less than five hours she would be meeting with Emily to finalize the script.

Should we use it? Do I dare mention it? Do I dare not to?

Chapter 83

"I WAS WONDERING HOW long it would take you to put two and two together," said Emily, with a sad smile.

"I can't begin to say how sorry I am," said Cindy.

"And to answer your unspoken question, this is not the reason I oppose the pipeline. Although, perhaps..."

"The intensity?"

"The intensity...You remind me so much of her."

Cindy could not bear it anymore.

"Please, I'm flattered beyond belief but I'm not a tenth of the person that Grace was. I've been camping exactly once. Fourth grade. I hated it. All those bugs."

Emily smiled at Cindy. "No matter. You're like her in the ways that count."

"I do wish you'd let me leak the information to the media about those dates on Steve Winters' petitions. It's all part of the public record. It might throw him off his game a little—"

"No," said Emily firmly. "He may become the party's nominee

and I don't want to hurt him. We're meeting each other on Monday."

Cindy looked at Emily in surprise. "What are you going to talk about?"

"Oh, things."

"Do you want me there?"

"I think not," said Emily. "I know you two have a history. I don't want to complicate things."

"Are you going to drop out?" asked Cindy, looking intently at Emily.

"No, I've made it this far. We'll let the voters decide. But I don't want to poison the well. Steve Winters is not the enemy. Jennifer Haley is. She's evil. I thought I stopped her before—"

"I know. That was such a close election."

"—but she escaped. And now poor Tracy. So unnecessary. That should never have happened. But we will remove Jennifer Haley, once and for all. You've studied her business dealings, I'm sure."

"I know she vigorously supports the pipeline. And that a subsidiary of her company was accused of polluting the James River."

"Oh, yes. That too. Cindy, thank you for everything. You have a phone bank organized for Monday evening, I understand."

"Yes, and we'll have fliers at all twelve precincts on Tuesday. I'm trying to staff as many as I can with volunteers."

"I believe I am one of those volunteers. At Manchester where I'm registered to vote. Well, I'll let you go. We'll be talking soon, I expect.

I would think so, thought Cindy as they embraced in a hug.

Chapter 84

SUNDAY JUNE 6, 11:00 A.M.

*I*F THIS IS *to be my last Sunday as a free woman, at least I'll go to the slammer well fed,* thought Cindy as she attacked the stack of chocolate chip pancakes.

The IHOP on Carter Road, two blocks down from St. Mark's, had been a Sunday morning ritual of Carl's for a number of years and today Cindy had joined him.

"I suppose you'll be reviewing the manual one more time today," said Cindy, "although I can hardly guess why. You have the stupid thing memorized by now."

"There are always changes," replied Carl. "Plus it's necessary to refresh. We all can forget things, you know."

He was using that same preachy tone that had infuriated her when they first met. The tone she had become so comfortable with.

"I don't know if you remember," he continued. "That first election we served together. The time I would have kept that woman from voting if you hadn't realized my mistake and interceded—"

"I certainly do remember," said Cindy. "It's down as one of the ten greatest moments of my life. A life that is apparently about to drastically change."

For a moment the conversation lagged.

"I called Valerie yesterday," said Cindy, breaking the silence. "I apologized for the other evening. For what I said. For what I was about to say. I'm getting pretty good at issuing apologies."

Once again, silence. And once again it was Cindy who broke it.

"I feel like our chance is slipping away. There are six suspects in Tracy's murder. Eight if you count us. Up until now, there has been one thing that ties us all together. That thing is Tuesday's primary. After Tuesday, folks will begin to disperse. Our interconnections will begin to loosen. Maybe not instantly and maybe not for everyone but they will loosen. I know it sounds irrational but I feel like if we don't discover something by Tuesday, as memories fade, all that will remain will be me, holding the bag."

Carl listened attentively. He wasn't sure what to say. The assurances that her innocence would win out seemed to wither in the shadow of what was soon to happen.

"The last couple of days, I've gone over it all one more time. I am still convinced it was Jennifer Haley. I don't dispute anything you have said about lack of opportunity. But somehow there is something we've missed. Emily, incidentally, agrees with me. Jennifer was so livid coming back from the deli. And one thing I've learned from researching her is that she is an action person. If she doesn't like a situation, she will change it."

"I wish I could agree with you. I did not vote for her, by the way."

"You voted for Palucci?"

"No. I voted a blank ballot."

Cindy laughed. "Between you and Val, the GOP is infested with RINOs."

They finished their breakfast in relative silence. Carl drove Cindy back to her apartment.

"If I don't see you before Tuesday," said Cindy, getting out of the car, "here is my cell phone. I turned on the Election Tracker app. It seems to work."

"Thanks but it won't be necessary after all. Terrence called me yesterday to tell me that the county cell phones have arrived. They'll be handing them out to the rovers when they pick up their stuff tomorrow."

"OK. Then, I guess I'll hold on to it."

"Good. Well I better be going."

Silence. An hour had passed since they had sat down at IHOP. Another hour closer to something that a few months ago would have seemed so unreal, so unthinkable. At that moment, all Cindy knew was that the last thing she wanted was to spend the day alone in her apartment. All alone. Waiting.

"Carl, I'm so scared."

"Would you like me to stay? I can read the manual at your place just as easily as I can read it at mine."

"Please."

"Of course."

She gave an audible sigh of relief as together they walked up the stairs to her apartment.

Chapter 85

IT WASN'T THE first time he noticed it. For the past two days it had been there. He had continually passed it by. Coming and going. In and out. Why had it caught his eye? There must be a reason. He was trained to notice things. Things that might have significance.

But no, he was over-imagining. It was probably nothing. Almost certainly nothing.

Chapter 86

MONDAY, JUNE 7, 9:00 A.M.

AND BEFORE CARL knew it, Monday, election eve, was upon him. As he had learned last November, the day before an election was almost as intense as Election Day itself. Pick up all your supplies at the Government Center. Visit as many precincts, as they are setting up, as possible. Handle last minute questions and concerns from the chiefs. Concerns that ranged from genuine problems to simple opportunities to vent.

The main difference from November was that school would be in session. As a result, none of the chiefs located in schools would be able to set up until the end of the school day. So during the morning, Carl concentrated on the other locations.

At 9:00 a.m. he arrived at the Pikesville Community Center. The previous fall there had been a misunderstanding over the voter parking places. The chief, Jessie McComber, had been slow to assert himself and a dispute had arisen that had required Carl's intervention. Carl arrived, greeted Jessie and his wife who were setting up, and proceeded to the administration office. Twenty minutes later he left, confident that the needs of the precinct were fully understood.

From there he drove over to Happy Acres, a campus-like senior citizen community. Last fall the chief, Patti McGrath, had insisted that no fewer than sixteen additional signs were needed to make sure people knew where the actual voting location was. At the time, Carl had felt this was overkill. Still, he had complied with her wish. This time he reduced the number to ten, which he went ahead and set up.

Next it was to the Government Center where Terrence was distributing supplies.

"All right, Rover Five. We have six packages of extra ballots for the Senate 48th, three for each party, sign here please. Here is your county cell phone, with the Election Tracker app installed, so we can track your every move. Two extra EPBs. Two extra *CreateBallot* machines. One extra scanner. An envelope with extra EPB flash drives. A notice from our illustrious electoral board about the Prohibited Activities sign. That should do it. Were you able to get over to the warehouse to pick up the extra signs?"

"Yes, and it's a mess over there. Dust all over the place."

"I know," said Terrence. "I was hoping that Rudy and his people would clean it up but it looks like the election area will be up to us. We will have a designated 'sweep and mop' day once the primary is behind us."

The afternoon progressed in an orderly fashion as Carl began visiting the schools where the chiefs and their officers were setting up. Sharon and Mandy, the chiefs at the two Manchester precincts, were overjoyed that they would be in the newly constructed gymnasium which was just inside the entrance. No more long walks down a dimly lit corridor. The other schools that Carl was able to visit all seemed in good shape: Wallingford, Chesterbrook,

Seneca Grove, Cooper. He could not visit them all but the chiefs could call him if there were any problems. No one called. Until…

"Carl, this is Kathy Gibbons, the chief at Hagerman."

Kathy had been a rookie chief the previous November and had done well, following the manual with exactitude.

"We may have a problem," she continued. "They told us last week that we were getting the gym but that has changed. We are now in a trailer which is in the rear of the school. It's OK, I guess, but the voters are going to have a tough time figuring out how to get back here. I've deployed the signs I have, but I'm not sure they're sufficient."

"I have a few extras," said Carl. "I'll come over right now."

Twenty minutes later he was pulling into the parking lot at Hagerman Elementary School. Almost immediately he saw the problem. There was ample parking in front of the school, with the wings of the school building embracing the lot like a horseshoe. At the center of the horseshoe was the main entrance where the voters usually entered. From there it was a short walk to the gym. That was what people were used to.

Carl looked around and saw a couple of real estate signs pointing to the left, toward the outside of the horseshoe. He followed the signs, wrapping around to the side of the school, along a side alley to the back. There he was greeted with a paved-over area that must have, at one time, been a second parking lot. There were numerous cracks in the concrete with weeds everywhere. And beyond that were the trailers. Carl could see the "Vote Here" sign in front of one of them.

He went up the ramp to the trailer and opened the door.

"Kathy," shouted a man. "I think the rover is here."

Kathy, a woman about Carl's age, was kneeling down in front of the open precinct cart, the manual in her hands. Getting up, she walked over to Carl.

"So you found us," she said, with a weary smile. "I've posted all the signs I had, but I'm afraid it's not going to be enough."

Carl looked around the trailer. There were four other officers there and they were in the process of configuring the room. It looked like they had a good handle on what needed to be done.

"I agree," said Carl. "I can give you three additional signs right now. I'll get them out of my car and post them. That should probably be enough."

Kathy nodded appreciatively. Carl went back to his car for the signs. He returned to the main parking lot and placed them in what he felt were the best spots. He then walked back to the front sidewalk to examine the view from the street. It wasn't perfect by any means, but he felt that if the voter was looking for direction, that direction was provided. At any rate, that was all he had.

The next few hours were smooth and relatively uneventful. Dinner at McDonalds. Visits to Carter Run and Danby which were the last two precincts to set up. Everything looked fine in both places.

It was 9:45 p.m. when he finally returned to his townhouse. It had been a long day. The day before an election was always tough because even though you were tired, Election Day lay right before you. Carl organized his supplies for the next day and prepared for bed.

The county cell phone buzzed.

"Carl, it's Jesse McComber, your chief at Pikesville. I'm sorry to bother you so late but there was so much happening today and getting all my things ready that I never realized but I should have realized but there was so much going on—"

"What is it Jesse? What's happened? Is the staff at Pikesville giving you a hard time like they did last fall? I thought we worked all that out this morning—"

"No, nothing like that. It's the envelope, you know from the sheriff's deputies..."

"Yes, what about it?"

"It's not here. They never delivered it. I didn't realize until just now with so much going on..."

The next few minutes were spent discussing the possible places the deputy could have left it. Negative. Jessie had searched everywhere. Carl then called the Office of Elections.

"All deliveries have been made and the deputies have gone home for the night. You'll have to sort it out in the morning."

Carl called Jesse back.

"They said all deliveries have been made. I do have extra flash drives for the Electronic Pollbooks so I'll come to your precinct at 5:00 a.m. and provide you with them. That will enable you to get the EPBs up and running."

"What about the list of absentee voters for my precinct?"

"You'll have to start without one. The EPBs will tell you if a voter has already voted absentee. I'll try and get the hard copy list to you tomorrow as soon as I can."

"And you will visit my precinct first? At 5:00 a.m.?"

"Absolutely. I can drive over to your home right now and deliver the flash drives if you'd like."

"No, me and the misses are about to retire. But I'll be looking for you tomorrow at five."

They said their goodbyes and hung up.

....*about to retire. Sounds like a good idea.*

Just then, Brad walked in the door.

"How goes it?" he asked.

"Hectic," said Carl. "But I think everything is under control."

"You'll be happy to know that the needs of your precious

little election has reached down into our ranks. I'll be in uniform tomorrow. From 6:00 a.m. to noon I'll be parked in a squad car, two blocks from the Hagerman precinct, ready to respond in a flash if there's a problem. Then from noon to 6:00 p.m., I'll be patrolling the neighborhood in Springdale."

"It's all in a good cause," said Carl.

"How is Cindy holding up?" asked Brad, turning serious.

"As well as can be expected. I talked with her on the phone earlier today. She was in the final stages of organizing a phone bank for Emily which has probably completed its run by now. And she'll be busy tomorrow making sure all twelve precincts are stocked with fliers. Which is good. It will keep her mind off.... other things."

For a few moments there was silence.

"I'm afraid I have some bad news," said Brad. "And mind you, you did not hear this from me..."

He waited for Carl to acknowledge.

"Understood."

"It's definite. Barring the unforeseen, Cindy will be arrested this Friday. At that time, prosecutors will ask the Grand Jury to return an indictment of first degree murder."

It wasn't exactly a shock, yet hearing the words was like having the wind knocked out of him. He tried to rally but words failed him. Finally after several minutes of complete silence, he spoke.

"She's seeing a lawyer on Wednesday. I'll break the news sometime before then. Probably tomorrow night. And I need to finish moving my finances around."

"Your finances?"

"To help with the bail."

Brad gave Carl a pitying look.

"Carl, this is a first degree murder indictment. Bail will be incredibly high if it's granted at all. More than likely she will be remanded in custody."

"Remanded. What, does that mean?"

"It means, she's going to jail."

Chapter 87

MONDAY EVENING, 9:50 P.M.

"YES SIR, SHE is the only candidate who truly understands the environment...not just the pipeline but other issues as well...need the strongest candidate to defeat Haley in November...that's right, her company, Gibbs Manufacturing, was polluting the James River...No, they settled out of court, but you know what they say...well thank you, and remember that the polls are open from 6:00 a.m. to 7:00 p.m....You're most welcome. Goodbye."

Cindy gave a sigh and leaned back in her chair. For the past four hours she had been on the phone. One registered voter after another. All with a history of voting in Democratic primaries. On the whole it had gone well. Dealing with people had always been one of her strengths which even the strains of the last few weeks couldn't erase. However, looking at the clock she saw that it was almost 10:00 p.m. Time to hang it up. Calling people after ten would probably do more harm than good.

They had used the office of an environmental lobbying group, which Emily was affiliated with, for the phone bank. The office had six phone lines but in the end Cindy was able to fill only four of the spots. Most of her friends were "too busy" to get involved.

"Let's call it a night," she said. "Deb, Mary, thank you so much for coming."

"It was fun," said Deb. "I'll be at Pikesville tomorrow when they open at six. I can give you four hours. I cleared coming in late with my boss."

"I wish I could help out tomorrow," said Mary, "But we have that audit and they need us for the whole day."

Cindy thanked them again and they departed, leaving her alone with Emily.

"I'm sorry I couldn't get more people to make calls tonight. I had hoped to get a few more volunteers."

"Don't give it a thought," said Emily, warmly. "You were wonderful. We've stressed the things that really mattered. I feel good about tomorrow."

"So do I," said Cindy, with more hope than conviction. "Now looking to tomorrow…"

"I'll be at Manchester at 5:45 a.m." said Emily. "I'll set up my table, go in and vote when the polls open, and spend the rest of the day pressing the flesh. Or at least as much as I'm able."

Cindy nodded. "As you just heard, Deb will be at Pikesville. Howard Morgenstein can give us a few hours at Seneca Grove and Mildred Purvis will do the same at Happy Acres. They all have their supplies. As for the rest, it will just be me, I'm afraid. I'll set up card tables with brochures at each of the precincts and rotate between them as best I can."

"Sounds like a plan. And you're all invited to my house once the polls close. We can wait for the returns and have a bit of a party."

Cindy gave a faint smile. The last thing she wanted was a party. They said their goodbyes and within a few minutes she was driving back to her apartment.

Her mind was saturated with words from four hours of phone calls. Words and images from two months of campaigning. It was almost eleven when she reached home. She wanted to phone Carl but he would be asleep by now. She needed to sleep herself. She set the alarm and got into bed.

Nothing. Those images kept drifting into her mind, refusing to let go.

...the only candidate who cares about the environment...

...the strongest candidate to oppose Haley in November...

...oppose the pipeline...

...subsidiary of Haley Enterprises polluting the James River...

...all those pipeline accidents...

...Gibbs Manufacturing polluting the James River...

...Grace Weston, 20, of Front Royal, Virginia...

... We did everything required by the government regulators...

...Gibbs Manufacturing...the James River...

...tents and sleeping bags completely melted...

...did everything required...Stone Hill spokesperson, Jennifer Gibbs...

...Grace Weston, 20, of Front Royal, Virginia...

...Gibbs Manufacturing...the James River...

...did everything required... Jennifer Gibbs...

...Grace Weston, 20, of Front Royal, Virginia...

...Gibbs...James River...Grace Weston...did everything required... Gibbs...pipeline explosion... Weston...Gibbs...Gibbs...

Chapter 88

TUESDAY MORNING, JUNE 8, 2:00 A.M.

C INDY WOKE WITH a start. She looked over to the clock. 2:00 a.m. She knew that she should try to get back to sleep but first there was something she wanted to know. Something she needed to know.

She walked into the dining room where the laptop sat on the table. Power on. Link to Google. Enter "Jennifer Haley." There's the Wikipedia article. And there it was. How had she missed it?

Jennifer Maureen Haley, née Gibbs...

For several minutes, she sat staring at the screen. And gradually she began to understand why that sweet, gentle, lady who loved the environment felt such hatred for her political opponent. It was more than just policy. It was personal.

But Jennifer was just a spokesperson for Stone Hill. She didn't cause the explosion. Surely Emily must realize that.

That said, Cindy could understand how infuriating it must have been. This spokesperson for a company that had apparently cut corners. How she was prospering, while her own cherished niece...

Cindy was now convinced, more than ever, that it was Jennifer Haley who had done away with Tracy. It seemed so obvious. Representing that company that had compromised safety for the sake of profits. Allowing her own subsidiary to pollute. Authorizing the voter fraud scam last year. And then when Tracy threatened to expose her. It was not only that she had the motive. It was in her character. In spite of it being two in the morning, Cindy was now determined to run through, one more time, the events of that awful day. To find out what they had missed. To discover that moment when Jennifer had seized the opportunity to poison Tracy Miller.

She tried to think.

When was Jennifer alone with Tracy's cup?

And once again it was the same tired scenario.

Jennifer was the first person to enter the warehouse. She went back to the election area before Tracy and I had the altercation. No opportunity there.

...then when Tracy arrived in the election area, Jennifer was already there. But so was Carl, Terrence, and Emily. There's no way Jennifer could have slipped something into her drink unnoticed. Then Steve came back. Then me. So now we have five potential witnesses to any shady doings...

...then Terrence announces that testing will begin. And Jennifer is one of the first to go back to the testing area. Leaving her cup behind...

...leaving her cup behind...that's right, her cup was right next to Tracy's, but still there's no way she could have spiked Tracy's cup without someone noticing...

...then they all go back to the testing area. All except me. So I'm alone with Tracy's cup...no wait...Am I completely alone?...

...Think... Would I have seen something?...I just remember staring

at the table, wallowing in my own guilt... Try to visualize...

Gradually the picture formed in Cindy's mind. And suddenly she realized that she had been looking at this all wrong.

But that would mean...No I can't believe that!

But it would explain everything.

Chapter 89

TUESDAY, JUNE 8, PRIMARY DAY

All Eyes Turn to the 48th

By J.C. Styles, Washington Herald

Virginians head to the polls today in a wide variety of primary elections with both houses of the Virginia legislature up for grabs as well as a plethora of local races. No contest, however, has drawn more attention, speculation, and even morbid curiosity than that of the Democratic and Republican primaries for the State Senate in Virginia's 48th district.

The seat is currently held by Jennifer Haley, a centrist, pro-business Republican, who is heavily favored over her challenger, right wing ideologue and perennial candidate, Anthony Palucci. It is the Democratic matchup, however, that has had the political community holding its collective breath for the past several weeks, a race that pits environmental activist Emily Weston against political newcomer Steve Winters.

Weston, who came within eleven votes of defeating Haley in last January's special election, is emphasizing environmental issues, especially her opposition to the natural gas pipeline project that has been proposed to run through the western part of the state. A Weston victory today would set up a dramatic November rematch as State Senator Haley has long championed the project.

In order to get that rematch, Weston must get past a formable challenge from Winters whose campaign has embraced a wider spectrum of issues. It is also believed that the youthful Winters may be more attuned to younger voters than the sixty-six-year-old Weston.

Democratic chairman Brian "Biff" Logan has steadfastly denied reports that the county Democratic apparatus is favoring Winters. "As always, the party organization is scrupulously neutral in this primary contest," stated Logan. "Naturally we want to see the strongest possible candidate prevail. Someone who can speak to the wide variety of issues that concern Northern Virginia voters and someone with the energy to run a vigorous campaign. Who that person is will be decided by the voters."

The shadow hanging over this race is that of the late popular news reporter Tracy Miller, who perished in a single car accident on the interstate just weeks after she announced her candidacy for the Democratic nomination. Police are treating this case as a homicide and it is believed that they are close to making an arrest. Winters, who had been serving as Miller's campaign manager, has dedicated his campaign to fulfilling the legacy of the fallen Miller. "The energy that flows from the bond that these two young people had for each other might be too much for the aging Weston to overcome," said WMML reporter Jimmy Forbes, in a recent interview. While no polling data for the 48th exists, local political observers sense that a Winters trend is developing.

An additional complication for the embattled Weston comes from her selection of Cynthia Phelps as her campaign manager. Phelps, who undisclosed sources are calling a "person of interest" in the Miller homicide investigation, has resigned her post although most observers believe she is still heavily involved in the Weston campaign. How much actual assistance Phelps, who ran for Soil and Water Conservation Board last year and finished last behind three other candidates, can provide is open for interpretation.

Voters are reminded that polls open at 6:00 a.m. and will remain open until 7:00 p.m.

Chapter 90

TUESDAY, 3:00 A.M.

CINDY NEVER RETURNED to bed. There was too much on her mind. At times she sat in quiet contemplation. Then the urge to move took over and she walked aimlessly around her apartment. She wasn't hungry; she didn't dare touch the bottle in the fridge; she had thrown out all her cigarettes. In the end, she spent most of the time sorting and resorting the brochures she would be distributing that day. Every few minutes she checked the time on her cell phone. Finally at 4:00 a.m. she decided the time had come to shower and get dressed. A half hour later she was ready to go.

By 4:30 she was on her way. There was no way that her sports car could hold all the card tables to be used so Val had loaned her the minivan for the day. Her initial destination was the nearby Chesterbrook precinct where she had first met Carl. She wondered where he was. He'd be heading off on his route, just about now. But it wouldn't be to Chesterbrook. Nancy Jordan was chief at Chesterbrook and she was as good as there was. Carl would not be needed here. He would go wherever things seemed shakiest.

It was comforting, thinking about all the election-based minutiae that she would encounter that day. There was a certain reassuring normality in it. Yet before the day was over, she would have to have the conversation. A conversation that she believed would reveal the truth. A truth that offered both sadness and hope.

It was exactly 4:45 when she arrived at the school. The parking lot was completely empty. The election officers would be arriving in a few minutes, but for now she was alone. She retrieved one of the card tables from the back of the van and proceeded up the walkway. Her flashlight illuminated the path; sunrise was still an hour away. And there it was. The tree that Carl had once assured her was exactly forty feet from the entrance to the school.

She set up the card table where it was most level and returned to the van. In a minute she was back with two sets of brochures. One that featured Emily; the other that stressed the pipeline. She placed them on the table and, using the flashlight, scanned the nearby ground. There. A couple of large rocks. She placed one on each pile and stepped back to admire her handiwork. She would be doing this at six other precincts.

She heard a car door slam. Then another. Nancy and her fellow officers were arriving. At another time, another place, she would stay and chat. But not today. They had things to do and so did she.

Chapter 91

TUESDAY, 5:00 A.M.

*R*EMEMBER, THE CHIEF *is in charge of the precinct.*

That was the mantra that Carl kept repeating to himself as he watched the election officers go through the various set-up tasks that were necessary to get the Pikesville precinct open by 6:00 a.m. The chief, Jessie McComber, had accepted with gratitude the EPB flash drives that Carl had given him. He then proceeded to put them down on one of the tables and began to engage his team in a general discussion as to the placement of the various tables in the room. Perhaps their set-up the day before had not been the best. No one seemed to be sure and everyone had a different idea. Finally after ten minutes, Carl interjected with the opinion that the set-up was probably adequate, given the light turnout expected, and Jessie needed to swear in his officers and get started.

At that point, things progressed...very slowly. The swearing in was done. Then Jessie started to explain to the officers where each of the signs should go.

Delegate the signs, Jessie! Get the EPBs and scanners up.

"Remember, the Prohibited Activities sign goes on the outside of the building."

"But's that not where we put it last year."

"But they said in the Chiefs meeting, Prohibited Activities have to go on the outside."

"What about the sample ballot. Where does that go?"

"Put it on the wall, near the check-in table."

"Are you sure? What about in the hallway where they first come in?"

"That's a good point. Let's see what the manual says…"

Carl couldn't take it any longer.

"Jessie, we need to get the EPBs set up. If you give me two of your people, I can make sure it happens."

Jessie looked at Carl with a startled expression on his face.

"Well, all right," he said, with a touch of annoyance. "Gladys, Phil, you work with Mr. Marsden here on the EPBs. Now don't forget folks, we need to get those voter parking signs in the correct places outside."

At that point, Carl took control of setting up the EPBs. Giving crisp instructions to Gladys and Phil, the set-up process was initiated. Confident that the EPBs were in hand, he scanned the room. The signs and posters were going up on the walls, mostly in the right places. That could be fine-tuned later. Over to one side, people appeared to be counting out sets of ballots. Someone else was getting the *CreateBallot* machine out of the cart.

On the whole, Jessie seemed to know what needed to be done. It was just the lack of organization and the lethargic pace that was getting to Carl. He remembered the first election that he worked with Cindy. She had made mistakes and had displayed a bit of an attitude, but she had been on top of things. She had been organized and had led them with purpose. He wondered how she was holding up now as she made her rounds.

He heard voices.

"Can we vote?"

"Not yet," one of the officers was saying. "Ten minutes."

Ten minutes. Carl looked up at the clock. Sure enough, it was 5:50 a.m. He looked over at the scanners. They were still sealed up.

"Jessie, you need to get those scanners up and running."

"What. OK, now Hank, don't you think that the Precinct Map might be displayed over there by the…"

"Jessie. The signs can wait. You need to get the scanners plugged in. Now! The polls open in less than ten minutes."

"Yes, I know that and…"

Carl went over to the scanners and with his key opened the lid of each of them. He then turned around to face an obviously annoyed Jessie.

"Jessie we need to get these scanners up and running now. Do you want me to do it?"

There was silence for a few seconds. Then,

"All right. Doris, please work with Mr. Marsden and get the scanners up. It was on my list to do but apparently not soon enough."

Doris walked over to join Carl.

"He's somewhat disorganized but he gets to things eventually," she said quietly.

"I'm sorry I came down so hard," said Carl, as they started the process to get the scanners up and running. "I hope I haven't offended him. I'll be sure to apologize before I leave."

Together they went through the opening sequence. A zero report was printed. The scanners were ready.

"I think it's time," said one of the officers, pointing to the clock.

"Very good," said Jessie. He started calling out assignments. "Gladys and Phil, you're at check-in. Doris, you're at the scanner. Rhoda, you're at the ballot table…"

Carl approached Jessie.

"Look, I'm sorry I've been so abrupt—"

"Not at all," said Jessie, who seemed relieved that everything was ready on time. "There is just so much and sometimes…. anyway, thanks for bringing the flash drives."

"No problem. I'll be on my way. Call me with any–"

That was when his cell phone began to buzz.

Chapter 92

TUESDAY, 6:15 A.M.

"**N**OTHING WORKS! IT'S a disaster! What do I do?"

Rosemary Pennington, the chief at Carter Run, was sincere, conscientious, and reasonably competent, but she often agonized over trifles. Carl had talked her off the ledge before. But this time, it sounded serious.

"Calm down, Rosemary. What's happening?"

"What's happening is that I have a line of angry voters and they can't vote. The scanners won't work. Neither of them. And the line is growing!"

"Both scanners are not working?"

"Exactly. One of them never even came up. It just flashed an "Election file not found" message when we turned it on. But the other one did come up. Printed a zero report and everything. But now it rejects the ballots. Every one."

"So no one has voted."

"That's right. And the line is growing. What do I do?"

"Rosemary, you can always have the voter insert the ballot in the auxiliary slot. Then we'll scan them at the end of the day. But before you do that, I need to ask you one thing. When the ballots are rejected, is there a message?"

"Yes, something about a missed ballot sequence."

Carl immediately knew what the problem was.

"All right, Rosemary. I need you to walk around to the rear of the scanner. Do not turn it off or unplug it. Invite any poll watchers there to observe."

"There are no poll watchers."

"Good, that makes it easier. There should be a metal bar. Do that now."

For a several seconds, Rosemary was silent. Carl could hear background noise. There seemed to be a fair amount of complaining.

"OK, I see the bar."

"Good, now push it down. "

A pause.

"OK, it's down."

"Good, now have a voter insert his ballot and see if it works."

"That's it?"

"That's it. The bar should always be down but sometimes it gets set incorrectly or dislodged during the move."

He waited for about a minute.

"It's working. Thanks, Carl. You're the best."

"Good, I'll be over as soon as I can to attend to the other scanner. At least now you're functioning."

They said their goodbyes and hung up.

Carl was standing on the sidewalk outside the Pikesville Community Center. The sun had come up and a stream of voters were entering the center. To one side he could see a poll worker for Jennifer Haley offering fliers to the passing voters.

On the other side there appeared to be competing tables. An earnest young man was distributing brochures for Steve Winters. From time to time he would glare over at the young woman at the neighboring table who had set up a display for Emily Weston. Carl recognized her as Deb Williamson, one of Cindy's girl friends, one of the few who had stuck by her. At that moment she spotted Carl and gave him a wave. Carl smiled and nodded. As an election official, he did not want to appear too chummy with either side. Besides, he needed to get over to Carter Run and see what was wrong with that other scanner.

Chapter 93

Tuesday, 6:50 A.M.

RUSH HOUR HAD begun. Carl was pretty sure he knew what the problem was with the other scanner. The message that Rosemary reported suggested that the flash drive was either unseated or missing. If it was unseated, it would be a simple matter to fix. Otherwise, it would be up to the Government Center to reprogram a new one.

Rover radio was relatively quiet this morning. At the beginning of the day, Carl had called in that he was going to Pikesville for the opening. The other rovers had likewise reported their initial destinations. These initial call-ins were more of a radio check than anything else. The Election Tracker app ensured that the Government Center knew where each rover was.

He arrived at Carter Run, parked his car, and walked toward the entrance to the school. There were a few voters entering, but not many. Unlike Pikesville, Carter Run was a small precinct. He noticed a card table with brochures for Emily Weston. Cindy had been here.

"Don't waste any time with that loser," said a lady, sporting a Steve Winters T-shirt. Then in a whisper, "Rumor has it that her campaign manager was the one who did in Tracy Miller."

Carl ignored her and went on into the building.

"Thank heavens, you're here," said Rosemary. "Here, let me show you the scanner. I tell you, operating with just one scanner has been so nerve-wracking."

They went over to the offending scanner. The message on the console was indeed "Election file not found."

"Still no poll watchers?"

"That's correct."

"Good, then let's do it. Rosemary, if you will, remove that sticker from the access door."

Rosemary gave Carl a doubtful look but complied.

"Now unlock the access door and open it."

She did as directed. Carl breathed easier. There was a flash drive but it appeared to be askew.

"If I may." He repositioned the flash drive and pushed down. Immediately messages started flashing on the screen, indicating that the scanner was coming to life.

"Close and lock the scanner," said Carl. "Here's a new sticker to cover the access door. You'll need to put the old sticker on the back of the machine certification form and write up the incident in the chief's notes. By the time you do that, it should be printing the zero report and you'll be ready to go."

Carl looked around the room as an appreciative Rosemary began to comply with his instructions. The set-up was good. Signs in the right places. Rosemary never exuded confidence but she got the job done.

Carl waited for the zero report to print. Rosemary removed it and inserted it in the appropriate envelope. A push of the button and the scanner was ready for the next voter.

It was time for Carl to move on. To move on to the precinct he was most concerned about.

Chapter 94

TUESDAY, 7:15 A.M.

"**G**OOD MORNING, MA'AM. I'm Steve Winters, your Democratic candidate for State Senate. I would appreciate your support today."

"Why you're the young man who's running in place of the reporter who was killed."

"Yes ma'am, I'm trying to carry on her mission. She dedicated her professional life to the truth. And I'm trying, however imperfectly, to follow in her footsteps."

"You certainly have my vote. The truth is so important. Keep on fighting."

"Thank you ma'am. Your support means so much to me."

Steve Winters was pressing the flesh outside Danby Elementary School where he had just voted. He wouldn't stay here long. There were other, more populous, precincts to be visited. The once steady stream of voters had slowed down to a trickle. He eagerly looked into the parking lot, trying to fix his eyes on whoever might be walking toward him. So eager in fact, that he did not notice the figure in the shadows.

"So truth is what we're selling this morning. I'm not sure if I should laugh or cry."

Steve continued to look toward the parking area but his pressed lips indicated that he had heard.

"Then again, it might be only me you lie to. Or about."

Steve continued to look straight ahead.

"I don't think we're supposed to be talking," he said.

"Carl says that either you killed Tracy or you believe I did."

"For once Carl is right."

There was a pause.

"Damn it, Steve. Look at me. I promise I'll leave when I've said my piece."

Steve slowly turned around.

"That's better. Now do you really believe I murdered Tracy?"

Steve's look was hard and unyielding.

"There's no other explanation."

"And that makes it OK to lie? Just because you can't think of another explanation? Well how's this for an alternative? You came upon Tracy's cup on the table outside the restroom. Emily and Palucci were back in the election area. Rudy and I were outside. And poor Tracy was still in the restroom. And there you were with all the opportunity in the world."

"And yet the police seem to have focused on you."

"In part because of the lie you told them."

A pause.

"I think we're done here," said Steve.

Cindy gave a sigh.

"Very well. I promised I'd leave and I will. Steve, I don't believe you killed Tracy. But it grieves me to think that you believe I did. And if this thing goes to trial and you perjure yourself on the witness stand, it will haunt you all your days…but then again, based on your track record with the truth, maybe it won't. Goodbye Steve. I really did care for you once."

Cindy walked past Steve toward the parking lot.

"Oh, and one piece of political advice," called Cindy over her shoulder, even as she continued walking away. "Grow a pair and come out against the pipeline. Read the brochure on Emily's table. It will give you all the reasons you need."

Chapter 95

Tuesday, 7:35 A.M.

CARL BECAME INCREASINGLY apprehensive as he drove down the road toward the Cooper Middle School. He had intended to visit Cooper first but his necessary stops at Pikesville and Carter Run had prevented it. He remembered all too well the report that Milton had given the last time Julia Hopkins had been chief. Of how not a single sign or poster had been displayed. How she had failed to call in the results after the close. And then the drama that had ensued when he and Cindy had navigated that hilly, icy road to rescue Julia after she had driven her car into a tree. What was the office thinking when they assigned her, once again, as chief?

There's the entrance to Cooper. And what's that? I don't believe it!

On the side of the road were two real estate signs each labeled "Polling Place" pointing in the direction of the entrance. Carl pulled into the parking lot and was greeted with another sign saying "Voter Parking" with the arrow pointing in the appropriate direction. "Voter Parking Here" signs (one of them labeled for handicapped voters) identified each of the parking places for the voters. Getting out of his car, he noted the necessary signs on the entrance door. There was even the much discussed "Prohibited Activities" sign in its rightful place.

As he approached the front door, volunteers from the Haley and Winters campaign approached him. He accepted each of their fliers. A card table with brochures for Emily and the pipeline gave evidence of Cindy's earlier visit.

He entered the building. Arrows taped to the wall directed him to the room where the voting was taking place.

"Carl!" came the cry. Julia Hopkins was sitting in the corner of the room. Carl noticed a walker next to her. He quickly scanned the room. It had been set up so as to easily handle the modest flow of voters expected for the primary.

"Everyone, this is the young man who rescued me on Duncan Hill Road last January," Julia was saying. "The young lady who was with him voted here about thirty minutes ago. I think she's working for one of the candidates."

That's right, Carl remembered. *Cooper is Cindy's home precinct.*

A silver haired man approached Carl. "Hi, I'm Lyle McCormick, the assistant chief."

"It looks like Julia and you have everything in hand," said Carl. He observed as a pair of voters entered the room and went over to the well-marked check-in table.

"I've served here a number of times as assistant chief with Julia over the years," Lyle quietly explained. "She called me a couple of months ago. Said she'd like to do it one more time if I would serve under her. Why not? We'll make sure everything is done right and I'll be the one to drive the stuff out to the Government Center tonight."

Carl wasn't sure what to say. He wasn't sure he approved of

what obviously was a "Chief Emeritus" situation. On the other hand this was hardly the first time that an Assistant Chief had been the dominant partner. And everything appeared to be going smoothly.

Any further contemplation of this unorthodox situation was brought to a halt as the ever-present rover radio sounded,

"Base to Rover Five. Base to Rover Five. We're receiving complaints from the Hagerman precinct. Voters are unable to find the polling location. Please investigate and resolve."

Chapter 96

Tuesday 7:55 A.M.

"Hello. Kathy Gibbons speaking."

"Kathy, it's Carl Marsden. What's up?"

"We're not doing well. People are having a tough time finding us back here. The ones who do find us are upset. But it's the ones who give up that I'm really worried about. One of my officers is wandering the halls, looking for the room where they teach Art. We're hoping to find some poster board and magic markers so we can make some signs. But the school day here doesn't begin until nine so most of the teachers aren't here yet."

While Kathy paused to take a breath, Carl raced through a number of possibilities. It was apparent that they underestimated the number of signs necessary to guide the voters.

"Look, Kathy," he began, "I don't have any extra signs but I'm pretty sure where I can get some. In the meantime, any homemade signs you can make would be great."

Twenty minutes later Carl was pulling into the parking lot at Manchester High School. Manchester housed two precincts, aptly labeled Manchester 1 and Manchester 2. It was one of the largest election venues in the county and always attracted a fair amount of media coverage. The previous fall had been especially difficult as the high school had been in the midst of a massive renovation project.

Now, seven months later, things had had improved considerably. Gone were the mounds of dirt and the trailers that had been there last November. A well-marked entrance door, with a clearly labeled handicap ramp off to one side, made it obvious where voters should enter. All four candidates had set up tables, with volunteers passing out fliers. He could see Emily Weston, standing by her table, being interviewed by a TV reporter.

"...and it's been a cornerstone of my campaign to ensure that voters are aware of the risks, both safety and environmental, that are created by the pipeline project. I have repeatedly asked Steve Winters to join me in denouncing the project but thus far he has been silent..."

Carl hurried past the candidates' tables, up the stairs, and through the entrance. Posters on the wall directed him to the newly constructed gymnasium.

"Carl!" called Sharon Goldman, the Manchester 1 chief. "Welcome to our election palace. It is so much better than last year."

A quick glance around the room told Carl that both precincts were running well. The normal procedure would have been to talk to the two chiefs, examine things in detail, and possibly offer suggestions. This, however, was not Carl's current mission. He'd come back later when he had more time.

"Sharon, do you have any real estate signs that you're not using?" With two precincts using the same location, Carl was hoping that the chiefs had not found it necessary to use all their signs.

"We used all of mine," she said. "But Mandy may not have used all of hers."

Even as Sharon was speaking, Carl hurried over to the other side of the gym where Manchester 2 was set up.

"Carl, this is a great location," said Mandy. "I can't tell you—"

"You can tell me later," interrupted Carl. He realized he was being a bit rude but he was on a case. "Do you have any real estate signs that are not being used?"

"I'm not using any of them. Sharon's signs were enough for the two of us. In fact—"

"Great. I need them. One of my other precincts got moved to an out-of-the way location and they're hurting."

"They're in the cart. Take what you need."

Carl walked over to the Manchester 2 cart and secured the six real estate signs and their wire frames. He assured both Sharon and Mandy that he would pay them a proper visit later and hurried to his car with the signs.

As Carl was putting them into his car, his cell began to buzz.

"Carl, this is Marianne Tomkins over at Wallingford. Listen, is the Hagerman precinct open? People are showing up here who normally vote at Hagerman. They say that there's no one over there so they've come here. Some of them remember voting here before Hagerman Elementary was built but that was at least ten years ago. What should I tell them?"

"Hagerman is open," said Carl, who was sensing, even more, the urgency of the situation. "It's in the back of the school. We're getting additional signage over there now but tell anyone who comes that they need to go around the side of the school to the back. It's well marked from there."

"Will do. But I tell you, people are not happy."

With that as motivation, Carl pulled out of the Manchester parking lot, where he was immediately treated to a line of cars waiting for the next red light to turn.

Ah, the joys of rush hour traffic!

Chapter 97

A s Carl pulled into the parking lot at Hagerman Elementary School, he could see the chief trying to affix a poster board sign to the side of the school.

He parked his car and got out the real estate signs and their wire frames.

"Thank heavens, you're here," said Kathy, coming over. "We made these signs but I'm having a tough time getting the tape to stick onto the brick wall of the school."

"It won't stick," said Carl. "At least not for long. Here, let's get these real estate signs set up."

They posted the signs in what appeared to be the most strategic locations.

"Let's hover and see if the voters seem to get it," said Carl.

For the next several minutes they watched as cars entered the parking lot.

"If this isn't sufficient, I can probably steal some additional signs from Happy Acres," said Carl. "The chief always asks for more signs than are necessary. She'll never miss it, if a few of them disappear."

"I don't think you'll have to," said Kathy, as she watched the cars coming into the lot. "See. They seem to be getting it."

Carl nodded, turning his attention to three cars that had just entered the lot.

"I met the policeman assigned to this precinct."

Kathy's statement came out of nowhere. At first Carl didn't understand what she was referring to. Then he realized.

"Oh, actually they're not supposed to be visible to you and certainly not to the voters. They usually park a few blocks away."

"Well he came by and introduced himself…"

"OK."

"He was very nice…"

"OK."

I think.

"His name was Brad Marsden…"

"OK."

Not OK. Memo from Carl to Brad:

Dear Brad,

Stay away from my chiefs.

"Is he any relation to…?"

"Yes. He's my brother."

An awkward silence. Carl had seen it so many times before. Brad had this effect on people. Or at least people of a certain gender. He briefly wondered why he had never made a play for Cindy.

"He's not married and to the best of my knowledge is not seeing anyone."

He said it quickly with no expression, eyes fixed on the cars in the parking lot.

Kathy said nothing. Carl could see out of the corner of his eye that her face had turned red.

Mercifully, his radio sounded.

"Base to Rover Five. Base to Rover Five. One of the scanners at Danby seems to be malfunctioning. Please investigate ASAP and report back."

Carl responded.

"Rover Five to Base. I'm on my way."

He turned to Kathy.

"I think you're OK now," he said, motioning to the signs.

"Agreed," said Kathy. "Thanks. For everything."

Chapter 98

TUESDAY, 9:00 A.M.

I T HAD TAKEN longer than she had expected but finally the last of the precincts had been done. The card table was firmly in place on the grass to the right of the walkway leading up to the entrance at Wallingford Elementary School. It wasn't the best location. The Haley and Winters camps had secured those, several hours earlier.

"You're a little late to the party," said a young lady, standing by the Winters table.

"Has it been a busy morning?" asked Cindy, trying to be sociable.

"Not really," said the woman. "It's been a bit boring, to be honest. I'm only doing this because the company I work for wants us to do a day of community service."

Cindy smiled.

Been there, done that.

"Did you think of volunteering inside? As an election officer?"

"Hell no," said the woman. "That's what my boyfriend is doing. He's trapped inside for the whole stinking day. And you know what? He's actually OK with that. Says is makes him feel good, like he's supporting democracy or something like that."

Sounds like a good guy. I wonder how he got stuck with you.

"I wasn't sure who to volunteer for, but then that reporter got killed. And of course, your candidate has that nutcase campaign manager, you know, the one who actually bumped her off. So bizarre. Oh, I'm Courtney Harrington, by the way. Pleased to meet, you."

Courtney extended her hand.

"Cindy Phelps," replied Cindy, shaking Courtney's hand. "The pleasure is mine."

Even as they were shaking hands, Courtney's demeanor changed. She studied Cindy's face, as if trying to remember where she had heard that name before.

"I'm the nutcase," said Cindy, flashing her brightest smile.

And I have a cup of antifreeze, just for you my dear.

Courtney's face registered a mixture of shock, embarrassment, and perhaps a little bit of fear.

"Well…uh…I didn't mean…of course…no, it's just…"

"I think we have a potential voter coming up the walkway," said Cindy, pointing to the lady who was approaching them.

Cindy hadn't planned to spend any time at Wallingford. Just set up the card table and move on to the more populous precincts. However, she was enjoying Courtney's discomfort too much to leave. Fifteen minutes here wouldn't hurt the cause. It was all time-filler anyway. Until it was time for the conversation. And that could happen only later. When voter traffic was at its slowest. Then they would have the conversation. Uninterrupted. And Cindy would learn if she was going to jail.

Chapter 99

TUESDAY, 9:10 A.M.

"*R*OVER SEVEN TO *Base. I'm at the Canterbury precinct. One of their EPBs has frozen. I tried rebooting. It's still frozen so I'll be swapping in a new EPB.*"

"*Copy that Seven.*"

"*Just be aware that this is my last spare EPB. Any more breakdowns will have to be replaced by someone else.*"

"*Copy that. Thanks for the update.*"

Terrence adjusted his headphone and leaned back in his chair. After a fairly calm beginning, the calls from the chiefs and the rovers had picked up. This was the second time in less than an hour that Rover Seven had to replace an EPB. And there were complaints from voters as well. All those unhappy people at Hagerman. And now Carl was heading off to Danby to investigate the reported bad scanner. He looked up at the large county map, projected on the screen. He could see the white dot begin to inch its way from Hagerman toward Danby.

"Those EPBs are not aging well," said Betty Mitchell. Normally she was in charge of the county outreach program which registered new voters at high schools and new citizens ceremonies. But on Election Day, she was in the Command Center with a headphone like several other Office of Election employees. Election Day was truly an "all hands on deck" event.

"I wish the county would come up with the funds to replace them," said Terrence. "Those new Poll Pads that I saw at the trade show last month looked great."

For a few minutes they sat in silence, enjoying a brief break in the action.

"Terrence," asked Betty. "How many rovers do we have?"

"Twenty," said Terrence.

"Oh."

"Oh, what?"

A pause.

"I think there are twenty-one dots on that screen."

"Impossible. There are twenty rovers. Hence twenty dots."

"Bear with me, Terrence. See, there are four dots in the southwest, three more up in the Benford area, four over by the river…"

"I can count, Betty. Let's see—"

"Base this is Rover Eleven. The chief at Sandy Springs is telling me that both EPBs have gone bad. He's reverting to paper."

"Base to Eleven. What do you mean 'both?' Did they both go down at the same time?"

"Eleven to Base. I think one went down earlier but the chief decided he could survive with just one."

"Not good. Base to Rover Eleven. Base to all Rovers. Instruct your chiefs to let us know when even a single EPB…"

It was so upsetting. Sandy Springs was going back to using paper pollbooks, all because the chief had failed to notify them in a timely manner. This was not acceptable. The rovers and chiefs needed to be on top of this. Counting the dots would have to wait till later.

Chapter 100

IT WASN'T THAT difficult, once you'd done it a few times. First invite all poll watchers to observe. Then write down the public count from the dead scanner. Now power down the scanner. Unplug the power cord. Remove scanner. Insert new scanner. Remove flash drive from old scanner and insert in new. Plug in. Power on. Hope for the best.

The scanner came to life. The public count matched the one that had been written down. Now all that remained was for the chief to complete the necessary paperwork. There was a Transfer form that both she and Carl had to complete. And it was done. Danby was back to full strength.

"Thank you, Carl," said Sylvia Moran, the Danby chief.

"You're most welcome," said Carl. Helping a chief out of a difficult situation and sensing their appreciation. This was the part of the job he liked best.

"I do have one suggestion," he said. Sylvia looked at Carl skeptically. Milton had advised Carl when he took over the route last fall.

The Danby chief is competent but headstrong. She will basically ignore anything you suggest.

"Actually, it's more than a suggestion." Sylvia's eyes narrowed as she looked at Carl.

"It's the Prohibited Activities sign," said Carl, plowing forward. "It's required to be posted outside the front entrance."

"It is posted," said Sylvia, defiantly. "Do you want me to show it to you?"

"The English-Spanish version of the sign is posted," said Carl. "I saw it. But we're also required to display the Korean-Vietnamese version of the sign. That was put into the regulations last year."

Sylvia said nothing, but walked over to the precinct cart. Carl followed.

She knelt down, opened the cart door, and pulled out what appeared to be a large poster. She spread it out on top of the cart for Carl to see.

It was indeed the Korean-Vietnamese version of the Prohibited Activities sign. Scrawled over the text, in bright red magic marker ink, were the words "Learn English."

"One of the voters informed me of this about an hour ago," she said. "I felt I had no choice but to take it down."

Carl nodded. "You were right to take it down. Do you have any idea who might have done this?"

"Not really. It sounds like something that could have come out of the Palucci campaign. There's a poll worker out there, peddling Palucci fliers. He seemed rather abrasive when I introduced myself to him earlier today, but I'm not in the position to make any accusations."

Carl understood. His experience had been that most of the party poll workers, even the zealous ones, treated their rival counterparts with respect and even cordiality. Over the years he had even seen instances where adversaries had become friends.

"Understood," he said. "I do have a replacement poster in my supplies and I'll go outside and post it. I'll also speak to the poll workers outside. Ask them, as a courtesy, to let you know if they see anything." He looked about the room. "Everything in here looks great, Sylvia. I'll catch you later when I do my afternoon rounds."

Carl went outside, secured the poster and tape, and returned to the front entrance. He could see the location where the poster had been. In a matter of seconds, the replacement was up. He was aware that he was being watched by the poll workers.

"I have a favor to ask," he said as he walked over to where the poll workers were. The Winters, Haley, and Palucci campaigns were represented. "Earlier in the day, someone defaced one of the posters. I'm sure you know that such an action is a crime. If any of you see something like that again, I'd appreciate it if you would let the chief know."

The Winters and Haley reps nodded.

"They should learn English," said the Palucci volunteer. "If they want to vote in our elections, they need to speak our language."

If they are registered voters, then it's "their" election, just as much as "ours."

"I'm not here to debate you," said Carl. "I'm just here to point out the law and ask for your support."

A pause.

"I didn't do it, if that's what you're thinking. I might know who did. Then again, I might not. But we'll keep an eye out so it doesn't happen again."

"I appreciate it," said Carl. He turned around and went back to his car.

Chapter 101

TUESDAY, 10:10 A.M.

"**T**HANK YOU DEB, for helping out. It means a lot to me."

"I wish I could stay longer but I need to get to the office."

"How's the morning been?"

"Brisk. The Winters guy and I spent the first hour glaring at each other, but eventually we worked it out. We stand on either side of the approaching voters, wave our fliers, give our best smiles, and whatever happens, happens."

Cindy looked over at the young man, wearing the Winters T-shirt.

How come all the Winters volunteers are so young?

"I saw Carl earlier. I waved and he gave me one of his 'I'd like to talk but I'm on official business' looks. Anyway, I'm off. Enjoy the rest of your day."

The two friends exchanged hugs. Deb was one of her now shrinking group of drinking buddies who she had been hanging out with since leaving college. Cindy appreciated her loyalty although in truth they were not especially close. They had never once talked about the cloud of suspicion that hung over Cindy.

Cindy grabbed a pile of fliers, nodded a greeting to the Winters volunteer, and focused on the parking lot. She did not have to wait long. Pikesville was a large precinct and every minute or so, one or more voters came up from the parking lot.

Unlike Manchester, Pikesville was not a Democratic stronghold. Hence a fair number of voters ignored the two Democrats entirely while the Haley volunteer did a brisk business. A few voters were even seen examining the literature that was on the unmanned Palucci table.

A small minibus entered the parking lot. It drove up the far aisle and pulled up in front of the entrance plaza of the Community Center. The driver opened the door.

"We have a dozen senior citizens here who want to vote. They'd like to do it out here if they can."

Discarding her fliers, Cindy immediately walked inside the front entrance and proceeded down the hall to the voting room.

"There's a bus of seniors outside," she said to the man who appeared to be in charge. "They would like to vote curbside."

"Oh dear," moaned Jessie. "This is always tricky."

Cindy remembered the first time she had been chief. There had been a bus of seniors. Carl had helped her get through the process. She wanted to help Jessie but realized that it was not her place to do so.

When she returned to the front of the building, she discovered that the Winters volunteer had climbed into the bus and was handing out his fliers.

I'm not sure if that's legal or not, but damn it, if he's going to do it...

She could hear the Winters volunteer talking to one of the seniors.

"That's right ma'am. Steve Winters is carrying the torch for truth and for Tracy Miller…"

"I'd get in there if I were you."

Cindy turned around. It was the Haley volunteer.

"Are you going in?"

He shook his head.

"Don't have to. Our win is a done deal. Palucci's all but conceded. But your race is different. Every vote counts. My guess is the people on that bus haven't focused on the race. Just here for an outing. Ready to be persuaded. Like I said, I'd go in there if I were you."

Cindy hesitated.

Why am I holding back? Because of some crazy theory I dreamed up in the middle of the night?

"…yes ma'am. Steve Winters. A mainstream Democrat who's best positioned to win in November…"

"What are you waiting for? If you believe in your candidate, get in there."

Still she hesitated.

"I don't know what I believe in anymore."

"What was that?"

"Oh." It was like she was coming out of a trance. "I need to get somewhere. Maybe…to Tower…That's right. Got to check and see if they have enough fliers."

And with that, Cindy hurried into the parking lot, toward her car.

Chapter 102

TUESDAY, 10:30 A.M.

"*T*HIS IS JIMMY *Forbes, WMML News, standing outside Chesterbrook Elementary School, with State Senator Jennifer Haley, who has just exited the school after casting her vote. Ms. Haley, how is your campaign for reelection shaping up?"*

"Good morning, Jimmy. I will answer your question in a moment but first let me acknowledge the dark shadow that hangs over all of us today, and especially over you and the WMML community. Tracy Miller was an outstanding journalist and a person of great warmth and integrity. Our community is greatly diminished by her passing. One of her last journalistic acts was to uncover the problematic policy of the local Democratic administration which promotes the practice of shredding perfectly good library books."

"Thank you, Ms. Haley for those kind words. We all miss Tracy very much. Now as to your own campaign..."

"We are taking nothing for granted. Anthony Palucci is a most able spokesperson for his wing of the Republican Party. We are confident that once the votes are counted this evening, we will all unite around

the Republican banner and go on to victory in November."

"Will it matter to you, which of the Democratic challengers you will face?"

"Not at all. Both of them come up way short, compared to Tracy Miller, who would have been a most worthy opponent. But beyond their shallow resumes, there have been developments concerning each of them that are troubling to say the least."

"Could you elaborate?"

"Very well. We'll start with Steve Winters. We were all surprised I think, that he was able to assemble all the necessary petition signatures to get on the ballot in just three short days after the passing of Tracy Miller. Now it appears that there were irregularities concerning his petitions that are most troubling indeed. We will be further expounding on these irregularities as we get into the fall campaign. As for Emily Weston, her fanatical opposition to the natural gas pipeline, a project that will reduce energy costs for all of us, puts her at the extreme end of the political spectrum. That along with her selection of a campaign manager who is, at best, mentally unstable and at worst... well, we'll let the police deal with that."

"I'm sure we will hear more about these things as we move toward November. Now on a final note, what are all these rumors we keep hearing of a Haley run for Lieutenant Governor in two years?"

(laughing) "Jimmy, we are getting way ahead of ourselves. The only thing on my mind is how best to serve the citizens of the 48th district in the State Senate."

"Thank you. We have been speaking with Jennifer Haley..."

Even as Jennifer Haley was wrapping up her interview, Carl was walking up the sidewalk to the entrance of Chesterbrook Elementary School. This was the precinct where he had served so many times as chief. It was the precinct where he had first met Cindy, the previous January. And it was the precinct he was least concerned about. Nancy Jordan had served with Carl for many elections and was one of the best. The precinct also had a strong contingent of officers, who returned year after year. After a fairly busy morning, Carl was looking forward to reconnecting with old friends.

"Everything is running smoothly," said Nancy. "We had one voter who tried to vote with a California driver's license. He wound up doing a provisional. Otherwise it's been pretty smooth. Jennifer Haley voted about fifteen minutes ago."

"Right. She's still holding court on your lawn, outside the forty foot limit. What are your numbers?"

"We're at 132 for the Democrats and 127 for the Republicans."

Carl nodded. Chesterbrook generally broke pretty even.

"Carl..." Nancy suddenly seemed hesitant.

"Yes?"

"We've been reading all these things about Cindy in the media. It's complete rubbish, of course. But we know it must be difficult. Could you let her know we're all behind her?"

Carl nodded and smiled. "Thanks. That will mean a lot to her."

How is she holding up? he wondered as he left the precinct fifteen minutes later. Should he reach out? Call? Text?

He got into his car, opened his cell, and typed a text.

Thinking of U

Chapter 103

CINDY SMILED WHEN she read the text. She had just arrived at the Tower precinct. Earlier that morning she had set up a card table with fliers and then left to go on to the other precincts. This was not as it should be. Tower was one of the largest precincts in the county. It should have had a full time poll worker. Well, she was back. And she would stay here until...

She crossed the parking lot, holding a fresh supply of brochures. She could see the table she had set up hours before. Volunteers for the other candidates were also there, offering their fliers to the voters as they passed.

"Yes sir, Jennifer Haley is the pro-business centrist we need in the State Senate. This brochure will tell you all about her."

The middle-aged man thrust the brochure into the voter's hand and then turned to face the parking lot.

"Cindy!"

"Mr. Hudgins!"

The two exchanged hugs. They had been poll workers at

Tower the previous November, each vigorously promoting their candidate. Their initial hostility had resulted in a standoff that had taken a special effort from both the chief and Carl, as rover, to resolve. Once that had been accomplished, the two had developed a certain camaraderie as the day progressed.

"My daughter got accepted by UVa. She is so excited."

"Awesome. Did you tell her about all the night spots I suggested?"

"Some of them," said Mr. Hudgins. "A few of them looked…a bit dodgy. A father can't be too careful."

"That's OK. She'll find them by herself. So what sort of hate-filled venom are you promoting today?" said Cindy, brightly as she gestured to the brochures in Mr. Hudgins' hands.

"There is no hate-filled venom," proclaimed Mr. Hudgins solemnly. "Jennifer Haley's pro-business agenda will put our state on the right track."

"Even as that miserable pipeline wreaks havoc with the environment."

"Even as that modern, safely constructed, pipeline reduces energy costs for us all."

They continued to fire their talking points at each other. Even as the exchange, which resembled playful banter more than a serious debate, continued Cindy was aware that he was staring at her.

Finally, as their dialogue petered out…

"Cindy, you look different."

Cindy was taken aback.

"It's still the same old me."

"Excuse me for asking…but have you been ill?"

"No."

Why would he think that?

"Oh, I'm sorry. I didn't mean to offend," said Mr. Hudgins, with a concerned look on his face. "But some of the things I've read....Just remember, these political causes we work on. Yes, they're important, but they shouldn't consume us. It's not like... you know...life and death."

"No," Cindy agreed. "It's not like life and death."

Chapter 104

*F*OR EVERY LIGHT *there is a dark. And for every Chesterbrook there is a Seneca Grove.*

Milton had warned him about Seneca Grove the year before. Its venue was, logically enough, Seneca Grove Elementary School. It was a small precinct. The school was modern and its staff reasonably accommodating. The problem was the chief.

Millard Hazlet had been chief at Seneca Grove for the past several years. The crusty curmudgeon, never that good to begin with, had become increasingly disorganized and sloppy with the passing of time. In addition, his frequent utterance of "politically incorrect" statements made him a less than desirable chief. That he continued in the position reflected more on the lack of willing alternatives than anything else.

As he made his entrance, Carl noted the absence of the Prohibited Activities sign. He suspected that would be the least of his worries.

Sadly, he was correct. A number of the required posters,

including the sample ballot, were nowhere to be seen. Only two privacy booths were on the table where people marked their ballots. The placement of the tables guaranteed that traffic would flow across each other at various points in the process.

"Hi Carl. Everything is going well, as you can see."

I don't think so, Millard.

Carl knew that he needed to pick his battles. The fact that the traffic flow was not the greatest was something they could probably live with.

"What are your numbers?" he asked.

"We're at 85 Democrats and 53 Republicans. It was busy the first hour. Not much since then."

"Were there only two privacy booths in the cart?"

"No need for more. Such a simple ballot. No one complained. Except that one lady. But that old biddy always complains."

"There should be six booths in your cart."

"So?"

"So use them. Please."

Millard shrugged. "Mike," he called over to one of the officers. "Get the other privacy booths and set them up."

From there Carl launched into the signage situation. The sample ballot was a must. Also the poster that showed the correct forms of voter identification. As they worked through the various problem areas it became apparent that Millard had delegated a number of tasks but had not provided any real supervision. Carl noticed that the officers at the check-in table were not repeating the names and addresses of the voters as they checked in.

As he made his points, the precinct was gradually brought into compliance. The Prohibited Activities signs were posted by the outside entrance.

By the time it was done, Carl had made a decision. He would

report, in no uncertain terms, that Seneca Grove needed a new chief for the fall. Small precinct or no, this could not continue.

As Carl walked back to his car, he checked his cell. There was a text message.

We may need to talk soon. I'll let you know.

Chapter 105

Tuesday, Noon

S HE COULD SEE that voters were still entering the school. She should have known. Manchester had the numbers. The Winters and Haley volunteers were actively engaging the people coming in from the parking lot. Not so with Emily. That had never been her style. She was on her feet, rearranging the brochures on her table. An occasional voter would stop and chat and even offer encouragement, but most passed her by.

"It's better this way," thought Cindy. *"It will make what I need to do easier."*

"Good morning, Cindy. Or is it afternoon?" said Emily, as Cindy approached. "I see you have more brochures although I'm not sure I need any more. How has the morning been?"

"Busy," said Cindy, with a faint smile. "With so many precincts to keep stocked, I've spread myself a bit thin. Plus I didn't get any sleep last night."

There wasn't any obvious need to say the last part but she wanted it said. It might make the transition easier.

"Pre-election jitters?" asked Emily. "I slept quite well, myself."

"Yes, pre-election jitters. And, you know, the other thing."

"Oh."

Silence. This was the part that Cindy had been rehearsing over and over again.

"Emily...the other day...when you said we both knew who killed Tracy..."

"Yes?"

"How can you be so sure?"

Emily looked intently at Cindy. "It all comes down to character. To take the life of another human being. Not everyone can do that. Even if that person feels threatened by another. Only someone who has shown a disregard for human life in the past. Who tried to excuse and minimize what was so preventable. That is the person who, when threatened, is capable..."

"Someone like Jennifer Gibbs?"

Emily looked at Cindy with renewed interest. "You are a clever little thing, aren't you? Of course, that's why I asked you to be my campaign manager. I've never been very clever myself."

"I thought it was Jennifer, too," said Cindy, determined to get it out. "Like you said, character. I wanted it to be her. But the opportunity was missing. She had already headed back to the election area when I had my encounter with Tracy. So, if it was Jennifer, it had to have happened in the election area. But she was one of the first to go back to where they were testing. She was never alone with Tracy's cup."

"Details," said Emily, shaking her head.

"But," continued Cindy, "her cup was next to Tracy's. What if she wasn't the killer? What if she was the intended victim?"

"I'm not sure what you're saying," said Emily. "Who would want Jennifer dead?"

For several seconds Cindy allowed the question to go unanswered.

"Who indeed?" she said finally, looking directly at Emily.

Emily's expression changed as she gradually comprehended Cindy's meaning. She gave Cindy a hard look.

"I don't like what you seem to be suggesting."

Cindy remained silent.

"Do you want me to deny it?"

"Can you?"

"Yes, I can and I do. I did not kill Tracy Miller. And as much as I despised her, I would never have killed Jennifer Haley."

A pause.

"You don't look convinced."

"I want to…"

"And because you don't seem to believe me, I think it's best if we sever all ties. Once this day is over, you will no longer be part of my campaign. Assuming I win and there still is a campaign."

"I'm sorry."

"And of course, if you do believe I killed Tracy, you would have to prove it. But you can't prove it, can you?"

"No, I mean…"

"And you won't be able to prove it…because I didn't do it."

Cindy found herself swimming in a sea of doubt.

"I talked with Steve Winters yesterday," continued Emily. "We had a very nice chat. If I win, he will serve as my campaign manager for the fall campaign. If he wins, I will campaign for him and he will formally oppose the pipeline. So one way or another, we will stop Jennifer Gibbs Haley. Of course, it was sad about Tracy. So very sad."

Cindy could not think of anything else to say.

"Here are your brochures," she said, weakly.

"Thank you. I'm sorry your stint as campaign manager was not more enjoyable. Perhaps Steve Winters was right. When he said that politics is no place for amateurs…and I see now that you are not at all like Grace. She was such a simple, trusting soul. And that's not you, is it? No indeed, that's not you."

Chapter 106

"*R*OVER SEVEN TO *Base. Rover Seven to Base. I am at Burns Elementary School. One of their EPBs has gone down. They need it replaced ASAP.*"

Terrence gave a sigh. It had been a rough day for the Electronic Pollbooks.

"*Base to Seven. Give them a replacement. Don't forget to fill out the Transfer form.*"

"*That's a negative, Base. Remember, I called in to you a while back. I've already given away both my spares.*"

"*Hold on, Seven. I'll get back to you.*"

"Damn," said Terrence, putting down his head set. "We need to get Seven another EPB. Now which one is Rover Seven?"

"That would be Brenda," said Betty, who was seated next to Terrence.

"All right," said Terrence, more to himself than anyone else. "I need a rover whose route is close to Route Seven and who still has spare EPBs."

"Route Five is closest," said Betty. "That would be Carl Marsden. I don't think he's called in any EPB transfers." Rovers were expected to call in to the Government Center any time they delivered a spare EPB to a precinct, although in the heat of battle they sometimes forgot.

"How close is he to Burns?" asked Terrence, looking at the electronic display.

"There's a dot at Seneca Grove," observed Betty. "That's pretty close. Oh and look. There's a dot at Manchester, as well."

"What?!?" exclaimed Terrence. "Two rovers in Route Five? Those rovers need to stay inside their route."

"Yes but remember I pointed out before that there appears to be twenty-one—"

"Base to all Rovers. Base to all Rovers. Rovers should stay within the confines of their route unless otherwise directed. I repeat, rovers should stay..."

Not for the first time that day, Betty emitted a quiet sigh.

Chapter 107

Tuesday, 12:30 P.M.

WAY TO BURN your bridges, Phelps.

Cindy sat in her car, going over and over her conversation with Emily. What had she expected? For Emily to jump up and say, *Oh yes, Cindy. I killed Tracy. How clever of you to figure that out.*

Any way you looked at it, their conversation had been a disaster. What could she have been thinking? To accuse that quiet, unassuming person of murder. That gentle woman who had dedicated her entire public career to preserving the environment. Of course, she would want to sever all ties with Cindy. Who wouldn't?

Cindy buried her face in her hands. She had no desire to visit any more precincts. She didn't give a damn who won this stupid election. She just wanted the day to be over. So she could get back to her life. So she could...go to prison.

"And of course, if you do believe I killed Tracy, you would have to prove it. But you can't prove it, can you?"

Those had been Emily's words. Cindy went over them in her

mind, not just the words but how they were delivered. The cry of a blameless person proclaiming her innocence. Perhaps. But might they be also the words of a murderer challenging her? Taunting her?

But of course, she couldn't prove Emily's guilt, any more than she had been able to prove Jennifer's. Emily had entered the warehouse, just as she was throwing the drink at Tracy. She was still there when Cindy followed Tracy into the ladies room but she was not alone with the cup. Rudy had been there as well and he had testified that she had gone back to the election area where she had remained. So if she did do it, it would have been back in the election area.

In the election area. She knew from Carl that Emily was already in the area when Tracy had made her appearance and put her cup down. But they were all there: Jennifer, Steve, Palucci, Carl. And after a minute or so Cindy, as well. Yes, Tracy's cup was next to Jennifer's. Yes, a person could have confused the two. But to locate the antifreeze and use it to contaminate either cup with all those potential witnesses on the scene? Impossible.

And then they had all gone back to the testing area.

Well, not quite. Cindy had remained behind. Overwhelmed by all that had happened. Not exactly in the best frame of mind to observe. But still the others had all gone—

"This is ridiculous. I have to trust the system."

Those words. It was what Emily had said. What she had said when she decided to…*stay behind!* But could she have done the deed? What were her movements?

I wasn't paying attention. Head down, staring at the table. Focused on my own problems.

Could Emily have done it? Taken advantage of Cindy's stupor and the others' absence?

It's certainly possible. But did she?

"...if you do believe I killed Tracy, you would have to prove it. But you can't prove it, can you?"

Let's assume for a moment that Emily did poison Tracy? How could I prove it?

Did I see her do it? Obviously, no.

Could anyone else have seen her do it? Again, obviously no. They were all in the testing area.

So, no one saw her do it. What's left?

Physical evidence.

There was Tracy's cup. But the police have that. Retrieved from the wreck.

The only other piece of physical evidence was…the container of antifreeze. The container that had gone missing. It was there when Cindy had arrived that morning. She had seen it. And it was gone when the police secured the warehouse the following morning. And the data from the security system had shown that no one had entered the building after they had all left the warehouse. So…

…the container must have been disposed of after Emily had done the deed but before they all exited the warehouse.

How could she have disposed of it? In the trash? No, the police would have found it the following morning. It was obvious from the questioning that they already suspected poisoning. So it would have had to be hidden.

But where?

Think. Think! Emily had been sort of wandering around the election area. Where could she have…?

And suddenly it became clear. And Cindy realized what she needed to do.

Chapter 108

TUESDAY, 12:45 P.M.

CARL'S CELL PHONE buzzed.

"Carl, this is Terrence. Where are you?"

"I'm just pulling out of the parking lot at Seneca Grove."

"Then who the hell is at Manchester?—No, never mind that right now. I need you to go to Burns Elementary School, ASAP. One of their EPBs is down and the line is growing exponentially."

"I can do that," said Carl, "but you do realize that Burns is not on my route."

"I know," said Terrence. "It's on Brenda's. But she's already handed out all her extra EPBs. They're dropping like flies. You're the closest rover to Burns who has any left. Brenda will meet you in the parking lot and show you where to go. I can give you the address—"

"Not necessary. I know where Burns is. I'll be there in fifteen."

Chapter 109

CARL WAS GRATEFUL that the call to go to Burns had come at midday. The school was located right off the interstate and things could get backed up if it was rush hour. He had half expected a call like this to happen. From the messages on Rover Radio it was obvious that the EPBs were having a tough day. Maybe this would motivate the county to purchase those Poll Pads he had been reading about.

He was about five minutes away from Burns, when his cell phone buzzed. He pulled over to the side of the road.

"Carl, it's Cindy. Can you talk?"

She sounded anxious. Breathless, actually.

"Always. How are you doing?"

"I'm not quite sure. I think I know who killed Tracy. It was Emily Weston."

Carl was shocked.

"Emily? We never seriously considered her. She's such a nice, gentle—"

"Yes, I know. A nice, gentle lady who wants to save trees. But she has that blind spot when it comes to Jennifer Haley. Haley was spokesperson for the company whose pipeline explosion killed her niece. Somehow, Emily's grief got twisted into holding Jennifer responsible. I know that sounds irrational but after my conversation with Emily a little while ago, I'm sure that's what happened."

"OK, but what does that have to do with Tracy's murder?"

"I think Emily poisoned Tracy's cup, thinking it was Jennifer's. The cups were next to each other."

She's desperate. Grasping at straws.

"Cindy, that's an interesting theory, but don't you think—"

"Carl, you should have been there when we talked. It was like she was a whole different person. It was so weird. It was almost like she was taunting me. She practically challenged me to prove it."

"I don't know, Cindy. Even if it's true, I don't see how—"

"How I can prove it? I think I may have a way. The poison would have come from the container of antifreeze that was on the shelf in the election area."

"The one that disappeared?"

"Exactly. I think I know where it is. Where Emily hid it after she did the deed."

"Where would that be?"

"In the books."

"The books?"

"You know, all those damn library books that are in the laundry carts. I remember that Emily was wandering around the election area while you were all off testing. She must have buried the container in one of those laundry carts. And when those books get taken away to be shredded—"

"Which is any day now—"

"The evidence will be gone."

Silence.

"What do you think?"

Carl considered.

"I think it's a long shot—"

"Of course, it's a long shot. It's all a long shot. The only thing that's not a long shot is that I'm going to jail."

Fair Point.

"Carl, I'm going to the warehouse. There are three laundry carts, all filled with books. It shouldn't take long to verify my theory. Emily would not have had time to put it very deep."

"Shouldn't we get the police involved in this?"

"The police won't do it. They think I'm guilty, remember. Look, I won't be disrupting or tampering any evidence. I've just left the CVS parking lot. The one down the road from Manchester High. I purchased a pair of sterile, disposable gloves. And I'll be careful. I won't actually touch the container. If Emily handled it, her fingerprints will be on it. Once I've verified that it's there, we can call the police. Maybe Brad can ease things for us there."

Carl wasn't convinced, but before he could say anything, Cindy continued,

"I have that paper that gives me access to the election area any time up to the primary, which is today. After today I'll no longer be authorized to go back there. If Rudy or anyone else questions me, I'll say I left some personal item during testing."

"Yes, I guess you could do that," agreed Carl, his tone reflecting the doubt that he felt.

Cindy sensed his doubt.

"Carl, I'm doing this whether you approve or not. In a few days I'm going to jail and I want to be able to say to myself that I did everything possible to prevent that from happening."

Carl knew better than to argue.

"OK, but be prepared for a mess. There is a whole lot of dust and debris in the election area that fell from the ceiling during the recent roof work. And just make sure Rudy doesn't see you rummaging through those books. They're zealous about protecting county property over there."

Cindy laughed.

"The last thing on my mind is incurring Rudy's displeasure. But I will be careful. In the meantime, please pray for me. I'll call you when I'm done."

"Is that a promise? Whatever you find?"

Or don't find.

"Yes Carl. That's a promise."

Chapter 110

TUESDAY 1:05 P.M.

"**B**ASE TO ROVER *Thirteen. I understand your situation. Give them a spare EPB and be sure to fill out the Transfer form.*"

"*Thirteen to Base. Will do, but just so you know, this is the last of my extras.*"

"*Copy that Thirteen. Keep us in the loop. Over and out.*"

Terrence took a deep breath and leaned back in his chair.

"Another one bites the dust. Betty, how do we stand?"

"Eighteen EPBs have failed," said Betty. "Three precincts have been reduced to doing it with paper pollbooks. It will be four if Marsden doesn't get to Burns on time."

"He's close," said Terrence, looking at the board. "But we need to get more EPBs out to the rovers. I know we have ten spares in the warehouse. If we can get someone over there to pick them up and bring them here...then the rovers with close-in routes can pick them up here. We can dispatch deliveries to the others."

"I saw Jack Vincent come in a short while ago. He'll be working in the absentee area later today but he was asking if anyone needed anything done now?"

"Good. Flag him down and get him on the road. We need those spares and we need them now."

Chapter 111

TUESDAY, 1:10 P.M.

CARL PULLED INTO the parking lot at Burns Elementary School. He parked and extracted one of the EPBs from the back of his car. He then started to scan the building for the voter entrance.

"Over here, Carl," came the voice. It was Brenda, waving from a near-by entrance.

"Terrence said it was ASAP," said Carl, as he joined Brenda.

"He spoke the truth. They're down to one EPB and the line is growing. Come on. Follow me. They're in the ridiculously tiny music room."

They entered the building and proceeded down a long hall. Carl could see the line that extended from out of a room, into the hall.

"How's your day been?" asked Carl.

"It's been a mechanical meltdown," said Brenda. "Three precincts have had EPB shutdowns. Another had a scanner that needed recalibration. Oh and the power brick on one of the *CreateBallot* machines went bad. And to top things off, one of my esteemed chiefs left his kit at home. And another chief, and you won't believe this…"

Brenda's narrative was cut short when they reached the music room at the end of the hall.

"I love you!" came the cry from the chief, upon seeing Carl.

"She loves me," said Carl to Brenda.

"No, she doesn't. She just wants your EPB."

Brenda's assessment proved to be correct. Once delivered, the chief's full attention was focused on getting the replacement EPB up and running. While that was going on, Carl worked on the required Equipment Transfer form.

"How's your day going?" asked Brenda.

"Smoother than yours," said Carl, double checking the serial number of the EPB he had just turned over.

"And how's your friend doing?" asked Brenda, quietly.

Carl hesitated. Brenda had never been privy to the investigation and he wasn't sure how much she knew. Still, there was no point hiding the truth.

"She's kind of desperate."

"I only met her the one time, last year at the warehouse," said Brenda. "She seemed nice."

Carl wasn't sure why but he suddenly felt the need to talk.

"I don't know how much you know but it's been proven that Tracy Miller was poisoned by some antifreeze that was administered in the warehouse."

"I've heard something like that," said Brenda.

"Anyway, its container is listed as missing. Cindy has a theory that it was hidden in one of those laundry carts that are full of library books. You know, the ones that are to be shredded. She's heading over to the warehouse now to see if it's there."

"I certainly remember those books," said Brenda. "If you

recall it was my complaint that started the whole brouhaha. But she won't find any antifreeze container in those books."

"I agree, it's a long shot—"

"It's not a 'long shot.' It's a 'no shot.' She will not find any antifreeze container among those books. Period."

"How can you be so positive?"

"Because George and I threw it out. Remember, we were tidying up the election area of the warehouse earlier that morning. The container was practically empty and it was taking up valuable space on that shelf. So we threw it out along with the rest of the trash."

"Hooray, it's up and running," shouted the Burns chief. "It's two lines everyone. Carl, thank you so much. You're a lifesaver. Let me sign that form and you can get out of here."

"The form...oh yeah...here," said Carl, in a daze, still looking at Brenda.

"So this means..."

"What it means is that Cindy is on a futile errand."

Chapter 112

TUESDAY, 1:25 P.M.

B Y THE TIME Carl returned to his car, he knew what needed to be done. He dialed Cindy's cell. Four rings, and then,

"Hi, this is Cindy. I'm out and about right now so just leave a message and I'll get back to you. Have a great day."

He left a message.

"Cindy, it's Carl. You need to abort your mission. The container of antifreeze was removed by Brenda earlier in the day. I'm sorry but you will not find anything but a pile of books."

He then sent a more cryptic version of the same thing as a text message. But he realized that Cindy was on a mission and might not be checking either her cell or text. He also realized that she needed to be stopped. The warehouse had been a crime scene and her snooping around might be misinterpreted by the law and make things even worse than they already were. Perhaps it had been worth a gamble when there had been a chance of success but not now.

But if she wasn't responding to his messages, that meant only one thing.

I need to get to the warehouse before she does.

But could it be done? She had about a fifteen minute head start. But she had called from the CVS parking lot near Manchester. That was several stop lights away from the interstate. Burns Elementary was closer to the warehouse and, more to the point, closer to the interstate. Could it be done?

I don't have time to do the calculations. I just have to do the best I can.

And with that, Carl turned on the engine, maneuvered out of the parking lot, and with all deliberate haste sped on his way to the interstate.

Chapter 113

Tuesday 1:30 P.M.

"Yes, Gordon. We've dispatched Jack Vincent to the warehouse to get additional EPBs...Yes, I realize that if even one goes bad...You have to understand, it's an aging technology...No sir, there are no excuses...Of course, we'll deliver a complete report...and going forward, you know the Poll Pads... right, not the time or place...very well, goodbye."

The line went dead.

"That was the Registrar," said Terrence. "He is not pleased."

"It's not like you didn't warn them," said Betty.

"This whole thing is giving me a headache," said Terrence, rubbing his forehead. "Please, no more bad EPBs. Did Carl get to Burns on time?"

"Yes, he did," said Betty. "Brenda just called it in."

"Good. At least that's resolved."

"Terrence..."

"What?"

"There's something on the board that I don't understand,"

said Betty, slowly.

"What is it," snapped Terrence, his patience at the breaking point.

"There were two dots at Burns. One is moving in a southwest direction. We can assume that's Brenda, resuming her route."

"And…"

"Look, the other dot, presumably Carl, is heading east. See that? Away from his own route. He's now in Route Twelve, Milton's area."

"What? He can't do that."

"And look, that other dot that was over at Manchester. That's moved well into Route Twelve as well."

Terrence was beside himself. "That dot has been out of his route all day. Did we ever figure out which of the rovers that is? This is not acceptable. I'm a patient man but that rover has to go."

"Terrence, I've been trying to tell you all day," said Betty, in exasperation, "There are twenty-one dots on the board. One of them, presumably the one that was at Manchester, is not a rover."

"You mean there's an imposter out there, masquerading as a rover?"

"Apparently."

"Well, we'll deal with that later. Right now we have to get Marsden back on the reservation."

Terrence dialed Carl's cell.

"He's not picking up, damn it!"

Terrence pounded his fist on the desk. Then in frustration, he pushed down on the radio transmit button with all his strength and bellowed into the radio,

"Base to all Rovers. Base to all Rovers. All rovers are to return to their preassigned routes. No one is to stray out of their routes without authorization from the Command Center. I repeat…"

Chapter 114

CINDY HAD NEVER seen the warehouse parking lot so full. There seemed to be trucks everywhere and all the parking spaces she had previously used were occupied. She was about to give up and look for something on one of the side streets, when she noticed a spot at the extreme end of the lot. Part of it was occupied by a large SUV which was partially over the line. Fortunately she had switched from Valerie's van to her tiny sports car after she had set up the last of the card tables. With great care, she was able to inch her car into the space.

She looked down at her cell phone. Carl had apparently left both phone and text messages.

Carl, I love you but this is my thing. You're not talking me out of it.
She deleted them both.

She then spent a few minutes trying to compose herself.

Deep breath. Relax. Time to turn on the charm.

She got out of her car and walked briskly to the warehouse entrance. Up the ramp. Open the door. The log-in computer was there, same as before.

"I thought you people were having your election today," said Rudy, looking up from his papers. "Didn't expect to see any election folks until they return the carts next week."

"I'm afraid I've misplaced my change purse," said Cindy, even as she was logging in. "I hope to find it back in the election area."

"Go have a look," said Rudy. "But don't go wandering around. We're moving a lot of stuff today. Pick-ups and all. It's not the safest place to be right now."

Cindy nodded and went over to the container and secured her green vest. Then, feigning an air of nonchalance, she headed back toward the election area.

Once she was safely past Rudy, she slipped into a side aisle, so as to be out of sight. She then opened her handbag to get the disposable gloves she had purchased earlier. Her hands were visibly trembling and it took her longer than she had anticipated to put them on. This was not good. She wasn't sure how long it would take her to sift through the books and she suspected that her prolonged presence in the warehouse would be noticed.

Cindy steeled herself. This was the moment she would verify her innocence. It was also the moment that would confirm that Emily was a murderer. She had so wanted it to be Jennifer. Or if not her, then Palucci. Even Steve was preferable to this. Still the confirmation of Emily's guilt, however tragic, was her doorway to exoneration. It had to be done. With renewed resolve, Cindy emerged from the shadows and headed back toward the election area.

Carl had warned her that there would be dust and debris everywhere. Something about work on the roof. Should she try and avoid making footprints in the dust? Not much point in that. Remember that her time was not limitless. Just do what you came here for. Plus, she was not seeing any dust at all. In fact, everything looked spotless.

Then Cindy came to an abrupt halt. It wasn't just the lack of dust. She looked all around, trying to make sense of what she was seeing. Or rather, what she was not seeing. Those laundry carts of books. They were gone!

Chapter 115

Tuesday, 1:45 P.M.

TERRENCE AND BETTY sat transfixed, watching two dots slowly move across the board.

"It looks like one of them has stopped," said Betty. "Is that a precinct?"

"No," said Terrence. "It's the warehouse."

"Well if I were to guess," said Betty, "I would say the other dot is heading in the same direction."

"We need some eyes on the ground," said Terrence, who was speed dialing his phone.

"Hello, Milton. We have a situation. I'm not sure why but Carl Marsden has decided to enter your route. Do you know anything about it?...No, we're at a loss as well. In addition, the tracker is picking up someone else in your route. We're not sure if it's another rover or not. That person is stopped at the warehouse which appears to be where Carl is heading. Can you go over there and see what's happening?...That's right. Jack Vincent should be over there as well, picking up some extras EPBs, but I don't have his number. Otherwise I'd ask him. So get over there and let us know what's happening…Good. Thanks. Talk to you soon."

Chapter 116

THE AISLE CONTAINED shelves upon shelves of "stuff." Boxes piled upon boxes. Some of the boxes had labels. Most did not. Cindy supposed that someone must know what they contained. She neither knew nor cared but she was thankful they were here. They gave her the opportunity to observe, without being seen, what was happening at the loading dock.

After the initial panic of not seeing the books had worn off, Cindy had made a decision. If those books were still in the warehouse, she would do whatever it took to track them down and the hell with the consequences. The criminal justice system could not screw her any more than they were about to, so what was there to lose?

It had not taken her long to locate the laundry carts. They were in the open area near the front of the warehouse where, apparently, items were being staged to be loaded into trucks. Perhaps this was the day they would be sent out to be shredded. Upon seeing them, Cindy had slipped into the aisle and stationed herself behind the boxes. There were two, no it was three, men in the area so it would be impossible to approach the laundry carts unseen. She had no choice but to wait. Wait and hope that the men would go to lunch, or to the bathroom, or to somewhere else.

The seconds became minutes. Two minutes. Three minutes. Four min—

What was that?

One of the men was approaching the first laundry cart. He was beginning to handle the books. Cindy pulled out her cell phone. If she could not go through the carts herself, then at least she could take pictures. Photos of the antifreeze container. Something to show to the police.

The man appeared to be pawing through the books. Wait…he seemed to have stopped. He was pulling something out.

It was not a container of antifreeze. It looked like a transparent plastic bag of some sort. There seemed to be something white inside. Cindy snapped a picture.

The bag was being placed in a nearby box. The man then went back to the laundry cart. Another man seemed to be doing the same thing with the second cart. Another transparent bag was being removed. And another. Cindy continued to snap photos.

"Can I help you, miss?"

Chapter 117

TUESDAY, 1:55 P.M.

CARL KNEW HE was in trouble. First there was the call from Terrence. Then the radio directive to all rovers. He had ignored them both. His career as Assistant Machine Coordinator was about to end. Probably his stint as a rover. But none of that mattered. He had to get to the warehouse before Cindy. He just had to.

He sat drumming his fingers on the steering wheel as he sat in traffic. Once again he went over it in his mind. If she had called him from the CVS lot, then there would have been four traffic lights to the interstate. Or was it five? But sometimes those lights were coordinated. Or were they? He wasn't sure. Perhaps she was already there. If so, maybe he could smooth things over with Rudy.

His cell buzzed.

Not Terrence again. But maybe it's from Cindy. Better check.

He looked down at the cell that was on the passenger seat. It was from Brad. He hesitated. What could he want?

I've already told Kathy that you're available. The rest is up to you.

But it wasn't like Brad to call when he was on duty just to chat. Carl picked up his phone.

"What is it Brad?"

"Carl I need to ask you a question and I need you to think carefully before answering it."

"Brad, if this is about Kathy—"

"No. Listen Carl. This is important. Very important."

Brad's tone matched his words.

"OK. What's your question?"

"Last week. Friday in particular. Where did you go?"

The light signaled green. Carl put the phone on speaker and stepped on the accelerator.

"Friday?"

"Yes, Friday."

"Let's see. I stopped at the Giant to buy groceries. And the post office. I had to mail some bill payments. And the bank to cash a check."

"Did you get out of the car at any of those places?"

"Yes, for all three."

"Anything else?"

"On Friday?"

"Yes Friday. The day it rained."

"Let's see. Oh yes, I was at the Government Center, sorting supplies. And I did go to the warehouse. To pick up the extra signs. Brad, what's this all about? I'm kind of in a hurry."

Carl pulled up to another red light. The warehouse was still ten minutes away.

"Carl, listen carefully. The shoes you were wearing on Friday. You left them inside the front door of the townhouse. There was some white residue on them that looked suspicious so I had the lab do an analysis. They just reported back. It's cocaine."

"What?"

"Do you recall coming in contact with any white powder at any of those places?"

"I'll have to think. Can I get back to you?"

"Please do. The lab reported that the sample appeared to be some high quality stuff. This might be the break we need to smash that cocaine ring."

"OK. Are you still doing watch duty over at Hagerman?"

"No, they have me in a squad car in the Springdale area. I thought I mentioned that."

The light turned green.

"Perhaps you did. Brad, I'm kind of on a mission right now. I'll give you a call when I've had a chance to think."

Chapter 118

TUESDAY 1:58 P.M.

"**W**HAT ARE YOU doing?"

"Uh...I was just heading out."

Rudy began to walk toward her. Ever so slowly.

I never realized he was so big.

"You were taking pictures."

"No, I was just looking around."

Rudy continued to slowly advance.

Cindy took a step backward. And another. And...no more. She was backed up against the shelf.

"Give me your phone."

Cindy was speechless. Desperately she looked for an avenue of escape. There was none. She would have to somehow get past him. Somehow distract him if only for an instant.

Damn, he's big.

He continued to advance. He was almost upon her.

"Here, take it," she shouted, throwing her cell phone as high in the air as she could manage. For the briefest fraction of a second Rudy looked up even as Cindy made to sprint past him.

"Not so fast, bitch," he cried, reaching out. But Cindy eluded his grasping hand. She was by him.

Kicking off her shoes, she ran as fast as she could toward the door. It seemed so far away and she could hear the sound of Rudy in pursuit. She dared not look back.

Faster. Faster. Closer. Closer. She was almost there...

...when a vice-like grip seized her arm. With incredible force she was spun around and thrown against the wall. The impact caused her knees to buckle.

"Please don't hurt me. Please..."

A closed fist came down upon her. And again. And again.

Chapter 119

Tuesday 2:00 P.M.

Jack Vincent was on a mission. Get those ten EPBs from the warehouse and bring them back to the Government Center ASAP. The fact that there was no room in the warehouse parking lot and he had to park a block away was not a deterrent.

Although he was eighty-six years old, Jack had the energy of someone twenty-five years his junior. At the time of his last check-up, his physician had declared him a "medical marvel." To be fair, he did take some daily medications. Blood pressure medicine and some vitamin supplements. But nothing to suggest he was slowing down.

About five years ago, it was decided that he would no longer be driving a route. Although disappointed, he had not wasted any time or energy brooding about it. He simply accepted whatever tasks and responsibilities were given. Frequently they were for important things that no one had anticipated. Like last year when he had tested those scanners on Election Day. The test that helped demonstrate that there were bad machines in the field.

As Jack approached the warehouse parking lot, he went over his plan of attack. Locate the ten EPBs. Then commandeer a dolly and use it to get them to his car. Then he could swing back to the parking lot to drop off the dolly and be on his way to the Government Center.

Up ahead, he could see that the front door of the warehouse was opening. He smiled and started to wave a greeting. But wait? Something didn't look quite right. In a flash, his old military instincts took over and he dropped to the ground. With rapt attention he watched the scene unfolding before him. Then ever slowly, he backed away and returned to his car.

Chapter 120

Tuesday 2:05 P.M.

CARL FELT A sense of relief as he pulled into the warehouse parking lot. He had arrived before Cindy. She had promised to call. No call meant she had not been here. The fact that the parking lot seemed to be full was but a minor annoyance. There was one partial opening at the far end, next to an SUV, but he doubted he could squeeze in his car. Returning to the street, he was able to find a parking place about a block away. He parked his car and walked back to the warehouse.

Now that he was here, what should he do? Sit on the stoop and wait for Cindy? The longer he stayed, the greater would be the wrath of Terrence. He considered calling Cindy again but what was the point? He had already left the message that explained the situation.

His mind wandered back to his recent conversation with Brad. Had he actually come in contact with cocaine? White residue. When had he come in contact with anything white?

He was still mulling this over when a car pulled into the

parking lot.

"Carl!"

It was Milton.

"What are you doing here?"

"What are *you* doing here?"

"I asked you first."

"Terrence sent me over here to round you up and send you back to Route Five where you belong. He's rather upset, to say the least. Now tell me your story."

"It's a long story. You see—wait a minute? White dust. There was white dust here. But it was from the plaster."

"What plaster?"

"You know, from the warehouse ceiling."

"Carl, there is no plaster. The warehouse ceiling is completely metal."

"Are you sure?"

"Go in and check if you'd like. By the way, did you see the other rover?"

"What other rover?"

"The one who was at the warehouse. At least that's what the Election Tracker app was saying. Terrence wasn't sure if it was a rover or not."

"Wait a minute…"

Information overload was setting in.

There was white dust near the laundry cart with the books. If it wasn't from the plaster could it be...no!

Carl turned around and ran up the ramp into the warehouse. He looked up at the ceiling. Metal, just like Milton said. He then sprinted past the log-in table and ran toward the rear of the warehouse.

"Hey, mister. You need to sign in."

He reached the election area. There was no dust. And no laundry cart.

He desperately tried to grapple with the situation. Had that white dust really been cocaine? Near the laundry cart...the books...Tracy's exposé...that day at the warehouse...Tracy at the laundry cart...

And then he remembered that look. That look of rage that Rudy had given Palucci because he failed to check in. But what if that rage had not been meant for Palucci but rather for the person directly behind him?

"Ah, those famous books. I wonder if that copy of Moby Dick is still on top of the pile..."

Had Tracy stumbled on to something? Something that may have cost her her life?

He would pass along his suspicions to Brad. Perhaps this new line of inquiry might spare Cindy from—In the meantime, what about Cindy? She should have arrived by now.

Carl walked slowly back toward the front of the warehouse. Where could she be? She said she would call.

And then he saw them. Not directly before him but over in a side aisle. Next to a pile of boxes, mounted on a pallet. He went over to the pallet and knelt down.

It was a pair of disposable gloves.

Oh my God. She's been here.

"You can't be snooping around here mister. You need to leave."

Carl got to his feet.

"Has a young lady been here?"

He could sense the panic on the workman's face.

"No. No one has been here. Absolutely not. You need to leave—"

Even as the workman was speaking, Carl elbowed past him

and raced to the front door. He opened the door and ran down the ramp.

She would have called. Where is she?

"Carl, what is it?" asked Milton.

Seeing Milton brought his mind back to their earlier conversation.

...did you see the other rover?

And then he remembered,

"...here is my cell phone. I turned on the Election Tracker app. It seems to work."

And suddenly Carl realized what he had to do. Opening his cell phone, he proceeded to make the most important call of his life.

Chapter 121

"I DON'T BELIEVE THIS. I do not believe this. You go rogue on us. You desert your route and then you ask me to—No, I will not. And you know something else. You're fired. You're never working another election—"

"Who is it?" asked Betty.

"It's Carl," said Terrence. "And he has the nerve to ask where that extra dot is. The one we've been following all day."

"Tell him."

"Absolutely not. He's been fired. I'm not going to—"

"Wonderful, he's been fired. Now tell him what he needs to know."

"What are you saying?"

"I'm saying that there are things going on now that we don't understand. I don't know what they are and neither do you but they must be important. Now you tell him or I will."

For a moment Betty thought that Terrence might fire her as well.

"Very well," said Terrence, at last. "But when this is over—all right, all right, I'll tell him."

Then into the phone.

"Carl, that dot seems to be stopped on Roberts Drive about halfway between 23rd and 24th streets. That's about three blocks from where you are. Now when this is over, I'll be wanting a full report—"

A pause.

Terrence looked at Betty.

"He hung up."

Chapter 122

"No, for now just record her as being checked out. We'll fix the database later, after I take care of things here...Not yet. I need to assess fully our exposure before...No, we're in the old Rumsford building...No one's used it for years...Right, and I'll let you know."

All during his phone conversation, Rudy had kept his pistol aimed directly at Cindy, who was kneeling on a tarp on the floor of the deserted warehouse. To one side there were piles of old furniture, mostly desks and chairs.

"You are causing us a great deal of inconvenience," said Rudy.

Cindy looked up at Rudy through blackened, swollen eyes, the result of her futile attempt to escape.

"You know my boyfriend knows where I was. He's looking for me—"

"Your boyfriend will never find you. No one will ever find you. I'm sure they will give you a nice memorial service but it will be without the benefit of your body."

Cindy's head was pounding from the earlier beating. Desperately she tried to think of ways to prolong the conversation. To delay what appeared to be inevitable.

"I sent those photos I took to the police—"

"I don't think so. We were watching you closely. You were too busy taking pictures. And once we destroy your cell, no one will ever—what was that?"

Rudy quickly looked over to the pile of furniture and the side door beyond it. He then focused back on Cindy, who had tried to inch away during his brief distraction.

"You know, with me gone the police will know I didn't kill Tracy Miller. They'll start looking for other suspects—"

"The police will think you ran away," said Rudy, a sense of agitation on his face. Perhaps he had not thought that part through. "Besides they'll just think it's one of the other politicos. It was actually quite amusing watching the police try to figure out those petty little entanglements you were all involved with. They never even considered that an ignorant warehouse foreman could ever be the person they were looking for. They kept questioning me about all your comings and goings, not realizing that I had the perfect opportunity to spike her drink. You and Ms. Miller were in the bathroom. The others were back in the election area. It was so easy. Plenty of time to wipe away any fingerprints."

"Did she know what you were up to?"

"I was never sure," said Rudy. "I think she suspected something. She seemed drawn to those books. We couldn't take a chance."

His cell phone buzzed.

"Good...OK, we'll wrap it up here."

Rudy closed his cell.

"Your car is on its way to West Virginia, where it will be transformed into a pile of spare parts. Now I think it's time for us to part company. I promise that it will be quick."

"Can I have a minute? To prepare myself?"

"No. You've had all the time you need—"

Whack!

What appeared to be a table leg came sailing from the pile of debris. It barely missed Rudy's head and landed on the floor with a clatter.

Rudy turned toward the pile and fired his gun. A crack could be heard and pieces of wood went flying in every direction. Rudy then fired again.

Suddenly a loud banging could be heard from the front of the building.

"What's that?" said Rudy as he turned his attention back to the front.

More banging. And the door was thrown open and the warehouse was bathed in bright sunshine.

And standing in the doorway was Carl Marsden.

Chapter 123

TUESDAY 2:30 P.M.

"**G**O BACK, CARL," shouted Cindy. "He has a gun."

But Carl wasn't going back. He started running, as fast as possible, straight at Rudy. Rudy slowly pointed the gun at him. Carl responded by weaving in a zig-zag fashion.

"This is what they do on that crime show," he was thinking.

"I'm begging you, Carl," cried Cindy, tears streaming down her cheeks. "Go back."

Rudy fired. The bullet exploded as it hit the side of the warehouse. Rudy cursed his carelessness. Sensing that he would not be so lucky the next time, Carl ducked behind one of the furniture piles.

"Come out in the open or I shoot your girlfriend."

"Don't do it. He's going to shoot me anyway," called Cindy.

"We've called 9-1-1. They're on their way," shouted Carl. "You better leave now."

"You're lying. Come out now, nice and slow or she's dead. You have five seconds."

If I come out slow like he says—

"Four."

—he shoots me and then Cindy.

"Three."

If I stay put, he shoots Cindy.

"Two."

So all that's left is Colonial Chamberlain at Gettysburg.

"One."

Charge!

Carl burst out of his hiding place and ran straight toward Rudy. Rudy aimed his gun directly at Carl.

"No you don't, you bastard," shouted Cindy as she came out of nowhere and flung herself at Rudy. He threw her off him, repositioned his gun at her midsection and fired. Almost immediately Carl barreled into Rudy and the two of them slammed into the wall. Carl tried to wrestle the gun away but Rudy's grasp was too strong. He raised the gun and brought it down on Carl, glancing off his head onto his shoulder. The pain from the blow staggered Carl. Rudy raised the gun a second time and came down hard. Carl fell to the ground, his head buzzing in pain. He looked up and saw the barrel of Rudy's gun pointed straight at him. He tried to get out of the way but his body would not respond. There was a loud popping sound. Then another.

Carl continued to stare at the barrel of Rudy's gun. Miraculously it had not been fired. Then he saw why. There were two bright red spots on Rudy's shirt, spots that were widening with each passing second. Rudy lowered his gun even as he fell to his knees and then pitched forward, face down on the floor.

"9-1-1, this is Officer Bradley Marsden. We need ambulances at 2314 Roberts Drive. There are two victims and one suspect down. We need the ambulances right away."

"Cindy!" cried Carl, getting to his feet. He looked around desperately.

She was lying on her back, moaning softly. There was a widening circle of red on the lower portion of her shirt. Carl rushed to her side.

"I tried...I tried to delay him..."

Sirens in the distance.

"You were great Cindy. Hang in there. Help is almost here."

"Carl, please...I need you to..."

"What? Anything?"

Sirens getting closer.

She looked up into Carl's eyes.

"Baptize me."

Carl was stunned by her request.

"You can do it," she whispered, rallying her last reservoir of strength. "It's allowed if someone is near....the end." Her hand gripped Carl's arm.

"No, it's not—"

"Please."

Carl realized that he could not allow himself to give in to the agony that he felt. He had witnessed adult baptisms as part of the Easter Vigil Mass. Desperately he tried to remember the sequence of questions that the priest had used. Fighting back the tears, he began.

"Do you reject Satan?"

"I do."

Sirens still louder.

"And all his empty promises."

Her grip on his arm seemed to loosen.

"I do." He wasn't sure if it was a whisper or she was just mouthing it.

"Do you refuse to be mastered by sin?"

Silence. Her hand fell from his arm.

"Cindy!"

A couple of shallow breaths. Then, "With God's help and yours...Yes, I do."

Carl tried to remember what came next. It seemed like there was supposed to be more.

"Carl...please...just get to the end part," whispered Cindy. He either saw or imagined the faintest of smiles on her lips.

"In here. The victims first. The woman straight ahead. And there's someone over by the furniture."

Water. Baptisms need water!

"Here, Carl." It was Milton, who was miraculously holding a cup of water.

Carl took the cup and threw the contents in Cindy's general direction. "I baptize you in the name of the Father and of the Son and—" Suddenly Carl was lifted off his feet and thrown to one side. He lost his balance and fell to his knees.

"We need oxygen over here. And we need to stop that blood."

Carl got to his feet. He tried to see what was happening to Cindy but three large paramedics blocked his view.

He started to move in closer but Milton restrained him.

"You need to let them do their thing," Milton was saying.

"But I want to help."

"You did help, Carl. And she heard you."

Chapter 124

"*Every time I look at you, I see more gray,*" thought, Valerie, with resigned indifference, as she sat in front of the mirror on her dressing table. She had in fact made very little progress since she had sat down ten minutes earlier.

"How's it coming?" asked Stan, as he came into the room.

"Just a few minutes more."

"How are you feeling?"

"It's a bit snug," said Valerie, running her hands down the side of her black dress. "I think tomorrow, I'll start with the maternity things. Could you get me my pearls? They're in the top drawer."

Stan retrieved the pearls and helped her put them on.

"Thanks. Now could you get my good handbag? It should be in the closet."

"The good handbag," repeated Stan, as he went over to the closet.

"You know, the black one."

"Uh…which black one?" said Stan, peering into the closet.

"I think it's on the floor in the corner," said Valerie with a brief, faint smile.

Stan retrieved the desired object even as Valerie started to extract items from her everyday handbag.

Keys. Wallet. Change Purse, Tissues. Mints.

"Oh."

Her hand had progressed to the bottom of the handbag. She pulled it out. It was the pack of cigarettes she had taken from Cindy.

Cyn, I think this time you've quit for good.

"Shouldn't we throw those out?" asked Stan.

"Tomorrow," said Valerie, putting the handbag down.

Twenty minutes later Stan was helping her into the car. It was a short ride. Less than fifteen minutes. Fortunately there was plenty of parking. An usher greeted them and pointed to a path that led up a gentle slope. They proceeded up the walkway where the others were gathered.

Carl was there. They embraced without saying a word. Terrence and Milton were there as well. And Brad.

Valerie looked around to see if any of the candidates had made an appearance. None had. She was not surprised. No, wait. There was Emily Weston, over there in the last row.

For several minutes they stood waiting. Occasional comments about the weather but mostly there was silent anticipation.

"Cindy should have been here," said Carl, quietly to himself.

"You know that's not possible," said Valerie to a startled Carl. He had not realized that his rumination had been overheard.

"Like hell it's not possible," came the defiant words from behind them.

Carl turned around.

"Cindy!"

She was leaning on a walker. Her face looked drained. Exhausted. But it also looked determined. At the bottom of the slope was an abandoned wheelchair.

A somewhat embarrassed aid stood by her side.

"She insisted on coming," said the aid. "I was afraid she'd do damage to herself if she did not."

"You're in no condition to be here," said Valerie. "I told you not to come—"

"And when I have I ever listened to you, dear sister?" said Cindy, with just a trace of her bright smile.

"I think they're ready to begin," said Stan.

"Carl, could you help me get closer?" said Cindy.

"I'm not sure that's wise," said Carl. "The ground is uneven. You might fall."

"If I fall, you'll pick me up, like you always do. Now please help me get closer."

"Dear friends, today we are gathered together..."

Carl and the aid helped Cindy move closer, guiding her short, measured steps.

"I could not miss this," whispered Cindy. "Not after what he did."

"For this graveyard service for Jack Vincent. On behalf of the family..."

"Somehow he realized what was happening and followed us to that awful place," continued Cindy. "And he hid behind that furniture pile. And did all he could to distract..."

She stopped, unable to continue.

"Blessed are they who mourn..."

"Eighty-six years, And he gave up what was left to save me. That means I need to try..."

"To try?" asked Carl.

"To try...you know...to live a life that's worthwhile, that matters, to honor what he did. Carl, you'll help me do that, won't you?"

"Of course, dearest. Of course."

EPILOGUE

ON JUNE 8, Steve Winters won the Democratic primary for the 48th State Senate district, defeating Emily Weston, 54% to 46%.

On the same day, Jennifer Haley defeated Anthony Palucci for the Republican nomination, 89% to 11%.

On June 10, arrests were made in five cities, busting the largest cocaine ring on the east coast. Five of those arrested were workers at the county warehouse in Springdale. The photos that Cindy had taken were instrumental in extracting confessions.

On June 11, the priests at St. Mark's met to determine the validity of Cindy's baptism. Unable to reach a consensus, they decided that using "an abundance of caution," she should receive a second "conditional baptism," which is sometimes given when an earlier baptism is in doubt. This occurred in the chapel of the county hospital.

On June 21, Jimmy Forbes, of WMML, reported a story that linked Jennifer Haley to the voter impersonation fraud attempt at the special election the previous January. Ms. Haley denied any involvement.

On June 22, Cindy was released from County Hospital and entered the Healthaid Rehab Center.

On June 26, Jennifer Haley, expressing a desire "to spend more time with her family," resigned her seat in the State Senate and withdrew her name as candidate for reelection.

On June 28, Emily Weston visited Cindy at the rehab center. The visit lasted ninety minutes. They talked, cried, held hands, and at the end, embraced. Neither one ever revealed the subject of the visit.

On July 12, the Republican Party committee met to select a nominee for the 48th State Senate district. An initial motion to offer the nomination to Anthony Palucci was overwhelmingly defeated.

On July 13, the Republican Party committee voted to offer the nomination for the 48th State Senate district to county school board member Valerie Turner. Mrs. Turner, citing her commitment to the school board, declined the nomination.

On July 14, the Republican Party committee voted not to field a candidate for the 48th State Senate district.

On July 15, Steve Winters came out against the pipeline project.

On July 23, Cindy was released from the Healthaid Rehab center. Three days later she resumed work at *MarketPro* on a reduced twenty-hour workweek schedule. Full hours were expected to resume on November 1.

On August 2, Mrs. Darlene McGovern of San Luis Obispo, California announced the engagement of her daughter, Cynthia Elizabeth Phelps to Carl Francis Marsden.

On August 3, Cindy offered her services as campaign manager to Valerie for her upcoming school board campaign. The offer was instantly, lovingly, and most definitely rejected.

ABOUT THE AUTHOR

BILL LEWERS WAS raised on Long Island in the 1950s and has been a political junkie for as long as he can remember. He holds B.A. degrees from Rutgers (mathematics) and the University of Maryland (history) and a M.A.T. degree from Harvard (mathematics education). After teaching high school mathematics for a few years, he commenced a career as a computer professional with IBM. He lives in McLean, Virginia with his wife, Mary.

Bill is a lifelong fan of the Boston Red Sox and this passion is reflected in his first book, *Six Decades of Baseball: A Personal Narrative*. This was followed by *A Voter's Journey* which is one citizen's sixty year romp through the American political system.

Bill began serving as a Fairfax County election officer in 1994. Two decades later he wrote *The Gatekeepers of Democracy*, which was dedicated to the women and men who volunteer to serve on Election Day. *The Gatekeepers of Democracy* has been described as the novel that defined the genre of "election officer fiction."

Reaction to *Gatekeepers* was sufficiently positive, that Bill decided to turn what was originally a stand-alone novel into a series. *November Third* (Book Two) examines things through the eyes of the "rovers," seasonal employees who support the election process in a variety of ways. Things take a more sinister tone in Book Three (*Primary Peril*) as "murder most foul" casts its dark shadow over the proceedings.

CPSIA information can be obtained
at www.ICGtesting.com
Printed in the USA
LVHW112035050319
609575LV00004B/454/P